THE HOTSHOT

PIPER RAYNE

Cover Design: Buerosued

1st Line Editor: Joy Editing

2nd Line Editor: My Brother's Editor

Proofreader: Olivia Winston

ABOUT THE HOTSHOT

Raising my cousin's three kids wasn't in my five-year plan.
Actually, it wasn't in *any* plan.

One minute I'm a single labor and delivery nurse living a
quiet life and the next, I'm navigating guardianship hearings,
meltdowns, and homework I'm pretty sure requires a math
degree.

Enter Hayes Carlisle.

My best friend's older brother.
Chicago Colts newest catcher.
And the man I once kissed and immediately pretended I
didn't.

So, when the custody battle I've been dreading becomes a
reality, I shouldn't be surprised that Hayes swoops in with a
wild idea—a fake relationship. According to him, pretending
we're together will polish his image and prove to the court
I'm not taking on an instant family alone.

But pretending to be Hayes' girlfriend is a terrible idea.
Because he remembers how to make me laugh.
Because he looks at me like our kiss wasn't a one-time
mistake.
Because the kids start asking him to read bedtime stories.
Because my heart starts wanting things my life doesn't have
room for.

I can manage the chaos. I can fight for these kids.
But pretending not to fall for Hayes Carlisle?
That might be the one thing I *can't* do.

The Hotshot

CHAPTER
ONE

Leighton

I tiptoe up the stairs, skipping the third from the bottom, craving distance from all the guests huddled in hushed conversations as they balance small plates of finger foods and repeat words like *tragic* and *unfair*.

Between Julianna's incessant nitpicking about what needs to be done and the guests exchanging glances and whispers at me, I need some air. My hand tightens on the banister, pretending I don't hear their judgmental comments.

"She's the one."

"Single."

"Not even a boyfriend."

"A labor and delivery nurse."

"You know the hours they work."

"How will she raise three kids with that schedule?"

I slip into the master bedroom and shut the door with the quietest of clicks. I should stay out of here—the doors to their room have been shut this past week as though it's a Smithsonian exhibit—but I'm desperate to feel Skylar, with hopes she somehow guides me from the grave.

My back hits the door, and I close my eyes, finally releasing the unsteady breath I've been holding since I watched a set of double caskets lowered into the ground this afternoon.

But when I open my eyes, the nightmare remains, and the peace I was hoping to find isn't here.

To an outside observer, there's nothing terrifying about this scene. The perfectly made bed. The picture frame of a happy couple on one nightstand, a stack of books on the other. A half full laundry hamper with clothes waiting to be washed. But the space is empty, somehow devoid of life. And worse, the entire room smells like *her*. Skylar's perfume would cling to my clothes from her tight hugs, and I'd smell it my entire ride home.

I push off the door and walk over to the dresser. Five smiling faces encased in picture frames grin up at me, posed for the professional photographer she'd book for every major holiday from Easter to Halloween to Christmas. The only candid photo is the two of us from when we were younger— me missing my two front teeth, looking at her as if she was the coolest person to ever exist.

The framed photo of us trembles in my hand, and I run my finger over our faces, her laugh ringing like an echo in my head. This wasn't our dream. Her dying at thirty-four, along with her husband, leaving behind three kids, wasn't part of the fairytale.

A soft knock lands on the door, and before I can say come in, Callie sticks her head in the room. "Sorry, but your mom is on the hunt."

I wave her in, and she shuts the door, flicking the lock. I put the picture down and blow out a breath, looking at my best friend.

"How am I supposed—" I ask for the millionth time between in my head and out loud to her.

"Have you eaten anything?" She doesn't entertain my question since we both know there is no answer.

I shake my head and walk across the room to the stack of historical non-fiction books on the nightstand. A smile curves my lips, remembering Skylar taunting Patrick before their trip that he was wasting good packing space and should invest in an e-reader like hers.

"Come down and eat."

"And listen to everyone question my ability to do this? No thanks." I walk around the bed, peeking into the bathroom.

Skylar always meticulously organizes—organized—everything, each item having a designated spot. I don't even put my clothes away from the laundry basket into the dresser. How am I supposed to replace her?

"They're assholes." I side-eye Callie, and she shrugs. "I'm not lying."

She's not. I lean my shoulder against the wall, and we stare at one another for what feels like an eternity. Everyone's questions about how I'll manage are unspoken between us. Her eyes are saying *fuck them* as mine say *I can't deny there's truth there.*

Her shoulders sink, and she steps closer. "Listen, this is a lot. Like, holy shit, a pivotal moment, a fork in the road, nothing will ever be the same." I quirk an eyebrow. "So English wasn't my best subject. What I'm trying to say is there are a lot of decisions to be made, but they'll still be there tomorrow. You need to allow yourself time to mourn them too."

"I think I'm still in shock."

I not only have to grieve my cousin, who was practically a sister to me, and her husband, but my mind won't stop replaying the lawyer's words, "They want you to be the children's guardian."

What was Sky thinking?

"Who wouldn't be? Which is why you have me. Come on." She holds out her hand. "Let's sneak into the kitchen and devour Sky's candy drawer."

Just another example of how opposite Skylar and I are. She'd never have a candy drawer.

"There's no way she has one."

"Everyone has one," Callie insists, continuing to hold out her hand toward me. "Hers just might be extra hard to find, but lucky for you, I'm like a bloodhound."

I accept her hand and take one more look around their space. It feels like a torture chamber. "You're going to come up empty."

She tucks my arm through hers and unlocks and opens the door. "I guess we'll have to see. And don't worry about everyone down there. The perfect distraction is on the way."

"Callie, I don't think a clown is appropriate for a day like today."

She laughs as we step into the hallway, but it dies a quick death when we see Monroe standing outside of her bedroom with her doll clutched in her arms. How careless of us to try to find any kind of levity today when there are three confused children grieving their parents.

"Cookie is hungry," she says.

I hold out my hand. "We're headed to raid the kitchen. Want to join?"

Monroe walks to us, her small hand slipping into mine.

The three of us walk down the stairs, and right when we get to the fourth step from the bottom, Monroe jumps and lands on the third stair, spurring a loud creak. My stomach drops as all eyes in the vicinity turn toward us.

My mom rushes over. "Monroe, honey, we were looking for you." She gives me a look—one that suggests *I told you this is going to be harder than you think.*

Nothing new about her underestimating me.

"Cookie is hungry." Monroe buries herself into my side.

I place my hand on Monroe's back. "I've got her."

My mom sighs and purses her lips. I know she's worried, and it's in her nature to step in, take control. The apple didn't fall far from the tree. But I told myself I wouldn't fret over all the logistics today. However, it's easier said than done.

"We're going in search of food," Callie interjects—as she has many times between my mother and me—turning to walk toward the back of the house.

"There's food right here." My mom points toward the buffet table under the giant television anchored to the wall.

"Yeah, different food." Callie places her hand on my mom's arm. "We'll be right back, Lil."

My mom nods, and I feel her gaze on our backs.

As the three of us walk toward the kitchen, I give everyone polite smiles and nods to assure them that we're all going to be okay, including the six-year-old clinging to me and her doll, even if I'm as doubtful as they are.

Freedom from the prying eyes is just steps away when the front door opens. Something has me turning to see who's coming through the door. Light floods into what feels like darkness, even though the drapes are wide open, and a figure stands haloed by the glow outside.

"Finally! It only took him forever," Callie grumbles.

My head snaps toward her. She didn't. Even only being able to make out that it's a tall, broad-shouldered man dressed in a suit, I know who it is.

"Hayes Carlisle?" Lincoln ditches the yo-yo that Patrick's father brought him and bolts off the couch, running over to him.

My heart plummets to my stomach. "You called your brother?"

Conversations pause mid-sentence, all of the attention transferred to the Chicago Colts' newest catcher.

Callie smiles and nods. "Like I said—a distraction." She

puts her arm around my shoulders, guiding me into the kitchen. She looks so proud of herself, but it's only because she doesn't know.

Suddenly, my mind isn't wrapped up in the unexpected deaths. My pulse races for an entirely different reason—the one secret I've kept from her during our friendship. It was so long ago that half the time, I don't even believe it happened myself.

I'm gonna need more than a candy drawer. I'm not sure a fully stocked vending machine would help me get through today.

CHAPTER
TWO

Leighton

Guess I worried for nothing. Hayes hasn't searched me out once since he arrived, and he has no idea I'm watching him from the kitchen like a stalker, eating a stale store-bought cookie that doesn't come close to fulfilling my sugar craving.

There was no candy drawer to be found. Though I'm sure there's a drawer Skylar used to organize all her charging cords that I can turn into a candy drawer. One point for me and zero for Callie.

You'd think Hayes was running for mayor, shaking everyone's hands with that damn charming smile of his in place. Lincoln excitedly weaves between him and everyone approaching, rambling questions about the other players on the team and if Hayes is happy to be a Colt now. Hayes ruffles Lincoln's hair and nods, entertaining every question. It's nice to see something other than confusion and sadness on the little guy's face.

Julianna breezes in, interrupting my tunnel vision. "This dip is going to go bad. We don't want people associating the funeral with food poisoning."

Sky would hate that I gave Julianna so much control over today.

I grit my teeth, swallowing down my comebacks. I'm not her biggest fan. She was always offering Sky unsolicited advice on everything from how to introduce new foods to the kids when they were babies to the importance of a Montessori education. Hell, I'm not even sure Arthur likes his wife very much. She clearly runs the roost in their household.

"I think we should talk." She scoops the dip out of the bowl, and it plops into the trash in one big solid mass.

"After." For someone who apparently has it all together, she sure can't take a hint. I've already told her ten times today.

She sets the bowl in the sink and grabs a new one. Did she already memorize what's in every cabinet? Other than some holidays and birthdays, they never really saw one another. Patrick and Arthur would go on their brotherly fishing trips every year. Selfishly, I was happy not to have to share Skylar and Patrick with them very often, so I never really asked questions.

"I have to go water the plants." I step toward the back door, seeking solitude once again, unable to handle these people and their sad looks at me as if I was dumped into that grave with Skylar and Patrick. My life isn't over because I have three kids to take care of. Although in just the week that I've been responsible for them, it's been obvious where my single life needs adjusting.

"Didn't it just rain?" Julianna asks.

"Yeah, you know how much Patrick loved his landscaping. We wouldn't want it to suffer." I don't wait for her to argue with me, opening the back door to their deck and hoping like hell she doesn't follow me.

Once I'm out there, I pull out a patio chair, and my legs relax in relief the minute I sit.

The sun warms my skin. How cruel of Mother Nature to give us the perfect Chicago spring day on a day like today. The sun shouldn't shine so brightly. The birds should still be south and not chirping with life in the nearby trees. Flowers shouldn't be budding, and green leaves shouldn't be yawning open on the tree branches.

I run my finger under my eyes to dry the tears bubbling up, wishing it were the middle of winter, when everything would be cold, dead, and empty.

Skylar didn't deserve to leave this world so young. She had an entire life to live, children to watch grow up into good humans because of her exceptional mothering skills.

The back door opens, and I straighten, my feet hitting the deck floor, and I run my palms over my cheeks to dry the tears.

A king-size Twix bar lands with a thud on the patio table in front of me, then the chair next to me slides out, a body falling into it. The scent of men's cologne reaches my nostrils, giving me an idea of who it is before I even turn my head to look.

Peeking, I catch his long, thick fingers wrapped around the arm of a patio chair. The button-down sleeves are rolled up to his elbows, showing off forearms corded with muscles.

I swallow back my rush of desire. This isn't the time to be crushing on Hayes Carlisle.

"I'll take half as payment," his deep voice says.

I face him, and damn, he looks as good as he did when I saw him six months ago. He's always been built, but more so since the last time I saw him. He was clearly hitting the gym in the offseason.

"And here I thought this was your condolence gift."

He leans forward, swiping the candy bar off the table and tearing open the top of the packaging. "It was until I had to entertain all your guests. You're welcome." He pushes the top of the first two bars out of the packaging, holding it out to me.

"Were flowers too cliché?" I slide out one of the bars.

He takes the other and puts the candy bar back on the table. Then he holds out his bar toward me as if it's a glass of champagne and there's something to cheers to. I knock my bar with his and get rewarded with one of his swoon-worthy smiles.

"I never understood flowers at a funeral." He props his feet up on the empty chair in front of him, crossing his ankles. "Why would I give someone who's grieving something that's inevitably going to die a week later?"

His teeth sink into the chocolate and caramel, and my gaze snags on the vision. I attempt to deny the memory of those lips on mine. In my top five worst decisions ever, that night battles for the top spot.

"I think flowers are supposed to make something beautiful out of a sad day."

He scoffs, biting off another piece. "I hope when I die, people aren't commenting on how beautiful the roses strewn over my casket are as I'm being lowered into the ground."

I laugh and instantly place my hand over my mouth.

"Don't do that." He pops the last piece into his mouth.

My forehead wrinkles. "Do what?"

"Act like it's shameful to laugh."

"It is a funeral."

"So, all our other emotions besides grief aren't supposed to exist anymore?" He arches a brown eyebrow.

"I'm pretty sure you were brought up with manners."

"Are the funeral police going to come and get you because I made you laugh?" He gives me a cocky grin.

I tilt my head. "Still conceited, huh?"

"When it comes to making people laugh when they're having a shit day, yeah."

I don't say anything because I'm unsure what to say. I'll still feel guilty for laughing, knowing Sky never will again.

"Besides, if I were the funeral police, I probably wouldn't have shown up." There's an edge to his voice.

"What do you mean?"

He shrugs and cracks his neck, moving it right and left. "I'm here because I can be a distraction, which is why Callie called me, but I almost didn't come because I'm pissed at her right now."

Embarrassment makes my cheeks heat. I'm sure he had ten better things to do than show up here today. "She shouldn't have called you. I'm sorry for ruining your day."

He stops mid-neck crack, turning to look at me. It's been half a lifetime since I've spent any real time with him, so I can't read his expression as well as I used to. "Ruin my day? Fuck, Leighton, I'm pissed that she waited until now to tell me what happened. I would've been at the actual funeral had I known."

My cheeks heat even hotter from wishing he had been there. "Oh."

"I knew Sky in high school."

The flush dies. Of course… how stupid to think he would show up for any other reason than to mourn a classmate's tragic death.

"I gotta say, this isn't where I thought she'd end up." He scans the backyard, taking in the perfect landscaping, the swing set in the corner of their small yard, and painted rocks lining the deck's ledge.

"What do you mean?"

"I thought she'd be some band's groupie or something. I remember her being pretty wild. The parties she used to throw." He shakes his head and chuckles, then faces me again. His smile fades, and I hate that he's giving me the same look as everyone else in that house. "Tough gig, huh?"

"Gig?" I repeat, still not wanting to address my new reality.

His gaze falls to the uneaten candy bar in my hand. "I had to endure five minutes with the clerk telling me what's wrong with the Colts to buy that for you."

"Maybe it's not my favorite candy anymore."

He nods and shrugs his shoulders. "Then I suppose it's another five minutes of my life wasted, but score, I get the whole candy bar." He holds out his hand, but I shake my head. "Yeah, didn't think so."

I finally take a bite. Whoever says sweets can't make your day a little better is a liar.

"So… want to tell me why you vanished at the hospital six months ago?" he asks, interrupting my momentary reprieve from the reality of today.

Hayes can never let things be. Of course he's going to bring up when his friends were having a baby, and by some weird twist of fate, I was their nurse.

"Well, I am a nurse. I had to go do important nurse things."

He chuckles. "Important nurse things?"

I take another bite of the candy bar, and a smug smile tips his lips because I'm enjoying the candy he bought me. Still a cocky bastard.

"I thought maybe you were still dodging me years later," he says.

I glance at the door to the house, then tilt my head and give him my bored look. "Get over yourself."

"Well, I, for one, thought our kiss was pretty great."

"You're probably getting it mixed up with all the other women you've kissed since." I take another bite of the Twix bar.

"You're the only one who ran away after I kissed them." His grin grows wider, and I toss the last piece of the candy bar at him, which he catches and tosses in the air, catching it in his mouth. "Did you forget what position I play?"

I roll my eyes. "Like you'd let me forget."

I pick up the rest of the Twix bar, take out a second bar, and hand him the last one.

"You always were a good sharer," he says, accepting the bar. "This is about the last thing I should be eating. Gotta keep in shape." He pats his stomach as if there's a beer belly hidden under his crisp white shirt.

"I'm sure a few extra pounds aren't going to detour all the women in waiting."

A piece of candy bar lands on my chest. I pick it up and pop it in my mouth, giving him a smug grin as if to say thanks. "So, you can catch but not throw?"

His tongue slides along his bottom lip, and he gives me a crooked smile that makes me forget the reason we've been thrown together today. "I have a lot to prove this year."

I wasn't going to mention the rumor mill. It would be like adding gasoline to an already blazing fire. "How did it feel to get the call from the Colts?"

He huffs, licking chocolate off his fingers. Is he trying to distract me? "Honestly, I was relieved. I thought I had ruined my chances of playing. Last year was..." He moves his head to the right, his neck cracking again. "Intense."

"And stupid."

He chuckles again, looking at me. "Very stupid. I just got lost in my head, you know?"

I'd seen the emptiness in his eyes during the games I caught on television. His love of the game had been on the back burner, and his attention was far away from what was happening on the field.

"I can't believe we're all grown up," he says, picking up the empty candy wrapper and folding it in his hands as if he's about to do origami with it. "Seems like yesterday you and

Callie were in my Corolla, and I had to drive you somewhere."

"I miss Cruella."

He rolls his eyes. "I'm still pissed that you guys renamed my car."

"It was Callie's by then. You were off at college."

If that small rust bucket of a car could have talked, it could have blackmailed Callie and me enough to be completely restored.

A hand lands on my thigh, and I stiffen, looking down. He runs his palm up and down my thigh. "I'm really sorry about Sky and her husband. Her kids seem great. Callie told me that—"

"Yeah." I'm not ready to hear anyone else say it out loud just yet.

"That's what I meant earlier with the tough gig thing."

I feel my lips tip and quickly press them back down. "I got that. Looks like we both have some uphill battles this year."

His head falls back, and his hand drops from my thigh as he stares at the sky. "I'm not sure ours are evenly matched on importance." He swivels his head, his dark eyes finding mine, and for a second, I forget how to breathe. "But if I had to bet on anyone, it would be you."

I swallow to coat the dryness of my throat. The last thing I should feel in this moment is desire. "I should go. The kids..." My chair screeches along the deck, tipping over behind me.

He grabs my hand, his calloused palms warming mine. "Leighton—"

The back door opens, and my head turns as fast as my heart rate skyrockets. Callie's eyes dart between us, then zero in on our joined hands.

I slip my hand out of his slowly as if I can convince her she was seeing things. "Hey, are the kids okay?"

She steps out onto the deck. "Hayes, you're doing a piss-poor job."

He stands and shoves his hands in his pockets. "I'm on a break." He winks at me, and my treacherous stomach somersaults.

Remember, you make bad decisions when you're around him.

"And you told me to help Leighton through today. I'm helping, aren't I?" He raises his eyebrows.

It's really unfair for someone to be so damn beautiful.

"He brought me a Twix," I say, and Callie's forehead wrinkles. My cheeks heat. I sound pathetic. "Excuse me."

I slide past Callie, stepping back into the house, but I overhear her say, "Hold up, big brother. You have some explaining to do."

CHAPTER
THREE

Hayes

The door shuts as Callie walks over to stand in front of me and lean against the deck railing. She scared Leighton off, which is the typical outcome ever since that kiss we shared.

My sister crosses her arms, giving me that same expression she does when she tries to maneuver a birth order role reversal, as if she's the big sister and I'm the little brother. I fall back into the chair, knowing this won't be a quick conversation.

"Whatcha doing?" She's not asking if I'm enjoying the nice spring day. No, she's always had her antenna up when it comes to Leighton and me.

Not that I think Callie has any idea that back in college, I may or may not have kissed her best friend. I assume Leighton never told her, otherwise I would've heard about it.

"*You* summoned *me* here." I feel the need to remind her, even if there's nowhere else I'd rather be.

"To distract the guests, not swindle alone time with my best friend."

Flirting with Leighton has long been a favorite pastime. But ever since she ran that night, I've tried to be polite and keep my distance. But this, what's just been thrown in her lap is some serious shit, and I want her to know I'm in her corner. My sister doesn't need to know any of this though. "You're paranoid."

"Am I?"

If I answer, I'll tell her the same thing I always do—that I don't want Leighton. There's truth in that statement but more lies than truth. Leighton being Callie's best friend would cause a lot of problems if I actively went after her. I'm not sure how my sister would take it. She wasn't a fan back in high school when her friends wanted to spend more time with me than her. The two of them are like sisters, and I would never want to cause trouble between them. So even though I do want Leighton, I'll try to keep myself on a tight leash.

"If you ask me, she's one of four people in that house who need a distraction. Not the bleach blonde trapezing around the room as though she's in a 'Be the Next Martha Stewart' competition."

Callie rolls her eyes. "I know, right? Her name is Julianna. She's Patrick's brother's wife. She's a know-it-all."

Well, that solidifies my opinion of her. But I don't want this conversation to get off track because I have a lot of questions that weren't appropriate for me to ask Leighton. "Sorry for being nice to your best friend."

She picks up the Twix wrapper and holds it in the air. "You remembered her favorite candy bar?"

"Don't be jealous. I brought you a Hershey's bar." I pat my chest before realizing I'm not wearing my suit jacket. "It's in my jacket."

She slides a chair out and sits across from me, dramatically crossing her legs to say we're really going to dig in now. "I'm your sister, you should remember my favorite candy, but Leighton isn't—"

"How many times did I drive you guys to the 7-Eleven?" I shoot down her line of thinking that I somehow stored that piece of information away because I've yearned for Leighton all these years.

She hums and leans back in her chair, tossing the wrapper onto the table. "Now isn't the time, Hayes."

I stare her right in the eye with the hope that she doesn't see through me. "Let's talk about something else."

She rests her chin in her palm. "I'm serious. I know you're back in town, but this season is top priority for you, and she has all this to deal with. It's not the right time." She gestures to the house behind us, which I assume is now Leighton's.

My chest grows heavy just thinking about how exhausted Leighton's mind must be from spinning. "Haven't you heard? I'm a manwhore and partier who almost torched his entire career." I might be deflecting, but I'm not lying.

"Come on, Hayes, talk to me." There's concern in her gaze.

I rest my forearms on my legs and clasp my hands together. "One for one."

She groans, not wanting to play the game we always play when we're both hiding something and want information from the other. My mom started it when we were young to spur *real conversations*, as she put it.

"We're adults now, you can't be serious."

"Deadly." My voice doesn't waver.

She rolls her eyes again, and I still get some kind of sick pleasure from annoying my sister, even as a thirty-two-year-old man. "Only if I get to go first."

I gesture with my hand. "By all means, you are the baby of the family."

She groans but doesn't fight me because she wants to

know something just as badly as I do. "With the season starting again… are you in a better headspace?"

"Well yeah." I rub my hands together. "You made the first question too easy."

She leans back in her chair, crossing her legs. "Just take your turn." She waves her hand between us, and I chuckle.

"Is Leighton really going to take this on?"

She nods. "And you make fun of my question for being too easy? Of course she is. She's Leighton. You know her."

I used to. Hell, Leighton went on family vacations. You don't spend that much time together without getting to know the person. Even now that we've kept our distance since the kissing incident, it's no surprise to me she's agreed to take on the role of guardian to her cousin's kids.

I open my mouth to ask another question.

"Nope… my turn." Callie taps her finger to her lips. "How's it going with your manager?"

"Listen, I'm just going to give it all to you at once because none of this seems very important in the grand scheme of why we're out on the deck with what's going on inside. Spring training was great. I'm meeting with Jagger in a couple of days. Vega seems good with me and is willing to give me a fresh start. I plan to work my ass off and win a Gold Glove this year to prove wrong everyone who said I was done. End of story. I fucked up last year…"

"Yeah, but—"

I cut her off because regardless of the circumstances, there was no excuse for all the partying. "My turn. Since you only decided to tell me today about Skylar dying, I'd like more specifics."

Callie blows out a breath. "I'm sorry, I should've told you earlier, but I didn't want anything too heavy on your mind. I'm honestly surprised Mom didn't tell you. She'd be here if she and Dad weren't in Europe." She smiles, and I can't help but match it. "Then I could tell Leighton was really getting sad and annoyed, and I just figured—"

"I wish you would've called me sooner. Hell, I would've brought over the entire team to get all those guests off Leighton's back."

"I know you would. I'm sorry though. I just… You two are weird together sometimes, and I thought maybe it would stress her out more."

Fuck. My sister *has* noticed the way that kiss changed the dynamic between Leighton and me. I'm surprised Callie's not asking me flat out what gives. "How did Skylar and her husband pass?"

She leans back and sighs. "No one is really certain on all the details. Sky and Patrick were up north at Patrick's family cabin for a couple's getaway. They were hiking, and it's not clear if one of them initially fell and the other tried to go after them, or what, but they were both found on a rock landing from what is suspected to be an accidental fall."

Shit, you go for quality time and die? I guess I can take hiking off my *bring the spark back* trip list for whenever I get married.

I let out a slow exhale. "That's crazy."

"I know. And then the lawyer comes and says they named Leighton—"

"She didn't know beforehand?" She had back-to-back blows. Fuck.

Callie shakes her head. "I'm sure they never thought anything would happen to them."

"I don't want to sound like I doubt her, but this is a lot for Leighton to take on."

And she'll do it for the sole reason that her cousin wanted her to. She's not someone who lets anyone down.

"Yeah, I'm going with her to the lawyer in a couple of days."

We both lean back in our chairs. I miss my sister. I haven't spent nearly the time I want with her since returning to Chicago. And now that I'm on the straight and narrow, away from clubs or anything that puts me in the gossip blogs, we won't be on the same Chicago nightlife scene.

"I can help."

She tips her head, knowing how busy I'm about to be. One hundred sixty-two games plus hopefully the playoffs are my next half of the year. I shouldn't care how Leighton will do it all. It's her business, and since she clearly doesn't want anything to do with me, I need to stay on my own course.

The door opens behind us, and I can't help but hope it's Leighton.

"Linc!" Leighton says, but the little boy is already in front of me with his mitt and ball in hand.

"Will you play catch with me?"

"Hayes has to go now." Leighton comes out and puts her hand on the little guy's shoulders. He can't be more than eight or nine.

"No, I don't." I stand up from the chair. "Do you have a glove for me?"

"Yeah, you can use my dad's." He drops his glove and ball and runs back into the house.

"You don't have to. I'm sure you have more important things to do." The dark circles under Leighton's blue eyes make my heart feel as heavy as lead.

I shrug. "I don't have anywhere I need to be."

Before I have time to enjoy the small smile creasing Leighton's lips, Lincoln comes back out and holds out a broken-in glove for me.

For the next hour, I play catch and hear all about Patrick, a man I didn't know but who was clearly a great dad.

CHAPTER
FOUR

Hayes

"Hellooo!" Jagger waves his hand in front of my face.

"Sorry." I straighten in my chair and pick up my fork again.

It's been three days, and I still can't get Leighton out of my head. This does not bode well for the season ahead.

"You need to get your head together. This is the kind of shit I'm talking about." He points his fork at me like a dad would at his teenage son who's on his fifth detention.

Jagger is the best agent in the industry, and I'm pretty sure it's because he doesn't sugarcoat anything. He doesn't boost our egos or baby us when we fuck up. He was all over my ass last year, but I didn't give a shit at the time. On the flip side though, he'll praise us and fight for us when our skills and talent have us at the top of the MVP list.

"Let me remind you, you're here because of me." He turns the fork around and points it at himself, then uses it to stab some of the scrambled eggs on his plate.

To some, that sentence might sound conceited. I didn't see Jagger busting his ass to get a D1 college offer, nor did I hear from him much when I was barely getting by in the minors. But I'm in Chicago now, playing for the Colts, blessed with a second chance to prove that I'm not a difficult player, so he's earned an imaginary gold ribbon for being the best fucking agent.

"Didn't you get my fruit bouquet?" I lean back in my chair.

His lips tip into an almost grin before he breaks out into a full smile. The other thing about Jagger is that he knows I'm deflecting and will play my game. "Quinn says get the one with more pineapple next time."

I fork my egg whites and avocado. "Done. Apologize to your wife for me. And sorry for not being completely here. It's just that my sister's best friend—"

He groans. "That sentence right there sounds like drama. The kind of drama you need to stay away from."

"It's not like that." That's a lie. If it wasn't anything, I'm pretty sure she wouldn't be on my mind every damn second.

Though there is some truth there, just for a different reason than Jagger suspects. Leighton isn't into me... and probably thinks I'm a shitty kisser since the only time I kissed her, I was on the heavier side of buzzed. Not that the alcohol running through my veins was the reason I kissed her—far from it. I think I noticed Leighton the minute she hit puberty, which probably makes me a creep.

"The way your mind is wandering again, I'm pretty sure it's exactly like that." Jagger frowns.

I drop my fork and pick up my water. "It's not. I appreciate this whole 'make sure you have your shit together' pep talk, but you didn't need to fly out here. I'm good. I told you that."

"All you athletes are so conceited. As if I'd fly to Chicago just for you." He raises his hand for the waitress when she passes by. "Excuse me, sorry, but I forgot to order something earlier. Can I have a pancake made into a flower? My daughter." He holds his phone out to her to see his screensaver. "She loves this place, and I promised to get one and eat it on her behalf."

The waitress smiles and stares at Jagger for a moment before coming out of her trance and heading over to the pancake maker behind the glass to put in Jagger's order. He's definitely got that salt-and-pepper good-looking guy thing. Plus, his suit says he's powerful. And rich.

"Does Quinn know you flirt?" I lean back in my chair, crossing my arms.

"Believe me, I got my head out of my ass a long time ago. Quinn knows she's the only woman I see or want. And if you think that was flirting, I can see why you're still single." He wipes his mouth and places the paper napkin back on his lap.

"I'm single by choice," I say.

"I used to say that too."

"I get that I fucked up last year, but I like to think I'm a pretty good catch."

He sips his coffee. "That's all you athletes' biggest problem. You attract the ones who want you for all the wrong reasons, and the good ones want nothing to do with the spotlight that comes along with your career. And if they can handle it, most of the time you're too blind to even see the good ones. I'll tell you though, the Falcons—"

"Here we go again." I groan. "You treat us Colts like we're your stepchildren."

"More like newborns. You're cute and all, but you whine and cry too much, and I often find myself having to clean up your shit."

The waitress places the flower-shaped pancake in front of Jagger. "Here you go. Anything else?"

"No, we're all good, thanks, Heidi." Jagger pulls out a

twenty and slides it into her palm. "Tell Erik thank you. She's going to be so happy."

She smiles and turns toward me, placing the bill beside my plate, and walks away.

Jagger pulls out his phone and snaps a picture of the flower pancake, his smile so big and genuine, something pulls at my heart. He's happy just because he knows his daughter will be happy. Sometimes I wonder if I'll ever be in a place to have my own family. My entire life has had one end goal, but that goal marker keeps moving. When will I feel like I can have it all?

"The bill is yours. You can pay it with the money from that shiny new contract I got you." Jagger puts syrup on one petal and eats it, takes another picture, then sips his coffee as he stands, ready to leave. The man is a machine.

"You got a percentage of that contract." I slide the bill toward him.

He picks it up and straightens his tie, pulling his wallet out. "Come on, you're not my only client."

I stand and grab my jacket from the back of the chair. "Which you always make clear. Off to see your golden boys?" I think he might be the Chicago Falcons biggest fan.

I follow him to the register, where I search for a mystery flavor Dum Dum in the complimentary bin by the register.

"Thanks, Val, see you next time I'm in town," Jagger says to the woman cashing us out.

"Tell the little ones I said hi and we miss them." Her long, manicured nails flail in the air as she waves goodbye.

I unwrap my Dum Dum and walk out of the pancake house onto the streets of Chicago. "You should ask for a back booth here. Have a constant rotation of your players in and out of the place." I stand on the sidewalk, out of the way of bypassing foot traffic.

"Coming here while I'm babysitting you toddlers makes it more bearable." He stuffs his wallet into the front pocket of his suit jacket. "We got off on a tangent, so let me lay it out there—I'm gonna give you three rules to follow."

Last year I would've blown him off, raised my hand for a taxi and pissed him off, only to get a voicemail with threats and demands from him later. This year, I'm different, so I stuff my hands in the pockets of my jacket and listen.

"Good boy," he says, noticing the effort I'm putting in. I don't even make a sarcastic comment about being a loyal dog. "One, you don't go out nights before a game."

I roll my eyes.

"Two, you are not seen with a million different women."

"A million? I'm impressed with myself."

"You know what I mean. Maybe try to find a girl to go on a couple quiet dinner dates with, go to the movies. Get your picture taken holding her hand. Do *not* find her in a club."

"A relationship is the furthest thing from my mind."

"Unless the Colts start winning, and then you'll be on a high. I've seen this more times than you. The highs are really fucking high, and you're going to want to celebrate with pussy. So, this year, steady pussy is the best option. Now… third… stay the fuck away from Foster Davis."

"What?" My forehead wrinkles. Foster's getting the blame for my behavior last year, but he had nothing to do with my mind being everywhere but on the ballfield. "He's my best friend."

"And he's my client, but he's not good for your reputation. Vega doesn't like him, so if you want a contract at the end of the year, in two weeks when you play one another, do not go out with him."

"This seems extreme. Vega isn't my dad, telling me who I can hang out with. I'm an adult."

Jagger looks around the sidewalk. Thankfully, it's midweek, so there aren't a ton of people, and no one has recognized me. "This is what you get when you try to blow up your entire career in a single year. Next year we can loosen the reins a little, but this year, you keep your head down, work your ass off, and stay out of trouble. A Gold Glove would be fucking awesome this year, just saying."

I scowl at him. "Like I haven't tried every year to get it?"

I've never been awarded one. Just another thing that pisses me off.

He steps closer. "Not last year, you didn't. We're in damage control mode. You're the best catcher in this league. It didn't take that much convincing to get Chicago to snap you up before the trade deadline because they know what you're capable of. But we have to clean up that shit off the field. When that happens and you have no distractions, you're going to have all eyes on you. Your career is going to peak. With you, Decker Davis, and Easton Bailey, the Colts have a shot at the playoffs. So please, do yourself and me a favor and listen to me—I promise the rewards are coming."

This is why Jagger is the most sought-after agent in the industry. I actually believe him. Minus the fact that he's mine, Decker's, and Easton's agent, so of course he thinks we're going to turn the Colts' shitty record around, but he actually makes me believe I'm indispensable. That the Colts are lucky to have me.

"Okay, you got it." I nod.

He holds out his hand, and we shake. "I knew you'd understand." A car pulls up to the curb. "Want a ride?"

"Nah, I'm gonna walk."

"Good. Good. Let the city see you as one of their own. Smile and wave and be approachable. Having them behind you can only help you."

I nod like an annoyed teenager at a family holiday. "Tell the Falcons I say hi."

He gives me his cocky grin. "You guys win it all like they did, and maybe you'll be my new favorites."

I roll my eyes. I get that they aren't his problem children. They're all married with kids and still killing it on the ice.

We part, and I turn toward the three-flat condo building that Decker, Easton, and I took over from the Falcons. It was meant to be ours—the rooftop overlooks Webber Field where the Colts play.

Being back in Chicago births new life inside me and makes me feel like the possibilities for the team and me are endless. I can totally do what Jagger is asking, and it's not as though I'll be around Foster much since he's still playing back in Seattle. Our paths won't cross often.

Walking up to my building, I see a cardboard sign on the black iron security door. Another attempt by the diamond girls to coin the name of our building.

Three of the Chicago Grizzlies lived here first, and the jersey chasers referred to it as The Den back then.

When the Falcons took it over, the puck bunnies called it The Nest.

And now the diamond girls can't seem to figure out what to call it. Every week a sign shows up with something new.

I pause in front of the gate to read the sign.

The Barn?

I tear down the cardboard sign. We're definitely not a bunch of smelly cows.

CHAPTER
FIVE

Leighton

"Why do you think lawyer's offices are always so stuffy and old?" Callie crosses her legs next to me in the conference room that the receptionist escorted us to. We've been sitting here for twenty minutes now, and with every second that passes, my anxiety ratchets up a notch.

"Probably to appear more serious."

"So, if they painted the walls lime green, people wouldn't think they're good at their job? All this dark wood and black leather is depressing." She spins her chair in a circle like Monroe would.

"I'll be sure to mention that their decorating is subpar on the comment card." I scroll through my phone, looking for a quick dinner recipe for tonight.

Gone are the days of microwave meals and takeout every night. Of all the challenges I knew taking on three children would entail, I did not anticipate that figuring out what to

make for dinner every night might be one of the most challenging.

It's been three days since the funeral. My mom and Aunt
Iris are watching the kids right now since they're not going
back to school until next week. Even then, I have to wonder if
it's appropriate for them to go back to school one week after
their entire lives blew up. I have no idea, which is another
indication that Sky may have made the wrong choice by
choosing me.

"They need something cheery, like wallpaper with a
flower or bird print. People are already coming to see a
lawyer for a crappy reason—lawsuit, divorce, custody
issues... maybe a little happiness would make the whole
experience less shitty."

"Maybe you should tell Mr. Notting that he needs a snow
cone machine and a balloon artist who makes you a flower
bouquet after you sign your divorce papers."

She stops spinning in the chair and glares at me. "It was
just a suggestion."

I inhale a deep breath. "I'm sorry. I'm just nervous. This is
all happening so fast."

Her hand covers mine on the long oval table that looks as
if it's polished every morning. "I know. I'm here for you
though."

"I know you are, but you have your own life."

"What life?"

I raise my eyebrows, and she tips her head right and left.
She doesn't need to put her life on hold for me. Callie's going
on tour for her podcast, *If I'm Honest*, in four weeks, and she
will be going—no matter how many times she tells me she can
reschedule it.

"You're going," I say before she can once again offer to set
aside her budding career.

"We'll see. I talked to Becca—"

"You're going. I'll call Becca myself."

There's a quick knock on the door and it opens. Mr. Notting strides in with his assistant, Peggy.

"Good morning. Sorry to keep you waiting, it's been a little crazy," he says.

His life has been crazy?

Okay, buddy, try being thrown into a war zone without any training. Sure, I was at Sky's house a lot and the kids know me and are close to me, but I never planned a dinner unless I was babysitting, and then it was anything that could be delivered. I'm unprepared for Lake's clothing crises, Lincoln constantly throwing a ball against the wall, and Monroe's *today I only eat this food*. Especially while we're all in the midst of grieving and trying to make sense of the loss of their parents.

"Crazy, huh? That many lives to ruin?" Callie raises her eyebrows.

I kick her under the table, but she doesn't flinch. She's become immune to it. Her eyes are set on Mr. Notting. He chuckles, and Peggy gives us an awkward smile.

If I had to guess, I'd think he's in his fifties—attractive and definitely keeps up with his health and fitness, with a trimmed salt-and-pepper beard and sparkling blue eyes. I think it's why he's wearing a blue suit every time I see him. Makes people get lost in his eyes and stop thinking about what he charges per hour.

"Good morning, Callie, nice to see you again." There's a flicker of amusement in his eyes.

"Morning, Mark. No coffee, huh?" She leans back, crosses her legs, and rests her forearms on the chair. "Is Leighton allowed to deduct her mileage and the cost of getting here off your bill?"

I have no idea why Patrick and Skylar chose Mr. Notting, but I do think he knows his stuff and can help me navigate this unfamiliar path.

He sets his gaze on me, ignoring Callie, and I'm sure if I

looked at her, she'd have a shit-eating grin across her face. "Now that you've had some time to think about the news and you've had the funeral and things are going to start settling down, I want to discuss how you're feeling about taking on guardianship of the children. If you want to move forward, we need to petition the court."

I glance at Peggy then back at him, looking for someone to help me understand. "Petition the court? They listed me as a guardian. It's a done deal, isn't it?"

Callie straightens in her chair, her alarm bells going off along with mine.

"Yes, Patrick and Skylar listed that their wish was that you would be the guardian to Lake, Lincoln, and Monroe. But now the court has to approve you."

"Approve her?" Callie's voice booms off the dark walls.

He gives Callie a fleeting gaze before he directs his attention back to me. "We have to say you want them—"

Panic hits, flooding my veins as if someone just pulled the fire alarm. All this time, I wondered what would happen if I said no. Would Aunt Iris step up? Patrick's dad? Where would the kids go? I felt trapped and lost, but now that Mr. Notting is implying there's a possibility I could not be approved, I can't imagine not doing it.

The idea of going back to my quiet, empty apartment feels like poison in my veins. I've grown accustomed to the chaos. I can't imagine how much I'd miss those kids if they were taken from me. Besides, it was obviously important to Sky and Patrick that I be the one to raise their children, and I want to make sure to honor their wishes.

"I want them." I turn to Callie.

A soft smile creases her lips as if she was waiting for me to be firm on my decision. Her hand wraps around mine in silent support. I really do have the best friend anyone could ask for.

Mr. Notting nods at Peggy. "Then we start by filing your Petition for Guardianship."

"But a judge has to agree that I'm fit to be their guardian?" Fear strikes me like a small itch that spreads into a rash. Quickly, my mind is calculating my job, my salary, my savings. Will a judge think I'm fit to take care of them?

"Why does she have to prove herself? Obviously, their parents thought she was the right person to raise their kids."

I squeeze Callie's hand. She's always the first to go to bat for me.

Mr. Notting raises his hand. "Let me explain what will happen moving forward. I'm sure you were a little stunned when I read the will. So..." He glances at Peggy again, and I suddenly feel like the third wheel on a date. They know what's about to happen to me before I do. "We file the petition, which tells the court that the will states you as guardian, and you do, in fact, want to take guardianship of the children. Then a notice will be issued to all other family members, and they will have the option to come forward if they wish to be the ones to raise the children." He must notice my face drain of color because he tips his head down. "I know, but nine times out of ten, nothing comes of this. It's just part of the process. If anyone should want to object, they can, and then temporary guardianship will be issued to one of the parties while the court figures out what is in the best interest of the children."

I spin toward Callie, and she squeezes my hand. I'm what Skylar wanted, and Patrick clearly agreed. I rack my brain on who might come forward. Aunt Iris said she wishes she could, but there's no way she could keep up with them. Though she offered to help me as much as she can. Sky had no other siblings. We were like sisters to each other since we were both only children.

"You're going to get them," Callie tries to assure me, but a haunting thought comes to mind.

"Art and Julianna," I whisper.

Callie shakes her head, but I'm not sure we can count them out. He's got a great job, and she's working now but made a point of telling me at the funeral that as soon as she gets pregnant, they can afford for her not to work. She was up my ass the entire time about how things should go and made more than one comment about how it seems like her motherly instincts might be better than mine.

"The brother?" Mr. Notting asks. "The one who got the house up north?"

I nod. The house Patrick and Sky were staying in before they died. I wasn't upset about that. I'd never want that house and reminder of what happened. I'm never going hiking again.

"I guess we'll find out if he has any interest in taking on guardianship. In the meantime, we'll file the paperwork. If no one comes forward before the hearing, then it will be easy."

"Good," I say. Callie and I share a look.

Art didn't show much interest in the children at the funeral. He hasn't been much of an uncle to them. Sure, he was upset about the news of his brother and sister-in-law's deaths, but he never said anything to me after finding out I was listed as the guardian.

"If someone does step forward, I'll refer you to a colleague, someone more experienced in that realm, but let's hope it doesn't come to that." He slides out of his chair and leans across the table, holding out his hand. "Thanks for coming in today." His smile shifts to Callie, and she giggles a little. "I'll be in touch."

I shake his hand, and when he shifts it in front of Callie, she slides her hand into his.

"Always a pleasure, Miss Carlisle."

I look between the two of them. There's a slight blush on her cheeks, and the way her teeth bite down on the edge of her lips… and she's getting a lot longer handshake than I did.

I clear my throat, and they part, Mr. Notting picking up his papers. "Peggy, do you mind seeing them out?"

"Of course," she says, unfazed by the exchange. Is he like that with all his clients' friends?

He walks out of the office, and I give Callie a look.

She shrugs. "I'm not his client."

"Well, I am."

"You didn't see me saying anything when you were holding hands with my brother the other day." She arches an eyebrow.

I'm surprised this is the first time she's brought it up.

I attempt to stare blankly, masking any reaction, as though I haven't replayed that interaction several times over the last few days. "I was not holding his hand."

"Okay, ladies, let's get you out of here. Surely you have things to do." Peggy smiles politely as she opens the door into the reception area. Polite but pointedly. She wants us gone.

We say our thanks then wait at the elevator.

"We weren't holding hands," I murmur, just to make sure she knows I'm not stepping over the line she was so adamant about when we were younger. Which I understood. Hell, every girl in our class wanted Hayes, and she had to deal with a lot of girls pretending to be her friend just to come over to see him. I swore I'd never do that to her.

Guilt weighs heavy on my shoulders, but I push it aside.

She puts her arm around my shoulders. "I know, but it's not my fault your lawyer has that hot-daddy energy."

I blow out a breath. "Callie…"

She laughs. "Relax, I'll wait until you're done with him."

The elevator doors slide open. "Ew, don't say it like that."

We step inside the small space as she laughs. "Why? Just because you've always had a thing for my brother, admitting that Mr. Notting is hot doesn't make you a cheater."

She laughs again, and I press the lobby button to be done

with this conversation, pretending she's delusional, although I think we both know she's not.

CHAPTER
SIX

Hayes

One Month Later

It's the last day of April, and that wouldn't be exciting to most people, but to six of us on the Colts, it ends a month-long bet between the infielders and outfielders. The winners get bragging rights and an expensive steak dinner.

"You just need to hit a double and we've won." Easton pats me on the back, coming into the dugout after Decker hit him home.

Now we're in a tied game with one out in the bottom of the ninth. Decker is on first, Torres is up to the plate, and I'll come in behind him. We just need to get Decker home.

"What the fuck has gotten into you guys?" Drew is stewing on the bench since we turned the tables on him and his outfield buddies, taking the lead in our little bet.

"Listen, DICs, this competition was your idea." Easton puts his helmet in the box, fixes his chains, and shakes out his hair before marking another five slashes on our makeshift scoreboard.

The fans out there would either think it's funny or irresponsible, or maybe just childish, that we're competing with one another over who can tag the most bases in a month.

"Will you stop calling us DICs!" Ian grabs his helmet because he's up after me.

"It's not our fault the first letter of all three of your names spells out DIC." I give Ian a shit-eating grin.

Our best day during spring training was when Easton figured that out. The nickname stuck immediately.

"We don't call you HED," Drew grumbles.

Easton's eyebrows raise at me, as if asking, *do we even have to dignify this ridiculousness with a response?*

"HED makes no sense. DIC does." Easton does end up responding because he likes nothing more than some good banter. Although Drew doesn't really offer the competition Easton thrives on.

"You guys have sucked all month, and on the last day of the month, you hit the ball like you've got horseshoes up your ass." Drew is pouting, as usual. Sometimes I think it's because between Easton, Decker, and me, we have the three biggest contracts on the team. My yearly beats Drew's, but he's young. If he's going to make it in the league, he'd better ditch this whiny-ass attitude.

Everyone shuts up as Torres steps up to the plate, talking shit to Greer.

I set up in the on deck circle, listening to Drew and Easton having it out behind me. I'm surprised Vega hasn't told them to cut the shit by now. He's entertained our game, but I think it's only because he thinks any competition between us will make us try harder.

Torres sees one strike and two balls before he hits a deep grounder to third and gets tagged out, but Decker makes it to second. I need a double to get Decker in to win the game—and the bet.

"Let's go, Haymaker," Easton shouts.

I look over to Paxton at third for my sign.

Even a month into the season with a decent batting average, the minute my cleats land in the batter's box, I start sweating. I haven't found myself in this kind of game-making situation yet this year. Every performance still feels as though it's a plus or minus on my contract extension for next year.

I run through the same drill I always have—run my bat along the outside of home plate, slide my feet, digging the front of my cleats into the ground. I ignore the shit talk from Greer, forcing myself to stay in the zone. *Be calm, be patient, and do what you know you can do.* I just wish the internal pep talk made a fucking difference. I'm still playing scared, which will never work long term for me.

The first pitch comes in—a strike just outside that I've struggled to hit my entire fucking life, so I let it go right by. I step up again, Greer continuing to talk shit, asking me where he should go tonight to find all the hot women since he figures I'd have a good hookup.

Fuck him.

The second pitch comes in, and it's way low, making Greer drop to his knees to block.

"Fucking hell," he grumbles.

"You look like you're used to being on your knees."

Ramos is getting tired on the mound, but Arizona will let him stay since there's only one out left to go. If I can throw Greer off and he misses a ball low in the dirt, it could get Decker to third and in scoring position.

"From eating your girl's pussy," Greer says. "Get ready, I see you going on a bender after you fuck up this opportunity to win the game."

I clench my jaw, the dig at my behavior last year hitting its mark.

The pitch comes in, and it's a ball, inside and high. Greer has to pop up to get it.

"Your boy is off," I say. "Go have a mound visit. Don't worry about me."

Greer squats again, making him one of the most selfish catchers in the league. There's no harm in giving your pitcher a little pep talk to get through the last batter. But all Greer wants him to do is throw a damn strike and go home.

The next pitch comes in and again, it's in the dirt, but this time, Greer can't get down fast enough. The ball hits his shin guard, shooting out toward their dugout. He goes to chase it down, and our entire dugout goes ballistic as Decker sprints to third.

All my teammates are up on their feet, cheering him on, and the pressure that was at a level I could manage is now rising so fast, my heart might leap out of my chest.

You can do this, Hayes. You were meant for moments like this. Hell, you've been in this same situation numerous times, from rec league to now. Just get in that box, swing the bat, and run like hell.

"This one is going to make you look stupid," Greer says as the pitch leaves Ramos' hand. It's a little high, but a strike, nonetheless. I should've gone after it.

"Fuck."

"Yeah, not going to get the ladies excited with that one."

I ignore Greer. My teammates are shouting, Vega looks concerned, and Decker takes his lead off of third, eyes Ramos.

Inhaling a deep breath, I think about what Greer will call and how tired Ramos' arm is. Then I reprimand myself for trying to predict and just go by what I was taught early—if I think I can hit it, swing the damn bat.

Ramos winds up, side-stepping, and releases the ball. Everything slows as the ball barrels toward me. It looks good, just outside and right in the zone. My zone. I shift my weight back, my hands in the perfect position, and swing for it. My swing feels right, the one I've been perfecting all year. My bat makes contact, and I see it sail right between left and center.

I drop the bat and run like hell to first base.

Decker must score because the entire stadium roars. I tag first base, the ball coming in right after my foot hits the bag.

God, this feels incredible.

The umpires call the game, the Colts win, and everyone is shouting and clapping. I forgot what it feels like when the entire stadium is on your side, the adrenaline from feeling that sense of accomplishment that comes from contributing to your team.

Easton hops over the fence, running right at me, and we jump and hit shoulders. "Way to fucking go! Fuck the DICs!"

I laugh, and Decker does the same, all three of us running and jumping into one another. We celebrate as if we won the division title.

Now I kind of understand what Jagger was talking about —I want to take this celebration out on the town with my teammates tonight and, yeah, bring a woman home. It just wouldn't be the one I really want.

As we walk off the field, Vega puts his hand up to us. "You three, interviews."

It's the first time this season I've been requested to go into the media room.

Maybe Drew's right, and someone did shove a horseshoe up my ass.

CHAPTER
SEVEN

Hayes

The three of us go to the locker room to shower and change.

"Reservation at seven, boys." Easton points at Drew, Ian, and Camden. "You have nice suits, don't you?"

"Fuck off, Kodiak," Drew says.

"That's Mr. Kodiak to you." Easton laughs and strips down before heading into the shower. He lives up to the stereotype that shortstops come with egos.

Camden doesn't seem to give a shit, undressing and preparing to head to the shower. He's quiet, a little like our Decker.

"Those two are going to come to blows at some point this season," Decker says next to me, slowly unbuttoning his jersey. "I bet that hit felt good."

I glance over, but he continues to unbutton and undress, not looking over. "It did. I'm just hoping this feeling sticks around until the next time I'm in the box."

He chuckles and nods. "Nothing harder than coming back from a slump, but you were great out there today. Behind the plate especially. Tell me Taz thanked you."

I shake my head and my mouth tips down at the corners. "Taz doesn't roll that way. I will say though, I know you and your brother aren't exactly besties, but Foster always thanked me before he stepped off the field."

Decker nods. "I'm not surprised. He has *some* good qualities." He pats me on the shoulder. "See you in there. Good game today, but I'd still love you even if you struck out." He winks and laughs, heading into the showers.

I sit on the bench and grab my phone out of my safe.

> Mom: I hope you're happy and proud.
> Love you.

> Dad: You're back in the saddle again…

I shake my head at how he always uses song lyrics to get his point across and scroll down to the next message.

> Foster: Sitting here watching your game-winning hit like a proud dad. At least my brother has one good quality, he can run fast.

There's no message from Callie, which is odd. She usually messages me win or lose, but she left for her tour yesterday, so I'm sure she's busy preparing for her kickoff show in New York.

I stuff my phone back into my safe and follow everyone else into the showers.

An hour later, we're showered, dressed, and out of the media room, which surprisingly went well. I guess that's what happens when you don't fuck it all up but actually help your team win.

Easton and Decker are grabbing their bags and talking

about how they're going to order every appetizer on the menu, and that soup and salad are a must. Decker says he'll order all the desserts and part of me feels bad for the DICs, but then again, they've been cocky assholes, saying it's the old men against the young bucks. Give me a break, I'm thirty-fucking-two, far from an old man.

My phone is vibrating as I open the safe, and I see ten missed calls from Callie and a slew of texts that go from nice to mean to meaner.

> Call me when you get this.
>
> You fuckwad, where are you?
>
> I'm going to strangle you.
>
> Haaaaaayesssssss… where are you?
>
> Your game has been over foooreeevver….
>
> Call me back as soon as you see these.

My stomach drops down to my toes. I dial her right back, fear like a class six rapid rushing through my veins. You'd never guess I felt so light and free a minute ago when I stepped out of that room where those reporters were praising me.

Callie picks up, sounding frustrated. "What the fuck, Hayes? Your game ended a long-ass time ago."

"What is it? What's wrong?"

"Oh shit, no… sorry… I didn't mean to panic you." Her anger dissipates, and I fall to the bench, the emotional roller coaster taking a toll on me.

"I got asked to be in the media room," I tell her, so she knows I wasn't dodging her.

She sighs. "Really? I'm the asshole then. How was it? Great? Dreamy?"

"Dreamy? What's going on, Callie?" I'd usually tell her

how much better this is than last year. Like winning the lottery when you're dirt poor. One day, your entire life changes with the scratch of a penny.

I appreciate her asking, but I want to know what has her in a panic, since usually there are only a couple of things—her podcast, our parents, and Leighton. With everything going on, Leighton is the most likely cause.

"It's Leighton," she says.

I pick up my bag and swing it over my shoulder. "What's going on?"

"She's having a rough night. Can you go over there and help? I know you're tired and all—"

"I thought 'now isn't the time,'" I say, using a faux female voice. She's too far away to pull my hair or wrap her hands around my throat when I throw her words back at her.

"I'm not asking you to fuck her. I'm asking you to go play catch with Linc or color with Monroe."

I chuckle, and she groans.

"I'm on my way."

"Really? Thanks, Hayes. And it's not like I need to say it, but keep your dick in your pants, okay?"

I shake my head, even if she can't see me. "I'll try, but sometimes he's got a mind all his own. He just pops up, you know?"

She pretends to gag. "I'm trying to eat my dinner here."

"Go and have a great podcast."

"Thank you! Love you."

"Love you too. I've got your best friend handled." She doesn't laugh, which spurs my own chuckle. "Fucking hell, Callie, relax."

We hang up, and it's then I realize Easton and Decker are waiting for me by the door. Shit, the dinner. Easton will probably tell me to bring Leighton and the kids just to punish the DICs, but I'm not gonna do that.

"Sorry, guys, I'm out."

"Out? You can't be out." Decker is the first one to object, which is surprising.

"The best friend?" Easton asks.

I filled the two of them in after I saw Leighton at the funeral.

I nod.

"Bring them," he says.

I'm a little amazed at how well I know Easton for only being friends for six months.

"Nah, but order my steak and all the sides and give it to Ruby or something." The woman who owns the bar on the street level of our building has a gruff exterior, but once you get to know her, she's not that bad.

Decker shakes his head, not giving me shit about this. "Do you need us?" He turns toward the exit, and Easton and I follow.

"No, I got it. I'll probably just order pizza, then freshen up on my stay-within-the-lines coloring skills." I'm not sure that's all I'll be doing. I'm guessing if Callie called me, Leighton must be losing her mind, since Callie's been very clear—she doesn't want me anywhere near her best friend.

"You should invite them to a game. I'd like to meet this best friend," Easton says, grinning.

"We met her," Decker reminds him.

"We did?" His dark brows draw down.

"At the hospital, when Tweetie had his baby."

The three of us are friendly with some of Chicago's professional hockey players.

We stop outside the stadium, since we're now headed in separate directions.

"The strawberry-blonde? Didn't realize that was who it was." Easton's eyes widen. "She's way out of your league."

Decker slaps him in the chest with the back of his hand. "And on that, I'm out."

"When can we talk about your sister? Are you a hands-off-my-sister kind of guy, or is it open season?" Easton laughs, walking backward in the opposite direction.

"Fuck you, East." I flip him off.

He laughs until he's almost at our building while I use my phone to order an Uber that comes in minutes, thank God.

When I'm in the back seat, I wonder if I should message Leighton, then wonder if the phone number I have for her is still hers. It's been years since we've called or texted one another, and even then, it was only on a group thread with Callie.

By the time I'm done debating, the Uber pulls up alongside a parked car by the curb outside their house. Guess the decision is made—my visit will be a surprise.

I thank the Uber driver, step out, and stand on the sidewalk, taking in the place. All the lights are on inside the house, and I spot Lincoln through the window, throwing a ball against the wall.

I jog up the stairs and knock on the door. The door opens almost immediately, and my gaze tracks down to Monroe.

"Monroe!" I recognize the voice as her big sister Lake's. She rushes into the entry area, sliding to a stop on her socks when she sees me. Lake quickly gets over her surprise and turns her attention to Monroe. "You know not to answer the door."

"I thought it was my bubble tea," Monroe whines.

"Doesn't matter." She slides in front of her little sister, urging Monroe behind her.

Lincoln peeks around Lake's shoulders, eyes wide. "Hayes?"

Lake bats her hands to keep him back, as if I'm a serial killer posing as a duct cleaning service, then she crosses her arms. "She's not here."

She sure gives off teenager vibes for an eleven-year-old. Or maybe this is what they're all like these days, thanks to social media.

"Yes, she is," Lincoln says.

Monroe peeks her head between her older sister's legs. "She's upstairs because she needs a goddamn minute to herself."

I have to press my lips together not to laugh at hearing that phrase come out of a six-year-old's mouth.

"Lake made her cry," Lincoln says.

The sister in question whips her head around. "I did not."

I remember being on the receiving end of looks just like that with my own sister back in the day. "Okay, guys, can I come in?"

"No." Lake spears me with a look.

"Tell me it's the bubble tea." I hear Leighton before I see her walking down the stairs.

"Even better! It's Hayes!" Lincoln makes me feel as if my number was retired and my jersey is hanging at Webber Field.

"Oh." Her surprised voice doesn't exactly sound happy. "Lake, you can go. I'll handle him."

I keep my gaze steady on Lake, and her eyes narrow for a minute before she steps back. Monroe gets caught in her legs and screams. Lake doesn't let her go right away, shuffling her feet out of the foyer.

"Lake," Leighton says in a very stern, very motherly tone.

"She has to learn at some point." She swings a leg over Monroe, who is on all fours. "I'll be upstairs."

Monroe steps past me out onto the porch and looks both ways down the street. She crosses her arms and huffs. "Where's the bubble tea man?"

I try to keep my eyes on the little girl, but Leighton is a fucking sight. If my sister knew the temptation she was putting in front of me tonight, she would've thought twice about calling me for help. Leighton is wearing a pink-and-white striped matching pajama set. The pants are thin and loose but still show off her figure. Her undershirt is tight and white, showing a sliver of her stomach because she hasn't buttoned up the pajama top, so it hangs open on both sides.

She's gone from girl next door to hot as fuck. Of course, Easton noticed her that day in the hospital.

Leighton crosses her arms like the other two girls in this house did. "What do you want?"

Definitely not the warm welcome I was hoping for.

CHAPTER
EIGHT

Leighton

"Can we play catch?" Lincoln tosses the ball toward me, but Leighton intercepts before I can catch it.

"We could've used you tonight." I'm hoping my joke will lighten the mood, but instead Leighton stares at Lincoln, no smile on her face.

"I said no more ball tonight." She keeps the ball, then grabs each side of her shirt, covering her tits that sit snug in her white tank top.

My hands clench into fists.

"Come on," Lincoln whines and looks at me as if I can save him, but I have no say here. And frankly, Mommy Leighton is a little scary. But also kinda sexy.

I hold up both hands. "Boss's rules."

A door slams upstairs, and Leighton's eyes close briefly as she draws in a breath through her nose.

"It's an inside ball, and it doesn't leave marks on the wall. Dad used to let me." Lincoln keeps pushing.

Leighton's chest rises and falls, which I notice, because apparently, I'm incapable of slacking my lust for this woman, even when children are present. Did I time travel back to thirteen? She's parenting here, on her last thread of patience, and I'm thinking about sliding my dick between her tits.

Clearly, I'm not meant for family life.

"Finish your math, and then we'll talk." Leighton nods toward the kitchen, her ponytail swaying back and forth. "And Monroe, the delivery guy will ring the doorbell when he arrives. Get in this house."

Monroe huffs but stomps inside, sliding by my legs as if I'm the bad guy in this situation. I step in to follow, but Leighton moves forward, stopping me outside the door.

"Tell Callie I'm fine."

She grabs the doorknob, her shirt coming open, and my gaze snaps right to her cleavage. God, why can't she be mine? All I can think about is what it would be like if there were no kids in this house and her lips were on mine.

I remember how soft and tentative our kiss started all those years ago. Then as I slid my tongue against her lips, she opened for me instantly, as if she'd been waiting to kiss me just as long as I had been. Just when it was getting good though, she ran. And that's probably the part I should remember most.

She clears her throat, and my gaze snaps up to hers. Under any other circumstance, I'd smack on my cocky grin and pretend I'm not embarrassed, but this isn't the time for ogling her as if I'm only interested in her body.

"Thanks for coming, Hayes, but I'm good."

She shuts the door a little, but I put my hand on it before she can entirely shut me out.

"Listen, Callie feels bad that she can't be here. She'd kill me if I left. Think of me here. I understand that you don't much like to be around me, but you'll feel bad when Callie twists my nuts off for not helping you."

She shakes her head, and a tiny smile forms on her mouth. I take her silence to mean that I might have a shot.

"You just finished a game. You have to be tired."

"He had a great game. That hit in the ninth!" Lincoln jumps in the air. "Leighton let me watch it, but I couldn't hear over Lake's yelling and Monroe's whining." The little boy rolls his eyes.

I'm starting to get a sense of what was going on before I arrived. Although Monroe and the bubble tea are still a mystery.

Monroe gives Lincoln a dirty look, then Leighton turns to me.

"I already ordered pizza. It's gonna be here in half an hour." I hold out my hands.

"Pizza? I don't want pizza! I have to have bubble tea!" Monroe shouts.

Leighton closes her eyes as though she has a migraine, and I wouldn't doubt that she does. She's clearly stressed out and trying to hold it all together. I wish she'd just give up this thing where she feels like she has to do everything herself.

"Just tonight. One night." There's a pleading note in my voice.

"I'm sure the bubble tea guy is on his way," I say to Monroe, and she smiles. I'll count that as a win. I zero in on Lincoln. "And I have plenty of time to play catch. But first, we're gonna do your math."

Who am I right now? I think I'm channeling my dad.

Leighton looks at me long and hard. "Lincoln and Monroe, can you give us a few minutes?"

They scramble out of the foyer and into the family room.

"Listen." She steps forward. "I get it, okay? Callie's your sister, and I'm her best friend, and we've been family friends for a long time. I know it's in your nature—your entire family's nature—to help people who need it. Had Callie called your parents, they'd have been over here."

"You're right, they would, but I'm not sure they would fly home from their once-in-a-lifetime trip to help you tonight."

She stares at me blankly, less than amused by my humor. "I'll take it tonight because I'm coming off a twelve-hour shift. Lake is throwing a fit about a sleepover she wants to go to this weekend. The teacher called about Lincoln, and Monroe… well, as you can see, she has a one-track mind."

She looks behind her again and steps a little closer. I smell the faint notes of her perfume, something she must have put on earlier today because it's not nearly as strong as the nights when she and Callie had me drop them off at a party. That scent would linger in my Corolla long after they were out of it. Or maybe with age, she's learned that less can actually be more, because the faint smell makes me want to lean in and run my nose up her neck, along her jawline.

"I want—I don't know—" She's hesitant to tell me whatever she wants to say, so I try to give her the space to come up with the words. Then she steps aside and opens the door a little more. "Thank you for coming."

She lets me step forward, past the threshold, and shuts the door, finally giving up the fight and accepting my help.

Lincoln jumps out from behind the wall. "Yay! Yay! Come on! Come on! Let's do math!"

He grabs my hand and pulls me toward the kitchen table, where there are a bunch of papers and pencils scattered, crayons and other coloring things on the other side.

Leighton stops at the staircase. "Do you mind watching them for five minutes while I go deal with Lake?"

I nod at Leighton and sit next to Lincoln at the kitchen table. He picks up his pencil and looks at his math sheet. Monroe stares out the front window, stalking the street like a mom waiting for her teenager to come home past curfew.

"He has to finish those two worksheets. And watch to make sure she doesn't open the door—"

"I got it, Leighton. Go."

She waits a second, as if she's still debating whether I should be here, but then she walks up the stairs.

"All right," I say, concentrating on the piece of paper. "What kind of math are we doing here?"

"I'd rather hear about the game. Were you scared?" Lincoln's eyes are wide and expectant.

Doing math homework isn't exactly the way I want to celebrate my best game in a long-ass time, but hey, I am sitting next to one of my biggest fans. He's a lot better than those fair-weather fans who love me when I play well and curse my name when I don't.

I tell Lincoln I'll fill him in on the game after he's done his homework and get him started on it. Then I turn my attention to Monroe. "What's up with the bubble tea?"

Lincoln groans, and I put my finger on the sheet of paper, indicating that he needs to keep going. He actually does.

Monroe turns around to face me, walking away from the window. I already felt pretty damn good after the game, but I'm rockin' this babysitting thing, and there haven't been any meltdowns. I want to pat myself on the back.

CHAPTER
NINE

Leighton

I stand on the stairs to listen in for a second and overhear Hayes ask Monroe, "What's up with the bubble tea thing?"

I'm curious if she'll share her obsession with him. After Sky and Patrick died, I completely forgot about her National Day list until she started crying one day out of the blue. Lincoln had to remind me, and ever since, I've been bending over backward to make sure we cross off the designated item every day.

My energy is already tapped from getting off shift three hours ago. It was my first day back after using my bereavement pay and personal days and vacation time. I won't be seeing that beach vacation I've been dreaming about any time soon. Single moms should walk the streets while people bow at their feet, I swear.

Luckily, I have my mom and Aunt Iris to watch them after school when needed. They do a good job as a duo, and I'm thankful for their help, but the minute I walked in the door, Lake was on me about the sleepover on Friday and Monroe about her bubble tea. Then Lincoln's teacher called, asking if I had five minutes to spare.

And now Hayes is sitting downstairs. Thanks, Callie.

When I came down in my pajamas, I assumed it was the delivery guy with the bubble tea and at least one of the crises would be averted. The last person I thought would be standing on the porch was Hayes. It was stupid of me not to think of him as a possibility, given that Callie was on the phone earlier when the chaos erupted. I shouldn't have answered the phone, but I wanted to wish her good luck on the podcast, and if I didn't do it right then, I'd forget and be a shitty best friend.

All I wanted to tell her was a quick "you got this" and "I'm in your corner," but then Monroe threw herself on the ground, saying she had to have bubble tea tonight, and Lincoln with that damn ball against the wall. *Pound, pound, pound.* He kept giving me recaps of the game and how well Hayes was playing, which spurred Hayes to infiltrate my already cluttered mind.

But Lincoln doesn't know that I've had a crush on Hayes for years. I haven't done anything about it because I value my friendship with Callie far more than any potential fling with her brother. And from what I've witnessed from the sidelines, he doesn't really do long-term relationships, so it would inevitably end and where would that leave me with Callie?

I shake my head to get rid of the thoughts and start up the stairs. I have way too much going on to be worrying about a relationship with Hayes that will never happen.

I knock on Lake's door. She doesn't tell me to come in. Not surprising. She's as stubborn as her mother—and me, if I'm honest. One thing I've realized is that being a guardian to three kids really puts my flaws into perspective.

I open the door and peek in. "Lake, we need to talk."

"The sleepover doesn't matter. Forget it. I won't go." She grabs a pillow, stuffing it in her lap, and hugs it to her body.

I blow out a breath. I hate that I need her so much. She's the oldest, so I have to rely on her to watch the younger kids sometimes. I worry though. She's just shy of twelve and too young to be so responsible, but I know Sky was already putting her in charge when she'd run to the grocery store or do a quick errand.

At the same time, Lake has lost so much—I don't want her to lose her childhood too. Then she'll end up a thirty-year-old nurse with no love prospects and trust issues.

"You can go. I'll figure something out. I'll get someone to take my shift, or I'll get a babysitter, but it's not for you to worry about."

Guilt fills Lake's sigh, and she looks away from me. Lake is old enough to understand a little more about the sacrifices that have to be made.

This new dynamic is going to change my relationship with Lake, and I'll have to mourn what we were or could've been because there's no changing it. I can't be her best friend, the one who sides with her against Sky so she can get her ears pierced. I wanted to be the fun aunt figure—the one who joked with her and gossiped about crushes. I don't want to be the one to discipline her or forbid her from doing something. But whether we like it or not, that's where we find ourselves.

I sit on the edge of the bed. "I'm sorry. I'd just gotten off shift, and it was a really long day. I'm tired, and I wasn't thinking. Well, I was only thinking about myself honestly—about how I needed to get us dinner and get Lincoln's homework done. I had an instant reaction when you asked, and I apologize, but you're going to the sleepover."

"I'm sorry too. It's fine. I don't have to go."

I shake my head and squeeze her leg. "You're going, Lake."

She holds the pillow tight to her chest, and god, she looks

so much like Sky did at her age. Tears come to my eyes, but I swallow them down.

I pat her leg. "I'll figure it out."

"I can go late. I can wait until you get home, and then I'll go."

Oh, Sky, you raised a good one.

"No." I shake my head. "You're going to go enjoy the whole thing."

She shouldn't have to sacrifice any fun. She lost her parents, for fuck's sake. I know she really wants to go, and it's not her being selfish—it's just that this is her world. And right now, her friends might be the only happy part of her world.

"Thanks, but honestly—"

"Nope. End of discussion. Now come on." I slide off the bed and hold out my hand.

"Okay, thanks." She accepts my hand, and I open my arms.

Lake steps into me, and we hold one another longer than we ever have before.

She's the first to pull away, and the smirk on her face says she's going to ask me something I don't want to talk about. "So, you let him stick around?"

An eleven-year-old should not be my confidante, but I don't have many options right now.

"Yeah," I say. "Well, Callie called him, because you know… he's Callie's brother."

"How come I never met him before? And why is he coming around? Do you like him or something?"

"No!" My reaction is way too quick.

Her eyes go wide. "Oh my god, you *do*!"

My head whips toward the door as if Hayes might be standing there. "No, I don't."

"Your face says you do." She laughs and circles her finger over my very heated face.

"It does not."

"You look like Jess when I ask her if she has a crush on Robbie."

"Well, I'm not Jess, and he's not Robbie, and there are no crushes."

"Your voice is doing that high-pitched thing. Just like that time Mom tried to get the number of that guy at Navy Pier for you."

"Okay, enough of that. Anyway, he ordered pizza, and he's helping Lincoln with homework, and Monroe is waiting for her bubble tea. Why don't you come down and finish your homework too?"

"I'm done with my homework. I finished it after school."

God, she's so responsible—classic firstborn daughter. She reminds me a lot of myself—taking on too much responsibility at a young age. I was twelve when I adopted my new role since my parents weren't able to keep their shit together. I won't let Lake go down the same path. She will have every experience a girl her age should have.

"Come and have pizza then."

She exhales and nods. Thank God—one crisis averted. Now I just need that damn bubble tea to show up and Lincoln to finish his homework. Then maybe this house will start to feel normal again. A sliver of hope winds around me that I can make this work.

I put my arm around Lake, and we walk toward the stairs. At the landing, we hear Monroe giving her play-by-play to Hayes, telling him about her goal for the rest of the year.

That's when it really hits me—the rest of the year. It sounds so daunting. I don't know why Sky or Patrick allowed her to do it, but I won't take it away from her. Monroe is going to reach her goal, just as I promised Lake she'll get to be a kid. And Lincoln—he's on cloud nine that Hayes is here. One thing I can give him is a major league baseball player to play catch with.

But as Lake and I reach the bottom of the stairs, and I feel like we finally have a small win, I hear Lincoln say, "Will you be my baseball coach? My dad was supposed to do it this year, but he died."

My feet slide to a stop before we can be seen. Panic mixes with devastation at his words.

Lake and I look at one another.

My body goes into reaction mode, and I scramble to get into the kitchen before Hayes has the chance to answer. This is not his responsibility—it's mine. I know him. I know Callie. I know all of the Carlisles. They'll step in, they'll help, they'll want to make it all work. But Hayes has his own things to accomplish this year, and I want him to have all the success he's dreamed of. Last year was a challenging year for the Carlisle family, and I want all of them to be happy. Hayes getting the Gold Glove—that would make them all so happy. I won't let my life detour his in any way.

The doorbell rings before he can answer Lincoln, but I see Hayes's stunned expression. He doesn't want to tell a nine-year-old boy, *I can't coach your baseball team. I'm really sorry your dad just died, but I play in the major leagues, kid, and I'm in the middle of my season.* Then he'll feel guilty, I'll feel guilty, and guilt is already drowning us in this house.

I'm about to tell Lincoln, "No, no, no, we can figure it out —don't put that pressure on him," when the doorbell rings again. Finally, the bubble tea.

Hayes bolts up from the table. "I'll get it. It's probably the pizza."

"Or my bubble tea!" Monroe trails him.

"Well, let's see if it is!" Hayes waits a second for her.

Lake puts her arm through mine. "Let's go get the paper plates."

This job is exhausting. One crisis is handled, only for another to pop right back up. How did Sky do this every day?

CHAPTER
TEN

Leighton

Lake and I head to the kitchen, but Hayes's hand runs down my forearm, giving it a tight squeeze when we cross paths as he walks to the front door. My breath hitches in my throat at the gesture of affection. Monroe is on his heels, hoping to God it's not the pizza man but her bubble tea delivery.

Lake and I go into the kitchen, where surprisingly, Lincoln is doing his homework instead of being distracted by the chaos. Although I see his pencil furiously sketching over the page, which tells me he may or may not be concentrating as much as he should.

"So, like… he's a big deal," Lake whispers to me as she grabs the paper plates, and I get the napkins.

I look at her. "What do you mean?"

She shrugs. "You know… like, he's a good player. I looked him up the other night."

"Well, he's a professional, so yeah, he's a good player."

"But, like, from what I saw, he had a rough year last year." She cringes, and I chuckle under my breath.

Thankfully, Monroe's squeal of excitement interrupts us because it doesn't feel fair to have this conversation with Hayes only ten steps away from me.

He comes in with two pizza boxes, and Monroe has already stuck her straw in her bubble tea and is drinking it as if she's in a race. Lake goes over to clean the table, clearing all the crayons and papers and answering one of Lincoln's questions about a math problem.

It's like a completely different house from the one I walked into earlier. I'm really hoping we're done with the chaos, if just for tonight.

Hayes opens the pizza boxes on the counter. "So, everything go okay upstairs?" he asks under his breath, and I hear that hesitancy in his voice. He's trying not to overstep, but he still wants to know. I'm not sure whether it's concern or curiosity.

"Yeah, everything's fine. She wants to go to a sleepover, and because I have to work, I originally told her she couldn't, and it just… devolved from there. But things are good now."

"Glad to hear it."

"So, I heard Monroe explain her obsession with bubble tea today?"

"National Days calendar, huh? What on earth was Sky thinking?"

I give Lincoln and Monroe slices of cheese pizza. "I don't know if it was her or Patrick, or if Monroe got her in some mommy guilt moment, but it's a thing now. She's put a check mark on every day they've already done." I gesture toward the fridge.

He stares at the laminated list. "I mean, there's something every single day."

"That is the point of National Day."

He pokes me in the side. "Smartass."

I look at the list and the long way we have to go until it's complete. "It's not going to be easy." I can't hide my irritation or my weariness at the idea.

"No way she wants to do all of them. I mean, there are some things—like what is this one?" He points. "What could she have possibly done for World Stationery Day?"

"Well, Hayes, we made our own stationery with stamps. My fingers were blue for two days."

He laughs, and the sound of it loosens something inside my chest. "At least you got some easy ones. High five day."

"Except she high-fived literally every single person we passed on the street, on the way to school, on the way back, and during her dance class."

He laughs again, and it's so genuine that it warms that piece of my heart that will always be drawn to him.

"What kind of sadist comes up with this? Was their goal to drive parents insane?"

"Believe me, I was ready to hunt down whoever it was by my second week in, but it's mine until the end of the year now, so I might as well accept it. Remind me, what do I have to worry about for tomorrow?"

He laughs and bites his lip, then looks back at the fridge before meeting my gaze again. "Space Day."

"Awesome, good thing it's an easy one." I shake my head. "What am I supposed to do for that?"

"Get her some of that dried ice cream. I remember always loving that from the museum as a kid."

"Sure, I'll just swing by the museum and grab some dried ice cream for her." I roll my eyes.

Hayes smiles. "The next one's pretty easy—Brother and Sister Day. And World Laughter Day."

"Thankfully, some are easier than others." I look at Monroe sitting at the table, happily sucking down her bubble tea and ignoring her pizza. The resentment I feel toward this whole endeavor melts like ice in the desert. "She looks so happy though."

Tears spring to my eyes because Monroe *is* happy, and that's all I want—for these kids to be happy.

Hayes must follow my gaze because he says softly, "Yeah, she really is."

We take our plates and join the kids at the table. Hayes sits next to me, and his thigh brushes mine. Shouldn't I be too bone tired to feel something spark inside me at being so near to him?

Lincoln puts away his papers, and I tell him I'll check them afterward. As we eat, Lincoln doesn't stop asking Hayes about the game. Hayes gives him the play-by-play, and god, my crush gets a little deeper when Hayes tells Lincoln how nervous he was stepping into the batter's box in the ninth inning, worried he wouldn't get Decker home, and they wouldn't win the game.

"You won though, right?" Lake asks.

Hayes nods. "We did. It was our day, which made it a good one. But not all days go like that. There've been plenty of times the game doesn't go our way—when I'm the one who strikes out."

"Go Colts!" Monroe says, raising her bubble tea.

"Yeah, Hayes, be happy. It's a great day for you." I place my hand on his arm.

He turns his head toward me. Our eyes lock, and for a heartbeat, I see the college version of him with his hat on backward. The one I couldn't stop wanting, the one who kissed me in a dark corner and made me forget everything else.

"Thanks." His voice sounds strained.

"You're going to have so many more great days because you're the best player in the league." I try to give him an unaffected smile.

Lincoln raises his glass, but I think he only does it because

Hayes is the only professional player he knows. I know there are other players on the Colts that Lincoln is obsessed with.

We continue talking about everyone's day, then Lake brings up the sleepover—how it's themed, and she needs to find some *Fancy Nancy* stuff to wear, with costume jewelry and a boa. She says she has to get a birthday gift too, and I make a mental note, knowing I'll need to write it down later, so I don't forget. My mind has been at max capacity, and I keep forgetting things.

"So, you're letting her go?" Lincoln asks me.

"Yep, she's going to go." Lake and I smile at one another.

"But then who's going to watch us?" Monroe asks with a frown. "It will be Nail Day! Who's going to do my nails? Lake was going to do my nails!"

Oh god, Nail Day. Geez. I want to find whoever made up that list and shove it down their throat.

Hayes intently watches our interaction.

"I'll figure it out. Right now, eat your pizza and enjoy the night. I have four days to work it out." I give Monroe a wan smile.

Hayes wipes his mouth with a napkin. "Friday? I'll do it."

This is exactly why I didn't want this brought up in front of him.

"You do nails?" Monroe asks, bright-eyed.

"She likes the fancy stuff," Lincoln says, giving Hayes a look that reads, *you should know what you're getting into.* "She likes to get the jewels and stuff like that."

"I can do it," Hayes says. "I mean, I could take you somewhere. We have an afternoon game, but I should be done by dinnertime. What time is the sleepover?"

He's mentally doing the math as though this is his responsibility, and I need to stop him. "Really, Hayes, I'll get this handled. You keep living your life. Don't worry about us."

His jaw clenches for a second, but it loosens so fast it's as if I was seeing things. "No, I'll do it. Nail Day sounds like fun. Maybe I'll get my nails done too." He winks at Monroe.

Monroe gasps and leans forward. "They massage your hands!" She raises her hands and widens each finger.

I could use a manicure. And a little massaging. Preferably by Hayes's hands.

No. No, no, no. Do not go there.

Thankfully, the conversation drifts off onto other topics while we all finish our pizza.

Lake saves me by saying she'll get Monroe bathed so I can check Lincoln's homework. Hayes cleans up the pizza boxes, putting leftovers in the fridge and taking out the garbage I meant to take out this morning. We're like a little machine, and I have to admit that it feels nice to share this with someone.

It won't be the norm, but I'll enjoy it for tonight.

After I check Lincoln's homework, I tell him to head upstairs. He's up next to shower. By the time everything's cleaned up, and I'm ready to say goodbye to Hayes, Monroe comes downstairs with her pajamas on, wet hair combed through.

Thank you, Lake.

She goes right over to Hayes. "Will you read me a story?"

"Oh, Monroe, sweetie." I walk over before Hayes can answer and run my hand through her wet hair. "Hayes has to go now, but I'll read you a story."

Hayes looks at the clock. I'm sure he's thinking to himself, *how many more minutes do I have to endure before I'm out of here?* But he surprises me when he says, "I've got time. Let's go."

They walk up the stairs, his big hand holding her small one, Monroe chattering about the National Days calendar and how excited she is for Friday and what color she wants for her nails. I see them together, and for a moment, I let myself dream. In another world—another lifetime—maybe that could've been us. Hayes and me and a family. The kind of life I used to picture.

But then reality settles in. I've stumbled into some distorted version of that life, standing in front of a futuristic Hayes who isn't really mine. Because as soon as Callie comes back, he'll go on living the life he's meant to have.

This isn't what he wants—and why would it be? He deserves someone who fits easily into his world. Someone gorgeous and free of complications.

Still, part of me can't stop wondering if he felt what I did that night.

If that kiss meant anything to him at all.

He never came after me. Never asked why I ran. And I've learned the hard way—if someone wants you, you don't have to guess.

CHAPTER
ELEVEN

Hayes

After reading Monroe a story, she instructs me on every step involved in putting her to bed. She tells me how to turn on her nightlight and tuck her in tightly, even though the sheets will end up on the floor by morning according to her. Then I have to check in her closet and under her bed, even though she insists she's old enough to know that monsters aren't real.

It makes me wonder—at what stage of life do we lose that? When do we stop being so open about what we need? At some point, we expect people to intuitively understand our feelings and guess what our needs are, and when they don't guess correctly, we think they're not the one for us.

Monroe is an amazing little girl. I'm impressed by her dedication to go three hundred sixty-five days with that National Days calendar, and I'm rooting for her to finish it. At the same time, I can't imagine how Leighton will handle it.

I walk out to the hall, slowly shutting the door, but when I turn around, I startle for a second. Lake stands in her doorway as if she were waiting for me.

"Did you need something?" I ask.

She crosses her arms and stares at me. Preteens are scary. They're a horror movie franchise just waiting to be made. "What's your, like, gameplay here?"

I swear she's eleven going on twenty-five.

"Gameplay?" I ask, shutting Monroe's door all the way.

"Yeah. Why are you here?"

I get it. Although she and Leighton probably go to war with each other—and will go to war many more times—Lake's protective of her. She doesn't want me to take advantage of her aunt. Or whatever the technical term for their relationship is, since Sky and Leighton were actual cousins but always like sisters.

"I'm just here to help."

"Yeah, but like, because you want something."

I tilt my head, wondering where she'd get that thought at such a young age. "I don't want anything from her."

"Okay, well, you know she can do it on her own, right?"

"My sister is her best friend," I say. "Callie's out of town, so I'm just helping while she's away at work, that's all."

"And then you're gonna leave?" There's more bite in her tone now.

"I don't know if I'm gonna leave. I mean, I probably won't be around as much because Callie will be here."

"Yeah. I figured. Well, good luck with your season then. Bye." She turns around and shuts her bedroom door.

I guess whatever I said isn't what she wanted to hear.

I walk toward the staircase, but on my way, I pass Lincoln's room—and I overhear Leighton talking to him.

"Daddy was going to be the coach. This is the first year he was going to have time to do it. Everybody else's dads are coaches. I wanted my dad to be the coach." There's so much hurt and confusion in his voice that my chest constricts painfully.

With everything else, I'd forgotten he'd asked me. I wanted to say yes and make that little guy's night, but that's a pipe dream.

"I know, Linc, but we can't ask that of Hayes. He's way too busy. With his schedule, it's just impossible." I hear her blow out a breath. "I'm sorry, but you can't ask him again. It's us now, just the four of us. I know that's really tough to hear, and I know you miss your mom and dad, but you can depend on me."

My temple rests on the wall, hating that there's truth in her words. I can't be here all the time. I can't coach his baseball team. I can't be who she needs, and I'm not sure I ever could.

"Would you want me to coach?" she asks.

Fuck, Leighton, what are you thinking?

"What do you know about baseball?"

I have to bite my lip from laughing.

"Hey, I know a lot about baseball," Leighton says.

It's in her tone—she so desperately wants to do anything and everything to make these kids not miss one opportunity. But how can she, when she's working and trying to juggle everything else? Then she's going to add on rec league coach too?

"The dads usually do it," Lincoln says.

Wrong response, buddy.

"Well, I don't care if it's the dads who do it—I'm gonna do it. So where do I go? The park district? Where do I sign you up?"

And just as I predicted, Lincoln gave her a little challenge, and now she wants to show the male coaches what she's got. It's a quality I admire.

"It's fine. I'll be on Jimmy's team again. His dad likes me. He plays me."

"No, I'm happy to do it. It will be fun."

"I'll think about it."

"Okay." She stands and bends down to kiss his forehead. "Good night. I'm really proud of you for doing your math homework. Was Hayes a lot of help?"

I feel bad that I'm standing outside the door eavesdropping, but I'm not moving now that they're going to talk about me.

"Yeah, he helped a little bit. But he was trying to teach me a different way than what my teacher does."

That new math shit can suck my balls.

"Yeah, well, that's because the way they do math now sucks. Oh shit—don't—oh god, don't repeat either of those words."

He giggles at her cursing. "Good night, Leighton."

"Good night, sweetie."

She tucks him in, and she doesn't have to be instructed on all the steps like I did because these kids have been a part of her life for a long time.

I tiptoe down the stairs, trying to hide the fact that I was listening.

I'd love to be Lincoln's coach. I enjoy helping kids, trying to make them better, to make them happy. Especially kids who have just lost their parents. But I don't see how I can do it without disappointing him. I'd instantly fail because there's no way to squeeze that into my schedule.

I walk down the stairs, my feet landing on that fucking third-from-the-bottom step that squeaks. "Damn it."

Leighton's laugh rings out from the top of the stairs.

CHAPTER
TWELVE

Hayes

"That step has squeaked since the day they moved in. You'll have to learn that."

My thoughts get stuck on the fact that she said I'll have to learn that—because that means she thinks I'll be around here again.

"Didn't they build the house?" I wait for her at the bottom of the staircase as she skips the third step.

"They built it, but it's squeaked since the day they moved in."

We face each other at the bottom of the stairs.

"Tired?" I ask, hoping she tells me no. I just want a few minutes alone with her.

"That's like asking a marathoner if they're tired after a race." She pauses. "Of course I'm tired, but I'm always wired after they go to bed. It's like I want a little me-time. I usually make myself a tea and sit in silence while I drink it—and then maybe watch some reality TV."

"I like tea and can be very quiet." I mime zipping my lips.

Sure, it's fun with the kids around—enjoyable, we laugh a lot—but I'd be lying if I pretended that I don't want some time that's just her and me.

"Well, there's only chamomile and peppermint tea in the house," she says. "So, what would you like?"

I follow her into the kitchen, mentally scoring myself a point that she agreed so easily. "I'll take the chamomile. I could definitely use something to make me sleepy."

She heats the kettle, lifts onto her tiptoes to grab the box of tea, and her shirt rises, giving me a little more than a glimpse of her bare stomach.

My hands itch to touch her hips. I want to press her into the counter from behind and press my dick into her lower back... reach around and slide my hands under that tight tank top until the weight of her breasts are in my hands.

Fuck.

I've got to get this desire—this want for her—under control.

"I'm glad you and Lake worked everything out," I say, forcing my gaze to the National Days calendar covered in check marks.

"Yeah." She puts the tea bags in the mugs, moving around the kitchen, and I can't stop watching her.

Why did I let her walk away that night? Why didn't I demand an explanation after our kiss was so fucking... earth-shattering?

There are so many questions I want to ask her, but they all feel selfish given her circumstance—what made her pull away, what made her run away. Could she ever give me a chance? Does she want me the way I want her?

The night we kissed, I swear she wanted it. I swear we'd been playing that game of *I really want you, but I shouldn't.* Maybe for her, it was just *Can I get Callie's older brother?* I'm sure plenty of girls played that game.

"I don't want Lake to become me."

My head snaps toward her at the admission, and I inwardly curse myself for letting my thoughts get off track. "Be you?"

"Yeah. I don't want her to think she has to take on all the responsibility. I don't want her to skip fun things because I need her here for her younger brother and sister."

"You're really worried about her." I know it has to come from her own experience growing up.

"Babysitting is fine. But I know she really wants to go to that party, and it killed me to tell her no. We're still getting used to the schedule. I just went back to work, and I can't believe how exhausted I am after a shift. I mean, I thought I was tired before. I was so naïve." She takes honey out of the cupboard. "I want her to be free to be her age." She pauses, appearing contemplative. "I was her age when my parents divorced. My mom always worked, so she would put me in charge of dinner, and I'd clean the house to make sure she didn't have to when she got home. She wasn't herself for a long time after that..." She peeks over at me, and I nod, remembering her parents' very public divorce.

More than anything, I want to walk over and draw Leighton into my arms, give her the support I think she needs right now, but I force myself to stay where I am.

"I don't know." Her voice is like a whisper. "A lot of shit went down back then."

"Yeah."

"It's bad enough that Lake is going to get all this attention —she's always going to be the girl whose parents died tragically. She's been branded with that for life."

A painful lump grows in my throat as I remember that Leighton was branded the girl whose father was found in an the school bathroom stall during a holiday play with a classmate's mom.

"I don't think you have any control over that." My voice is gentle.

She shrugs, bringing the kettle over and pouring water into the two cups. "I can control what happens here though. I thought I was doing okay until I went back to work."

"Has anybody brought up whether you'll be able to keep working? Like, Patrick and Sky—did they leave anything financially to help?" I've been wondering, because going from a single nurse living in an apartment to a house with three kids is a significant increase in expenses. "Will you be able to live off what they left?"

"As of right now, I don't get anything until the custody thing is handled. But the estate pays for the house and things like that during this process."

I must've heard her wrong. I thought she was getting custody. That she already had it.

My forehead wrinkles. "What do you mean, custody thing?"

"I had to petition the courts for custody. If anybody else comes forward, they can contest it—say I'm not fit—and then it'll be an even longer process."

There's a chance she may not get the kids? After everything she's done—everything she's sacrificed—they might take them from her? Just hand them off to someone who looks better on paper? Anger is like a raging bull with its head down in my chest, horns scratching against my sternum.

"That's bullshit. Who would protest?" I ask.

"Maybe no one. But if anyone does, I think it might be Patrick's brother, Art… and his wife. I think they've been trying to have kids for a while, and she might see this as an instant family."

The Martha Stewart bleach-blonde from the funeral.

"Well, I hope they see the connection you have with the kids."

"Yeah, me too. Anyway, once that gets cleared up, the house and everything will be paid out of the estate. For now, living expenses are covered. But you might want to think long and hard before you have a family. They're expensive." She chuckles, but there's no humor in it, then she sighs. "Regardless of whatever happens and if there's the option for me not to work, I still want to. I love my job. I'm just not sure I can do both right now."

I look at her, then step over and take the two mugs of tea so we can go into the living room.

"I don't know what to do," she says softly. "It's strange. I've always been so decisive, so sure of what I want. And now I'm not."

Doesn't that mean she was sure when she ran away from me? That's not promising.

She shakes her head. "Anyway, let's just drink our tea, then you can go home and get some much-needed sleep. You must be exhausted."

There's a part of me that wants to fix everything for her—to take away the pain in her eyes, the lines of her face, and the rigidity of her shoulders. But she's not the type of woman who would ever let me step in and fix things for her. And I'm far from the right person to take over that role with her. My profession doesn't allow me to be who she needs.

Even now, sitting beside her on the couch with this small gap between us, all I can think about is how badly I want to close it. I want to take her tea and place it on the coffee table, then press her into the couch with the weight of my body. I want to pull down her pajama pants, put my face between her legs, and eat her pussy.

But it would be a fleeting moment, one night, and then what can I really promise her?

I'm in no place to take on a fatherly role to those kids upstairs.

I'm starting to wonder if our paths just aren't ever meant to merge into one.

CHAPTER
THIRTEEN

Leighton

I give my coworker the info on all my patients before I grab my lunch. I go to the outside patio and sit at a table away from everyone else. It's another nice spring day, and I tip my head back to feel the sun on my face before I call Callie. She told me she'd make sure to take a break because it was going to be bestie bitch time.

She answers before it rings twice.

"I miss you. I'm going through Leighton detox. I wish you were here with me." The sadness in her tone is another realization of how much my life has changed.

"I should've been, but then my cousin died."

"God, Leighton, you just ruined the moment."

"Sorry." I sigh and get more comfortable in my chair.

"So, tell me everything." She jumps to another topic as she always does. "I have your entire lunch hour marked off as bestie bitch time. I've told everyone not to bother me, that this time is reserved for Callie and Leighton, and if you're not named Callie or Leighton, fuck off. So, tell me, how are things going?"

I blow out a breath. "I really don't want to ruin this conversation with all my drama. I mean, I'm not joking, Callie, it's a different world. I keep thinking someone should've given me a map or a manual. Every day there's some new crisis. I feel like someone just picked me up and plopped me in some remote place—I might as well be in the middle of the jungle struggling to survive."

"First of all, did you miss the most important word in our ritual? Bitch. So..." She sighs. "Get everything off your chest." There's kindness and genuine love in her voice.

"I thought I knew what Sky's life was like, but I had no fucking clue. You don't get a minute to yourself. You don't even get a second. I was in the bathroom the other day and I'd just gotten out of the shower and Monroe just sauntered in. She opens the door and doesn't even flinch at my naked body. I reached for a towel so fast—"

Callie bursts out laughing. "Oh my god. Well, good thing it wasn't Linc."

"Yeah. He at least knocks. But Monroe—my god—she thinks every place in the house is hers."

"Well, she's six," Callie says.

"I'm gonna have you babysit for a week, then you'll understand where I'm coming from." I stab my salad, wishing it were anything else, like two rolls of sushi.

"All right," Callie says. "So, Monroe is a little peeping Tom now. What else?"

"And then Lincoln... Your brother was over the other day, you know. By the way—thanks for recruiting him to come help me." I'm slightly upset she put it on him, but at the same time, he was so much help that I can't even be that mad about it.

"Oh, come on. I know Hayes doesn't check the boxes on

your Safe Guy Shortlist, but he was happy to help. He needs something to do anyway since he has to be on his best behavior. He can't go out with the guys. He can't celebrate in a bar."

She's delusional. She has no idea that she's playing with fire every time she asks him to help me. Because every time our eyes meet or his arm brushes mine, that slow, burning spark I try to ignore flares up. And for a split second, I imagine what it would be like to give in to my desire for just one night. One night where he helps me forget every responsibility and problem.

"Thanks for the reminder to add *ready to be an instant father* to the Safe Guy Shortlist." I try to deflect the conversation away from Hayes.

I'd rather listen to her rant about my list with the qualities I need in a man in order to feel like he won't hurt or disappoint me. She thinks it's ridiculous, and maybe it is, but I like lists, and it's a reminder that the men who can't check off the boxes will eventually break my heart.

"God, you and that list." I can practically hear her roll her eyes. "You're keeping Hayes busy—think of it as *you* helping *him*." Usually, my diversion tactics work better on Callie.

"I am not helping him, believe me. Lincoln asked him to be his rec league coach."

She laughs but stops abruptly. "That's perfect! Yeah, totally. He should do that."

I wish I could live with her blind optimism. Where does she think her brother would fit that into his schedule?

"No, he shouldn't! He's a professional baseball player who plays 162 games a year. He's literally home for, what, seven days this month? Then he leaves again right away—not even a full day off. He's got a travel day, then he's on the field the next day. He does not have time to coach a bunch of nine-year-old boys."

"Huh. Someone's keeping tabs on my brother's schedule."

I grunt, and a couple at a nearby table glance over at me.

"Stop it. Everyone knows the life of a pro baseball player is demanding."

"I don't know," she says. "I think he'd enjoy it."

"You think I should let him do everything. And stop calling him to come over, all right? It's bad enough what he's doing on Friday… one thing just steamrolls into the next."

"What am I missing?" she says in a singsong voice, and my head drops. That was a stupid slip on my part.

"When he was over helping me the night you overheard all the screaming in the background, which, by the way, I *had* handled."

"I believe you," she says with a laugh to say she didn't. She might be right on that one.

"I would've had it handled. Sure, I might've had a good cry after they went to bed, but I could've gotten through it."

At least the crying every time they go to bed has subsided for now.

"Well, if you—"

I cut her off. "I started talking about this National Days thing with Monroe. Can I tell you what I've done this week? Hayes actually gave me a good idea—to get space ice cream for Space Day. I ordered the freeze-dried stuff. Thank God for Amazon. What did we do before Prime delivery existed?"

She laughs.

"Then there was Brothers and Sisters Day. That was easy. I took them out for ice cream. World Laughter Day? I bought a joke book, and we told jokes all night. Orange Juice Day was handled by seven o'clock that morning. It was like I won the lottery, having an entire day without that weighing me down. But of course, when he was over, Monroe brought up Nail Day."

"That might be above his pay grade."

"Yes, and I have to work. Then Lake wanted to go to a birthday party, but I was going to have Lake do her nails because I figured that would be the easiest. I mean, do people really take a six-year-old to a salon?" I barely take a breath, my salad long forgotten. "So yeah, Lake was going to do it because Monroe looks up to her—just like I looked up to Sky all those years."

I pause, realizing I'm rambling. But Callie is the one person I can tell everything… well… except anything that has to do with her brother.

Still, it would be *really* nice to tell her that I kept seeing his eyes on my body the whole time he was over, how that sparked a sick desire inside me. Because how can I even want sex with everything going on in my life? With everything I've lost? Besides, I feel gross most nights after they go to bed. I'm constantly running around, sweating in areas I didn't know could sweat. The word relaxed is a foreign concept nowadays. But then Hayes looks at me, the way his jaw tenses and his teeth bite his bottom lip, and suddenly all I can think about is sex.

"Are you lost in your head?" Callie interrupts my thoughts.

Thank God, I do not need to be in that thought realm.

"Sorry. Anyway, this is what happens to me now. Motherhood, apparently. You have all this shit in your head, and you're shuffling through it like a stack of tax papers that you don't understand. Just warning you."

She laughs. "That's a long way off for me."

"Anyway," I continue, "so they're talking about Nail Day, and your brother just says, 'I'll take her to get her nails done.'"

"Ah! I'm so proud of him! Hold on a second. I'm having a proud sister moment," Callie gushes. "I didn't think he had it in him. He's doing so well—I want to send him a 'you go' meme."

"Callie, you're not helping."

"Yeah, I know, but let me have this."

"Fine. You get one minute."

She giggles. "Okay. Moment over—turns out, it only took ten seconds."

The sun is warm against the side of my face, the glare bouncing off metal benches.

"So yeah, he wants to come over today to watch Monroe and Lincoln and take Monroe to get her nails done for Nail Day."

"I don't see the problem," she says. "He wouldn't agree if his schedule didn't allow for it."

"This can't be a long-term solution though. I have to figure out how to navigate all of this on my own. Your brother can't be the savior. He has his own life."

"Are you sure that's it?" Callie asks. "Is that the real reason you don't want his help? Could it be because you feel like you have to do it all by yourself?"

I squeeze my eyes shut. "Callie, don't start with this shit. Please, I'm in no mood."

"Sorry, it's my duty as your best friend," she says gently. "Only best friends can tell you the truth when you don't want to hear it. I think you're afraid to lean on him because you never want to lean on anybody."

I tear a napkin into strips, my knee bouncing. A gust of wind carries the faint smell of cafeteria fries my way, and my stomach grumbles. I should've eaten from the cafeteria today.

"Callie, I don't want to have this discussion." I look around, making sure no one's nearby. The couple that was closest to me is gone.

"Of course you don't. No one wants to hear about their flaws—and I'm sure, at some point, you'll tell me about mine."

"Would you like me to start a list now?" I say, flicking the napkin scraps into my salad container.

"Oh, okay, is that how we're playing it?" she teases. "I was just trying to tell you that you can depend on Hayes. I don't think he'll let you down."

I squint against the sun, shading my eyes with my hand. "Let me down? He's not anything to me. Why are you talking like that?"

"Because Leighton, come on. Let's not play dumb. You know."

"Oh my god." I roll my eyes.

"You know what I mean. Your parents' divorce. Their fighting over having you. That asshole boyfriend from your freshman year of college."

I groan softly, tossing what's left of my lunch into the bag. "Your list of flaws is going to be so long."

"I'm not trying to call you out. I'm just saying that sometimes you get stuck in a pattern. You feel like you have to do everything yourself because you don't want anyone to disappoint you. It's a just wound. Everyone has them. I have them. People develop new ones every day."

I pick up my water bottle and swirl the ice around. "You talk too much. That's at the top of your list."

She laughs, and the sound is muffled as though she's flopped back on her hotel bed. "In the end, I think he's someone you can trust. That's all."

"Okay, well, you're related to him, so of course you think that. But I don't need to trust him because he is not my savior, and I'll be fine without him."

Will I? What would I have done if he hadn't offered to help tonight?

An ambulance blares nearby. I glance at the hospital doors, picturing how I'll be back in there soon, pretending I'm the cool and calm nurse my patients can depend on.

She says all this, assuming her brother and I are platonic. That we'd never cross the line she's drawn.

"Just let him do it," she says. "You'll survive even if he stops helping, but you might as well take the help while you can. Get through this guardianship thing—you should know about that soon, right?"

"Yeah." As I'm about to continue, another call beeps through. I pull my phone away from my ear, nearly dropping it. "Oh—it's Mr. Notting. Hold on one second."

My heart lodges in my throat. I really hope this is good news.

CHAPTER
FOURTEEN

Leighton

"Ask him whether he's a boxers or briefs guy for me." Callie laughs.

I click over to the other call. "Hi, this is Leighton."

"Hey, Leighton, Mark Notting here. I'll get right to it. You know I track my hours, so I don't want to waste minutes and have your bestie come to my office to tell me off."

"Aren't we wasting them now?"

He chuckles, and I'm glad he got my humor. "Fair point. I hate to be the bearer of bad news, but someone has come forward and contested you being the guardian."

All the comfort I felt in getting to connect with my best friend splats against the ground, gasping for air. My mind spins. I know who it is before he has to tell me. If it were Aunt Iris, my mom, or Patrick's dad, they would've had the decency to tell me themselves. It has to be Art and the she-devil.

"It's Art and his wife, Julianna." Mr. Notting confirms my

worst fear. "So now the process changes. We go to court, and the judge will appoint temporary custody while an investigation is done."

My stomach lurches and I swallow back bile. "An investigation?"

Does that mean visits from social workers, people looking into my finances? Shit, I have six loads of laundry to do, and I hope the store I bought my vibrator from online has a discreet company name on my credit card statement.

"What does that entail?" I should get specifics before my head travels too far away from my body.

"It means you'd better get your ducks in a row because you're going to have to prove that you're the fittest guardian for the dependents."

All my concerns from the past month flood back like a tsunami of doubt. Every mistake I've made with the kids, every moment I got wrong or thought I could've done better. The slammed doors from Lake, Monroe throwing fits on the floor, Lincoln and that damn ball... all of my horrible parenting moments rush back.

Hell, maybe they don't even want me to raise them?

Of course the judge will find me unfit. I'm barely functioning. Julianna can quit her job if she needs to. And if she doesn't, they're a two-income family. How can I compete with that? Sky will haunt me if I lose the kids and allow them to be raised by Julianna. She never had anything nice to say about her.

"Okay, listen," Mr. Notting says, "I can tell your head's racing. There are a lot of factors to be considered. It's not just about being married versus single. The parents' wishes will hold a lot of sway over the judge. Skylar and Patrick left the kids to you—so don't panic. Nothing about them says they're better than you."

I actually find comfort in his little pep talk, and I'm not sure I thought he had it in him, in truth.

"I know you love them, Leighton," he says, "and we're going to do everything we can to make sure they remain with you. Court will likely be next week. Be prepared to make it clear that you want the kids."

"I do," I say. "I told you I do."

"I know. Just make sure the judge knows too. Relax and sit tight. I'll call my colleague, and we'll get things in motion. I'll keep you updated."

"Okay. Thanks for calling."

"Of course. I'll be in touch. You'll need to put down a retainer for your new counsel. If you don't like my colleague, you can interview whomever you like."

"Okay. Whatever I have to do."

"Sit tight. I'll call soon."

"Okay. Bye. Thanks."

"You're welcome."

I hang up with Mr. Notting and switch back to my call with Callie. She's mid-conversation with someone in the room with her.

"Hey," I say, my tone a stark difference from before.

"Hey! Sorry—bestie bitch time. See you later," she says to whoever's with her, then returns to our conversation. "What's up? Did you find out what he's wearing under those expensive suit pants?"

"No."

She must hear it in my voice because she drops the teasing. "What did he say?" I don't even have to tell her. She knows. "They contested. They want them." She makes a noise that sounds a lot like a growl. "Art and Julianna?"

"Yeah."

"Okay. That's fine. They can want them. Doesn't mean they'll get them. You're going to get them because you're the best person for the job. That's it. End of story."

Callie sounds so sure. I wish I had her confidence in my

abilities. If she'd been here this past month, she might think differently.

"When's the court date? I can rearrange my schedule."

"No, Callie. Stop. You're not rearranging your schedule. This tour has been planned for months. You're staying, you're rocking it. By the way, I've been following along—you're amazing. I know I haven't been the best cheerleader lately, but I'm so proud of you. You stay put."

"My parents are coming back from Ireland soon."

"Stop it, Callie. I can handle this. Please stop recruiting your family."

"But you shouldn't have to do this alone. It's my guilt."

I know I'd be the same. If her life blew up and she had as many balls in the air as I do, I'd want to ditch all of my shit to be there next to her, but her podcast going on tour is way too big an opportunity for her to give up. She's worked for too many years to make this dream happen.

"I can handle it," I say again.

"Leighton, I know you can, but you shouldn't have to."

"I'll be okay." I think for a moment. Another ambulance's siren blares as it gets closer to the hospital. Someone is having a much worse day than me. "Whatever you do, do *not* tell your brother, okay? I can handle this. I'm used to doing everything myself."

"Isn't that the problem though?" Callie asks.

I ignore her comment. I'm not in the mood to self-diagnose. "All right, Callie, let's talk about something else. Tell me about the podcast."

She's quiet for a moment. She doesn't want to tell me how good her life is while mine's falling apart. But I want her to. I need to live through her if I'm ever going to survive this.

"Please," I say softly.

She's only silent for a few more seconds before she dives in, telling me everything, but with a little less gusto than I would've thought. Her life sounds so magical, so bright. I wish I could have a *Freaky Friday* with her, just for one day.

But I'm also so proud of her. She's worked hard. She deserves all of the success she's getting. I have to believe that one day I'll be right alongside her—both of us living happy, fulfilled lives.

In this moment, it's tough to picture though.

CHAPTER
FIFTEEN

Hayes

I'm jogging down the stairs of our condo building to catch an Uber so I can get to Leighton's before Lake has to be at the party. I'm behind because I was asked to be in the media room again, which is a good thing. But it wasn't ideal today when I don't want to disappoint the one person who is used to being disappointed. Definitely not a good way for me to get in Leighton's good graces. I don't want Lake to have to call Leighton at work and ask her where the hell I am. Plus, Leighton's mom is watching the kids right now, and Leighton told me her mom has some big auction event with her friends tonight, so if I don't get there ASAP, I'll be on all the Sinclair women's hit lists.

I open the security gate and run into Decker and Easton on the sidewalk.

Decker's holding another cardboard sign that was left behind on the gate. "The Paddock?" He holds up the sign where I see girly script in black Sharpie spell out the word. There're also a few phone numbers and lines like *I'll be the easiest home run you've swung at* and *hit me out of the park*.

Easton grabs it from Decker and tears it in two. "We're not a bunch of horses that can be caged up. We're wild mustangs." He walks over and drops the sign in the trash can.

Decker and I look at one another with raised eyebrows.

Is it annoying that we find these signs? Hell yeah. Does it suck more that they know where we live? For sure.

"You're really taking this name thing to heart," I say, looking down the street for my Uber and checking my phone.

"It's just that there was The Den, then The Nest, and now we're the fucking Barn or The Paddock? We need something cooler."

"I don't think it's that heavy," Decker says, and I agree.

Easton pats me on the stomach. "We're heading over to Peeper's. You want to come and boost your ego? The old guys are on our side after our win today."

I scoff. The regulars who line the bar at Peeper's always have an opinion on our game. They complain when we play shitty and still give us pointers when we win.

"You know they're waiting to give you shit about not getting Tremble out in the fourth, right?" I pointedly look at Easton.

"I missed him by, like, an inch. Plus, he's fucking lead off, he's fast as shit. Give me a break."

Easton. I love him when he makes excuses and acts as if nobody should be calling him out for anything. In truth, it was a hard play and shows off his amazing glove skills, but the old men like to pick apart everything.

"I gotta pass. I've got somewhere to be." I look down the street again, tapping my foot on the concrete.

"The best friend again?" Easton shakes his head.

I haven't told them much about what's going on with

Leighton, except that she's now responsible for three kids. It's not that I don't trust them. After all, Decker is the twin brother of my best friend. Then again, I haven't told Foster anything either.

I have no reason not to trust Easton and Decker. I should probably be straight with them. "Yeah, I'm the babysitter tonight."

"Babysitting?" Decker scratches his chin. "Wow. Good luck. Hope you get paid more than I ever did when I babysat."

"You were a babysitter?" I ask.

Easton and I cross our arms and stare him down. Not that I'm surprised—Decker has the patience to deal with kids, for sure.

"Didn't everybody babysit?" Decker looks between Easton and me.

"Fuck no, I didn't babysit," Easton says with a scowl.

"I was the most requested babysitter in our area." Decker puffs his chest out a little.

"The most requested—please stop." Easton snorts, trying to hold back his laugh. "I had to watch enough of my cousins for free. No chance I was signing up for more even if I was being paid."

"That's because you come from one of those freakish families who have, like, nine kids," I say.

"It's not freakish. And I only have one sibling. It's Dad who has eight. There're no parties better than ours though. One day you're coming up to Alaska with me."

"And I'm sure you're the entertainment at said parties." I step closer to the curb, hoping my ride is close. "Anyway, it's National Nail Day, so I gotta go deal with that."

Easton puts his hand on my chest to stop me from walking to the curb and leans forward as if he didn't hear me right. "I'm sorry, what?"

"Should've kept that one to yourself." Decker shoves his hands into his pockets.

"The little girl is doing this National Days calendar thing, and today's Nail Day, so I'm taking her to get her nails done."

Easton looks like Vega just told him to play right field. "Fuck, tell me you're at least sleeping with this best friend of your sister's."

"Here we go. Peeper's, remember?" Decker thumbs in the direction of the bar.

I narrow my eyes, offended that Easton thinks I need to be getting laid to do something nice for a woman. "Why would you say that?"

"Because you've been totally preoccupied with this woman. You barely go out with us anymore. I'm assuming you're doing all this to get in her pants."

"Sorry, am I not showing you enough love? You'll always have a place in my heart." I cover my heart with my hand.

"I'd better. You were lucky to get me the first time. Second time you have to work for it." Easton's cocky grin is prominent.

Decker shakes his head at Easton. "I think it's nice that you're doing this for her."

Of course he does, because Decker is known as the nice guy of baseball. He rarely talks shit about anyone, even though he's probably got the most dirt. Since he's so quiet, people feel comfortable saying shit in front of him.

"She's my sister's best friend. My sister asked me to help out."

"Why didn't you say so? I'd do it for Callie too." Easton waggles his eyebrows.

"Would you stop? I'm not one of those brothers who's gonna be pissed off if one of my friends date her, but I don't really know if I want her dating *you*."

"Shit, man, that hurts." He puts a hand over his heart and

stumbles back. "I'm just a baseball player looking for a girl to change me."

Decker snickers.

"Callie's not that girl," I deadpan.

"Says who?" Decker and I both give Easton a look, and he scoffs. "All right, so maybe I'm not ready to settle down yet, but I don't think I should be getting judgment from either one of you. I don't see a ring on any of your fingers."

He's got me there.

"This has been fun, but my Uber's here." I walk over to the dark car pulling up to the curb.

My hand is on the door handle when Easton says, "Deck, we got nothing going on. Why don't we go get our nails done?"

"Works for me." Decker's already at my back.

"This isn't a group outing." I don't open the door, purposely keeping them out.

"That's mean-girl behavior." Easton looks around, baffled as to why nobody would want him in the car. "And my nails are hideous. What about you, Deck?"

"My cuticles are way overgrown," he says.

I glance at my watch. I need to go. "Fucking hell—let's go. But you're not staying the whole time."

"We'll make sure to be gone when it's time for Leighton to play with the nanny." Decker slides in as soon as I open the door.

"The *manny*," Easton jokes, going right after him.

"Shut up or we're dropping you off at the next corner." I slip in last, the three of us wedged in the back seat like sardines.

Once we're driving and the driver confirms where we're going, Easton tries to unwedge his shoulder to shift and look at me. "Tell me more about this National Days calendar. This seems like something I could be into."

I give him the gist of Monroe's goal for the year, and I

honestly feel as though he's going to print out a calendar and check off the items himself, because his interest is way too piqued. If he thinks I'm going to be doing cartwheels with him on the baseball field for Cartwheel Day, he's wrong.

We pull up to the house, and I spot, Lillian, on the porch with her purse tucked over her shoulder, Monroe and Lincoln sitting on the front steps.

"Who's the evil Mary Poppins?" Decker mumbles.

CHAPTER
SIXTEEN

Hayes

"It's Leighton's mom, and I just made a piss-poor impression," I mumble, hopping out of the car. I weave through the parked cars to the front steps, holding my hands up, hoping she'll hear me out. "Miss Sinclair, I am so sorry. The game ran a little late."

"Miz," she clarifies.

"Right. Ms. Sinclair."

She looks past me, and I'm really regretting allowing Easton and Decker to join me.

Lincoln jumps off the stairs and walks right by me. No high-five. No great game. Reason number two I should've come alone. Look how easily I've been replaced.

"Easton Bailey? Decker Davis?" Lincoln's voice reflects his awe.

Monroe comes down the stairs and tugs on my hand. "Can we go?"

"In a minute." I give her a smile.

"You're late, and the ladies are waiting for me. Try to pay attention and not lose one." Ms. Sinclair walks down the stairs. "Are these your reinforcements because you can't actually handle two kids by yourself but want Leighton to think you can?"

"No, no—I can handle them. They're just clingy." I laugh. She doesn't. She's already walking down the sidewalk. "I apologize again."

"Another disappointing man. Nothing I'm not used to," she mumbles as she walks toward the sidewalk. "Stay with them, Lincoln and Monroe. One pair of long legs and they'll forget all about you." She waves then disappears around the corner.

"She's fun," Decker says.

"Yeah, I guess you're not on the Mommy-Approved list," Easton says and laughs.

I've never spent any real time with Lillian Sinclair, but from what Callie said, the divorce and the cheating scorned her to the point that she'll never trust another man, and she's seen to it that Leighton sides with her. I hate that Leighton has never found a man she could trust. But maybe I'd hate it more if she had.

Lincoln jumps up and down next to us. "Can we all play catch?"

"No, we're going to get my nails done," Monroe says. "We have to get there before it closes."

"All right, first—where is Lake?" I head up the porch stairs and into the house, everyone following. I need to walk Lake to the party.

"She already left. Aunt Lil got her ready, and we walked her to her friend's house." Lincoln walks into the family room and grabs his glove. "Now can we play catch?" He tosses the ball, and Decker catches it, tossing it back to him.

"Then I guess it's off to the nail salon," I say.

I spot a note on the table, in Leighton's girlish handwriting, along with a key secured on a silver half-heart keychain.

"Did you break her heart already?" Easton eyes the keychain as I shove it in my pocket.

"Stop meddling." I shoo him away with my hand.

"He's good at meddling. Says he learned from his Grandma Dori," Decker says.

I laugh, remembering Easton taking credit for getting Tweetie from the Falcons back together with his ex.

Monroe and Lincoln stare at us since they don't understand what we're talking about.

I clap my hands. "All right, let's go!"

"Are you guys going to the nail salon too?" Lincoln asks.

"Thinking about it." Easton holds up his hands and wiggles his fingers. "We're playing Texas, so what do you think about Fu—"

Decker swats him in the back of the head. "Easton!"

"Shut up," I whisper.

Easton recovers quickly. "Right. I'm gonna get them to paint Boo, Texas."

"That's so cool. Can I get the same thing?" Lincoln looks at me, excitement glimmering in his eyes.

"Sure, nails for everyone I guess." I shrug.

"You'll love the massage," Monroe says to Decker.

She's ditching me too? I guess he really was babysitter of the year.

"I'm gonna be just like Easton Bailey. And I'm gonna tell everybody that I knew Easton Bailey was getting his nails done before the game," Lincoln says proudly.

It's official. I've been replaced. I was like a rock star, and now he's all over Easton. But Easton is a favorite of the Colts' fanbase since he's played here longer than Decker and me.

When we reach the salon, we head inside and it takes me a minute to get used to the overpowering chemical smell. They take Monroe first, then Easton somehow finagles a spot for him and Lincoln, using his charm to get the same thing done to both of their nails. Decker sits in the corner on his phone, not really talking to any of us, so I slide in next to him.

"So be straight with me."

"Straight with what?" He doesn't look away from his phone, continuing to scroll.

"Was he right? Like… that I'm doing this to get in Leighton's pants? Is it gonna come off that way? Because I do like her," I whisper.

He turns away from his phone and quirks an eyebrow at me. "Easton owes me fifty. Thanks for that."

I frown. "What?"

"He was baiting you. You know… reverse psychology. Make you do what you're doing now, convincing yourself you shouldn't be into her."

"I just want to make sure I'm not doing it *because* I like her."

But he doesn't clarify why he and Easton are betting on whether I like Leighton or not. They've never even seen us together except at the hospital six months ago.

"I wouldn't say you're doing this because you want to get in her pants. You're the kind of guy who helps a lot of people out," Decker says.

"Who do I help out?"

"I'm not going to boost your ego by saying I think you could be captain material by next year."

"Captain material?" I've never thought of myself as a captain. He's just being a nice guy—per usual.

"You help all the guys on the team. I mean, you're even nice to Drew. And Drew is a complete asshat."

I shrug. "He's young. He's new in the league. You know how it was."

"Yeah, I do know how it was, and we all earned our

stripes the hard way. Drew needs to get knocked down a couple of pegs if he's ever gonna get respect from the team."

I don't really want to get into the rookies with him, but I've always had a soft spot for the underdog, because I can relate to them.

"It sucks that you actually like her, though, because you're never gonna do anything about it. She's your sister's best friend, so that makes her off-limits."

Decker is such an admirable guy. I could leave him in a dark room with Callie giving him a lap dance, and he'd still lock his hands behind his back. Not so sure I could say the same about his brother, even if Foster is my best friend.

Decker will think less of me if I tell him about the kiss, so I keep it to myself. First, for going behind Callie's back, and second, it's embarrassing. I'm sure none of them have ever had a girl kiss them and literally run away.

"She's a family friend of yours. I'd be doing the same thing."

"Yeah, but I want to make sure my intentions are honorable," I say.

I don't know why it's important to me. I don't want Leighton to ever think I was doing all this just to sleep with her. It'd make me yet another man who has failed her, and I can't stomach the idea of that.

"You can still want someone even if you're helping them. If you feel like your intentions are honorable, then I'd say they are," he says.

"Yeah, I guess."

I lean back in the chair and think about it. When Callie first called to tell me what was going on, I wanted to get to the house to see how Leighton was holding up. Sure, I care about Leighton, but I'm not expecting any payback or even trying to get her in bed. Once she gets herself in a good routine and Callie comes back to town, I'll step back, and we'll move on like we used to, occasionally seeing each other. The thought of it hurts my chest though.

I look over at where Monroe's legs swing under the chair, back and forth, and she smiles. God, she looks so happy. It was totally worth the hassle of getting here.

Decker isn't one for conversation right now it seems, so I go to Monroe and lean over her to see her nails. "What color did you end up picking?"

"Purple, pink, and blue—three colors."

I can see the nail tech doing every other nail a different color. "That's pretty cool."

"I know! Can we put diamonds on?" Her eyes are so big and expectant.

"Diamonds?"

"They're rhinestones," the tech says.

Then I see the little container of jewels sitting off to the side. "Yeah, anything you want."

"Can I get nail art?" Monroe asks.

"Sure."

"I love daisies, can you do daisies with the diamonds?" Monroe tells the woman exactly what she wants.

The woman nods, looks up at me, looks back down, then peeks up at me again. If she recognizes me, she doesn't say anything.

I'm not a guy who flashes around the fact that I'm a professional baseball player. I'll leave that to Easton.

By the time we're done at the nail salon, Easton and Lincoln have the same nails, and Monroe is skipping along the sidewalk as though she's hopping over clouds in the sky. She keeps putting her hands in the sunlight to stare at them. Her happiness is kind of contagious.

"All right, where are we going for dinner?" Easton asks. "I'm starving."

I thought for sure he and Decker would be making some

excuse to leave by now. Having them here for my first time alone with the kids has been comforting though. Since they're opposites of one another, it evens things out. I mean, sure, I can throw a ball with Lincoln, but how do I manage Lincoln and Monroe at the same time?

It's kind of nice to have reinforcements. Hopefully this is how Leighton feels when I'm around.

"What does everyone want?" I ask.

"I haven't cooked out in ages," Decker says.

"Yeah, let's cook out," Easton agrees.

"Grocery store it is."

We stop at the grocery store on the walk back to the house and pick up some meat, hot dogs, buns, and Decker adds a couple of premade salads to the mix. When Monroe picks up a package of cookies, Decker and Easton turn into the Bickersons.

"Is she supposed to have that much sugar?" Decker looks at me, and I shrug.

"She's a kid. Don't all kids live off sugar?" Easton looks at me too.

"How the hell am I supposed to know?" I point at Decker. "You're the babysitter." Then I shift my pointed finger to Easton. "And you have, like, twenty-five nieces and nephews."

"Yeah, true." Easton looks at the ceiling, thinking. "All right, let me see... I have one pretty strict cousin. Her kids have to eat like rabbits. Another cousin lives on fast food. My sister is really easy, and her kid puts a whole new meaning to swinging from the rafters. So, I'd say one package of cookies isn't gonna hurt."

Decker, not wanting to argue with Easton anymore, says, "Put them in the cart."

I leave the four of them to get the rest of what we need while they play rock, paper, scissors in order to decide who gets to choose what flavor of cookie to buy. I have no idea what Skylar—I mean, Leighton—has in her fridge.

I'm excited to see Leighton's reaction when she comes home to see that we have dinner ready. Jeez, when Callie's back, and it's my time to leave, I'm going to miss all of them —but Leighton the most.

CHAPTER
SEVENTEEN

Hayes

I can see why Leighton is exhausted. I'm tired too. I did over two hundred squats during the game and warm-ups today, but that's likely nothing compared to Leighton coming off a shift in labor and delivery.

As soon as we get back into the house, Monroe rushes into the kitchen, opens a drawer, and grabs the marker. "Okay," she says extra loud, "everyone ready?"

Lincoln groans. "She does this every time."

We all circle around and watch her use the marker to put a check mark over today's date where Nail Day is written in the box. We all clap and give her high fives while she jumps up and down in excitement.

I fire up the grill, wondering if Sky or Patrick were the last ones to use it, then inevitably think about the last time they cooked—how they didn't know it would be their last time.

Easton and Lincoln play catch in the yard. Easton is helping Lincoln learn how to field the ball correctly, while

Decker paints rocks with Monroe. She's telling him a story about the last time she did it and how her parents got into a big fight because pink paint got on the expensive patio chair, and Mommy said Daddy should have put something down and he's old enough to know better.

I'm surprised at how even her voice is. Part of me wonders if she really understands what's going on. I can't help but wonder if some time will have to pass before she realizes the permanency of what it means that her parents are no longer with us.

Decker gives Monroe a sweet smile and says, "That's what happens with mommies and daddies sometimes. My mommy and daddy used to fight too."

I don't know his whole story, but I do know his parents are divorced, and that he and Foster grew up in separate households for most of their teen years.

I'm walking inside with the burgers, putting everything out to make an assembly line and debating if we should eat inside or outside, when the front door opens. Leighton is wearing her scrubs. She's got a lunch bag, another bag swung over her shoulder, and a big water bottle in hand. She stops and leans back against the door. She takes a deep breath, and I watch her chest rise and fall.

Then she opens her eyes and sees me. Her face flushes with surprise and slight embarrassment. "You guys are back?"

"We decided to cook out."

"Amazing. Your sister completely monopolized my entire lunch today." She smiles. "Just kidding. My salad wasn't cutting it, so I'm starving. Nobody brought anything good into the break room today."

She drops everything on the bench by the front door, then toes off her shoes and walks into the kitchen. Damn, scrubs look good on her. They're snug in all the right places. And now I'm thinking about naughty nurse role plays with this woman.

She peruses all the items I've set out on the island. "I love burgers."

"We went to Mariano's. There are pasta salads in the fridge."

"Tell me somebody bought the broccoli pasta salad." She opens the fridge. I have no idea which salads Decker picked out. "You guys spoil me. You did buy it."

Decker gets credit for that one. Unfortunately.

"How was Nail Day? Was it horrendous? Did you have to wait a long time?" she asks.

"Well, I don't think every six-year-old in the neighborhood follows the same National Day calendar as Monroe, so we were lucky. We got in right away, and she got them done. So did Easton and Lincoln. I really hope Lincoln doesn't end catching shit about it when he goes to school."

"Easton Bailey went too?" she asks. "You just jumped twenty rungs on Lincoln's favorites ladder." She steals a chip and leans against the counter.

"Decker Davis is here too."

Her hand and half-eaten chip fall to her side. "Seriously?" She breaks across the room and looks out the window. "And he's painting rocks with Monroe?" She turns back toward me. "Take a picture of that, and he'll have women lined up outside your building. What are they calling it now? The Saloon?"

"Saloon? Colts are horses, not drunks."

She chuckles. "Sorry for not keeping up with the diamond girls."

"But you did know they're debating what to call our building?" I lift an eyebrow. It shouldn't feel as good as it does that she's keeping tabs on me. Sort of. In a roundabout way.

"It's not a big deal… but honestly, Tweetie Sorensen has a

big mouth and kept carrying on about it when Tedi delivered their baby."

And there goes that hope, popped before the balloon even blew all the way up.

"What's your opinion?" I slice the tomatoes.

"I don't have one, but if I snap that picture and post it, all those girly notes that get left at your building will only be for Decker." She nods toward the back patio, veering our conversation in a different direction.

"Now you're making me jealous."

She giggles, not taking me seriously, although I'm about ready to ditch the meal prep to go paint rocks.

"Ah, don't worry, you're feeding me. I'll take that over being nice to a little girl any day." She reaches past me for another chip. She's so close, and the way her strawberry-blonde hair is pulled up in a messy bun, exposing her neck, makes me want to bend down and place my lips there.

"Good to know. Food wins for you."

What a fucking lame line. Jesus, do better, Carlisle.

"Food and massages." She pops the chip into her mouth.

"You're heartless." In my mind, she's not wearing scrubs. She's naked under me as my hands roam her body.

She gives what I interpret as a flirty smile. "What did the boys get on their nails?"

"Easton wanted to say, 'Fuck Texas,' but he ended up having to say, 'Boo Texas.' Because, you know, we're with a six- and a nine-year-old."

She laughs again. It sounds really nice, and I realize how much I've missed it.

"Do you mind that they're over? Can I introduce you?" I wipe my hands on the dishcloth and motion toward the back door.

"Couldn't handle the kids yourself?"

I take the jab and open the back door. Now, all four of them are painting rocks. They all look up mid-stroke.

"Hey, best friend." Easton smiles and waves.

She turns to me, and I shrug.

"Easton Bailey, this is Leighton Sinclair. Leighton, Easton. And this is Decker Davis. Leighton, Decker."

They all say hello, and she takes a seat with them. Monroe ditches the painting and crawls into Leighton's lap.

"Look." She wiggles her fingers. "Pretty."

"I love daisies—they're my favorite," Leighton tells her.

"I know." Monroe holds them up in the air, admiring them again. "And look—Lincoln got his done."

Lincoln lifts his hands.

"Oh, I like it. The Colts' colors." Leighton flashes him a smile.

"Yeah, because the Colts are gonna kick Texas's butt."

"Yeah, we are," Easton says, knocking Lincoln's elbow.

It's weird to have this mix—my friends and her and kids I didn't know until last month—but I like it. It makes me trust the boys a little more, and although I didn't want them to come at first, I'm glad they did.

Now, how do I get them out of here before bedtime?

CHAPTER
EIGHTEEN

Hayes

Baseball doesn't come up in conversation at dinner, which is a nice change. Sometimes I feel as though all I ever talk about is baseball.

Instead, Leighton tells us about a patient she had in the labor and delivery unit today.

"The baby was crowning, and her mother and the doctor were gushing about this new restaurant on Dearborn and how mouth-watering the steaks were. They were going on and on as this poor woman was pushing. I saw her keep giving them dirty looks and knew she was going to lose her patience. Then she starts yelling at both of them every time she pushes. The baby arrives with no problems, and once she's resting, she starts crying because she brought her baby into the world hearing his mother yelling."

"She doesn't sound nice," Monroe says.

"She was frustrated. She hadn't eaten for over eight hours.

She was hungry, exhausted, and in pain. It's understandable." Leighton smooths Monroe's hair, giving her a soft smile.

Monroe brings her knees up, resting her feet on the edge of the seat, her palms flat on her thighs, looking at her nails for the millionth time.

"I guess she's done with that conversation." Leighton wipes her mouth and puts the napkin on the plate.

Easton points at me. "That's the restaurant you missed out on the other night. It was so good, right, Deck?" Easton looks from me to Decker.

"It was okay," he mumbles and buries his head in his plate.

The alarm bells go off in my head. This conversation needs a detour and fast. If Leighton finds out that I missed that dinner, she'll feel guilty.

"Okay? Rarely do you get a new restaurant that lives up to the hype. Don't tell my uncle Rome, but they make a better ribeye than him. And the best part was we didn't have to pay a dime." Easton continues to tell the story even though no one but Leighton seems interested. "But don't worry, we'll beat them next month, and you can join us then. I'll be more than happy to go back to that place... ouch." He grabs his leg and glares at Decker.

Leighton turns to me. I'd rather eat a charred ribeye than tell her the truth.

Easton covers Lincoln's ears. Lincoln doesn't bother stopping him because Easton's his new hero. "Deck... man." He nods at Monroe.

"Monroe, cover your ears for a second?" Leighton asks her, and she does it. "They get the drill."

Easton lets Lincoln's ears go, and Lincoln replaces them with his own hands.

I say, "We have this competition with the DICS and—"

"What are the dicks?" Leighton asks.

I stretch out my sore arm by putting it across the back of

her chair. "Drew, Ian, and Camden. The three outfielders. They have this childish competition with us."

Leighton leans back and crosses her arms and legs. "Tell me more."

"I knew I liked you," Easton says, but Leighton puts up her finger.

"Watch the language, okay?"

Easton nods, and Leighton touches Monroe's arm. "Do you two want to go get your shoes on, and we'll go for ice cream?"

"Yay!" They both run for the front door.

Once they're gone, Leighton nods to Easton.

"We're in teams of three, and whoever has more bases—whether stolen or hits—at the end of the month has to buy the other three dinner."

"And you guys won in April?" She looks at me when she asks.

I nod.

Her head tilts. "And when was this dinner?"

"Jackass," Decker mumbles.

Leighton's eyes don't leave mine. She's waiting for me to tell her, but I don't want to see those eyes filled with guilt. Because I was happy to be here and not at a steak restaurant.

"I don't like red meat." It's a lame response from a guy sitting here eating a burger.

A small smile forms on her lips, and our eyes hold. Does she know how beautiful she is? How the curve of her neck is so appealing, you'd think I was a vampire?

"Tuesday," I finally say.

She nods, and the guilt-ridden eyes are there, but then her smile grows wider. "I guess I'll have to take you there then."

"No need, we'll beat them this month," Easton says. "Ouch. Fucker." He glares at Decker.

Leighton pushes her chair back and gets up.

I glare at Easton.

"It was really good, thank you all." She takes my plate and hers.

Both kids run back in with their shoes on.

"I had more fun than a night out with Drew," Easton says. "And I get to show off my nails tomorrow." He looks at Lincoln, who holds up his hands to show off his matching nails.

"Can we go now?" Monroe asks.

This is the perfect time for Decker and Easton to tap out, make an excuse, and I'll stay. I lean back and shake my head at the guys.

"Sure," they say in unison.

My hand fists around my napkin, wishing it was a fork and I could throw it at them.

"I'm gonna go change out of my scrubs." Leighton heads toward the stairs.

Decker and Easton join me in the kitchen to help clean up.

I don't really talk to them or entertain their conversation about playing Texas and who is pitching, because I'm annoyed and confused. Annoyed because I want to be alone with Leighton, to have all her attention on me, but what is the point when we're both in such different places—neither of which seem right to pursue a relationship.

"Something wrong?" Decker asks.

"Nothing." I put the salad lids on and put them in the fridge.

"Oh, he wants us gone." Easton pushes himself up on the counter, not helping to get things cleaned up.

"She's Callie's best friend," Decker says, ever the voice of reason.

Easton rolls his eyes.

Before I can tell Decker that I'm not as admirable as he is, Leighton comes back downstairs wearing a shirt and a pair of jeans—jeans that hug her ass so tightly, I even catch Easton looking.

I give him a scolding look while Decker nudges Easton with his shoulder.

"We're gonna head out," Decker says.

Lincoln and Monroe instantly whine, obviously overhearing from the other room.

"Sorry, boys, you're committed now. You have to see it through." Leighton grabs Monroe's hand, and the two of them leave the house.

Lincoln is right at Easton's side, and Decker and I follow behind. Decker gives me an expression to say he tried. And he did. Just not hard enough.

CHAPTER
NINETEEN

Leighton

Monroe and I lead the pack as we walk three blocks to the ice cream shop. I haven't felt this unburdened since Sky died—all thanks to Hayes. Decker and Easton too, but it was Hayes who put this whole day into motion. It's rare for me to trust someone completely, and even rarer for it to work out.

Rounding the corner of where the ice cream shop is, I freeze. A long line wraps around the block, but what really stops me in my tracks is the ripple of recognition traveling through the patrons. Heads turn, elbows nudge sides, and fans peel away from their spots in line, drifting toward us.

Monroe steps beside me and squeezes my hand, while Lincoln comes along my other side. Within seconds, Hayes, Decker, and Easton are surrounded by fans clamoring for photos and autographs. One guy even dashes over to the counter and asks for a pen and paper. Only minutes ago, they were regular guys sitting around our dinner table. Now they're celebrities.

Everyone wants to talk baseball, giving compliments with play-by-plays from today's game. One guy won't stop going on and on about Easton's glove in the fourth.

Monroe tugs my sleeve. "I want my ice cream."

Hayes must hear her because he glances up after giving an autograph. When he sees us standing to the side, he smiles, then peels away and joins us. "Let's get our ice cream."

His hand slips to the small of my back, and I can't deny how much I want to lean into his touch. He ushers us into line, his other hand on Monroe's shoulder as we wait our turn.

"So, what are you getting, Linc?" Hayes asks. The way he shortens his name twists something in me, as though he's part of us.

"I want cookie dough," Lincoln replies. "What's your favorite?"

"Mint Oreo—not to be confused with mint chocolate chip," I say, already wishing I could take it back.

Hayes's fingers flex along my back.

"How do you know?" Lincoln asks me with a confused look on his face.

I have nothing to be embarrassed about. Logically, I know about Hayes—I'm his sister's best friend. I went to Myrtle Beach with his family more than once, and who doesn't get ice cream on a beach vacation?

"I've known Hayes a long time. And when someone is really picky about their ice cream, you tend to remember." I try to keep my voice casual and light, but I'm not sure if I succeed.

"Picky?" Hayes leans in, his warm breath brushing my neck. "They're completely different flavors."

"Both mint." I smile.

"I want sprinkles." Monroe inches up on her toes to see how much closer we are to the front of the line.

I'm happy for the interruption and change of topic.

"You can have anything you want." Hayes's voice is warm and indulgent.

For a moment, I imagine that tone in bed, asking me what I want him to do to me.

I swallow hard and push that thought out of my mind. "You can go back with the guys. I have this handled." I motion toward where Decker and Easton are still conversing with fans.

Hayes leans in. "I'm right where I want to be."

My pulse stutters. I need to get my reaction to him under control.

We move up in line, and a man who's walking away from the counter with his ice cream sets his gaze on Hayes. "That passed ball in the eighth almost cost us the game. It's only a matter of time before you poison this team. I told my friends they never should have taken you."

Hayes stiffens but says nothing. Good for him for holding his tongue, but who the hell does this guy think he is?

I step in front of Monroe, putting her between Hayes and me. "Excuse me? Why would you think that's appropriate to say to someone you don't even know?"

There's so much more I want to say, but Hayes puts his hand on my shoulder. "Let it go, Leighton. He's not worth it."

I narrow my eyes at the guy.

I'm so angry that I don't notice Lincoln walking over until he stomps on the guy's foot. "You're a bully."

The guy peers down at Lincoln and scoffs. The woman he's with pulls him away, the two of them slinking off around a corner.

My hands fist at my sides. "Oh my god, I want to follow him and—"

"Our turn!" Monroe shouts and rushes up to the counter.

"Stop. It's fine. Everyone has their opinion." Hayes is stoic, but I can see the muscle twitching in his jaw, as though he's using every ounce of his strength not to react.

I hate that he's learned to be the bigger person because he's so used to people judging his mistakes.

Hayes asks Monroe, "Chocolate or rainbow sprinkles?" ending the conversation about the jerk-off baseball fan.

Decker and Easton squeeze in last-minute orders. I pull out my wallet to pay, but Hayes places his hand on mine and says he's got it.

As we wait for our ice cream, Hayes takes Lincoln to the side, and Decker slips free from the new group of fans, leaving Easton behind.

"Everyone gets praised or ridiculed, especially on game days," Decker tells me.

"I don't understand how you guys handle it. I'd like to see that guy squat all game and catch hundred-mile-per-hour fastballs."

Decker laughs. "He'd do a shitty job. Probably quit. But how Hayes responded is exactly what he needs to do. After last year... well, he's the dark horse. But he'll be on top by year's end."

My heart clenches. After the decades of work he's put into his career... one bad season and people stop believing in him.

Hayes ruffles Lincoln's hair, and they come over and join us. I assume he told Linc that he can't stomp on people's feet, but I don't ask because that guy ruined our night enough. I'm not giving him any more attention.

We get called up for our ice cream, and we all agree to walk home and eat it there so the guys can enjoy theirs without the constant interruption from fans.

On the walk home, Monroe sticks to Decker and Lincoln to Easton. They seem to have found their favorites. And I have too—Hayes and I fall back. I'm not sure there's a better time in Chicago than early spring. Then again, maybe autumn can compete. Hayes's face plays peekaboo with every street-light as we walk back to the house.

It's a reminder of that night—our kiss. We were tucked in the corner of a party with the strobe light flashing from the aspiring DJ's booth. Callie was in a room with a guy, and Hayes was keeping an eye on me, probably at her insistence. His hat was on backward, his arm on the wall above me, his eyes on my lips. My body was strung tighter than a bow. No kiss since has lived up to that one.

I push away that memory. Nothing good can come from it —the one time I gave in to weakness.

We reach the house, and the kids say goodbye to Easton and Decker on the sidewalk, then the guys slide into the Uber they ordered on the way home. They all have an early flight tomorrow.

"I'll walk you up," Hayes says.

"Not necessary."

"Humor me." He holds out his arm, and the three of us walk up the stairs.

"Say good night and thank you to Hayes," I tell the kids, unlocking the front door.

They each hug him, and Lincoln tells him good luck tomorrow.

"Hit me a home run?" Monroe asks, jumping up and down, probably from a sugar rush.

Hayes laughs and runs his hand down the back of his neck. "I'll try. If I get a hold of one, it's for you." He winks at her.

Her eyes widen, and she looks at me. Then the two of them go in, and I shut the door.

I wasn't prepared to be alone with Hayes on a porch after a great night together, and my heart picks up its pace.

"I'm gonna need you to go in and flip the lock so I hear it." He nods toward the door.

"Funny thing, I've managed well all these years on my own without you telling me what to do."

"Well, that was before I promised my sister to make sure you're good."

His reminder that he's only here because of Callie feels like a plunge in Lake Michigan in the middle of January. He's not here for me, but for his sister.

The lightness I felt dissipates with the warm breeze.

Why am I standing here all googly-eyed over this man? I have real problems to worry about. A court appearance that will help to decide whether I get to keep the kids or not. His words were painful, but they were the reminder I needed.

"Thank you," I say, my voice all business now. "Today was a really shitty day, and this was… nice."

His forehead wrinkles, and he opens his mouth and closes it. "What happened?"

I shrug, not wanting to involve him anymore than he needs to be. "Go kick Texas's ass, okay?"

He leans forward, and I want to tell him all about how I have to fight for these kids, how scared I am. But he needs to do what he needs to do. As Decker said, Hayes is the dark horse, but this year will change that. Not if he's playing house with me though.

"Leighton?"

I shake my head. "I'm fine. Just getting used to all this. Thank you so much for a great night." I put my hands on his shoulders and turn him around. "Now, go, so you can get some sleep and play a great game tomorrow."

He hesitates but walks down two steps. "Can I have your phone number?"

"You have it," I say, although I'm not sure how many more times I can do this with him.

Having him help me, seeing him with the kids and how he is with me… it's making me want him—a lot more than just a crush on my best friend's older brother.

His eyes widen. "So same number?"

I nod. "Same."

And you never used it.

"You should go." I point toward the Uber.

He glances over his shoulder. "I'll call you." Then he jogs down the rest of the steps.

"Go Colts," I blurt, raising my fist like an idiot.

I don't wait for him to get in the car. I go into the house and lock the door, so I don't run after him. My heart pounds, but I take a few breaths, reminding myself that the fairytale I envisioned a long time ago will never come true. They were just the imaginings of a naïve girl.

Now, I need to stick to my Safe Guy Shortlist and remember that's the kind of guy who is ready for commitment, sadly, Hayes Carlisle isn't him.

CHAPTER
TWENTY

Hayes

I trudge down the stairs, every step excruciating because I don't want to say goodbye. I want to climb back up to Leighton, take her face in my hands, and press my lips to hers. God, I wish we were in different spots in our lives. I give her one last wave from the bottom of the stairs, then she says something about the Colts and goes inside and shuts the door.

"Oh, fuck. You got it bad," Easton says after I climb into the Uber. "You couldn't take your eyes off her the entire night."

"Neither could you, asshole. It's impolite to ogle the ass of your teammate's—" I stop, because technically she isn't anything to me. She's not my girlfriend or even a woman who's interested in me.

"Crush," Decker finishes for me.

But it feels like more than that.

I pull out my phone and click on Callie's name as we drive

through the dark streets of Chicago back to our building. The abrupt change in Leighton's demeanor is bothering me, and I want to get to the bottom of it.

> What the hell's going on? Why is Leighton so upset?

The three dots appear, disappear, then reappear. I grip my phone tighter, growing impatient.

> New phone who dis?

> Callie...

> Maybe she's just having a bad day? PMS? Work shit? Grieving? The fact that she's the guardian to three kids and worried she's never going to get laid again?

My dick twitches in my pants. I'd volunteer as tribute to fuck her. Jesus, there is something seriously wrong with me. Still, the image of Leighton beneath me, her hair spread across my pillow, flashes through my mind before I can stop it.

> I'm serious.

> And I'm not?

I'm about to throw my phone when it vibrates again. The frustration building in my chest is almost unbearable.

> Fine... twist my arm why don't you...

Still nothing. My thumbs are ready to hammer out another message, but hers comes before I send her the middle finger emoji.

That jackass Art and his annoying wife are contesting her guardianship. There's a court hearing next week.

My stomach drops. Those kids are her life now. The thought of someone trying to take them away from her makes my blood boil.

"Calm down over there, you're going to break your screen." Decker looks over at Easton who's looking at me, curious about what the problem is.

Give me the info. I want the date and time and where.

You're being really bossy.

My jaw clenches. God, my little sister can be so fucking annoying, even as an adult.

I'm not supposed to tell you any of this.

And that has stopped you when?

True. But this is like BFF code. I was specifically told not to tell you and that you were not to go to the court. It was a big no-no, Hayes.

I get the point. She doesn't want me.

The words hurt to type. More than they should for someone who's just a friend. It only makes me want to be there more though.

Did I say that? I don't remember saying that.

Give me the information.

The three dots appear and disappear, and I'm growing more annoyed by the second.

> If Leighton asks, you DIDN'T hear it from me.

She sends me the details, and I check my scedule. I think I can make it work—I have a practice that day, but no game. I don't care what I have to do—I'll be there, whether she wants me there or not. If I learned anything last year, it's that sometimes you don't know you need someone until they're standing next to you.

CHAPTER
TWENTY-ONE

Leighton

I have never been this nervous in my life.

I was more at ease deciding which house I wanted to live in, my mom's or my dad's, when I was thirteen. Back then, walking into the courtroom, I felt the weight of everyone's expectations as the judge asked me questions. Now, I feel as though I'm in my parents' shoes, anxious that I won't get what I want before I even enter the courtroom.

In the hallway, I spot my mom and Aunt Iris sitting on a bench. My dad is leaning against the wall a few feet away. My mom stands immediately, rushing over and wrapping her arms around me. My dad joins us, both of them competing to comfort me.

"Oh my god, leave her alone, you two," Aunt Iris says, always my guard dog when it comes to their tug-of-war games.

I glance down the hallway and see Patrick's dad a couple of benches away, but there's no sign of Art or Julianna. Every time I've gone through something major, I had comfort from Callie, and if not her, there was Sky. Now, Sky is dead, and I told Callie a million times she was not to leave that tour. My family surrounds me, yet I feel entirely alone. They're not the most comforting people, to say the least.

"So what's the deal? What do we have to do?" my mom asks, her need for information palpable.

"I don't know. Mr. Notting said I would meet him and the other lawyer here. He thinks she's the best option, so that's who I'm going with."

"He should be here already. The court is supposed to hear your case in ten minutes," she insists, worry creeping into her voice.

"I know, Mom. I just… I don't know what to tell you."

Her gaze shifts to my dad. "You should've helped her figure this out."

Aunt Iris glares at Patrick's dad. "I can't believe he's just sitting there letting us all go through this when he knows it should be you who has the kids."

I agree. I don't understand why he isn't more involved either. He never was. We kind of adopted Patrick into our family, and while his dad, Art, and Julianna had their moments with us, we were rarely all together.

Just then, the elevator doors open, revealing Mr. Notting and a tall blonde with a sleek bob. She's impeccably dressed in a black suit and heels. I glance down at my outfit, feeling like the big-box-store version. I live in scrubs and comfy clothes most of the time.

They're talking and laughing, and for a moment, I see Mr. Notting as a real person, not the serious lawyer I've known. He's dressed in his usual expensive suit and polished shoes, and that salt-and-pepper beard that I know drives Callie crazy is perfectly groomed as always.

I wait for them to reach us, my mom and dad anchored to my sides. As usual, them being together feels like an actual anchor weighing me down. Aunt Iris takes a seat back on the bench, her rheumatoid arthritis likely flaring up today. This additional stress isn't good for her.

"Leighton." Mr. Notting extends his hand while he's still steps away from me. He glances behind me but doesn't acknowledge my parents, which I'm sure reinforces my mom's belief that all men are slime.

My dad steps forward. "Lenny Sinclair, Leighton's dad." He offers his hand.

"Nice to meet you," Mr. Notting responds before turning to my mom.

"Lily Sinclair, Leighton's mom." My mom gives him a purposeful stare, and I can't help but wonder how, at my age, my parents are still competing over me.

"Nice to meet you, Mrs. Sinclair."

"It's Miz," Mom clarifies, and I take a big cleansing breath.

"My apologies, Ms. Sinclair." Then he glances at the bench. "Is this another family member?"

Aunt Iris lifts her hand in greeting. "I'm Iris. Lily's sister, Skylar's mom."

"I'm very sorry for your loss, ma'am." Mr. Notting gives her a solemn nod.

"Thank you." Her voice is choked with emotion, but she swallows it down. Her usual stoicism is a trait I think was ingrained in their generation—feelings are meant to be hidden.

"Everyone, this is Vivian Dupont. She's going to be your legal representative when we go in there." He motions to the blonde at his side.

A small part of me feels a bit calmer from her kind smile. I extend my hand. "Nice to meet you."

"Same. And don't call me Miss Dupont." She shoots a teasing glance at Mr. Notting. "Just call me Viv."

"Okay." I manage a small smile.

She sets her briefcase on the bench with Aunt Iris, then

comes back over, taking both my hands. "Look at you. Try not to worry, okay? You're in the best hands with me. I'm"—she nudges Mr. Notting with her elbow—"as Mark believes, a great lawyer. Even better than him."

Her camaraderie with Mr. Notting eases some of my tension. He hasn't done me wrong yet.

"So, this is how it's going to work…" She explains the process, going through the details, and it's as if someone flipped a switch. The caring woman who was in front of me a moment ago has been replaced with a take-no-shit attorney. "I have the will, which is an updated will. There's nothing fishy about it, and it was executed by Mr. Notting and witnessed. So, we're golden there."

"But…" my mom whispers, dread coloring her tone. Always the pessimist.

"Well, the people contesting the guardianship are family members. A closer family relation than you." Viv holds up her hands in a placating gesture. "I'm not saying that to upset you. I'm just explaining what the judge will consider and what the other side will probably argue. He's an uncle, and you're a cousin once removed."

That title hits me hard. I never considered how that might look in court—that I'm a more distant relative… oh my god. Panic rises within me, and it's hard to breathe.

"No, no, no, please don't do that. We're going to be fine. I'm going to do everything in my power to make sure those kids end up with you, okay, Leighton?" She talks to me in a soothing tone as if she thinks I'm one more word away from fainting.

Which I might be.

"I know you and Skylar were practically sisters. We might need more proof of that—pictures showing your relationship, photos of you with the kids—but we'll handle that later. Today, our focus is on the will stating that you've been chosen as guardian by the deceased, and that you've taken care of the kids for the past six weeks. We need to show the judge that remaining with you is in their best interest, okay?"

"Okay. All right. Okay." My mind is a jumble. What if I don't get the kids? What if tonight I'm in that big empty house all by myself? Or worse, I'm back in my apartment and Julianna is sleeping in my bed?

"One fight at a time," she assures me. "Today is about getting them to stay with you. So just let me do the talking, and we'll be fine. Their lawyer is probably going to—"

At the sound of shoes clicking against the tile floor, we all turn our heads in that direction.

"God, there they are," my mom says, disgust dripping from her tone.

"Oh, relax, Lil. They're trying to do what they think is best." As always, my dad's attempt to calm her down is lacking.

My gaze catches Julianna's, and she holds it longer than necessary before looking away. Art doesn't even glance in our direction. I want to stomp over and scream and yell that these are my kids to care for.

"Of course, I shouldn't be surprised by who their lawyer is," Viv says.

"What's wrong with their lawyer?" I can't help but ask, looking at a man who appears the same age as Viv.

He has blondish-brown hair, is clean-shaven, and I'd think he was quite handsome if my libido was into guys like him. Unfortunately, it has a thing for guys who kneel in the dirt all day. The thought has me kind of missing Hayes right now.

"He's an asshat," Viv says.

"Oh my god," I murmur.

Viv laughs lightly. "Don't worry. It'll probably be me getting arrested today." She squeezes my hand. "Are you ready?"

"I guess..." I worry my bottom lip.

Mr. Notting interjects, "I think I'm going to—"

"You can go if you want, Mark. I've got this from here." If I wasn't so stressed, I might actually chuckle at the way Viv dismisses him.

"I'm going to see this one out. I'm invested," he replies firmly, nodding at me.

"Whatever you like," Viv concedes, and she's all business, appearing even cooler than before. She grabs her briefcase off the bench, then comes back to me. "Let's go. It's time."

"All right, we're right here with you," my mom reassures me, sliding her arm through mine.

"Yes," my dad pipes up, stepping closer. "We're here, right by your side. Your biggest supporters."

"We love you," my mom says. "We're going to make sure you get these kids. Anything we have to do."

"My checkbook is open. You need anything, you let me know." My dad can't help but add his classic phrase.

And then we're walking toward the courtroom. Mr. Notting opens the door, waiting for us to file through.

"Leighton!"

At the sound of a man's voice, I turn and look behind me. Hayes is jogging down the hallway.

CHAPTER
TWENTY-TWO

Leighton

"Oh my god, is that Hayes Carlisle?" Mr. Notting asks.

"It is." I think I might sound a little breathless.

"You know Hayes Carlisle?"

"He's Callie's brother," I explain without looking away from Hayes.

"Callie's brother is Hayes Carlisle?" I can hear the shock in his voice.

"Oh god, what is that guy doing here?" My mom can't help but show her disapproval. "You don't need the distraction of him."

"Give the guy a break. You don't even know him," my dad says.

I turn to both of them, not in the mood to deal with their bullshit right now. "Mom, Dad, go inside. Take Aunt Iris and get her settled," I say firmly. "I'll be right in," I tell Mark.

"All right, hurry though," he says. "You don't want to be late."

"I won't be."

They walk into the courtroom, and the door shuts behind them. Hayes approaches me, hair slightly damp, dressed in slacks and a button-down, sleeves rolled up to his elbows. He looks breathtakingly handsome, as he always does.

"What are you doing here?" My voice is sharper than I intended, the shock of seeing him here making my usual wall falter. My heart skips a beat—not from annoyance, but because I want to walk into his arms and let him hold me, which isn't an option.

He fixes his dark eyes on mine with an intensity that makes me want to look away. His lips curl into the smile he uses when he knows something I don't. "What do you think I'm doing here?" His tone is teasing, but there's an edge to it that hints at annoyance.

So, great, we're both annoyed.

"I don't know," I lie, my voice quieter but no less strained.

My fingers fidget with the hem of my blazer as I glance around the hallway. People are milling about in hushed conversation, their eyes occasionally darting toward us—or him really.

"You don't have to be here." I try to keep my tone steady. "You don't have to keep helping me."

His teasing smile vanishes, and his jaw tightens. He takes a step closer, closing the distance between us until I can feel the heat radiating off of him. "I'm not here to fucking help you, Leighton." The raw honesty in his words cuts through me. "I'm here to stand by your side."

For a moment, I'm stunned into silence. The weight of his words hangs between us, and my chest tightens under the pressure of his confession.

"Did Callie tell you?" My voice is laced with frustration—not just at him making my mind a jumbled mess of emotion, but at Callie too. She's been ignoring my boundaries, and this feels like yet another breach of our trust.

His gaze doesn't waver as he crosses his arms. "Well, she only had to tell me because you didn't." There's no accusation in his tone, just a simple fact that makes my stomach churn with guilt.

"This doesn't pertain to you." Even as the words leave my mouth, they feel hollow. My hands clench into fists at my sides as I try to maintain some semblance of control.

He grabs my hand—not roughly, but firmly enough that I can't pull away without causing a scene—and guides me away from the door. Before I know it, my back is pressed against the cool marble wall as he steps into my space. The air leaves my lungs in a rush, and I look up at him with wide eyes.

"How can you say it doesn't pertain to me?" he asks quietly, his voice dropping low enough that only I can hear him. His dark eyes search mine, and for a moment, something flickers there. Hurt? Anger? But it's gone before I can identify it. "I've spent time with those kids. I'm invested in them now, okay? You don't get to shut me out of this just because you're scared or stubborn or whatever your reasons are for being hell-bent on doing this alone." He gestures vaguely toward me with one hand before letting out a frustrated sigh.

I open my mouth to retort—to tell him he has no idea what he's talking about—but he cuts me off before I can form the words.

"I want you to have this," he says, his voice softening further as he looks at me with an earnestness that makes my throat tighten. "I'm going to be there to support you. And if that means sitting in the back row while you pretend I don't exist? Fine." His lips twitch into a smile. "But this is a public courtroom—I'm pretty sure anyone can walk in if they want. So yeah… I'm going in. And I'm going to be there whether you want it or not."

I stare at him for what feels like an eternity but is probably only a few seconds. The sheer force of his persistence presses down on me, and I mutter under my breath, "Fine."

His small smile widens into a grin. Not the smug smirk from earlier, but a softer, more genuine one. My chest aches in a way that's both infuriating and… something I don't want to give any space to right now.

"Well, geez," he says lightly, his tone returning to its usual teasing cadence as he steps back and releases my hand. "You make it so easy to do nice things for you, you know that?"

I roll my eyes and don't bother responding because what am I supposed to say? Instead, I glance at the clock on the far wall and jolt because there are only two minutes until we're supposed to start.

"Leighton." Viv has opened the door to the courtroom and poked her head out. Her voice has a note of authority to it.

I hesitate for half a second before straightening and smoothing down my blazer. "If you must."

"I must." Hayes falls into step beside me, and we go into the courtroom.

And for reasons I can't quite explain… a small part of me is glad he's here.

Everyone in the courtroom stares as we enter.

I follow Viv to my chair just in time for the deputy to call, "All rise for the honorable Judge Northcott."

The intensity of the moment grows. This is it—the moment that will determine the course of my life. There are so many ways this could go, and all I can see are those three pairs of eyes at home waiting for me.

CHAPTER
TWENTY-THREE

Hayes

I sit on a gallery bench with Leighton's family, beside her Aunt Iris, who I know was Skylar's mom. The only thing I really remember about her is that she worked a lot. And that's because Skylar used to take full advantage and throw parties while her mom was out of the house. But now, from what I've heard from my own mother, Iris has rheumatoid arthritis and doesn't have nearly as much energy as she did when she ran her own house-cleaning company and worked as a waitress at night.

Iris pats my leg—the only one of the three of them who is welcoming. Though I don't think Leighton's dad really even knows who I am.

"So nice of you to be here for Leighton. Did you have a game today?" She glances at my damp hair, and I realize that her eyes hold a sweetness her sister's never do.

"Just a practice, but I was cutting it close. Almost had to come in a T-shirt and sweats."

She laughs softly. "You should have worn your uniform."

The judge clears his throat and knocks his gavel on the desk, pulling everyone's attention. "Excuse me, is the conversation over there more important than what we're here for?"

"No. No, sorry," Iris says. "It's just this is Hayes Carlisle, you know, the catcher for the Colts."

Iris says it as if that's an excuse. My mom would kill me if she were here.

The judge's gaze shifts to me. I really wish Iris hadn't done that. Today is about Leighton, not what I do for a living.

"Nice to have you in the courtroom," Judge Northcott says. "Good luck this year. I think you guys might have a shot." His tone is very businesslike. "Anyway, back to the case at hand so I can get to lunch. I'll hear from you first, Miss Dupont."

Leighton's lawyer, who looks as though she could run Fight Club in the back alley, approaches the bench. "Sir, the will states that Leighton Sinclair is to be the guardian. Both of the parents, who are now deceased, listed and signed the papers appointing her. It was their wish for Miss Sinclair to have guardianship of the children, and we would like the court to abide by it."

She hands the will to the deputy, who brings it to the judge. He puts on his reading glasses and glances over the document, paging through it.

"Well, it definitely states Leighton Sinclair." He turns to the other counsel. "And your clients are objecting to this? They want to take guardianship of..." He scans the paper. "The three underage children?"

The other lawyer stands, giving Leighton's lawyer a smirk. "My client is the biological brother of the deceased father, Your Honor. He is married, and he believes that the children should be left with him and his wife, Julianna. Their household would be best suited for the well-being of the children."

"Oh my god," Lily gasps, leaning over the edge of the pew. "Grow a pair," she says to an older male on the other side.

Leighton's dad tugs at his ex-wife's shirt.

Leighton turns around to shush her mom, and her dad waves as though he's desperate to tell Leighton he's not part of it.

"That may be, Mr. Lochs, but the deceased named Leighton Sinclair. I'm going to need more than a marriage license to reverse what were very clearly their wishes," the judge says.

The lawyer looks back at his clients—Patrick's brother, Art, and that Martha-Stewart-wannabe blonde—and says, "We believe that Skylar persuaded Patrick into signing the will."

Leighton's lawyer laughs. "You've got to be joking. That's your argument? Do you have any proof of this?" She turns to the judge. "Your Honor, we cannot dictate whether a deceased person was coerced. And it doesn't matter. He signed the will, and I have the executor, the lawyer who prepared it, in the courtroom with me today. He can testify that Patrick signed the will of his own free will."

She holds her hand out toward a perfectly dressed man with a salt-and-pepper beard, sitting a little too close to Leighton.

The judge nods. "I have to agree with Miss Dupont that we cannot go by what we think a deceased person was thinking or feeling at the time they signed, unless you have some evidence to suggest otherwise. Do you have anything else before I make my ruling for temporary custody?"

The other lawyer frantically looks through a few papers, while Miss Dupont leans her elbow on her podium, staring at him with a cocky grin as though she's won already.

Julianna nods at the lawyer, and he blows out a breath.

"Leighton Sinclair works twelve-hour shifts three nights a

week—which leaves, from what we know, the two grandmas, Lily Sinclair and Iris Richards, in charge of the children. She has no other help. Whereas my clients have a beautiful home —four bedrooms, enough for each child to have their own. They are in a committed relationship, married, with two incomes. The kids would want for nothing. On top of that, my clients are able and willing to support them on a single income so that the children would have a stay-at-home guardian. They would have love *and* security in my clients' home."

"They would have love and security with me," Leighton says, glaring at Julianna.

Atta girl.

"Yes, but she cannot raise three children on her own. She's thirty years old and actually lives in a one-bedroom apartment."

"Oh my god. How does he know where she lives?" her mom whispers.

"Because they're doing recon on her. They know every-thing about our daughter," Leighton's dad mutters.

Art's lawyer continues. "Miss Sinclair isn't in a committed relationship. She cannot raise three kids with her piecemeal babysitters. They need the consistency and stability that my clients can provide. We would like you to appoint temporary custody to Arthur and Julianna Sullivan."

Leighton's lawyer raises her hand and narrows her eyes at the other lawyer. "First of all, I don't think 'piecemeal babysit-ters' is an appropriate reference to the children's grandmother and great-aunt watching them. Plus, Miss Sinclair being single has no bearing on her ability to be a guardian. Mr. Lochs, there are plenty of single mothers raising their kids while juggling work schedules."

Mr. Lochs turns to Miss Dupont. "To their own children. These aren't her children, so the court gets to decide who should raise these kids. My clients offer a more ideal living situation than your client."

Miss Dupont blows out a breath. "Are you suggesting, Mr. Lochs, that those parents aren't doing what they should for their kids?"

"No, Miss Dupont. I'm suggesting that, given the option—and there is one now that my clients are contesting guardianship—it is more preferable for these children to be with the brother of their father, who's in a committed marriage. Julianna could turn in her notice, and they would still be fine financially. They can give the children the love and routine and security similar to the household they had before their parents' untimely death."

"You've got to be kidding me. You are such..." Miss Dupont pauses and looks at the judge. "The will states that Skylar and Patrick Sullivan named Leighton Sinclair as the guardian to their children. We cannot overturn that decision, as I'm sure it was not made lightly. We must abide by their wishes for the children."

She straightens her back, glances at Mr. Lochs, then returns her attention to the judge. "It does not matter whether or not Miss Sinclair is married. It has no bearing on this case. Her schedule as a nurse—does it matter? Yes. But she has already figured out a solution to that. There are plenty of people who work and raise children without a partner."

"Very true, but that's not what these kids are used to," Mr. Lochs argues. "They're used to a mom who stayed at home. And they're used to a dad who went to work. And they're used to a mom who volunteered..."

He goes on and on while Leighton's shoulders sink a little every time that man says something she can't do.

"My clients will have time to spend with the kids. They can do the bake sale. Be part of the PTA. I hate to say it, but Miss Sinclair can't. She doesn't have the time in her schedule to devote to these kids' needs like my clients do."

Leighton leans forward with her hand on her forehead.

Fuck me. My hands fist on my thighs in an attempt to contain my anger before I jump over the railing and punch Mr. Lochs Mike Tyson-style.

Miss Dupont shakes her head. "You cannot honestly be—"

The judge raises his hand, and both lawyers quiet down. "At first, when I saw the will, I thought this was a clear case—that the temporary custody would be granted to Miss Sinclair. But hearing Mr. Lochs's argument, I have to say these children are going through a lot of change, and to have a similar routine with somebody so close as the biological brother does seem like it may be a better fit for the kids."

"With all due respect, Your Honor, the children have been in the care of Miss Sinclair for the past six weeks," Miss Dupont says more calmly.

"I understand that. And I'll take it into consideration." Then the judge sets his gaze on Leighton. "Miss Sinclair, hearing the two arguments, do you honestly believe that what you're capable of giving the children is the same as what Mr. and Mrs. Sullivan can give them? That you have the time and energy to care for these kids while they are grieving their parents?"

Leighton stands, staring at the judge. "It was a big adjustment for everyone, but we're fine, Your Honor."

"With all due respect, 'fine' doesn't really cut it when it comes to three children's well-being," Mr. Lochs chimes in.

Fucking hell. I'm gonna bite his ear off, Mike Tyson-style.

"There's no comparison. She cannot do this by herself," Mr. Loch adds.

The judge puts his hand up to stop him.

Hearing him state outright that Leighton can't do this has the words rushing out of my mouth before I can stop them. "She isn't!" I stand.

All heads swivel in my direction as my palms grow clammy.

"Excuse me," the judge says. "Mr. Carlisle, what are you saying?"

My gaze sets on Leighton, hoping I'm doing the right thing. "She has me. I'm in a committed relationship with Leighton Sinclair."

Lily gasps. "What? Leighton?"

I've always lived with the philosophy of go big or go home, and this is no different.

CHAPTER
TWENTY-FOUR

Hayes

"And what does that entail?" the judge asks.

I think my crazy idea born of anger and frustration might be working. "It entails exactly what you think. I'm her boyfriend. She's my girlfriend. I've helped her with the kids this week. We're as solid as any married couple."

Jeez, keep throwing shit out there, Hayes, and see what happens I guess.

"This is ludicrous. They're clearly not in a relationship. They would have already used that to plead their case. He's lying," Mr. Lochs interjects.

"Your Honor, I'm a public figure, and I like to keep things private for the benefit of the ones I love. Leighton and I were going to keep quiet, but hearing Mr. Lochs say she doesn't have someone over and over again, I can't sit here and listen to it when I know she's the best thing these kids could ever have—aside from their parents, of course. Regardless, she—and they—have me."

"Oh dear," Iris murmurs next to me.

Miss Dupont blinks at me. "Yes." Her tone sounds as if she's convincing herself. "My client is in a committed relationship." She eyes Leighton, who is biting her cheek. "Hayes Carlisle is Leighton Sinclair's boyfriend, is willing to help, and clearly has the financial means." She turns to Mr. Lochs with a wicked smile, and he exhales. "Does she still work as a nurse? She does. But she clearly has a committed partner to juggle their schedules with. "

"A baseball player who's gone more than he's home?" Mr. Lochs looks at me.

"During the season. And I have home games, and as Miss Dupont said, I have the money to care for any of the financial needs the kids have. We can hire whatever we need done to make sure they want for nothing. But I'm telling you this." I look at the judge. "I've been at that house during this transition. Leighton is amazing with those children, and they love her. Her intentions are always for what is best for them. She's doing this National Days thing with Monroe, and she's going to coach rec league for Lincoln. And her and Lake—well, they have a special relationship."

The judge stares at me, and I worry that he can see that I'm lying about my relationship with Leighton. If I end up in jail, then my career will really be blown to pieces.

"You know it's against the law to lie in court, right?" One of the judge's eyebrows arches.

"I do." I keep it short with the hope he doesn't see through me.

He nods. "We're going to take a five-minute recess. I'll be in my chambers. I'm going to think this over and weigh some options. I'll be back with who I think should have temporary custody."

The deputy stands. "All rise."

We all stand, and the judge leaves the courtroom.

Leighton rushes over to sit next to me. "What are you doing?"

"You're the best person for those kids, Leighton. I couldn't listen to that asshole say you weren't for one more fucking minute."

Her shoulders sink and she stares at the ceiling, blinking back tears. "I mean, his points were valid."

I put one hand on her thigh and another around her shoulders, spurring her to look at me. "They were not valid. Don't even think that."

Iris leans over. "Just so you guys know, we can hear you, so you might want to hush and maybe act all lovey-dovey.'"

We glance at Art and Julianna, who are staring at us like a mama bear might look at humans who have come too close to her cubs. They probably suspect I'm lying, since at the funeral we weren't together, but we could've gotten into a relationship in the last six weeks, right?

The judge returns and we all stand, Leighton going back to her spot.

The judge instructs us to sit. "Okay, this is where I am. Clearly, because of the challenge to the guardianship of the children, we have to conduct an investigation. We'll start that, but in the meantime, temporary custody remains with Leighton Sinclair. I believe the will is valid for one, and the second is that between Mr. Carlisle and Miss Sinclair, they've made it work these past six weeks. To uproot the children when their needs are being met seems unnecessarily cruel with all they're dealing with. But I will stipulate that during this investigation, the children spend two weekends with Mr. and Mrs. Sullivan. We'll set a date to award final custody once social services have finished their investigation. Court adjourned." He smacks the gavel on the desk.

My chest tightens and loosens at the same time, as if someone's squeezing my heart while lifting a weight from my shoulders. We have to figure out what happens next with this whole fake relationship charade I've gotten us into, but looking at Leighton tells me everything. Her smile reaches her eyes for the first time today, and her shoulders are free of tension. Whatever mess I've gotten myself into, it's worth it.

CHAPTER
TWENTY-FIVE

Leighton

Oh my god, did I actually get temporary custody? I look at Viv, needing confirmation that I'm not delusional. She nods with a big smile before she steps away to converse with Mr. Lochs.

Mr. Notting squeezes my shoulder. "I told you she was the best."

"Yeah, you should be dating her."

He chuckles. "Yeah, well, we tried. It was unsuccessful," he adds with a teasing grin, glancing around the courtroom. "Where's Miss Carlisle?"

"She's on tour with her podcast."

"She has a podcast?" His eyes widen with interest.

Based on that, maybe I should tell him not to bother if he's looking for something more than just one night. Callie's far from ready for anything serious. If she piques his interest too hard, he'll be waking up to an empty bed.

"It's called *If I'm Honest.*"

"Oh, interesting. I'll have to look it up."

Viv comes over. "Okay, that's it for now. I'll have my assistant call you, and we'll schedule something, okay? We can go over how the whole process will work. But this is excellent news." Then she looks at Hayes. "Our savior."

"You really think he wasn't going to give me temporary guardianship?" I ask.

She shrugs. "I believe you're the best person for these kids. Besides the fact that it's what their parents wanted, you seem like a very sweet, capable person, Leighton. But I can't lie—their marriage—whether or not it's a happy marriage, it's a marriage on paper—their finances, and their ability to slot the kids into a life very similar to the life they had will appeal to the judge, as sad as that is. So, I think the fact that you and Hayes are finally coming out with your relationship…" She kind of hems and haws as though she maybe doesn't believe it. And why would she? I mean, why would Hayes Carlisle and I be together?

"It puts you on more equal footing. But no matter what, temporary custody is temporary custody, and now we have to prove that you can raise those children in a loving home. So, I'm going to tell you right now… for the home visit—when the social worker comes—you both will be there, understand?"

"I'll be there," Hayes says.

"But how do we know the social worker's schedule will align with Hayes's?" I ask.

"I'll talk to the department when everything is being filed requesting the home visit," Viv says, "and I'll tell the department that they need to make sure they're working around your schedule and who exactly you are. Now, they should be accommodating, but sometimes they're not. But if you have a game, I understand that—well, let's not get ahead of ourselves."

"I'll make it work," Hayes says with a firm nod.

He's insane. As if I'd ever allow him to miss a game.

"Okay, then I'll be in touch. We'll talk more about the specifics, but don't worry, Leighton." Again, she grabs my hands and squeezes them. Viv opens her briefcase. "There is one topic we've yet to talk about that always makes me uncomfortable." She reaches into the briefcase and pulls out a piece of paper. "I hate this part of the job."

"But you love the paycheck," Mr. Notting adds.

"I do love the paycheck. So unfortunately, this is the invoice for my retainer."

My dad plucks the paper out of Viv's hands. "I'll take care of it. Whatever she needs. Have your assistant call me."

"Here we go again, just throwing your money around like it's love," Mom says.

I try to center myself and ignore their bickering.

"I'm helping our daughter. There's no way she can afford to pay for that," my dad says.

"Do you want the judge to hear that she's broke?" my mom whisper-yells.

"I'm not broke," I argue.

Mr. Notting leans forward, lowering his voice. "Once this custody thing is established, everything will be left to Leighton. Patrick had a very good job and good life insurance, so she will be fine."

They all look at me with pity in their eyes.

"I have money." I sound begrudging. Not what I assume Patrick and Sky had, and I have nowhere near what Hayes has, but I have money and savings.

"We know you do, sweetie," my mom says in that condescending voice. "I always told you, you should've gone for your doctorate instead of just being a nurse."

I inhale a deep breath, and a hand falls to the small of my back. Hayes steps into me, and I'd be lying if I said I didn't take comfort in his touch.

"I'd like to take responsibility for the retainer," he says to my dad.

Hayes has no idea the challenge he's in for. Like trying to get a hit of heroin out of an addict's hands.

"Oh no. You don't need to do that."

"Rarely do I have people fighting to pay me." Viv smiles and nods to Mr. Notting as though she has to go.

I don't want to keep her with my family's antics. "Thank you so much, Viv. I really appreciate everything that you did today."

"You're very welcome." She eyes Hayes and me. "You guys make a cute couple."

I open my mouth to rebut her statement, but Hayes's hand slides around to tighten on my hip, reminding me that we need to keep this relationship looking very real.

Now all I want to do is go back to Sky's house and clean every nook and cranny. Dust every corner and organize every cabinet so that when that social worker comes, she has no excuse to write a single bad thing on that form.

Viv moves to walk away but then turns and comes back to stand directly in front of me. "I'm just going to tell you this because woman to woman—there's nothing wrong with you working. It's great if they can afford for Julianna not to work, and it's great that Sky didn't work. That might work for some families—but it doesn't always, and that's okay. It doesn't make you any less fit of a guardian. Unfortunately, there are people in the legal system"—she glares toward the judge's desk—"who just don't agree with all that. They still believe that a woman's only place is at home, and they think kids can't have a healthy upbringing if both parents are working. All that being said, just keep doing what you're doing." She winks then faces Mr. Notting. "Mark, want to walk me out?"

"Sure." He squeezes my shoulder, his teasing demeanor resurfacing. "Tell Callie I said hi."

"Callie, my sister?" Hayes asks, watching Mark leave with a confused question in his eyes.

After they leave, my parents are on me again, both of them swinging their arms around my shoulders, hugging me and telling me how they'll be there for anything I need.

"Thanks, Mom, Dad. Try not to kill each other on the way to the parking lot." Then I hug Aunt Iris. "Thank you so much for coming."

"Of course, sweetie. I'll do anything you need me to do."

And I know she will. She's the sweetest woman I've ever met—the polar opposite of my mom. Which always makes me wonder if my mom was once like her and it was just her experience with my dad that made her so jaded.

But unfortunately, Aunt Iris can't help me—no one really can right now. This fight is mine and mine alone. Whether Hayes thinks so or not.

"Okay, bye, guys. I'm gonna talk to Hayes now."

"Oh yes, Hayes," my dad says. "I forgot to introduce myself. Lenny Sinclair, Leighton's dad."

"Yes, sir, I know who you are. Nice to meet you." Hayes extends his hand, and my dad shakes it. "Honestly, I'm more than happy to take over the financial—"

"Oh no, let him to do it. It's how he shows his love," my mom says.

I sigh. I'm used to being embarrassed by my mother and father, but in front of Hayes, I feel a little more self-conscious than normal.

"Ms. Sinclair, good to see you again." Hayes emphasizes the Miz, which tells me there's been a discussion or a lecture at some point.

"Yes, of course. I see that the kids are still alive, so it's good to know you were able to keep them safe, although you needed two other baseball players to help you."

I shoo my parents away with my hand. "Maybe go eat and

get rid of that hangry vibe you got going on. Hayes and I have to talk."

My parents finally leave, fighting one another to give me extra-long hugs and kisses on the cheek, as always.

I hug Aunt Iris again, and she tells me it's gonna be okay. "Everything will work out."

Can she please rub off on me a little?

After they're all gone, Hayes slides his hand in mine. "Food sounds really good right now." I glance at our joined hands, and he snickers. "We never know who's watching. We have to play the part, right?"

As he leads me out of the courtroom, neither of us says anything, but a sense of security flows through me from our adjoined hands. For the first time today, I don't feel so alone. I wish that were a good thing.

CHAPTER
TWENTY-SIX

Hayes

We step out of the courtroom, and the door swings shut behind us. My adrenaline is racing as though there are two outs in the bottom of the ninth with a runner on third, and I need to make damn sure a ball doesn't get passed me.

It felt right in the moment, but now that we're alone, I'm terrified of how Leighton will react after the high of winning temporary custody dissipates.

She slides her hand out of mine. "You want to walk around the courtyard?"

Okay, she's calm. That's a good sign, right?

I'll let her take the lead here. "Yeah, sure."

"You have time?" Again, wanting to talk about it rationally. We're still in the green.

"Yeah. I'm off for the rest of the afternoon."

We wander toward a few concrete benches—public limbo for people waiting to learn their fate in the courtrooms. She hugs her arms around herself against the cool breeze. I shove my hands into my jacket pockets, so I don't reach for her again.

Once we're away from any prying eyes, she whirls around. Shit, this is a blaring red light.

"God, Hayes, why did you do that?"

My back goes up, and automatically, I'm stumbling for words. "I just… I couldn't sit there and listen to them act like you're unfit because you're not married. You don't need anyone. You don't need me. You're doing an excellent job with those kids, and it pissed me off."

She throws her hands in the air. "It pissed *you* off? It pissed me off. They were saying those things about me and my life."

"It was completely unfair. Total bullshit."

We're on the same page. I'm not sure why she's mad at me then. It was a desperate times, desperate measures kind of thing.

"Why are you helping me so much? I don't understand why, and I just…" Her eyes lock with mine, and I don't shift my gaze away. In a lot of ways, it feels as if this standoff is way overdue.

My confession is on the tip of my tongue, but I don't think that pouring out my feelings to her right now is ideal. Today has been a lot for her. Instead, I change tactics.

"Why are you so resistant to letting anyone help you?"

She throws up her hands and walks away. "We're not doing this. Your sister psychoanalyzes me enough. What is it, a Carlisle family trait?"

"We're on your side. You're going through a really shitty time, but we can help ease the load if you'd let us, you're just so fucking stubborn."

She whips around, her strawberry-blonde hair flying in a wave, before I see her seething face. "It's not stubbornness keeping me from wanting your help, Hayes."

"Then what is it? Me? You don't want to be near me?" I step forward, our faces inches from one another.

Her anger dissolves for the briefest moment, and I take that as a good sign, but it sparks right back to life. "You don't wanna know. Just go back to The Barn or whatever they call it, pick up a diamond girl, and leave me the hell alone."

She whirls around to walk away, but I grab her wrist, tugging her into a nearby alley and pressing her back to the wall. "Diamond girl? So, you think of me just like the rest of them? That all I want is fun and parties and take nothing in my life seriously, most of all my fucking career?" Now I'm the one seething, my jaw so tight my teeth hurt.

Our mingled breaths are heavy, and our eyes have matching fire in them. Neither of us turns away, as if we're in a stupid stare-off and the first to blink has to lay all their vulnerabilities out for the other to judge.

Her shoulders fall and the fire in her eyes diminishes into a flickering flame. "I don't think of you that way. I understand why you were that way last year, it's just…"

"Why won't you let me help you?" I'm desperate to hear why she fights me at every turn.

Leighton turns her face to look at the sidewalk, but I bring my forefinger up and force her to look at me. Again, our gazes hold, and for a minute, I have to use every ounce of willpower I have not to lean in and kiss her.

"It's inevitable." Her voice is soft, broken.

I search her face. "What is?"

Her chest rises and falls, but she doesn't look away from me. "You leaving." She slides out around me, walking deeper into the alley. "My entire life, people have disappointed me. Shit, Hayes, you saw my parents in there. All I am to them is a prize. Did they ever think about what that does to me? No. Did my dad think about me having to go to school and have people whispering behind my back—or worse, when they'd say it to my face? It's just easier this way.

So, I made a list…"

"What kind of a list?"

She turns away, and mumbles something under her breath.

"What?" I inch forward.

"It's stupid, but it's a reminder for me."

"I'm lost, Leighton."

She pulls out her phone, opens her Notes app, and hands it over to me.

"Safe Guy Shortlist?" I glance up at her. "Texts back promptly… treats service workers well… not a risktaker… ready for a family?"

She takes her phone out of my hands and closes the screen, shoving it back in her purse.

"Do not tell me that's what you're using to find a man?" I can't hide the judgment or annoyance in my tone.

"This way, there are no expectations, and I don't have to feel like anyone disappointed me. Because… I wrote the list." She turns around as the sun peeks out from behind a cloud, warming her face in a soft glow.

"So, they have to check every box?" I need specifics if I'm going to squash this.

"The majority… yes."

"Done."

She frowns. "What?"

"I can be that man."

"I hate to break it to you, but you're far from that guy." Hurt stabs at my heart, but I splash on a cocky grin to mask it.

"Why do you say that? You looking for an accountant or some office guy who works Monday through Friday, nine to five?"

"Listen, Hayes, you're great and yes, you check off a lot of those boxes, but I don't want to put you in that position."

"What position?"

She shakes her head. "A position where I'll hate you."

I'm still so confused. "Help me understand this."

She walks back toward me, looking resigned. "Fine, you want to know everything? Here it is—I always had a crush on you, but you were Callie's brother, and we both know how she felt about her friends crushing on you." She raises her hand above her head. "Right now, you're here, Hayes. And if I let you keep being my savior, inevitably you're going to be here." She brings her hand all the way down to her knees.

I'm still processing the first part. She liked me? "You had or have a crush on me?" I break the distance.

"That's what you got from that?"

"The rest is bullshit, and nothing I can't prove wrong."

She snakes along the wall, trying to escape me, but I step in front of her. Her back presses against the brick just like before.

"That's why you ran when I kissed you. You were worried about me hurting you."

Finally, some clarity after years of thinking I was a shitty kisser, and she didn't want me. But I was wrong. She was just as into that kiss as I was. That's why it was so damn good.

"You're not understanding me." Her hands splay along the brick at her sides.

"I'm not going to hurt you. I prom—"

She puts her hand over my mouth. "Don't say it. Please don't say it."

I take her wrist and lower it from my mouth, ready to tell her I mean it.

"You're in no position right now, Hayes. You're in the fight of your life to renew your contract at the end of the season. You can't do both. You can't have both."

When Callie first called me six weeks ago, I came to comfort Leighton, to make her life more manageable, but now I find myself wanting to see her, to give her a reason to smile. I want to spend time with her and be in her orbit. The kids are a bonus for sure, but it's her that I want. But she's so adamant that I can't do both that I worry it's just a pipe dream that I can be one of those players who has a family and a career, both going full steam without any conflicts.

I'd do just about anything to cage her in and kiss her right now, but her mind is made up, so I step back. I swear there's a flicker of disappointment in her eyes, but we can both ignore this pull between us if that's what she wants.

"Then I'm not doing this to help you. You're going to help me."

She frowns. "What?"

"We're going to date, and that will help my image with the fans, the team, and the front office. If I show I'm in a committed relationship with a woman who is a guardian to three kids, it helps to put my behavior from last year behind me." It's all bullshit. Sure, it will help me, but I would never ask Leighton to do this if she weren't so hell-bent on me not helping her.

"So, the fake dating benefits both of us?" Her eyes light up.

Ah, she likes the idea. Now we're getting somewhere.

I nod. "I get something out of this too, but you'll have to be seen in public with me."

"I'm in public now."

"My agent says I need to look settled down," I tell her. "You'll come to a few games. We'll take pictures. Make it seem like you're my girlfriend."

Fear, uncertainty, maybe curiosity are all doing a tug-of-war behind her wide eyes. She's not really a public kind of person.

I stick out my hand. "What do you say? Deal?"

She stares at my hand, and I can see all the arguments warring in her head.

"You're going to so much trouble for me, it's the least I can do." Her soft hand falls into mine, and we shake.

"No takebacks."

She laughs and I tug her away from the wall, wrapping an arm around her waist—partly for show, partly because I want to know what it feels like to hold her without an audience.

"What are you doing?" she asks, though she doesn't pull away.

"Playing the part."

She arches a brow. She has no idea what that look does to me.

Because the part I'm playing has a little too much truth in it.

CHAPTER
TWENTY-SEVEN

Hayes

It's no surprise when I tell Jagger about me having a fake girlfriend that he demands an in-person meeting, asking to be introduced to Leighton. He uses the same tone of voice he did when a picture of me passed out in a bar's VIP lounge circulated. Unfortunately, that required me to send a text message to Leighton, asking her to please set aside a little of the free time she doesn't have to meet my agent.

I walk into Peeper's—Jagger's choice, which is fine since it's right under our condo building. It's afternoon, and the Falcons don't play until tonight, so it's dead except for the usual crew of regulars that line the bar.

I stop at the edge of the bar instead of going to the back-room Ruby reserves for us to keep the diamond girls and fans from bothering us. She definitely has a softer heart than she lets on. Ruby has a Doberman exterior, but more of a Labrador interior.

"Why are you here?" she asks, filling a beer for one of her regulars.

"Jagger wants to meet me here."

She glares at me over the beer handle. "What did you do?"

I blow out a breath. "Other than being a saint, nothing."

I smile at her, but she doesn't return it because Ruby finds very little to smile about. Plus, she probably thinks I'm full of shit.

Ruby's one of those take-no-shit, you-do-what-I-want types of people. The funny thing is, according to the Falcons players, she's loosened up a lot over the years. I imagine the fact that the last few tenants living above her have been professional athletes helps—she's probably used to our bull-shit by now.

She's one of those hardcore Chicago-will-persevere types you just can't help but love, even if she shows no love toward you. Though once you get to know her, you realize she does, only in her own small ways.

"I'll bring it in," she says, so I go into the back room and turn on the TV, finding a cornhole competition on the sports channel.

Ruby comes in a little bit later and slides a beer in front of me.

"Thanks, Rubes."

She pulls out a chair and sits. "Are you getting traded? Am I gonna have to get used to some new boy toy on the third floor now?"

When will people stop thinking I'm a screw-up?

"I have a contract until the end of the year."

"I know, but I've seen a lot of shit with all of you athletes—"

"Sorry to disappoint you, but you're stuck with me, Rubes."

She doesn't say anything for a second. "You're doing good

out there." She nods in the direction of Webber Field. "Even the regulars say you are." She stands and slides her chair into the table. "I'll go fix Jagger his usual, although he'll probably come in with one of those green shakes or some healthy shit. God, those California types. I don't understand them."

I chuckle, but she squeezes my shoulder and walks out of the room, probably thinking Jagger coming here means my ass is about to be handed to me. She may be right.

My phone vibrates on the table, and I pick it up to see a text from Leighton.

> I'm running late, but I promise I'll be there as soon as I can.

I wanted to tell Jagger to fuck off when he asked for this meeting. I didn't want to put anything else on Leighton's plate, but I also know how important it is to tell your agent what the hell is going on in your life. I didn't bring him into the fold last year, and that proved to be a massive mistake.

> Take your time. I'm sorry you have to come here in the first place.

Her text pops up immediately.

> It's fine. You've done me all kinds of favors. I can do this one for you.

> I'm not keeping score, just so you know.

> Then good for both of us that I'm a list person. 😊

I want to flirt back, but I'm struggling after our conversation in the alley. I can't help but wonder if she thinks I'm still that guy from last year but doesn't want to tell me. Every part of me wants to prove her wrong, but something stops me— can I have it all? Can I be the baseball player I aspire to be, a good partner to her, and have a role in the kids' lives? I'm not sure, so I text back the only thing I can think of.

> Me: Just be careful and take your time.

The minute I put my phone on the table, the door opens and Jaggar strolls in.

I do a double-take. "Sorry, this is a private room."

"Haha, asshole."

"Joggers, a T-shirt, and running shoes? Who are you and what did you do with my agent?"

"Who am I?" He sits across from me at the table. "Apparently I'm the only one who uses the gym I pay for all you fuckers to have access to."

"We go there… sometimes." I smile before sipping my beer.

"You do know I get reports of who's scanned in and out, right?" He puts one leg up on the chair beside him and stretches.

"We're in season. So get on the Grizzlies." I take another sip of my beer.

"I don't have time to meet with them because I spend all my time with your sorry asses." He groans, putting his one arm across his chest to stretch.

"Need me to call you an ambulance?"

He flips me off.

"It's okay, no one is here, you can tell me how I'm your favorite." I smile wide with arrogance.

He glances at the door and back at me. "My favorite problem child."

"Problem child? I'm a new man this year. Give me some credit."

"You had some until you adopted a whole fucking family. What the hell, Carlisle?"

I laugh because, as much as his opinions aren't always my favorite, Jagger's still always seen my worth and believed in me. That's harder to find in this industry than you'd think.

"You told me to do this." I arch an eyebrow at him.

"I told you to get on the straight and narrow. Find a girl and go on a few dates, take a few pictures. I didn't say find a girl who is a guardian to three kids and pretend to be a family man."

The door opens in the middle of our conversation.

"Oh shit, Daddy's here, and he looks mad," Easton says as he swaggers in. "What did our little Hayes do this time?"

Easton and Decker both shake hands with Jagger. He compliments them on their performance lately.

"This is a Jagger-and-me conversation, so you guys can go wait outside." I thumb in the direction of the door.

They both look at one another, then Easton shakes his head. "Nah, we'll stay."

"They're your housemates even if they are the world's worst babysitters." Jagger scowls at them.

I don't bother correcting him that we might be building mates, but we don't share the same apartment.

Ruby comes in with Jagger's usual drink in a highball glass, and a beer for both Easton and Decker.

"I love you, Ruby," Jagger says.

She doesn't say anything before leaving. It's either getting busier outside of this room or she's not in the mood to deal with Jagger's shit.

"I don't think she likes me." Jagger looks legitimately hurt.

"Decker is the world's best babysitter. Didn't you know that, Jagger?" Easton turns to Decker. "I feel like your agent should know that fact about you. It's a selling point."

Decker drinks his beer and rolls his eyes.

"That's great news, you can babysit Hayes's new kid crew he's taken on." Jagger sends a look my way.

Easton's head rolls back. "Ah, should've figured that's why you're here. The best friend."

"Good, you told them. It's about time you all start bonding and knowing shit about one another. Make a little family here." Jagger brings his glass to his lips.

I look back at the door, hoping Ruby isn't stopping Leighton from getting in. I should have told her we were expecting her. "I didn't tell them."

Jagger's eyebrows lift. "But you guys all hang together. Don't you? They should know this kinda shit."

Easton and Decker turn to one another, then set their eyes on me, expecting me to answer.

"The Falcons would know this about one another," Jagger grumbles, only adding more fuel to us being pissed about his favoritism.

"Stop comparing us to the Falcons," Decker says.

Jagger holds up his hand in defense mode. "Sorry, but they were like this golden age, you know? I just want the same for you guys. There are some differences though—like there are only three of you, and there were four of them. Well actually—" He stops abruptly and looks at Decker for a longer beat then shakes his head. "That's about all, I guess."

"Whoa, whoa, whoa." Easton raises his hand. "What aren't you telling us?"

Jagger shrugs. "Nothing. I don't keep secrets from you."

Decker glances between Easton and me, then back at Jagger. "Bullshit."

I have to agree with them. Jagger keeps plenty of stuff from us. He's always been a fan of the dramatic and surprises. Like when he got the Colts to trade for me, he knew I wanted it badly and didn't tell me they were even interested. Then one day, he shows up in Seattle, asks who my daddy is, and tells me to pack my bag.

"It's nothing. There are just some talks going on, but it's early stages, so I can't say anything." Jagger lifts his drink to his lips again.

What talks could be happening? And why is it related to there maybe being four of us? Who the fuck would be coming to Chicago? For his comment to make sense, he'd have to think it's someone who would want to hang out with us.

No, no fucking way. Could Foster be making a trade? But he has at least three more years in Seattle, so I can't see that happening. Not to mention Vega hates him. He's the only guy I'd want to see come here. But then I glance at Decker, and from his scowl, I think he's wondering the same thing. The last person he'd want to show up on this team's roster is his twin brother.

Jagger turns the conversation back to the topic at hand. "Well, boys, let me be the one to tell you. Hayes has decided to throw his hat in for Father of the Year. He's adopted a fake family with a fake girlfriend and fake kids. Don't you think it's a brilliant idea, what with this being his comeback year and all?"

His sarcasm isn't lost, and fuck, the way he says it makes me feel as though it might actually be a massive problem.

"So, you made a special trip?" Decker asks, not showing any reaction.

"Yup," Jagger says.

My hand tightens around my beer. "No. He was coming here anyway because one of the Falcons—Conor or Tweetie, whoever—had an endorsement deal he had to be a part of."

Jagger's lips thin, and his eyes drill into mine like a displeased father. Whatever, I already have a father.

"I think it's great. I mean, she's great. The kids are great," Decker says, always the one trying to keep the peace.

"Yeah, they are great. I mean, I will say that kid Lincoln—I'm not joking, Jagger, that kid fucking loves me." Easton leans back in his chair, grinning.

"Get over yourself." I roll my eyes.

Easton knows it pisses me off, so he gives me a thumbs-up.

Jagger studies me.

"What?" I ask, annoyance in my tone.

"Are you attached?" He looks at Decker and Easton. "Is he attached?"

"No." My tone of voice reminds me of some preteen kid getting teased about his crush. "I'm not attached."

Easton smacks me in the chest with the back of his hand. "Our boy is, in fact, attached. They both like to pretend they don't like each other. It's some eighth-grade bullshit."

"She doesn't like me." If they heard her yesterday in the alley, they'd know she used the word crush, which means she likes the way I look but doesn't trust me with her heart.

"See, eighth-grade bullshit." Easton shrugs.

"You're blind, Hayes," Decker says.

"Did he tell you it's his sister's best friend?"

I wish I could punch the shit-eating grin right off Easton's face. Instead, I narrow my eyes at him. "Were you the tattle-tale of your big Alaskan family?"

Easton sticks his tongue out at me.

"I already told him to stay away from fucking drama this year, but here we are." Jagger leans back and looks at his watch.

"How about you guys talk like I'm actually in the room?"

"It's the forbidden," Easton says, nodding as if he's all-knowing. "Temptation."

"It's a red flag," Decker says.

Easton groans. "You need to live a little."

"Callie's not like that." I swallow hard. Other than the one time when a girl cornered me at a party when I was a senior and they were sophomores. She was Callie's friend, and Callie pushed me into our parents' bedroom and yelled at me to stay the fuck away from her friends. "It's fake, guys. We're in it for her to get the kids."

Jagger blows out a breath. "I don't know how you come to Chicago for a fresh start and end up here. We have our plan—we're gonna have this banner year where you're gonna work out nonstop, work with the coaches, become the player no one can deny is on top of his game, and now you've decided fuck all that, I don't want to be Hayes Haymaker Carlisle, the best catcher in the league. I'd much rather play Ward fucking Cleaver."

I was right, Jagger is pissed at me.

It's not going to change my plan.

"Who's that?" Decker asks as if Jagger's nostrils aren't flaring.

Easton raises his hand. "Sorry, I'm on board with Deck. Who is Ward Cleaver?"

"You guys are useless." Jagger shakes his head, and now he's even more pissed off, which worries me for when Leighton arrives. "Let me think of a reference you'd know. Phil Dunphy."

"From *Modern Family*?" Decker nods.

"Hayes isn't Phil." Easton shakes his head.

"Can we just stop this conversation?" I cross my arms.

"Let me get to the point because Quinn came with me on this trip, and I'd really rather be with her. You know, my *real* wife?"

I wave. "Then get to the point already."

Jagger straightens and puts his hands on the table. "Now that you have adopted a family, we might as well make it public so it will help your career."

"So now it wasn't a shitty career-ending decision?" I raise my eyebrows at him.

"I'm making the best out of what you're giving me, but let me start by saying this is not your brightest decision."

I just want this over with, so I don't respond with a smartass remark. I pick up my phone to check my texts, but there's nothing from Leighton.

The door opens a bit but slams shut. Then I hear two female voices arguing on the other side.

We all look at one another.

"Be on your best behavior, jackasses." I slide my chair out and get up to go save Leighton from Ruby.

CHAPTER
TWENTY-EIGHT

Leighton

After getting off the train, I stop and huddle closer to the building, so I don't get trampled by the foot traffic. It's warmer than I expected, so I strip off my sweatshirt and tie it around my waist. Being more economical sucks, but having three kids to support means the L train and buses rather than cabs or even Ubers.

I glance at the GPS on my phone, walking up the few blocks to where Hayes lives. I'm supposed to meet him in the back room of a bar named Peeper's Alley. I've heard of it, of course. It's the bar you go to if you want to sleep with one of the three Colts players who live in the building. The back room is like some makeshift speakeasy you can only get into if one of the guys invites you in.

Sometimes when I see the posts from the diamond girls talking about spotting Hayes and his friends, or when they say they slept with one of them, it's hard to believe that it's Hayes they're talking about. Even if I wasn't a new guardian to three kids, I don't think I'd want that life, or a boyfriend with a lifestyle that left me in constant competition with a bunch of other women.

Then again, the way Hayes looked at me in the alley the other day… his body pressed against mine, his arm above my head. Everything in me begged to just let him kiss me. Have fun with him and see what happens. Then I heard the logical voice in my head—that isn't your life anymore. You can't have the pleasure of sleeping with a guy and seeing where it goes. Those days are long gone.

I heave for breath after the uphill jaunt to their condo building that's nestled in the Colts' little area of the city. Bars litter the streets, and all the stores have to do with baseball or Chicago sports teams. Three-flat apartment and condo buildings with rooftops to watch a Colts game line the street. Hayes lives one happy life.

I stand in front of their building, and it feels like a tourist destination when I see a cardboard sign with The Corral written in a girly script. There are a few white pieces of paper on it, more promises of a good time. I can't imagine coming home and finding a slew of messages from guys with invitations to massage my feet and spoon-feed me ice cream. The life of a professional baseball player.

I sigh, ignoring my annoyance with the notes and mental images of Hayes entertaining one of the girls' promises. Peeper's Alley has a nice wooden sign with black lettering. There are a few neon beer brand lights in the window, but it's definitely an older vibe than the other bars around here.

It takes a moment for my eyes to adjust to the darkness inside the bar. There aren't a lot of people in here except for at the stools along the bar, all filled with men who look as though they have designated seats and if they show up and someone's in them, they're told to get the hell out.

I scan the room, seeing a door in the back that says Keep Out. That's where Hayes told me to go, so I heft my bags on my shoulder and weave through the tables, my eye on the door.

I'm not sure what Hayes's agent wants to talk to me about, but Hayes has done enough for me that I can do this for him. Even if it meant asking my dad to pick up Lake from her after school activity and driving her home before her friend's mom picks her up for a sleepover. With my mom watching Monroe and Lincoln, their paths will collide, and I'm sure it won't be pretty, but hopefully they'll keep it in check since the kids will be around.

I start to open the door, but a hand covers mine and slams it shut.

I blink and draw back, turning to see an older woman with red hair glaring at me.

"You're early but let me give you some advice—around here, the early bird doesn't get the worm." The short woman moves to stand as a sentinel in front of the door and crosses her arms.

"Excuse me, I'm looking for Hayes. Hayes Carlisle."

Her drawn-on eyebrows raise. "Yeah, not gonna happen."

"He's expecting me." Surely, she'll let me in once she finds out who I am.

"Come up with something original."

I glance over my shoulder to see if there are television crews around. Am I on one of those prank shows? But all I see are all the older men with beer bellies hanging over their pants, staring at me.

I circle back around and smack on a smile. "I think there's some confusion here."

The doorknob twists in her palm, but she tightens her hand and her teeth clench from the strength it's taking to not allow whoever is on the other side of the door to open it.

She points at a table in the corner with her other hand. "You can wait for him to come out if you're that desperate. But I'm telling you, you don't have a shot with him."

My head rears back. "Maybe I don't want a shot with him." I should throw it in her face that just the other day he wanted to stick his tongue down my throat. Have that, crazy lady.

She finally releases the doorknob and wrings out her arm.

Hayes stands in the doorframe, and yeah, I do want a shot with him. In another life, obviously, because any shot we might have had in this one is over.

"Leighton."

I lean forward, wanting him to say my name like that again, as if he's been waiting all day for me to show up.

The red-haired woman throws her hands in the air. "I give up. You guys are just asking for it."

She moves to walk away, but Hayes quickly scurries out of the room and puts his arm around her shoulders, guiding her back over to me. "Rubes, I want to introduce you to Leighton. My girlfriend."

He winks at me. I guess the whole fake dating thing has begun.

"Her?" Her eyebrows raise another inch.

I glance down at myself. "I look better out of my scrubs."

Hayes smirks, and his gaze flows down my body and back up.

"I bet," a guy on one of the stools says.

"I like to play doctor," another one says.

"You two are out!" Ruby points at them. "What do you think this is, a brothel? You don't say that shit to a woman."

To her credit, the two men mumble an apology and toss cash on the bar top then leave.

She looks back at Hayes. "She looks too nice and too cute for you."

I preen under her compliment even if I'm being compared to who she's most likely seen on Hayes's arm before. The supermodel types—gorgeous and stunning. Not me with my strawberry-blonde hair and freckles along my cheeks and nose.

"Well, Rubes, you always know just what to say." He motions between us. "Leighton, this is Ruby. She owns the bar, and she's like our bodyguard. Excuse her brashness, that's just her."

I put out my hand. "It's nice to meet you."

She rolls her eyes and circles out of Hayes's arms. "What do you drink? Never mind, I'll just bring something the girls like."

I raise my finger. "I'll just take a water. I have to get home to the kids."

Her eyebrows go another inch higher, but she disappears behind the bar.

Hayes's eyes find mine. "Hey," he says in that drippy, sweet, lazy way again, as if he's been counting the minutes until he could see me.

Get a grip, Leighton. Fake—remember?

He holds out his hand and leads me into the room, shutting the door behind him.

The room is a definite man den with a pinball machine, dart boards, and a giant round table with a bunch of chairs around it. There's also a ton of Colts paraphernalia on the walls, along with some televisions. It's a man's paradise apparently.

My gaze snags on Decker and Easton, who I didn't know would be here, but at least I know them.

A man I don't know stands and puts his hand out in front of me. "Jagger Kale."

I slide my hand into his, lifting my bags higher on my shoulder. His palm is smooth, free of calluses, and has a softness that says he's not big on manual labor. But damn, he's good-looking in a rich kid bad-boy-with-money kind of way. "Leighton Sinclair."

"Nice to meet the woman who's been able to tame this guy." He puts his hand on Hayes's neck and squeezes.

"We heard you met Ruby?" Decker asks. "She grows on you."

She'd have to, I don't say.

"I am so sorry I'm late." I heft my bags another time, but Hayes takes them from my grip, sliding the straps down my arm.

"Oh look, doing the boyfriend moves already," Easton says.

"Have a seat, Leighton." Jagger goes back to the table and pulls out a chair for me.

Ruby walks in and places a bottle of water in front of me and sets down some refills for the guys.

"Ruby, did you meet Hayes's fake girlfriend?" Easton laughs.

Jagger throws a balled-up napkin at him, and it pings off his forehead. "Dumbass."

"Ruby isn't going to tell anyone," Easton argues.

I have nothing to worry about. I doubt social services are going to come here and ask her about me.

"Fake?" Ruby eyes Hayes.

"It's a long story," he says.

"You boys and your games. Leighton, do whatever you have to do, but I'm not getting attached." She walks away, and the door slams shut behind her.

Jagger glances at me. "At least you picked a girl next door, sweet and wholesome."

I want to scoff, but I narrow my eyes at Jagger. "Just what every woman wants to hear."

"She does *not* look like the girl next door," Easton mumbles.

Hayes shoots Easton a death look.

The thought of Hayes possibly being jealous shouldn't make my stomach flip a little, but it does.

Easton raises both hands. "I'm just saying—she's not the girl next door."

Hayes inches closer to me and puts his arm around the back of my chair.

"I'm sorry. I married a girl-next-door type, so it was meant to be a compliment. Are you into romance novels?" Jagger asks.

"I'm sorry?" It takes me a beat to make sense of the words since this conversation is going in a very different direction than I expected.

"Do you read romance novels?"

"I don't know. I—maybe, like, sometimes. Not in a while. I haven't had the time." I shrug.

"Right. I heard about your loss, which I am very sorry about."

"Thank you." I'm trying to be polite though I still don't understand why he needed to meet me.

"My wife is a romance writer. So, if you're ever in the market, I'll give you her name."

"Ah… sure. That would be great." I glance at Hayes, but he seems nonplussed with Jagger's segue into this line of conversation.

"She has the best inspiration for her heroes, so of course they're the best," Jagger says.

"Clearly." I cringe. "That sounded sarcastic. I didn't mean for it to sound that way. I'm sure you are her inspiration."

Hayes squeezes my shoulder.

"I'm going to make this quick." Jagger blows out a breath. "Thanks for coming, Leighton. But unfortunately, you're not going to get my charming personality that most of the girl-friends and wives do because you two have put yourself in a situation that could end up being really bad for Hayes if it's outed. So, what we have to make sure is that this whole fake thing stays a secret. All of us in this room know. And thanks to Easton, Ruby knows, but she's like a vault. I'm not worried about her. No one else outside of this room needs to know."

"Well, the kids," I say.

He shakes his head. "No, the kids do not need to know."

I glance at Hayes, not wanting to lie to the kids. But they're all so young. I don't think they could really understand anyway. Plus, I don't want them overly worried that they won't be able to remain with me and letting them in on this plan would certainly up their anxiety.

"Does your lawyer know?" Jagger interrupts my thoughts.

"I think she suspects," Hayes answers.

"She does, I'm pretty sure." I nod.

"Well, you can let her suspect, but don't ever give it any weight or admit it. From here on out, you guys are a couple. Every time you are seen outside of closed doors—you are in love. Hayes, your hand is either in hers or on her every single time you walk out of a building. You're gonna nuzzle your head into the crook of her neck, and you're gonna give her little kisses on the cheek and on the lips. You're gonna run your hand along her back, around her thigh."

Panic sparks in my veins. To have Hayes touching me as if I'm his? How will I ever be able to keep my feelings straight?

"I think you've been reading too many of Quinn's romance novels," Easton says.

"I agree," Decker says. "I mean, next you're gonna have him fucking her in the alley."

"Also, why doesn't Hayes get touched?" Easton asks.

Jagger rubs his chin, looking as though he's considering their protests to be real suggestions. "I wouldn't be opposed to it. Get a picture taken of the two of you, hot and heavy in Ruby's alley? Have at it. I'll call somebody and get a picture out to the world—"

"That's not exactly like a relationship. That's a hookup," Decker says.

"It is what people in a relationship do," Jagger counters.

"At least a good one. And Leighton can give our boy a little thigh rub and fingers in the hair on the back of his head now and again."

"I'm not a dog," Hayes says with a frown.

Everyone laughs.

Jagger points at the two of us. "Lucky for you guys, I have a charity gala for the Children's Hospital you can attend together as a couple. I'll volunteer Decker to babysit for you."

"Gala?" I'm sure they must hear the strain in my voice.

They all smile as though it should be the easiest thing in the world for me.

I should have told the judge the truth because I'm way out of my league here.

CHAPTER
TWENTY-NINE

Leighton

Our meeting with Jagger wraps up, and I couldn't be happier—he's an intimidating man. He obviously knows about Hayes, but he's a straight-talker. I didn't even think about the repercussions of what would happen if our fake relationship was discovered, how bad it could be for Hayes. People would question his character once again.

So as soon as we step out of Peeper's, Hayes does his part, slipping his hand into mine.

He nods at the black security gate on the right side of the building. "Do you want to come up?"

"To your place?" That's an idiotic question. He's not going to take me up to Easton or Decker's.

He chuckles, gripping my hand a little tighter, and I pretend it doesn't send a fission of electricity rushing up my arm. "Yes, to my place."

"Sure." Damn my curiosity for wanting to see where he lives, since he knows exactly where I spend my nights.

It's so you can visualize it later when you get off.

Ugh, I need my sex drive to shut off.

"Am I deserving of seeing what's behind this guarded gate?" I turn and walk backward, his hand still in mine. In the short time I've been here, someone has added another sign on the gate. "Oh, there's a debate now. The Corral or The Stable?"

My hand slips from his, and I tap my finger on my lips and playfully point at each sign, alternating back and forth. He comes up behind me, chest pressed into my back, and reaches around me, tearing both signs off the gate.

"Ah, what fun is that?" I circle to see him walking to the trash can. "You're getting rid of all their bubblegum and notes. Tell me, Hayes, is your dick as impressive as your bat? Inquiring minds want to know."

He shakes his head. His cheeks have a hint of pink, and not from the tease of summer today. "Unfortunately, this stuff comes with living in this condo."

"Well, it is kind of an iconic building."

He punches in the security code and opens the gate for me. I step in, wondering if some woman is lurking around, wondering who I am. I'd have to say I'm a nobody. But then his hand touches the small of my back, playing the part perfectly until the gate closes behind us. I don't want to be a nobody. I wish I really was here to find out his dick size. But I'd keep it all to myself.

"Unfortunately, I'm on the top floor though."

"I bet you usually just carry all the women up the stairs," I tease, and he knocks me with his shoulder, causing me to bump into the first-floor unit. "Whose place is this?"

"Easton's."

"I bet that door sees a lot of action, huh?"

Easton seems like a decent guy. A family guy, from what I witnessed at my house. I shouldn't believe the rumors I hear, but if the gossip is to be believed, he definitely enjoys his life as a professional baseball player, especially the nightlife.

"You interested?" Hayes cocks his eyebrow at me.

"My nights are getting a little lonely."

He stops us mid-step, crushing me against the wall, his hands on my hips. "Just say the word, and I'll fill the vacancy in your bed."

I'm flushed and at a loss for words. His eyes brim with lust, and I can't deny I feel the same way. "How come you're always caging me against a wall?"

"'Cause you're always one second away from running."

We stare into one another's eyes, and god, I could sink into him so easily. Allow all these feelings to rise to the surface and take advantage of the sexual tension that feels as though it's always the third party in a room with us.

"No one's here. You're wasting all your good moves when it's just the two of us." My voice is way breathier than it should be.

His fingers mold to my hips. "Believe me, Leighton, if I ever get you behind a closed bedroom door, you'll see this is just the warm-up."

He steps back, and my body instantly misses the heat of his. He jogs up a few stairs and looks back at me, a cocky grin in place because he knows what he just did to me.

I follow, his ass at my eye level, probably something he did on purpose. "Didn't your mom ever tell you it's not nice to tease a girl?"

He stands at his condo door, his finger hovering over the keypad as he smirks. "Just tell me when you want me to do more than tease."

The space between my thighs throbs with his comment. "I think we're playing with fire."

He punches in the code and opens the door. "Sorry, it's hard for me when I know you had a crush on me."

I scoff and slide by him into his apartment, hoping he has

a dog or a cat I don't know about to act as a distraction. "I crushed on a lot of people, don't hang your pride on it."

It's a lie. Hayes has been my number one crush my entire life.

"Always one to pull my head from the clouds." He steps inside and closes the door.

"Oh, did I bruise your ego? I'm only one woman. If guys were leaving notes on my door every day, I wouldn't let one man chink my armor." I look around his private space. I'm just joking with him, but being in his space, a place I don't think he shares with many people, does make me feel a little special.

"Have I not made it clear how uninterested I am in anyone but you?"

My heart stutters to a stop for a second. Sure, we've had some heated moments, and I admitted to a crush, but what is he implying?

I twirl around, pressing my hands on the back of his brown leather couch. "Too bad there's a list of reasons you need to move on."

It's easier not to ask him directly, to let his comments just hang in the air. That way they won't lead to disappointment.

"I don't believe in lists like that. You'd come with more pros than cons anyway, Leighton."

God, the way he says my name makes me want to squeeze my thighs together. "Ha."

I walk through his family room area. It's a bachelor pad for sure with all the dark wood and brown leather. At least he doesn't have black leather. I swear they must sell the stuff at some store named Bachelors 'R Us. So many of the guys I've dated had black leather couches. It's clearly a guy's space, but there's a homey feeling about it. Maybe it's the pictures on the wall and the end tables. The fact that he took time to get photos of the people he loves framed. His family, Callie, high school and college friends, even Foster Davis made the wall.

I hear him walk in my direction, then his shoulder hits mine as he looks at them with me. There's no reason for me to be hurt that I'm not in any of the pictures. We haven't been a part of each other's lives in a really long time. But I find myself wanting to be on that wall. Knowing that some other woman will be there one day is a hard truth to stomach.

"So, you're really that close with him, huh? I thought it was just, like, a teammate thing." I point at the picture of him and Foster. It must have been taken after they won something important because Hayes has his catcher's helmet resting on top of his head, and he's wearing his full uniform, a huge smile on his face.

"That was after we won the division two years ago, before things…"

He doesn't need to finish his sentence. We both know how he went from the highest of highs to the lowest of lows.

"Callie said you two were really in sync. That you worked well together." I turn away from the wall to face him. "Do you miss him?"

He smiles, then leans his shoulder against the wall. "I do. We're great together when he's on the mound, and I'm behind home plate. Maybe that's because we're such good friends, I don't know. I miss playing in Seattle with him, but I'd rather be here. Now I play with Decker, and they don't get along, so it's always weird talking with Foster and telling him what his brother has been up to. I've heard shit from Foster about Decker, and now Decker—although he doesn't say anything bad about his brother. Mostly when Foster's name gets brought up, his attention wanders off. They're both good guys though. I don't even know what happened." He shrugs.

"Yeah, well, sometimes family relationships can be complicated. Just look at mine." I smile wide, hoping to mask the trauma from adolescence that somehow still has a way of affecting how I live my life.

His lips tip down.

We're not doing this. I shouldn't have brought it up. "You saw them in the courtroom."

He pushes off the wall and heads toward the kitchen. "This place must seem pretty small compared to Sky's place."

I'm not sure if he's purposely giving me an out, but I'm going to take it.

"It's a great location, and you don't need a lot of space. You're a bachelor. I really like it though." I scan the place again and see an open door that must lead to his bedroom on one side of the kitchen.

"What have you done with your apartment?" he asks.

I walk up to the breakfast bar to see that he's taking a bag of microwave popcorn out of his cupboard and placing it in the microwave. "It's still mine. My lease isn't up for a while. I'm stopping there on my way back to pick up my coffee maker. Cross your fingers I don't have any rodents that have moved in and think of the place as theirs now."

"Sky didn't have a coffee maker?" He tugs the popcorn out of the microwave and opens it, dropping it on the counter when all the steam billows out.

"Tough guy there," I joke, and he glances at me through his long eyelashes. "I tried to use Sky and Patrick's fancy machine, but all I want is a regular cup of coffee, you know? So, I'm just gonna go get mine and bring it back there." I shrug.

He dumps the popcorn in a bowl and buries his head in the fridge, pulling out two waters. Then he reaches into a cabinet and drops a bag of licorice on the counter. "Won't you have to move everything out and find room at Sky's for all your things?"

He's right. Assuming I maintain custody of the kids, moving is inevitable, but I'm still in the guest room next to Sky and Patrick's bedroom, living out of my suitcase and a laundry basket. It just doesn't feel right to take up residence in their bedroom.

"I'm guessing all your clothes are there by now?"

His questions make me realize that I haven't really moved in. I'm still living like a guest in a house that might end up being mine. I've made a couple of quick trips, grabbing a bag here and a bag there, but anything personal is still back at my apartment.

He must notice me thinking and probably clocks the worry etched on my face.

"It's not anything you have to decide now. Anyway, what do you think of this place now that you've seen it?" he asks, changing the subject again.

"I really like it. If I ever envisioned where you live, this is what I would think."

He smiles big, as though that means something to him. "Who's watching the kids?"

"My mom, but they all have places to go tonight. Lake is at a friend's house, and Lincoln and Monroe are going to the same house to hang out with kids their own ages. I have to pick them up…" I glance at my phone. "In a couple of hours."

"So, you have a few hours to yourself?" He picks up the bowl of popcorn and cradles it in his arms.

"I do. And it's still light outside. Amazing."

He bites his lower lip in what seems like it might be a nervous gesture. "Would you be willing to spend those hours with me?"

The teenage girl in me is swooning right now, but I do my best to keep from outwardly reacting. "That depends on what you have in mind." I glance at the items in his hands.

"I'd like to show you the rooftop." Again, his teeth nibble on his bottom lip.

If I was in charge of choosing the theme for today's National Day, it would definitely be known as the day Hayes Carlisle Looked Nervous in Front of Me.

CHAPTER
THIRTY

Hayes

This could be a bad decision, but Leighton shared her fears with me. She was open and honest with me and deserves the same in return.

Leighton opens the door for me, and I tell her the keypad codes to get up to the rooftop. The bar up here is closed since there's no game, and it's only rented for private parties while games are happening at Webber Field. Our private entrance opens into the bar with the giant windows that walk you out to the stadium seating on the rooftop.

"How are you allowed access up here?" she asks.

"Cooper Rice from the Grizzlies owns this building, and he gave us the code."

She turns around, her jaw hanging open. "You professional athletes have a little secret society none of us know about."

I laugh, and we walk out of the bar area, up the stairs to

the rooftop seats. "He's a great guy. Used to live here. Years ago, before he was married and had a family."

We rarely see Cooper, but that's the same with the Grizzlies and the Falcons. They're off living their happily-ever-afters. Good for them.

"I feel like I'm in some rom-com, special access." She giggles, looking around as though she's afraid she'll miss something. "I always wondered what it was like up on these rooftops."

"You should bring the kids one day. I can get you tickets." I wait for her to pick a row, and I'm surprised when she goes all the way to the top.

"They'd love it." She sits in the middle of the row, staring down at the field. I hand her a water, and she takes the bowl of popcorn, letting me get situated next to her.

I realize she's still wearing her scrubs. "I could've given you something to change into."

"Have you ever worn scrubs?" She puts her feet up on the seat in front of her and opens her water.

"I like to leave that to the professionals." I lean back as well. Even after all these months, sometimes I still can't believe I get to play on the field I grew up watching ball games on. That people fill those seats, in part, to see me play.

"I'll get you a pair. You'll love them. So comfortable." Her hand digs into the popcorn, and she tosses up a kernel, catching it in her mouth.

"You gonna share?"

She snags another handful and hands me the bowl. "So, why am I here?" Leighton meets my gaze.

I've never thought of myself as a closed-off person, but I've been stalling. I want to put myself out there with her. I trust her not to discuss my vulnerabilities with anyone else, but that doesn't make it any easier.

"You don't see the players down there on the field?"

She laughs and leans her head on my shoulder all too

briefly before she straightens to continue eating her popcorn. Still, she remains quiet, waiting for me to fill the silence, waiting for me to tell her why she's here. Why I asked her to stare at an empty baseball field.

"Last year—"

"No!" Her feet fall off the back of the chair in front of her, and she swivels, putting her hand on my thigh. "I told you, you don't need to explain yourself."

"I want to."

"It won't change my opinion of you—which is pretty great, I have to say. I only said that shit in the alley because of my own issues and being scared. You owe me nothing. No explanations."

"And that's why I want to tell you."

She smiles softly as her palm runs down my thigh. My dick twitches in my pants. If she were mine, I'd probably be trying to figure out the logistics of how I could fuck her in these uncomfortable seats.

"Okay. If you really want to." Her voice is soft, tender.

I look at the green grass, the brown basepaths, the empty stadium seats. "I was already struggling at the beginning of last year. I was pissed that I didn't win the Gold Glove, and the chip that's been on my shoulder my entire career just grew bigger."

"Chip?" She frowns. "I never thought—"

"It started way back with Coach Linden."

"He was an asshole." She'd know, since he was the gym and health teacher at our school.

"Well, he didn't believe in me—said I was only there to make the pitcher look good. And played games with my playing time."

She sips her water. "Weren't you All-State?"

I nod. "After Coach Linden retired, my senior year. But him telling me he didn't think I had what it took always stuck with me. Then when I hit the minors after college, I was a throw-in to a trade package for another player." I shrug, remembering how I doubted myself and my worth at that point. Figured I'd never even see a professional field. "There's a lot of ups and downs in this career."

"But you've persevered. So many fans love you, Hayes. You've proven Coach Linden wrong. You made it."

I laugh, and it sounds hollow as fuck. "I've never won a Gold Glove. I've never gotten any accolades for my performance. Sure, I'm consistent and steady as far as my play goes, except last year, but I'm replaceable. That's why the Colts only took me on for one year. They're probably just buying time until the next hot catcher comes up, and then I'll be out."

"That's not true," she says. "They're lucky to have you."

I open the Twizzlers package and pull one out for myself. "Anyway, I was pissed that I'd had my best year in the league and was still passed up for the Gold Glove. I always believed that if you work hard enough, the reward will come, but that didn't seem true for me. So, I decided I didn't give a shit anymore. I was halfway into that spiral when my mom and dad showed up unexpectedly at an away game." I hold out the Twizzlers bag. "Sorry, I'll stock some Twix at my place for next time."

She gives me a smile that says *don't dodge this with humor*, but she takes one.

"For them to come to an away game that wasn't in Chicago raised my red flags, but Callie wasn't with them, so I figured if it were something bad, she'd have been there too."

I remember wanting to text Callie in the locker room before the dinner that would change everything. But then I thought that I was the oldest, and my parents were telling me whatever it was first so that I could be there to help Callie through it. Turns out I was the last to know.

"Neither of my parents said anything about my game and how horrible I'd played. It might've been my worst game that year. We went out to eat, and that's when they told me my mom had done a routine medical exam, and they found something. After an ultrasound and a biopsy, it confirmed what the doctors thought—she had cancer."

A short, strangled noise comes out of Leighton.

"They already had her chemo schedule. They knew what steps the doctor would take and explained to me exactly what would be happening going forward. The milestones they hoped she'd reach. I should've been there with them during those doctor visits."

"They understood." Leighton turns to face me and takes my hand. Her thumb runs along my pointer finger, and just that small contact feels like so much comfort.

"I was in shock at first, I think. I didn't say anything… just excused myself, put my napkin on my chair, walked right to the bathroom, and wept." Tears sting my eyes, but I suck them back, not wanting to remember how my dad came in and hugged me so tightly, his tears wetting my white silk shirt, the two of us terrified we were going to lose her.

"And after that, I didn't give a shit about my average, or stops, or wins. I just wanted to be here in Chicago with her, holding her hand during her treatments, making her laugh to distract her from the poison being delivered to her bloodstream. But she told me I couldn't, that her greatest joy would be to watch me play the game she knew I loved. So, I stayed, and I managed to screw that up too."

Leighton throws herself on me, her arms wrapping around my neck. My water bottle crinkles in my hand, and the Twizzlers press into my body.

"She loves you. You've never disappointed her," she whispers in my ear. Just when I think I can't hold the tears back anymore, she draws back and stares right into my eyes. "You're a great son, a great brother, and a great baseball player."

Her words mean so much to me, but I'm not sure I can believe them.

"I just don't want you to think that the man I was last year is truly who I am. It isn't. It was the most fucked-up version of myself."

She leans back, and I miss her comfort as soon as she's back in her seat. "Thank you for trusting me with all this. It can't be easy, but I never thought that was who you are. I thought you were going through the worst chapter of your life and not dealing with it well."

"I partied to forget, but there weren't that many women. Fewer than you probably think."

I don't miss the way she stiffens slightly. "Why are you telling me that? It's your business, not mine."

"It matters what you think of me. I wanted to clarify where my head was at. Although you ran away from that kiss because you thought I would hurt you, so maybe that says something about my character even back then."

She stands and walks over a few seats, wrapping her arms around her stomach. She stares at the field, and it's obvious she's struggling with something. I just have no idea what it could be.

Finally, she turns to me. "There's something you don't know about that night."

CHAPTER
THIRTY-ONE

Leighton

My stomach riots at the idea of telling Hayes the truth, but I have to be honest with him.

"What don't I know?" He straightens in his seat, abandoning the Twizzlers, popcorn, and water.

"I'm a bad person."

He huffs. "I doubt that, Leighton. You're the nicest person I know."

I stare at him for a moment. "Thank you for sharing all that with me. I was an outsider, seeing what your family went through last year. I tried to comfort Callie, and I would go visit your mom during some of her treatments at the hospital during my lunch break. You didn't have to tell me all that for me to know you aren't really the guy you were a year ago. I know how close you all are and how hard it had to be on you. And I understood it"—my head lobs back and forth—"to an extent, but I wish you'd had someone to lean on."

Me particularly, but we're not going to go there.

"You never had to worry about what I thought of you, but I guess this is good. Like a cleanse before we embark on a fake relationship. It will make us closer. Which is why I'm going to confide in you..."

His eyebrows raise.

"I'm not an admirable person, Hayes. When I ran away from you the night of our kiss, it wasn't because I thought you would hurt me. In truth, I hadn't processed that thought at that point, but it's probably the conclusion I would've come up with."

"Knife lodged and twisted."

I break the distance and sit in the chair next to him. "Don't. It's a me thing. I mean, I actually have a list of..." I wave my hand. "Forget that... That night at the party, I um... I had a boyfriend."

He stares blankly at me. So much that I wave my hand in front of his face.

Hayes blinks. "I'm just shocked. You kissed me when you had a boyfriend?"

I squeeze my eyes shut. "Yes. God, hearing you say that out loud feels like you have your finger on a bruise that is my guilt."

"It's just... all these years, I thought it was me. Was I drunker than I thought or was I a bad kisser. I mean, I didn't really believe that last one, but if I was wasted and didn't realize it, that might have made sense..." Now he's the one rambling, and somehow, it's endearing.

I'm just going to put it all on the table. Then there's nothing between us. No secrets. "I had been dating this guy, Colby, and he'd already cheated on me once before freshman year, but I forgave him because we were technically broken up for a few hours. Anyway, we promised to make it work—"

"You used me to get back at him?"

"No!" I practically shout and look around, but we're alone

of course. "I kissed you because I wanted to kiss you. But after the kiss…"

"The amazing kiss, you mean?"

I roll my eyes. "After the amazing kiss—or during, I guess—something jarred me, and I felt so dirty and gross."

"This conversation is a real self-esteem booster. Tell me more about how my lips on yours made you feel," Hayes deadpans.

I chuckle, unable to hold back.

"I was my dad." I shake my head, hating the feeling that saying those words out loud gives me. "I did to someone what my dad did to my mom, and even though I really enjoyed it—well, that's why I ran."

"Please feel free to continue to tell me how much you enjoyed the kiss." There's a cocky grin on his face now.

I swear I could still feel his lips on mine if I close my eyes and replay it in my head.

"It was like seeing a side of myself I never thought I would," I say. "I swore for so many years I'd never do that to someone. Never. Not after I saw the effect it had on my mom. On me."

His head rocks back, finally understanding why I ran.

"I gave in to temptation. I made a shitty decision that was going to hurt people. Callie, Colby, and you, although Callie said you found my replacement pretty quick that night."

He tilts his head and studies me, frowning. "What?"

"Callie came home the next morning and said how mad she was because she saw you making out with a girl and apologized on your behalf for abandoning me."

His eyebrows raise. "And did the girl in question have strawberry-blonde hair?"

I shake my head. "No." I narrow my eyes. "It was a blonde. Because there were two girls you made out with, and I'm strawberry-blonde."

I don't blame him for moving on after I left, but it still stung to hear about it.

"So, Callie saw me making out with someone with blonde hair in a dark room with a strobe light going?" He picks up his bucket of popcorn and leans back in the seat as if a movie is about to start.

"Are you insinuating it was me she saw you with?"

"Well, since after you left the party, I went to look for you and then just sat by the bonfire, yeah. There were no other girls who had their lips on mine that night."

"Oh." How did that never occur to me? I thought Callie was upstairs with that all-star pitcher who'd just been drafted. "Are you sure?"

He nods. "I wasn't that drunk, Leighton."

"Really? All these years, I thought you just moved on."

"All these years, I wondered what made you run. You could've stayed, and we could've talked about it and cleared it up. We might have been a couple by now."

"That would have been a very mature decision for a girl my age who'd just kissed her best friend's older brother." I smile, unable to imagine me being that grown-up then.

"I guess." He shrugs.

We both sit facing forward and staring at the field, deep in our own thoughts.

"I have one more thing to tell you." I want to put everything out there. To be the grown-up version I should've been back then. Maybe the truth will set us on the right track, so we both understand there's no option for us to be together, regardless of if we're attracted to each other or not. "I can't be your reason for not doing well this season."

His forehead wrinkles. "Why would you be?"

I turn to him, and he's so casual, leaning back as if he doesn't have a care in the world. My confession doesn't seem to even have fazed him.

"Because you've been drawn into all my drama. You're

going to pretend to date me so I can win custody, and that means all your free time will be taken up with me. I'm sure you would've used it to work out or train or whatever you need to do to get that Gold Glove."

He shakes his head. "Newsflash, professional athletes do have lives. They have wives, kids, families. Sure, it's more challenging during the season, but not completely impossible."

My shoulders fall. "I know, but—"

"Listen." His feet hit the floor, and he ditches the popcorn, taking my hands. "We're in this together. Don't worry about me. So far, I'm already worlds ahead of where I was last year. And seeing you through this matters to me. I don't really know why, other than I want you to have those kids. I'm sure if I dug down far enough, it would probably be because I wasn't here last year when my mom needed me the most. And I want you to be there for those kids when they need you most. Maybe not. But you do need to know something."

"I'm starting to think we should pitch in for our own personal therapist."

He squeezes my hands. "I know it's the wrong time and all that, but I'm sorry to tell you that I like you, Leighton."

My hands go limp in his. This is not the way I thought he'd ever confess his feelings for me. To apologize as if it's a horrible thing.

"But I'm going to respect your wishes."

What wishes were those?

Oh yeah, for nothing to happen between us. I have too much going on, and neither of us is in a place to start something.

"Oh… yeah… thanks." I play it off, even if I want to ditch the holding hands and go right to lip-smacking.

"I'll keep my distance until you say go."

Would he think less of me if I said go right now? Yes, because he needs to win the Gold Glove, and I need to win custody, and if we try to start something and we fail, then both of our lives will be upended.

I'm a jumble of emotions, and it's hard to make sense of any of them. I'm ecstatic that Hayes likes me in that way, but full of disappointment because it doesn't change anything.

"I should go." I stand, sliding my hands from his.

Thankfully, he doesn't fight me on it. "I'll walk you out."

And that's that, I suppose. He confesses he likes me and is willing to start something as soon as I say so, then I just run away again.

"Can I ask you something before you go?" Hayes asks as we reach the bar area on the roof. His voice sounds pained.

"Um, sure."

"Can I have a hug?" His smile is sheepish and endearing. I could never say no. "You know, therapy and all that. I'm feeling vulnerable, and hugs release oxytocin." He opens his arms wide.

"This is such a bad idea," I mumble, but I step into his arms anyway.

He wraps them around my waist, palms flat against my back, pulling me flush against him. His chest is broad and solid, but he holds me as if I'm the prized teddy bear he won at the fair.

His chin angles down, nuzzling into my hair. The sensation is dizzying and unreal. I've spent years avoiding Hayes, and now he holds me as though he understands me and the trials I'm facing. I don't know if and when I'll get this again, so I try to memorize the feel of him. The scent of him. But this is a terrible idea, and if I ever have any hopes of moving on from him, I can't let it continue. So, I pull away, but he clings tighter.

"Twenty seconds." His breath warms my neck.

"That's a very specific number," I whisper, fully engulfed in his intoxicating bubble.

"Google it," he whispers back. "That's how long it takes for the oxytocin to kick in."

His fingers stroke up and down my spine in a soothing, repetitive motion. The rhythm is so hypnotic, I sink into his arms a little deeper. He buries his face in my neck, inhaling, exhaling, as though he's trying to calm himself but failing. Because when my hand weaves between us and I lay it over his heart, it's practically beating out of his chest.

"Leighton."

I've never heard my name spoken with such reverence. The one word like a plea.

"Hayes," I answer with a similar tone, but more of a surrender. My tongue wets my lower lip, a subconscious acquiescence.

We're like a snagged ribbon, both our consciences fraying the longer we're entwined.

His cheek brushes mine once, then twice, and our lips find each other's. A soft, tentative press that lingers. Neither of us pulls away, so we continue tempting fate until a collision of hunger erupts that's years in the making.

His mouth is on mine—hot and demanding, salty from the popcorn, and his tongue slides against mine with an urgency that ignites a moan low in my throat.

Hayes's hands are everywhere—roaming up my sides, trailing down to my hips, cupping my face with a gentleness at odds with the bruising intensity of his kiss. I clutch his shirt, pulling him closer even though there's no space left between us.

At some point, we stumble against the wall, my back thudding into the cold brick. He pins me there, hips flush to mine, and the friction is electric. One of his hands tangles in my hair, angling my head so he can kiss me even deeper, and the other grips my thigh, urging it up around his waist.

We're both gasping, the sound obscene in the empty bar. I

lose all sense of time. There is only this—his body, my body, and the red-hot spark of what we've never allowed ourselves.

He breaks away first, resting his forehead against mine, his eyes dark and wild and searching, breath ragged. "I'm sorry," he whispers, though he doesn't move away. "I shouldn't have—"

I lift on my tiptoes and press my lips to his again. He wastes no time taking control of the kiss, and I grind my center along his hard length, forgetting every reason we said this is a bad idea.

Screw rules and lists and all the shit I worry too much about.

My hands wedge between us, and I flick open the button of his pants. I am lust personified. My fingers grab the top of his zipper. I'm going to take this for myself.

The sound of a door slamming shut reverberates through the small space. We both strip our mouths off one another and turn our heads.

Hayes groans. "Impeccable timing as always, Kodiak."

CHAPTER
THIRTY-TWO

Leighton

I'm in the guest room, essentially my room, putting away the clothes I've left in suitcases and laundry baskets since I moved in. I've been through this house the past two days, trying to get it neat and tidy and organized for the home visit tonight. Hayes is supposed to be here any minute, and we'll tell the kids that we're a couple. They won't know the fake part of it because we can't chance them blowing our secret.

After that kiss in the rooftop bar though, I'm kind of wishing we were a real couple. I would've slept with Hayes that day, then we'd be in even bigger trouble. Thankfully, Easton interrupted us, and when Hayes walked me down to the Uber, we both agreed that it shouldn't happen again.

Every night since, I've masturbated to what might have happened had Easton not interrupted us. Every time I think about it, a flash of heat flows through my body like lava, slow-moving and scorching. I've never been kissed like that.

Lincoln runs into the room and throws himself onto my

bed, effectively forcing me to stop thinking about the feel of Hayes's dick pressing against my core.

"Did you put your clean clothes in the dresser?" I ask, hanging my clothes in the closet.

"Yep."

"And nothing is falling out? The drawers are all closed?" I eye him, piling my sweatshirts on the shelf.

"Yep."

"There's a lot of room in this closet." I continue putting away my clothes.

"You should paint your room," Lincoln says. "What color is your room at your apartment?"

I look around the room. It's probably the smallest bedroom, but I'm not complaining. "A boring cream color. I wasn't allowed to paint at my apartment."

Lake comes in and sits on the edge of the bed. "Why don't you move into Mom and Dad's room? Then you'd have your own bathroom."

That has been the only downside of living in the guest room. I share a bathroom with Lincoln and Monroe. Lake has her own attached to her room, but the three of us share the main bath. I usually end up doing my makeup downstairs.

But the idea of moving into Sky's room… "I don't know about that."

Lincoln says nothing, probably because he thinks we should leave their room untouched.

"You're going to so much trouble." Lake crosses her legs. "Who cares if your clothes are in your suitcase?"

"Because it makes it look temporary. Half in, half out." I take out my bag of shoes and put them in the bottom of the closet.

Lake lies down, resting her head in her palm, watching me. "I think this whole home visit thing is stupid. Why don't we have a say?"

I've already talked to the three of them about this. "You're not old enough. We need to make a really good impression today. But don't forget you're going to stay with Uncle Art and Aunt Julianna next weekend."

Lincoln rolls over and flails his arms and legs. "They're sooo boring. Aunt Julianna bought me a puzzle for Christmas last year."

"It had all the MLB teams on it," Lake says and eyes me as though she's trying to make it better, even though I know she doesn't want to go either.

"Who wants to do a puzzle? Boring."

I throw a pair of my shoes in the closet in the far corner, because I doubt the social worker is going to reach back there. They hit something that doesn't sound like a wall or the floor.

"It's weird that you sleep in here. No one ever sleeps here," Lake says, looking around the room. "We never have any guests."

"That's not true. Daddy used to sleep here sometimes," Lincoln says.

I stop reaching to find out what's in the back of the closet and turn to face Lake. She's not disagreeing with her brother.

"Your dad slept in this room?" I ask. Sky never told me about them having any problems. It must have been an occasional thing when they had a fight. Or maybe Patrick snored.

"Yeah, on the bad nights," Lake says.

The doorbell rings, and Lincoln catapults himself off the bed and out of the bedroom.

"Be the best niece and let Hayes in?" I ask Lake.

She rolls her eyes but gets up, screaming at Lincoln to wait for her.

I crawl to the back of the closet, seeing a black overnight bag shoved in the far corner. If no one sleeps here, why is this here? I sit back on my heels and open the bag.

Inside is a bottle of perfume and red lingerie. Not Sky's usual perfume, and she once told me she hated red lingerie.

What am I missing here?

Footsteps sound up the steps, and I hurriedly shove it all back in the closet, positioning the bag under my shoes so the kids won't find it.

"You say we can never kiss again, then I come in here to see you on all fours. You're playing games, Leighton Sinclair."

Hayes's deep voice prickles my skin, and our kiss, that grinding, rushes back through my mind.

"Look, Hayes!" Lincoln runs back in the room and jumps, bouncing off my bed, effectively dousing my heated libido.

"That's cool. I love making beds bounce," Hayes says.

I glare at him, and he shrugs, a grin on his face.

"Want to give it a try, Leighton?" Hayes leans his shoulder on the wall.

"Not right now," I say. "Come on, Lincoln, time for the family chat before the social worker gets here. Go get Monroe."

He groans and tries to get Hayes to bounce on the bed, but Hayes tells him he has to talk to me for a second.

Once Lincoln is gone, Hayes blocks the doorway. "I think we should let them catch us kissing."

His fingers hold on to the trim above the door, and his shirt rises above the waistband of his pants, showing off his happy trail. I swear the universe is testing me.

I place my hand on his stomach, even though I shouldn't. I just can't resist. "I think we both know that's not a good idea."

His hands drop to his sides. "Tell me that kiss sucked," he whispers. "Because I can't stop thinking about it."

"Hayes, we need to go talk to the kids." I move to go around, but he steps in front of me.

"You know how many times I've beat off, imagining where your hand was going before we were interrupted?"

Probably the same amount as me.

He takes my hand, running his palm down mine.

"What are you doing?"

"Trying to memorize your hand so I can picture it wrapped around my dick later. Shit, you have some soft hands."

"Ready!" Lincoln yells down the hallway.

Meanwhile, my cheeks are flushed, and my palm wants to become intimately acquainted with his dick. I too find myself wanting to know what my hand would look like wrapped around his shaft.

But no. We agreed.

I unwind my hand from his. "Let's go."

I slide by Hayes and walk down the stairs before I make a massive mistake and kiss him again.

CHAPTER
THIRTY-THREE

Hayes

It has been pure and utter torture since Easton interrupted us on the roof. All I can see every time I blink are Leighton's swollen lips. All I can feel is her ass in my hands. All I can hear are her soft little moans. I'm in way over my head. I thought I could control my appetite for her—keep my shit together until she gives me the green light—but I'm starting to wonder.

I force myself to sit on the couch in the family room. "Did you hire a maid?"

"No, I did it myself." She lights a candle on the table.

Everything looks meticulous. It's the most put-together I've seen this house look.

"I take offense to that by the way."

"She made us do stuff all day." Monroe groans.

"Okay, guys," Leighton says and sits next to me. She places her hand on my thigh. I have to think of something shitty before my dick joins our little party. "Hayes and I have some news."

Lake's eyes zoom in on Leighton's hand on my thigh, and I straighten, pulling her hand off to hold it. "We were trying to keep it a secret, but during the court hearing, we had no choice but to tell the judge."

They don't say anything. Monroe is flicking her bee headband for National Bee Day. She's dressed in yellow and black, and it's cute as hell.

"Hayes and I are a couple. A romantically involved couple," Leighton says.

"What does that mean?" Lincoln frowns.

"They, like, kiss and stuff," Lake says.

"It's like Mom and Dad, except we don't live together, nor are we married. We are dating. He's my boyfriend."

"Hayes is going to be my uncle!" Lincoln screams and raises his fists in the air.

Leighton squeezes my hand.

I clear my throat. I assume that's her subtle way of telling me to tag in. "No, buddy, but maybe..." Another squeeze. Leighton has a Miss America smile plastered on as she crushes my knuckles together. Does she realize that's how I make my money? "We're taking things slow, and nothing is changing. I'll be coming and going like I have been."

"Are you going to sleep over? National Sleepover Day is coming soon," Monroe says.

Leighton's grip gets even tighter. "Um... we'll see. But we didn't want to keep any secrets from you guys."

"When did you start dating?" Lake tucks herself into the corner of the love seat, pointedly staring at us, then our adjoined hands, and back to our faces.

"Um..." I look at Leighton because I'm not sure what to say.

"Well, I've known Hayes a long time."

I release Leighton's hand so I can have feeling in mine again and wrap my arm around her shoulders. She leans against my chest. Fake or not, this feels damn good.

"I know that, but you weren't dating before, so when did you start?" Lake asks.

Is it hot in here? I crack my neck, and Leighton looks at me with an expression to say I suck at faking it.

I've never been good at lying. Even when I was a little kid.

"I don't know the specific date, but it doesn't matter," she says.

Lincoln tosses me the ball in his lap, and I go to throw it back, but earn a look from Leighton that says we're still talking.

"In a little bit, Linc." I place it next to me on the couch.

"Do you not like that we're dating, Lake?" Leighton asks.

She shrugs. "No, I just wonder why all of a sudden."

Leighton puts her hand on my thigh again, and my leg jumps a little. She squeezes it to keep it in place.

Lake's eyes are on Leighton's hand again, and I feel uncomfortable. Almost like the father of a teenager watching me grope his daughter in front of him.

"It was just time, I guess. We've been spending time together," Leighton says.

"Hmm. Okay, is this family meeting over then?" Lake twirls her finger in the air.

"Yes. She'll be here any minute, so just be yourselves."

The doorbell rings, and I couldn't be happier that this uncomfortable conversation is over. Leighton gets up to answer the door, Lincoln and Monroe following her. Lake stays in the chair, her gaze on me.

She totally knows this thing is fake, but I decide to tell her the one thing that is true.

"I like Leighton. A lot. So, whatever you're concerned about, don't be."

"I don't care who you are. If you hurt her, I have a lot of friends with social media accounts."

I purse my lips, trying not to smile or laugh. "Message received."

She nods, and I let her think she made her point, but I'll prove her wrong—I won't ever hurt Leighton.

CHAPTER
THIRTY-FOUR

Leighton

I show up to the baseball field with Lincoln and Monroe, a bag of T-shirts the park district gave me, and some equipment. After the home visit, Hayes stayed for a while and demonstrated some exercises I could have the team do to build their skills. Between those and the ones I researched, I was feeling pretty confident until now.

Lincoln is still doubtful that I can coach this team, and as he was going to bed, he begged Hayes to be here to help tonight. I'm sure Hayes would, but they had a game this afternoon and then a press thing, so Lincoln promised to give him a recap tonight on the phone.

Lake has been on me for details about my relationship with Hayes, but I'm keeping firm on my decision not to tell any of the kids that it is indeed fake.

"Where is everyone?" Lincoln whines, already in his T-shirt and shorts.

Monroe picks up a ball. "Why can't I play?"

"This is just for nine-year-olds, but Aunt Lily is going to come and watch you during practice." I try to force excitement into my tone, but who am I kidding? No way will my mom let Monroe go play at the park with all the other siblings.

Lake decided to go to a friend's house, and maybe I should've told her I wanted her to come to watch Monroe with my mom, but I don't want her to take on any more than she already has. She deserves to be a kid.

Lincoln and Monroe throw the ball back and forth, and thankfully, Lincoln is being cautious. Then again, he knows that Monroe is his only teammate at home, so he better make sure she enjoys playing catch. Lord knows his older sister isn't going to throw the ball around with him.

A few families arrive, and the parents come over to introduce themselves to me and get their child a T-shirt. I'm surprised when they all stick around instead of just dropping off their child.

Guess I'm doing their first practice with an audience. Awesome.

"You look like you need some help there," a man says. I look over to find that he's dressed in athletic shorts, a matching T-shirt, and hat with the initials PBR. Professional Bull Riding? Huh. That's cool.

His kid must be the last one I was waiting for. I check my clipboard and cross the name Rawlings off the list. After shaking the dad's hand and handing out the T-shirt, I turn to go back to where the boys are messing around, ready to get started.

"I'll help you." He jogs to catch up to me.

The league told me that it would be hard to find assistant coaches since I grabbed the last spot, and no one else seemed to want it, so this is a pleasant surprise.

"Oh, thanks."

A few of the moms on the other side of the fence are

talking to each other, but I can't hear what they're saying. I worry it might not be good things about me.

"I used to play shortstop back in the day. Rawlings has an older brother, Wilson, who plays shortstop now."

"Oh, that's cool." I give him a smile. I look at my list of instructions, thankful for the help but more nervous now that I'm not alone with the boys.

"What's on the clipboard?" His head is suddenly right next to mine, peering at my papers.

I bring them down to my side. "Boys, pair up and throw to one another." I turn to… "I'm sorry, what's your name? I'm Leighton."

"Mike, but people call me Butter."

I nod. "Nice to officially meet you. I think I'll call you Mike."

"Ah." He waves. "Butter is good. It's a nickname from back in high school. Smooth like butter…" He skates his hand in a flat line in front of him, but I don't really get the reference. "My glove skills." His expression tells me he's upset that I didn't understand. "So, do you mind if I check out your list?" He points at the clipboard.

"Oh, it's just some drills that my boyfriend wrote up for me. In case I needed them." I don't hand him the clipboard.

"Doesn't think you have what it takes for this team to make it to the championship?"

My eyes scrunch. Is that what the expectation is? That I win this team a trophy? I glance to the outfield where the boys are throwing balls at one another. And I only say throwing because I don't see a lot of catching, but I do see a lot of running after errant balls. I think I might have bit off a little more than I can chew.

"He just wanted me to have a starting point. He played a little too." I'm not going to get into exactly who my boyfriend is because for one, he's not my actual boyfriend.

"Yeah, cool. I'm sure he wanted to show off the fact he

played rec ball once too." Mike elbows me and laughs. "I'm gonna be honest with you." He widens his stance and crosses his arms. "I wanted your coaching spot."

I blink at him. "Oh. The office said—"

"I was on vacation." He shrugs with one shoulder. "And Bill—you know, the organizer for rec baseball—he was supposed to hold it for me, but he was out on medical leave. Anyway, I'm happy to take over for you. I mean, I coached my older son, and I've been coaching Rawlings since he was little. No offense. You just look a little in over your head."

I glance at the other parents. There are mostly moms by the dugout, and there are a few dads at the fence line, instructing their kids on how to catch the ball. Then there's another group of dads in the outfield, hanging out over by the fence.

"I really appreciate the offer, Mike—"

"Butter."

"Butter," I say. "But I'd like to do this myself. No offense. You probably don't know this, but Lincoln's parents passed away in an accident a couple of months ago, and I think it would mean a lot to him if I coached. But I really appreciate the offer. The assistant job is still up for grabs if you want it."

The last thing I want is this guy assisting me, but I don't see any other parents volunteering, so I'll have to grin and bear it. Then again, maybe if he can't bulldoze me to the side to be head coach, he and Rawlings will hightail it to another team.

"Oh damn, which little guy is it?"

"The one with the Colts hat." I don't mention that it's signed by three Colts players.

"I'm sorry, and yeah, I'll totally assist." Mike runs his hand down the back of his head and pulls at his neck, looking at one of the other fields. "Actually, I have a buddy who coaches the other team, and he was saying we could scrimmage. You know, if you're up for it. Might show you who should play where, you know?"

I glance in the direction he's looking, where there's a shorter man also wearing the PBR hat, but his T-shirt says PG. I have no idea what the PG stands for, or that there are so many rodeo fans around here.

To be honest, when Hayes was showing me the drills, I wasn't taking the best notes. I was mostly watching him and his legs, his hands, and his strong thighs that I so badly wanted to straddle. It's hard not to imagine riding them, they're so muscular. What they might feel like grinding against my clit—

"Leighton," Mike says.

I blink my eyes out of my daydream. "Sure. Sounds good." I press my hand to my cheek. "I'm just going to get some water."

"I'll go tell Randy." He jogs away, and I'm thankful for the reprieve.

When I make my way to the bag near the dugout, one of the moms there grabs my attention.

"Did he try to take over your coaching job?" she asks as I swallow a gulp of water. "He's been talking a lot of shit the last couple weeks. I'm Aimee." She holds out her hand.

"Hi, Aimee, I'm Leighton."

"Don't let him bully you. Stand your ground. We'll back you up." She turns to the other moms. "Her name is Leighton, ladies."

They each come over and introduce themselves, telling me which child is theirs. I'll never remember, but I'm glad to hear they weren't talking shit about me.

Mike jogs back over. "Randy's in."

"Oh, I thought it was his idea." I frown, pulling out the catcher gear the district gave me.

He waves off my comment. "Yeah. Yeah. That's what I meant."

I call the boys over, already done with Mike or Butter or whatever he wants me to call him.

Once they've all made their way over, I address the group. "We're going to play a scrimmage with the other team."

All the boys look at the team walking over. They all have their matching orange shirts on, and each boy has baseball pants, belts, eye paint, and is that an elbow guard on the one? What did I sign these poor kids up for?

CHAPTER
THIRTY-FIVE

Hayes

The Uber drops us off at the park. Easton and Decker insisted on coming with me, saying that they're like family too. Whatever.

"So, are we just not gonna talk about how you had your tongue down her throat the other day?" Easton asks for the millionth time.

Mental note. Easton and secrets don't mix.

We follow the signs to the baseball fields, passing a shit-ton of soccer fields. "No, we're not."

"Didn't look very fake to me," Easton says.

"And you're going to keep your mouth shut about it. It's not happening again."

He puts up both hands. "Shit, sorry. You two looked hot though. I mean, Deck, her leg was over his hip, and our boy here was grinding into her, his tongue so far down her throat I'm not sure she could breathe."

"I don't need or want the play-by-play," Decker says, shaking his head. "Does Callie know?"

Easton blows out a breath. "Man, you need to worry about the rules a little less. Live a little."

"No, she doesn't know, and she won't because it's not happening again. Now let's just find Lincoln's team. I wanted to be here earlier, but you jackasses tagged along." I shut down the conversation about my make-out session with Leighton, eager to see her in action.

She was so worried the other night. I didn't want to over-step, but she asked for some help, so I showed her some things she could have the kids work on. Having her watching from the patio chair and me in the yard with Lincoln felt really nice, like we were a family.

"I give up. Where the fuck are the fields?" Easton throws his hands in the air. He's a little pissy after going oh for three today at the plate.

"That sign says the baseball fields are this way. Let's go." I point at the sign, and we head in that direction.

We reach a hill, and when we crest the top, all three of us stop.

"Holy shit, there's a million of them," Decker says.

He's right. Little yellow bodies, little red bodies, little green bodies all running around in organized chaos.

"Lincoln's team has maroon jerseys," I say, scanning the area.

"There." Easton points.

"I think that's red." I pull off my ball cap and run my hand through my hair before fitting it back on my head.

"No, there." Decker points.

"Are you color blind? That's brown." Easton crosses his arms.

I finally spot them mixed together with the orange team. Why are they playing a game when every other team is prac-ticing in the outfields?

"There they are." I point in their general direction. I lead the way and the guys follow.

"Some of these kids are really good," Decker says.

"Hopefully, since she has their team in a game, she got some more advanced kids. It would make it easier for her," I say.

As we approach the outfield, I overhear a couple of the dads talking.

"I don't get it. Why doesn't she just let Mike coach? They're going to fall back this year now."

Easton's eyebrows raise, and Decker mouths, "What the fuck?"

I decide to slow my steps and lean against the fence line. "New coach, huh?" I ask, lowering my baseball hat.

Easton and Decker do the same, standing on either side of me.

None of the dads take their eyes off the field, so I'm pretty sure I don't need the ball cap.

"Yeah, and she's clearly never coached before. She's got my kid in right field. He's a third baseman." The man shakes his head in disgust.

"And mine plays second, but she's got him in as catcher. He hates playing catcher."

"That's a tough position," Decker chimes in.

"Not as a professional, but at this age, yeah. Kids can't throw strikes. Jack is going to be exhausted tonight. I'll have to ice his legs."

Easton laughs but masks it with a cough.

"Who's your kid?" one of the dads asks.

I scan the field. "Second base."

Right then, a kid hits the ball, and it goes right to Lincoln. He fields it and throws it to the first baseman, who misses the catch, so the runner is safe. I'm super proud of Lincoln, and I'm going to tell him it was a great play.

"That's all me," Easton brags.

"At least she got your kid's position right," the dad says. "Maybe we should vote her out or something?"

Easton puts his hand on my back. "I want a closer look, come on."

It takes every ounce of my willpower to walk away from these dipshits who think their kids are preparing for the major leagues at nine years old.

As we walk along the fence line, the inning ends, and the guy at first goes over to Leighton. He almost looks as though he's whispering, his arm around her back, resting on the top of the fence behind her.

"Oh shit, things are about to go down," Easton says.

My jaw clenches, but Decker knocks his shoulder to mine and shakes his head. He'd probably die if I made a scene at rec baseball.

Lincoln is up to bat, and I stand back from the other parents, so he doesn't see us. I don't want him any more nervous than he probably already is.

"What is he doing?" Easton asks.

"Did you tell him how to position his bat?" Decker turns his head to look at me.

"He's nine. We've only ever worked on fielding and catching." Even I bite my cheek.

Lincoln swings and misses. He's pulling his head out, and his upright stance isn't doing him any favors.

"We have to get our boy to the cages," Easton says, crossing his arms.

"We'll start with the tee," Decker adds.

"And then soft toss," I say.

Poor Lincoln strikes out with only three pitches, and some guy in a Perfect Game T-shirt says the game is over.

All the boys line up, and Leighton does too. The jackass talking to her earlier walks behind her, and if I see his eyes stray to her ass even once, I'm going to be over the fence.

We finally walk the rest of the way over, and Monroe spots us immediately.

"You came!" She jumps up from the blanket where she's playing with another girl her age. A paperclip necklace swings around her neck as she runs over to us.

Lily stands and folds up her camping chair, not offering us a smile.

I squat and wait for Monroe to run into my arms, but she attaches herself to Decker's legs instead, squeezing hard and closing her eyes.

"Damn, you've definitely been replaced." Easton laughs and walks over to the dugout. He nods to the moms gawking at him as he passes by.

"Will you take me to the park, Decker?" Monroe asks, still wrapped around his legs.

"Sure, but I'm gonna need that necklace. It's not safe to climb with that on."

She takes it off right away. "It's Paperclip Day."

"Cool, another checkmark." They high-five each other and take off.

Dickwad is talking Leighton's ear off while she packs up the bag. He's head to toe in Prep Baseball Report gear, and I shake my head. I detour through the dugout, the boys staring at me in awe, even though I don't think they exactly know who I am. I don't have to explain that we play for the Colts, Easton's doing enough of it for the three of us.

Once I'm on the field, Leighton catches sight of me, and the smile she gives me… shit, it's one most men would dream about. It has to mean something. I understand her not being ready with everything she has going on, but no one smiles at someone like that if they don't want more.

"Hey, babe." I come alongside her, wrapping my arm around her waist and pulling her into me.

"Hey." She steadies herself with a hand on my chest.

"This must be the boyfriend." Dickhead holds his hand in

front of me. He's so arrogant that he's yet to look me in the eye.

"You bragging about me, babe?" I kiss her cheek.

"I just said you played some baseball too." She smiles wide, and I can assume from her tone and her comment how the conversation between the two of them went. "How was the game?"

"We won, and your man went two for three."

Dickwad's eyes snap up, and as recognition hits, his jaw falls open. "Your boyfriend is Hayes Carlisle?"

"Oh." Leighton's voice is syrupy sweet and drips with sarcasm. "Did I not mention that?"

He clears his throat. "I think you forgot that part."

"Honey, this is Mike, but he likes to be referred to as Butter. You know, smooth as butter."

I'm about ready to bust out laughing from her tone of voice.

"Mike is good," he says, shifting in place.

I hold out my hand. "Pleasure." We shake. "How did my girl do?"

"Great. She did great."

"I told you you had nothing to worry about. That some helpful dad would volunteer to help. Thanks, Butter—"

"You can call me Mike…"

I ignore his response. "Excuse us, we need to get home and feed the kids." I reach for the bag of equipment. "Let me get that." I keep my arm around her waist and lead us away. "See you, Mike."

"Yeah, bye." His voice is distant.

I tap Leighton's ass with the hopes he's looking to make it very clear that she's mine.

"What are you doing?" Leighton says under her breath.

"Just playing the part, babe." I kiss her cheek. I'll take any excuse I can get to be affectionate.

"All right then. When I come to a baseball game, I'll grab you by the dick."

I laugh. "Do you think you'd hear any complaints from me?"

She leans her head on my chest, and I tuck her in a little tighter. I'll fake it until she believes there's nothing fake about what's happening between us.

CHAPTER
THIRTY-SIX

Hayes

I'm walking into the hospital when my phone vibrates in my pocket. I'm hopeful it's Leighton telling me she wants to eat lunch with me or maybe inviting me to hang out during her break since she knew I'd be here today.

Sadly, it's just my sister.

> Why are you two hiding things from me!?

> I'm on my way up to mom's appointment.

> Do you think I didn't talk to mom this morning? I know that. Now tell me about how you and my bff are now fake dating. I caught up with Leighton last night…

I chuckle, leaning against the wall near the elevator.

> Sorry, I don't remember having to run things by you.

When it comes to Leighton, you do.

Well then, we're in a relationship.

FAKE news, big brother.

And then she starts in with her rapid-fire texts, as I knew she would. She's so easy to bait. I wait until I make it to the floor of my mom's doctor before I respond.

You hurt her, and I'll kill you.

I will disown you if she sheds one tear because of you.

Keep your dick in your pants and your tongue in your mouth.

Don't you have anything to say for yourself?

I could play this one of two ways, but I'm still a big brother who likes to poke his little sister.

What can I say? I like your best friend, and I'm not sorry about it.

Gotta go.

Almost Mom's appointment time.

I'll let you know how it goes.

See ya.

I put my phone on silent and stuff it in my pocket, opening the door to my mom's doctor's office. My dad waves, and I walk over to them in the corner of the room near the windows that face Lake Michigan.

"What are you so smiley about?" Mom asks when I bend over and hug her.

"I was just pissing off Callie."

She holds me tightly for a second and chuckles. "Why do you have to do that?"

I shrug. "Because it's fun."

I hug my dad, then sit in the seat across from them. Leighton and I decided that I'd tell my parents about our situation when I saw them today. They know her, and I don't want them getting any ideas and being disappointed. But now that I'm sitting with them, I'm wondering what we were thinking.

My mom is here to get the results of her one-year scan. She seems in good spirits, but her mind has to be spinning. Then again, it would distract her, and it won't upset her, I don't think. She'll understand why we're doing it.

I look around the room and lean in closer. My mom takes the hint, leaning in, but my dad is still looking out the window at all the sailboats in the water.

"I have to tell you something," I whisper.

No one is close to us, and the people who are might not even know who I am, but I need to be careful.

"Did you get a tattoo?" my mom whispers.

My eyes crinkle, and I shake my head.

"Because I don't care anymore. That's the good side of this disease. You just don't care about the small stuff."

"I didn't know you were against tattoos?" My head cocks to the side.

"I'm not. Now." She shrugs.

"Well, that's not it."

"Okay." She looks at my dad. "Dave, any guesses what Hayes has to tell us?"

My dad looks at me. "What's the game?"

This is the result of a family who treats everything like a game.

"We're not playing a game," I say.

"I thought you wanted me to guess?" My mom looks confused. "You bought a farm!"

I hate to tell her she couldn't be further from the truth because she looks so happy.

"I'd rather you buy a lake house. If you're going to spend your money, you should be on a lake where you can fish." My dad goes back to looking at the water gleaming in the sun. "Or a sailboat would be nice. We could take lessons together. Father and son bonding."

"Oh, that would be nice. Wouldn't it, Hayes?" My mom smiles at me.

"Sure, I'll think about it. Anyway, that's not what I have to tell you." My mom opens her mouth, but I raise my hand. "No guessing."

Her smile falters, and she draws back in her chair, crossing her legs as if I just ruined her fun. "Fine. What is it then?"

I glance at my watch and see that we have about five minutes before her appointment time. Even then, they're always running behind from what Callie has told me.

"Well, what is it?" My dad looks at me.

"You know about Leighton and the kids, right?"

My mom sits up straighter. "What about them? Did something happen? I forgot to tell you how proud I am of you stepping up to help her." She pats my leg.

"Yeah, well, there's the whole custody thing and all that, so we sort of told the court that we're dating." When my mom's eyebrows raise up to her hairline, and she grins, I quickly add, "But we're not."

My mom frowns.

"I don't understand," my dad says. "You are or you're not?"

"Not. But you're going to see pictures of us on the internet and stuff because we're telling everyone we are. I just didn't want you to think we were a real thing, and then… well, I didn't want to lie to you."

"Why aren't you dating her?" my dad asks. "She's a sweet girl, and you'd be lucky to have her."

Thanks for the dagger to the heart, Dad.

"Oh, I get it." My mom elbows my dad but gets him right in the ribs, and he holds his side.

"You definitely have your strength back," he says.

They both laugh.

"So you're actually together, but you're telling people it's fake in case it doesn't work out. Like a no-pressure thing." My mom taps her temple. "Sorry, Hayes, you can't fool me," she singsongs.

"Mom, I'm serious, it's fake."

She winks. "Okay, sweetie." She mimes zipping her lips shut and throwing away the key.

My dad pretends to catch the key and put it in his pocket.

I shake my head. "Mom, seriously, it's not real."

"And I said okay." She exaggerates a wink.

"Guys—"

"Jennifer Carlisle, for Dr. Apostolos."

My mom stands, and my dad joins her. Before she walks over to the woman who called her name, Mom bends down and pinches my cheek. "I, for one, couldn't be happier that you're *not* dating Leighton."

She winks—again—and walks to the other side of the waiting room.

"Hi, Margot." My mom crosses her fingers. "Today's the day."

I walk over and join them.

My dad puts his hand on my shoulder. "This is our son, Hayes Carlisle, the catcher for the Colts."

"But he's got a girlfriend, so hands off." My mom chuckles.

We file through the door, and if no one knew it was me, they do now.

Thanks, Mom and Dad.

We walk out of the doctor's office, full of gratitude and excitement that the scans showed no sign of cancer. We were all so happy that my parents hugged the doctor at the same time and waved me in to join. Dr. Apostolos will probably never forget that moment. He doesn't seem like a touchy-feely guy, but my parents didn't give him much of a choice.

"Let's go celebrate," my dad says, a huge smile on his face.

"Our usual?" Mom and Dad smile at one another, and I'm clearly missing the inside joke.

"My treat, where are we going?" I'll take them wherever they want. It was a challenging year, and since I wasn't here enough, I want to make today memorable.

"What floor is it on?" my dad asks, standing in front of the elevators.

"Second is the walkway to the garage, but we'll just take an Uber to the restaurant and come back here for you guys to get your car." I press the down button.

"I think it's on third," my mom says.

"No, it's on the second," I say.

"The cafeteria is on the second floor?" My dad's forehead wrinkles.

"Cafeteria?" I look between them. "That's where you want to celebrate?"

"Your mom loves their cookies."

We get in the elevator, and my dad presses the button for the third floor.

"Cafeteria it is," I say.

We ride the elevator down, and I send Callie a quick message about the results and tell her we'll call her after we eat in the cafeteria. She sends back a party popper emoji followed by the puking face emoji.

We wind our way through the cafeteria, go through the line, and get the food my parents have an affinity for since they've eaten here so much.

As we're checking out and I'm fighting with my dad over who's going to pay, my mom hits me in the arm. "Your girlfriend is here."

"Excuse me?"

"Leighton. She's right there." She points across the room at a couple sitting in the corner of the cafeteria, both dressed in scrubs, laughing with one another. He says something else to her, and she reaches forward and touches the top of his hand, laughing again. "Oh honey, I guess it really is fake, huh? I thought you were just saying that." She frowns.

My dad throws his hands in the air. "Woohoo, I won."

He's celebrating being able to pay because I'm too awestruck watching Leighton be so taken with a man who isn't fucking me.

"I just want to go say hi. You won't be mad, will you?" Mom whispers and heads in Leighton's direction.

"Hold on, Dad, I forgot a knife," I say.

To stab myself in the fucking eye.

CHAPTER
THIRTY-SEVEN

Leighton

Elias is telling me a story about this weekend when he went on a mountain biking trip with his friends from medical school up in Wisconsin, and one thing after another went wrong. He's been telling the story to anyone who would listen today.

"It was unbelievable. By the end, he was covered in mud, with bird guts splattered on him, and his shorts were shredded from his seat popping off."

I lean back in my seat, covering my mouth before my chewed-up fries spray across the table at him.

"He'll never live it down. That's who he's going to be now for eternity." Elias hands me a napkin since tears are leaking from my eyes from laughing so hard.

Then our eyes lock for a moment too long, and there's something in his that I'm sure doesn't match mine.

"Will you go out with me?" he asks, and all the laughter turns to ash on my tongue.

Did I give him the wrong idea? When he asked me to lunch, I accepted because everyone was saying how funny his story was, and I wanted to hear it. I've worked with him quite a bit, and I've never thought he was interested in a relationship as more than friends and colleagues.

"Oh, um…"

"Well, that's not a good sign." He rubs his hand down his face.

"No. I mean…" I have no idea what to say. I have a boyfriend. Although it's fake—at least, it's supposed to be fake—if I could resolve my childhood traumas, I'd like it to be more. But it's my best friend's brother, and that brings up its own problems.

"You can just say no, Leighton." His voice pulls me out of my head. My head that always seems to be on Hayes.

"Leighton!"

Elias and I both turn to look toward the person who called my name.

"Mrs. Carlisle?" I whisper.

Oh, that's right. Hayes said it was her appointment today and had suggested we get lunch, but then we were interrupted by Monroe begging for a cat so she could hug one for National Cat Hugging Day. I never got the time they'd be here.

"Great timing," Elias says. "You've been saved by a brown-haired middle-aged woman who is 'Not Slim and Kind of Shady.'" He sounds confused reading her sweatshirt.

I can't help but chuckle. "Just give me a minute."

I stand, but she reaches the table before I can get some distance from Elias.

Her arms were out three tables away, and she swamps me in one of her tight hugs, swaying us right and left. "I'm cancer-free."

She says it so loudly that the tables around us clap. She pulls back, her cheeks growing red and waving for people to stop cheering for her, but when they don't, she preens under the attention. It's well deserved after everything she went through.

"Congratulations," I say, hugging her again.

My eyes stray to Hayes and his dad at the cash register. Hayes is staring at me, then Elias, then back at me. He looks just like he did that day at the ice cream parlor when that guy made the shitty remark about his play.

"I know. And I heard about you and Hayes," she whispers—not nearly quiet enough, but that's always been Mrs. Carlisle. Callie got her loud personality from her mom. "Your secret is safe with me, but I'm so happy." She throws her arms around me again, swaying us, and nausea erupts in my stomach. "I always wanted you for a daughter-in-law."

Oh boy, she's laying it on thick.

"Leighton," Mr. Carlisle says, carrying over the trays. "Let me put these down." He steps over to the table with Elias. "Hi, son, you don't mind, do you?"

"By all means." Elias leans back in his chair, eating his apple, watching the entire scene unfold.

"Mrs. Carlisle was just telling me the great news. You must be ecstatic." I hug him, but I'm not really in the moment. My mind is on the large figure approaching us, his jaw tight, holding a stack of napkins.

"Thank God. This was the worst year of my life," he whispers in my ear.

Tears prick my eyes, and I tighten my arms to comfort Mr. Carlisle. I understand how relieved he must be right now.

"Introductions, Leighton," Elias says.

Mr. Carlise pulls away and holds out his hand. "Dave Carlisle, and this is my wife, Jennifer."

Elias introduces himself and gets up and shakes both of their hands, then goes to pick up his tray. "I'll leave you guys to catch up."

"Nonsense." Mr. Carlisle sits down next to where Elias was. "We don't bite."

Elias's eyes meet mine, questioning what he should do. I'd really like him to leave—

"Hayes, what took you so long?" Mrs. Carlisle puts her arm through his, bringing him over.

He drops the napkins on the table but doesn't sit.

"Hayes Carlisle?" Elias asks, causing Hayes's gaze to move from me to him.

Hayes smacks on a fake smile and puts out his hand. "Yeah."

"Hayes, this is Elias. He's a doctor on the OB/GYN floor," I say.

They shake hands, and I watch Elias give a slight grimace, making me wonder how hard Hayes is shaking his hand. "You've been playing out of your shoes this year."

If I thought Hayes's jaw was stiff before, it's granite now. Although Elias meant it as a compliment, Hayes still holds so many wounds from last year.

"I know, he's having an amazing year." Mrs. Carlisle puts her free arm in mine. "I think it's because of a certain someone." She winks at me, but Hayes has yet to even acknowledge me.

"He should be a shoo-in for the Gold Glove, and if not, it's all rigged." Mr. Carlisle put dishes in front of the three empty chairs at the table. "Come and eat, the food's getting cold."

"I'll be back. I'm going to the restroom." Hayes doesn't wait for anyone to respond, just walks away.

My gaze follows him.

"Sit, Elias, tell me whatever you were telling Leighton that had her laughing so hard," Mr. Carlisle says.

Mrs. Carlisle sits next to Dave, looking just as intrigued as her husband.

Elias lowers to his chair, eyeing me the entire time. I

should save him, I really should, but instead, I place my hand on Mrs. Carlisle's shoulder. "I'll be right back."

She taps my hand with hers. "Take your time, sweetie. I might go back for more cookies. I'm celebrating."

I squeeze her hand, so happy that she got good news today.

"Leighton?" Elias says as I step away from the table.

I raise my hand. I should offer a more thorough explanation, but I need to clear this up with Hayes.

I walk down the hall, dodging all the visitors and staff going to get lunch. I weave through people, my footsteps increasing in speed, trying to reach Hayes before he reaches the bathroom. When I get close enough, I call his name. He doesn't stop, so I set off in a light jog, trying to be inconspicuous, which is hard since I'm jogging through a hospital hallway.

I grab his arm. "Hayes," I say, catching my breath.

"Don't worry about it. Go back and eat before you have to go back to work."

I tug him out of the way of the people, closer to the wall. "It's not what you think."

He gives me a fleeting glance, refusing to look me in the eye. "It's fine. It's fake, remember? I can't be mad."

"But you are?" My voice wavers because it kills me to see him hurting. Does he think I can't read his body language? Hell, Monroe could, he's making it so obvious.

"Just go back to your perfect guy. He checks off all your boxes, right?"

"Hayes." I don't want to talk about my safe guy list when my entire body aches for him.

"He's a safe bet, right?" He steps in, closing us off from the chaos, his thigh sandwiched between my legs. "The one you can depend on?"

He pushes his leg against my core, and my hands grab his arms on instinct. His strong biceps bunch under my touch.

His hand goes to my hip to keep me in place. Heat radiates from him. Frustration, want, and possession all mixed together. And God help me, I'm greedy for whatever he'll give me.

There are so many people walking by, I'm hoping we look as though we're just having a conversation, and I'm not seconds away from begging him to push his thigh up a little more.

"You think he won't hurt you, but I will?" The pain and frustration radiating out of Hayes's dark eyes is my undoing.

"I never said that." My voice is breathless, and he pushes his thigh into me. I shamelessly grind down, just a bit, my hands clinging to his arms.

His gaze strips away from me, then his thigh is gone, and I'm whimpering as he drags me around the corner, our steps uneven, his head moving back and forth, searching both sides of the hallway. He opens a door, looks both ways, and nudges me inside.

I realize it's a janitorial closet when he flicks the light, which is a pale yellow, barely lighting up the space. The air in here is hot and dusty, but it's closed off from prying eyes, leaving him and me and the desire coursing between us.

My back goes to the racks, and he steps into my space again.

"Now, where were we?" He wedges his thigh between my legs again, and I let out a soft whimper. He tucks a piece of hair behind my ear with a gentleness that belies his intensity. "You were going to tell me how you want that guy because he's a safer bet?"

"I wasn't. I'm not." My hips betray me, greedily rolling forward. He keeps pressing his thigh in the right spot, and all I want to do is grind on it until I come apart.

"That's not what it looked like to me. Do you think he can make you feel what you're feeling right now?"

"No," I whisper, shaking my head.

He holds both my hips, and I press my hands down on his wrists, anchoring myself so I can grind along his hard, muscled thigh. The pressure sends sparks up my spine, and my nipples pebble in my bra, begging for friction of their own.

"Do you think he can make you forget your name? Make you tremble with need and scream in ecstasy?" He bends forward, running his nose along my jaw.

I shiver, my skin igniting into goose bumps everywhere he breathes. His scent surrounds me—the crispness of his cologne and something that defies explanation. It's just him.

"Tell me, Leighton. Is he the one you want?"

My hands skirt up his arms and wind around his neck, running through the hair at the back of his head. I'm trembling—not from fear, but from finally being able to stop pretending he's not the one I think about every time I touch myself. "Please, Hayes."

He shakes his head. "You're not getting off that easy. Who do you want, Leighton?"

Another press of his thigh between my legs, and I groan. I can feel the slickness of desire wetting my underwear.

"Do you want him?" he asks again, his hand snaking under one thigh, lifting it so we're in the same position we were when Easton interrupted us.

"No." The truth rips free, breaking through the surface.

My pussy is still pressed to his thigh, but he's not kissing me, and it's complete and absolute torture to be this close to what I crave and still be denied. His hard heat presses against my hip, and I'm needy in a way I've never been before. Desperate for it. For him.

"Then tell me, Leighton, what do you want?"

His hands, his lips, his body entwined with mine. I don't have it in me to fight anymore. I'm exhausted from fighting my feelings for him. The more he touches me, the more my walls turn to dust.

"You." I finally grant him the word he's been waiting for.

His head rears back, searching my eyes as if he wants to double-check before we go any further. But there's no denying this thing between us, how powerful and all-encompassing our need for each other is.

"About fucking time."

CHAPTER
THIRTY-EIGHT

Hayes

My lips are on hers, and my tongue dives into her mouth, my hand sliding higher up her thigh as she melts against me—wanting more, needing more, ready to take whatever she'll give me.

I can taste how much she wants me. Her desperation for me is an aphrodisiac. I'm done pretending this thing between us is nothing, that it can be stifled, set aside.

I untie the bow on her pants and push her scrubs down. She shimmies, pushing off her shoes and helping me get her pants free. My hand slides under her ass, lifting her higher so her heat grinds where I know she wants it.

She thinks she wants a safe, controlled man? Fuck that. She was made to come apart for me.

"Wrap your leg around me," I say against her parted lips, dragging her closer, not giving her a chance to pull away again.

She clings to my shoulders, her breath shaky, as she does

what I say. I slide my fingers along the inside of her thigh. Her skin is exactly as I dreamed—silky and soft. I can't wait until I can bury my head between her legs and taste her.

"Hayes—" she whispers as though she needs me, and only me, to take care of her desire.

It fuels the possessive fire already roaring through me, burning up my sanity.

"Say it again." I push the heel of my hand against her center, and fuck, she's soaked and swollen and so fucking ready for me.

She gasps then moans, a melody I'll never get out of my head, chasing it every minute for the rest of my life.

"Hayes," she moans louder.

"I got you."

My mouth drags down her neck, my teeth scraping against her beating pulse. Feeling her desperation makes me want to make her come ten times in this janitor's closet. She won't be walking out of here wanting the safe option anymore. She'll finally realize I'm exactly what she needs, what she wants.

She grabs my face and presses her lips to mine, claiming me, and fuck, it feels good.

Take what you want from me, baby.

"You belong with me," I practically growl, lifting her so her back hits the metal shelf with a clatter. "Not with some guy who doesn't know how to give you what you need."

My dick presses almost painfully against my zipper. I'm desperate to be inside her, so deep she forgets every man who isn't me. I slide her panties aside, fingers slipping through her slick heat until she gasps against my lips.

"Look at me," I say, voice low and commanding. "I'm the one making you lose your mind."

Her beautiful blue eyes drag open, pupils wide. She's almost ready to come just from the brush of my hand. Pure male satisfaction fills my chest.

"Who's the only man who can get you this wet?" I demand.

"You," she breathes. "Only you."

"Damn right."

Victory finally feels like it's mine. She's done pretending she doesn't want me as badly as I want her.

I lower her just enough so her thighs straddle my lap, and she can use her back against the shelf for leverage. My fingers go to the button of my jeans. I flick the button, and I'm ready to lower the zipper when her fingers cover mine.

"Let me." Her voice is husky, and I watch her fingers manipulate my pants.

My aching cock bounces free of its confines. Leighton wraps her hand around my length and strokes me. Fuck, I'm gonna blow.

Somehow, I shimmy my pants and boxer briefs to my ankles, more desperate than ever to feel her sweet heat surround me.

I wish we had time for her to play with me. Fuck, just the thought of her mouth on me almost makes me come. But we don't have the time, nor the space to explore each other right now.

"Hold on to me." I bring myself to her entrance, her slick heat welcoming me as though I'm fucking home.

She digs her fingers into my hair. "Hayes—"

Her desperate pleas keep unraveling me more every time.

"Yeah, baby. I know." I push into her in one slow, brutal stroke, claiming every inch she's been denying me.

Her breath breaks on a raw gasp.

Holy hell, perfection.

I could die right now, and it would all be worth it.

She tightens around me, and I curse under my breath, gripping her hips to keep from embarrassing myself and spilling inside her already.

"You feel that?" I thrust shallow then deep. "That's *me* making you feel good."

Her nails drag across my shoulders, urging me on. All of her hesitation about us has vanished. "Hayes…don't stop."

I pull back just enough to see her face. It's flushed, and her lips are swollen from our kissing. But most of all, her big blue eyes are practically begging me to give her what she needs.

"Never," I promise, because she's not getting away this time. I will chase her if she runs again. "I'm never gonna fucking stop." I punctuate each word with the thrust of my hips.

I drive into her again—hard—a claiming she welcomes.

I thrust again, deeper this time, and her entire body arcs into mine. Her breath stutters against my cheek, and I bury my face in her neck because I can't get close enough.

"Oh god…" Her fingers press into my skin.

I grip her thighs tighter, holding her exactly where I need her. The angle lets me grind against that perfect spot inside her, and she bites my shoulder to keep from screaming.

"Scream," I hiss, rolling my hips again. "Let them know who's making you fall apart."

Her walls clamp around my cock and my vision blurs. Fuck, she's right there.

"Say it," I demand, breath hot in her ear. "Say you're mine."

I slam into her once, twice—and she breaks.

"Yours," she cries out, her legs squeezing my waist. "I'm yours—"

"That's right," I growl, thrusting through every pulse of her orgasm because she's dragging me under with her. "Leighton…"

She grabs my jaw, forcing me to look her in the eyes as I fall apart. "Come for me."

All my restraint snaps.

My hips thrust forward as my release tears through me.

Burying myself as deep as I can, breathing her in, I slam my mouth on hers as I spill inside her.

When she's done milking me, she rests her forehead against mine, our breath mixing, both of us completely exhausted and euphoric.

I brush my thumb over her swollen bottom lip, my possessiveness settling deep and immovable in my chest. She's all mine. Finally.

"We have a problem," she says, breaking my trance.

CHAPTER
THIRTY-NINE

Hayes

Fear wasn't the emotion I thought I'd see from Leighton after we had sex for the first time, but that's what's staring at me.

"I'm gonna be honest right now, Leighton, if you tell me you regret what we did, I'm going to walk out of here, and you'll never see me again." The words fly off my tongue even if I know they're a lie. More than likely I'd get down on my knees and beg for her to give us a chance.

She giggles.

I frown, not understanding.

She stops herself, although she's still smiling. "No. I just…" She looks down between us, where my dick is slowly softening inside her. "We didn't use anything."

Now there's fear in my eyes. "Fuck. I'm sorry." I slide out of her as if that changes the fact that my seed is running down the insides of her thighs. "Fuck. That's on me. I should have…"

She laughs again and opens a package of paper towels sitting on the shelf. She's so calm. How can she be so unaffected by this?

"I'm on the pill, so no worries about pregnancy." She twirls her finger. "Turn around though."

She hands me a stack of paper towels, and I circle around, facing the wall as I clean myself.

I push a hand through my hair. "Still, it was careless of me, but I was just so…"

"Lost in the moment? Me too. It's okay, but Hayes?"

I circle back around, and she's pulling up her pants.

Janitor closet sex is hot until you have to figure out how to clean up after. She gets a trash bag and holds it out for my paper towels.

"This seems so weird," I say, and she laughs.

"This is sex without a condom. But, Hayes, I hate to ask, but—" Her eyes soften.

I pull up and fasten my jeans. "What?"

She hesitates. "Have you been tested recently?"

"Oh fuck, yeah, of course." I take the trash bag and place it on a shelf before taking her into my arms. "Yes, I was tested, and I'm good. No worries on that front."

"No worries on my end either."

I tug her closer, and her smile grows. "I am sorry though."

She rests her forehead on my shoulder. "I like that we were so in the moment, we didn't stop to think about it."

"Then why aren't you looking at me when you say that?"

She shrugs. "It's embarrassing. I've never had sex like… I mean, I've never…"

I stiffen. "You're a virgin? Fuck." I release her and run my hands through my hair. "Callie's going to kill me. I took your virginity in a janitor's closet?"

She laughs and wraps her arms around my back, running her palms up my chest from behind. "I wasn't a virgin. I just meant…"

I circle around in her arms.

"I can get in my head a lot during sex so…" She shrugs, and that pink tinge on her cheeks says she really doesn't want to talk about this. "I think this is a conversation best for when your parents aren't in the cafeteria, wondering where we went. And poor Elias."

I bend down and kiss her lips. "My parents are fine. And maybe I should feel bad for Elias, but I don't."

She tips her head back, eyes serious now. "He's just a colleague."

I blow out a breath. "I was really fucking jealous."

She laughs. "I know. You don't hide your emotions very well."

"But we're over the whole 'I don't want you' thing, right? Like this…" I nod between us because I don't want to take my hands off her. "We're a thing."

"Yes." She lifts onto her tiptoes and kisses me. "We are definitely a thing. But can we wait to go public officially to all our friends until I can tell Callie?"

"I'll pull my phone out right now." I shift, but she tightens her hands on my shirt.

"In person."

My shoulders deflate.

"Hey, no, it's not some attempt to push this off. We're together. Everyone already thinks we are, but maybe only we know it's real until she gets back. I just want to assure her that nothing will change with her and me. The thought of doing it while she's away—I don't want to do it that way."

I can't say I blame her. Callie keeps telling me to stay away, and I do worry she'll be mad. If so, if she can see us together, we'll be more likely to convince her this is a good thing.

I kiss her again. "Okay. But you're good with this? Us as a couple and everything it entails?"

Her forehead crinkles, and it's so damn cute. "Yes. Now,

we can revisit this tonight, but we need to get back to the cafeteria, and I need to get back to work."

I bring my lips down to where her neck meets her shoulder. "Call in sick and spend the day in bed with me."

A shiver racks through her body. "I wish, but I have to be a responsible parental figure now."

"Fine, use me for my body." I take her hand and open the door, slowly stepping out and bringing her with me.

"You can't really blame me. I mean, it's a great body."

"Just great?" I joke as we walk down the hallway toward the cafeteria.

"I haven't seen enough of it yet."

"Tell me about it. I still haven't seen your tits. Do you know how crushing that is?"

She laughs, and a few people look at us, but I don't care. Having her hand in mine and knowing it's because she wants it there makes me feel as though I just won MVP after the World Series.

We get to the cafeteria and find my parents still talking to Elias. I assumed he'd be bored out of his mind, but it looks as though he's actually enjoying the conversation, and my parents are just as enthralled.

"Oh, I ate your cookie," my mom says when we approach the table.

Elias checks his watch. "Where have you guys been? I need to get back to work." He stands and holds his hand out to my dad. "Nice talking to you both, and congratulations, Jennifer." He nods at me but doesn't say anything. "I'll see you up there, Leighton."

"Yeah, I'm right behind you." She grabs her bag of chips and her drink off the table before hugging my mom from behind. "Congrats, Mrs. Carlisle. Hayes can make a reservation at a fancy restaurant, and we'll all celebrate."

My mom turns her head and kisses her cheek. "I want to meet the kids too."

"Definitely, we'll plan something." She moves to my dad too and hugs him from behind. "Bye, Mr. Carlisle."

Then she comes over to me and winds her arms around my neck, rises on her tiptoes, and kisses me as if she's been doing it for years. "I'll see you tonight?" she says in a soft voice.

My hands slide down so they're half covering her ass. "Text me when you're off shift."

We kiss, and I want to deepen it, but that would be highly unprofessional in the middle of the cafeteria. She says one more goodbye, then I watch her walk away until she's out of view.

"So, sex is included in fake relationships these days?" My mom bites into a chocolate chip cookie.

I'm not sure why we thought we were fooling them.

I start walking back toward the counter. "Want another cookie?"

My gaze strays one more time toward the hallway, hoping for another glimpse of Leighton. Damn, it's been a long time since I've been this happy.

CHAPTER
FORTY

Leighton

The kids are having dinner at Art and Julianna's tonight, which hasn't done much for my anxiety level. And now I'm waiting for Hayes to get here and hopefully distract me—preferably with his dick or tongue—or even better, both.

I'm too young to get a hot flash, but every time I think about us in that closet, my entire body feels as if it's about to go up in flames.

The doorbell rings, and I bolt off the couch, sprinting before forcing myself into a walk, telling myself I don't want to seem too eager, but who am I kidding? This has been a decade in the making.

I pull the door open, and there he is, hair damp from showering after his workout, dressed in sweatpants and a T-shirt.

Hayes's gaze rolls down my body like a wave and back up. "Fuck, you're beautiful."

I purposely wore my white tank top sans bra and the same

pajamas he couldn't get enough of the first time he came over. The pajama top is unbuttoned so it hangs open. "You have a key. You can use it."

He shrugs. "Felt weird. I'm here for a date, not to take care of the kids." He's still standing on the other side of the door.

"Why are you still over there?"

He shrugs again.

Why is this so awkward?

"You haven't invited me in."

I grab his T-shirt and pull him into the house, shutting the door. Then I trap him against the wall for a change and press my lips to his. He takes my not-so-subtle signs and slides his tongue into my mouth. His hands drift to my ass, pulling me up from the floor, and I wrap my legs around his waist.

God, I can't get enough of him. Our kiss is so frantic, it's practically bruising, and when he ends the kiss, I groan.

"Fuck, I'm already rock-hard."

"Sorry." This whole being-horny-for-him-all-the-time thing is a little surprising for me too.

"Don't apologize, that was hot as fuck. You can throw me around anytime."

I smile and bite my lip, still a touch embarrassed even if he liked it. My body is humming to feel him inside me again.

I slide my hand between us and cup his thick length. "I love this easy access."

"That wasn't my intention when I got dressed. You know we don't have to…"

I arch an eyebrow. "You don't want to?"

"No, I want to, I just don't want you to think I'm only here for that."

"Oh." I wave him off. "I don't."

I inch forward to kiss him again, and he rears his head back.

"Is there a problem?" I frown.

He shakes his head, but sighs.

I loosen my legs and climb off of him. "What is it?"

"Vega got fired today."

"Shit." I walk farther into the house, and he follows me into the kitchen.

"I was riding high after everything that happened with us and my mom. I felt like today was the best day ever, but then bam. We were told it was something with the upper office. An argument. The details are sketchy about whether he was fired or quit, but whatever it was, it's obvious they weren't going to come to an understanding. So, now they're trying to find an interim manager for the rest of the year."

I go over to the fridge and pull out a water and a beer. "Which one?"

"Beer, please." He props himself up on the counter, and I grab two beers and walk over to him. "I'm ruining our time together."

"No, you're not."

I hand him his beer, and he twists off the cap before taking a long pull. Then he grabs mine and twists off the cap before handing it back to me. I scoot up on the counter next to him.

"This could be a good thing," I say, trying to see the silver lining.

"Or it could be a manager who already has an opinion on me based on last year."

"But you've already made up for that this year. Any manager who comes in will know that last year was a one-off."

He kisses my cheek. "You're sweet."

"I'm serious. You're doing the work and making good choices. If he doesn't like you or wants to put you in some designated box, then fuck him."

He laughs and puts his arm around my shoulders, pulling me into him. "God, Leighton, why is it so sexy when you swear?"

I smile and hop down from the counter. "It could end up

being a better manager, you know. One who is more on your side than Vega."

He tilts his head in agreement. "True."

"Let's eat your feelings and see that there could be a brighter side to this." I reach for some chips from the cabinet, stretching, trying to get a finger on the bag, but still having no luck.

"Take off your shirt." His voice is deeper, more commanding, and my nipples pebble at just the sound of it. I turn to him, and he's staring at where my tank is rising up my stomach. "Please?"

I drop down to flat feet and turn to face him. His gaze is on my tits. Slowly, I slide my arms out of my pajama shirt, letting the fabric drop to the floor and leaving me in my white tank top.

"You had to go no bra, didn't you?" His tongue slides out of his mouth and runs along his bottom lip.

The sight of it makes the space between my legs ache in the best way.

I guess the entire manager dilemma is done, and we're back to us.

I shrug. "You said you wanted to see my tits."

Using that word feels a little weird. I've never been one to talk dirty or be vocal when it came to sex.

"I can't wait to feel the weight of them in my palms." He sucks in a breath and crooks his finger at me.

I walk over to him, and his eyes never stray from my tits.

When I get close, he slinks down from the counter. "Do you know how sexy you are?"

I'm not sure how to answer. I've never felt sexy except when he looks at me. Cute is the word I hear most often, never sexy.

He brushes his finger over my shirt where my pebbled nipples poke out. I inhale a sharp breath.

"You like that?" His brown eyes seem even darker somehow.

I nod. He does it again, earning the same reaction, except this time my back arches into his hands, wanting more. With his left hand, he palms my breast, running his thumb over my nipple with such soft pressure, my pussy quivers. A wicked grin crosses his face, and he dips his head, taking my right nipple into his mouth through my tank top.

Oh shit, that feels really, really good.

He swings an arm around my waist, lifting me and propping me up on the counter, mouth still on my breast.

"Perfection," he murmurs against the wet fabric, grabbing the hem of my shirt and slowly pulling it up my body.

I raise my hands, and he tosses it somewhere behind us.

Then he stares at my tits for a moment before lifting his gaze to mine. "Just like I imagined when I was beating off all these years."

The thought of him masturbating to thoughts of me makes that quiver in my pussy turn into an ache.

I take his hand and bring it to my breast. "They're yours now."

His lids grow heavy, and he pinches my nipple. "Fuck yeah, they are."

Then he takes my hand and leads it down his chest to the waistband of his sweats. He's going commando, and his hot, thick cock twitches in my palm. "And this is yours."

I'm not sure I can breathe. This is really happening, right?

He slips my hand out of his pants and picks me up, carrying me over to the couch. But he doesn't place me on the cushions. Instead, he lets my feet hit the floor and falls to his knees before me.

Staring up at me, he hooks his fingers on either side of my pajama pants, sliding them down my legs. He doesn't look at my pussy slowly being revealed, as if he wants to see it bared for him all at once.

Our gaze holds, and after I step out of my pants, he gives me another wicked grin before he presses a kiss to my stomach and leans back. "Sit down, babe."

I do.

Then he spreads my legs and takes in all of me. And I mean all. The impulse to shut my legs rears up, but when I see the awe on his face, I relax.

"I bet you taste like fucking heaven." He swings my legs over his shoulders. His thumb traces circles over my clit, and my head falls back against the cushions, my eyes closed. "Oh no, you're going to watch."

I pick up my head and watch him play with my pussy, knowing even my fantasies haven't been this good. His touch is slow and methodical, taking the time to learn what I like and what pleases me. I'm slowly breaking apart, and his mouth hasn't even been on me yet.

Hayes looks up at me, making sure I'm watching as he leans in closer. And when his tongue laps at my pussy, the air leaves my lungs in short, shallow bursts. Any other thoughts I had scatter like sparks from a fire as he drags me closer to the edge.

"Hayes." His name is barely audible as my hands fall to his head.

My orgasm builds, wave by wave, with every stroke of his tongue, suck on my clit. His fingers dig into my ass, bringing my pussy closer to him.

And then I'm dangling from that cliff, and every time he glances up at me and our eyes meet, I slip a little more until he sucks hard on my clit, and I'm falling off the cliff. I don't cry out, I whimper, my orgasm traveling through me with hard, undulating waves instead of a bolt of electricity.

He slows his pace before falling back to his heels. His mouth is wet with my juices, and as though I didn't just come, I am desperate to have him inside me.

"Jesus, Leighton, I'm about to come in my fucking pants."

"How about my mouth instead?"

His mouth falls open, and I slide down to the floor, making him trade spots with me.

We make the best of our time before the kids return. Three orgasms for me, two for him, but not nearly enough, since I still crave him even more.

CHAPTER
FORTY-ONE

Leighton

"Hi," Monroe says to a group of strangers on our way to find the seats Hayes got us for tonight's Colts game. "Hi." She waves to another group. "Hi." Yet another group.

I inhale, trying to channel a Zen state. Lincoln is practically bouncing off the walls, Monroe hasn't stopped saying hi to everyone we pass, and Lake's been in a sour mood since we left the house.

"And then she made me do my homework at the kitchen table and said I couldn't have dessert until she checked it over. Does she even know I have straight A's, and I'm in honors classes?"

Lake has been going on and on about how horrible her time at Art and Julianna's was. Although I didn't love that they were with them, they are still her family, and my time with Hayes was enjoyable.

"She took away Monroe's Play-Doh, and Uncle Art wouldn't play with Lincoln outside. He said he was tired from work. Why do they want us if they're not going to spend time with us?" Lake asks.

"Hi." Monroe waves at a guy also wearing a Carlisle jersey, and he tries to high-five her. "No, just hi today."

He laughs and nods. I offer him a soft smile, and he continues on his way.

"You can high-five him." Lake groans then turns to me. "I'm not going again, so you can tell the judge that."

"They want you because they love you. You're family." I'm not sure what's appropriate to say, and I probably shouldn't be secretly happy she doesn't want to go back.

"They don't love us!" Her voice gets louder.

Lately I've been thinking that it may be a good idea to get the kids into some kind of therapy to talk about everything going on in their lives, and this outburst from Lake tells me I was right. I make a mental note to look up some good options tomorrow when I have time.

"Hi." Monroe waves to the guy selling beer.

"Can you tell her to stop saying hi to everyone?" Lake snipes.

"What do you want me to do? It's National Say Hi Day." I roll my eyes.

This is so much worse than National High Five Day.

"I don't know, but she's drawing attention to us." She looks around at a bunch of people who probably think Monroe is a cute little girl wearing a Hayes Carlisle jersey.

A group of fans wearing Milwaukee jerseys walks by.

"No hi for you," Monroe says. A group of Colts fans walks by next. "Hi."

Lake growls, and her hands clench into fists.

"Monroe, sweetie, is there a maximum number of people you can say hi to today?" I ask.

She stops, and her forehead scrunches.

"Never mind. Let's just get to our seats." I turn to Lake.

"And then she'll already have said hi to everyone around us, and we'll be done for a while."

We're at the top of the stairs in our section when Lincoln sees Easton and Decker come out of the dugout and bolts toward the field. "Easton!"

"Oh boy, okay, let's get going." I scramble to get us down the stairs, but Monroe is taking one at a time, stopping and doing the Miss America wave while she says hi to every row of fans.

I urge Monroe forward with my hand on her back. I'm carrying a bag full of activities in case she gets bored, along with my purse. My shoulders will be sore by the end of the day.

"Hi. Hi. Hi. Hi." Monroe says it to everyone we pass.

Lake huffs. "We look so stupid, all wearing his jersey."

I turn to look at her, while making sure Monroe doesn't trip and fall down the stairs since she's so hell-bent on saying hello to every person in this damn stadium. "We're supporting him. Just like he supports us."

Easton comes over to the railing, and I catch a few people getting up to join Lincoln there.

Monroe sees Decker. "Hi, Decker!" She lifts her hand and runs down the steps before I can grab her. "It's National Say Hi Day today!"

She gets swallowed up in the group of people wanting to talk to the two players.

I rush down the stairs. "I'm sorry, I just need…" I slide my hand between a group of kids, getting a hold of Monroe. "She's mine."

I guide her out, but she continues saying hi to everyone who's ready to trample her to get an autograph. I lift her, and she swings her legs around my middle.

"Sorry, Hayes is in the bullpen." Decker points in that direction, but I can't see him.

The new manager is a guy with the last name Ripley. He

was an assistant in Seattle, so Hayes has been nervous the entire week, but he said the guy doesn't seem to be holding anything against him.

"That's okay." I reach for Lincoln, tugging on his arm. "You guys go get ready for the game. Good luck."

Lincoln doesn't come willingly, continuing to talk to them the entire time I pull him back to me.

Once I have both kids, I take a breath and see Lake sitting in our seats, her feet propped up on the empty seat in front of her, phone in her hand.

"Let's get to our seats." I hold on to Lincoln and keep Monroe in my arms.

"Hi," Monroe says to a couple behind us. "Hi." She waves to the next group of people.

They all smile and say it back, but I swear I never want to hear the word hi again in my life.

I set Monroe down and sandwich the two of them between Lake and me. "Now let's all just sit and get our bearings for a minute, okay?"

"Your face is really red," Lake says.

I narrow my eyes at her. She has no idea how exhausted I already am, and the game hasn't even started.

"I think next time I come to a game, it might have to be alone," I mumble.

I pull my phone from my purse to take a few pictures of us and send them to Callie and Viv, since she said I need to show I'm doing family things with the kids. I guess that doesn't include dinner and bath time because she wasn't too interested in those.

"Smile," I say, and right as I press on the screen to take the picture, a text comes in. I snap the picture and, surprisingly, Lake has her smile back.

Did you find the seats okay?

I look toward the field, knowing he's out there some-where. I'm so excited to see him play.

> Yes, I'll have a perfect view of your ass the entire game.

> Why do you think I chose them?

> I'm not sure I'll be able to control myself.

> Good, then you'll already be halfway there when I see you after the game.

I send him a picture of all three kids.

> I think you forgot about these guys.

> They go to bed eventually. I have to go, but I wanted to make sure you made it to your seats okay. I can't wait to see you after.

We haven't done a sleepover yet, mostly because I don't want to confuse the kids and the thought of it makes me feel irresponsible.

> Good luck today. You have your own little cheering section.

I tuck my phone into my bag.

"Why are you staring at your phone like that?" Lake asks.

A half hour later, after Monroe has personally greeted everyone in our section, we're all asked to stand for the national anthem.

Hayes comes out onto the field with his shin guards and chest protector on. He searches us out, and Monroe screams hi to him. I make Lincoln swap seats with her before Lake covers Monroe's mouth with her hand.

After the national anthem, Hayes waves to us.

"Turn around, guys," I say.

"Seriously?" Lake whines, but she does it.

We show him all of us wearing his jersey, and when I turn around, Hayes has his hand over his heart. I blow him a kiss, and his smile only grows wider.

Then he disappears into the dugout, and we sit back down. When it's the Colts' turn to be on the field, he jogs out with his helmet resting on top of his head. He slows and eyes us. He checks to see the pitcher is still walking to the mound, so he runs over and presses his hands on the netting.

"Hi," he says directly to Monroe.

She giggles. "It's National Say Hi Day." She jumps up and claps her hands.

"I know. That's why I said hi." He looks at me, and I really hope the netting prohibits him from seeing the tears filling my eyes. "See you guys after."

He winks, then he's squatting behind home plate.

"That was embarrassing," Lake mumbles.

I ignore her because I'm right in the middle of feeling very, very smitten with Hayes Carlisle.

CHAPTER
FORTY-TWO

Hayes

It's hard to concentrate knowing Leighton and the kids are in the stands. Between every inning, I smile over at them when I make my way back to the dugout. Lake looks mostly disinterested, Lincoln is on the edge of his seat, and Monroe usually has her back turned, talking to the people in the row behind her.

Even though I feel more pressure with their presence, I like having them see me in my element. It gives me a little extra jolt to show off.

My first time at the plate, I got a double to right field that was just on the line. Even Lake was on her feet, cheering. I should've been looking at the dugout, but I looked at Leighton first.

Things have been so good since we crossed the line. Her insatiable sex drive is addictive as hell, but it's not only that she's just as into the sex as I am. It's everything else too. Coming home to her after a home game, snuggling on the couch with her legs swung over mine, the fact that we figure out dinner together.

She gave me a phenomenal thank-you blow job the other night after the kids went to bed when she came home from work and I had finished the laundry and dinner was on the table.

And turns out her hands are good at a lot of things, massages included. My legs have never felt better.

Ian drives me in with a single, and as I cross home plate, I glance in their direction. They're all cheering, and I give them a wave.

"Man, you're on fire," Decker says when I reach the dugout.

"It's the power of Leighton," Easton says.

"That the girlfriend?" Drew asks.

"Yup." I pick up my drink and take a swig.

"You should think about getting one, they're good for the mojo," Easton says, turning around from the railing to smugly smile at Drew. "You could use a little luck." He points at our makeshift board. Right now, us infielders are ahead on bases for the month.

Drew scowls at him. "I don't need a chick to make me play well."

Easton goes at him again. "If you had one, maybe you wouldn't have struck out today."

"The umpire has a shit zone," Drew snipes.

"It's always something, right?" Easton winks at him.

Thankfully, Ripley waves me over and I get a reprieve from the Easton versus Drew battle.

"What's up?"

Our new manager was on the staff in Seattle, and at first, I wasn't sure if he'd hold last year against me, but he doesn't seem to be.

"What do you think about Taz? How's he doing?" He never takes his eyes off the field.

I glance down the dugout to look at Taz. He was a little off the last inning, but I think he has more in him. "I'd say one more."

"Me too. You two will go back out there, but be prepared for relief."

I nod. "Sounds good."

"You're hitting great lately." He nods toward the stands. "That your family?"

"Yeah, my girlfriend. She just got guardianship of her nieces and nephew." Saying it that way is easier than trying to say cousin once removed and explaining the whole situation.

He nods and glances at me. "You seem really… good."

"I am." And I am. It makes me a little afraid that something bad is coming my way.

He smiles briefly, then dismisses me by not talking anymore and concentrating on the game.

I get the rest of my gear on and get ready to go. When the inning ends, I jog out and meet Taz on the mound. He shakes me off all the time, but since this is likely his last inning in this game, I'd like us to be on the same page, even though he thinks he knows more than I do. It pisses me off, as if I don't do my research.

"You don't have to visit me. I want to start with the curve," he says.

"Your sinker is looking good today. I say we start with the sinker and then go into a slider."

He's shaking his head before I've finished my sentence. "Curve, four seam, slider."

"No sinker?"

I hate dealing with pitchers like him. Makes me miss Foster. He was by far the best pitcher I ever caught for. When he was at the mound, it felt a little more like a partnership. He always took my opinion into account.

"Not unless I'm at full count," Taz says.

I lower my mask to hide my expression. "You got it." On

the way back to the plate, I grumble, "And I bet you last one fucking batter."

I squat in place. I still call the sequence I want, but Taz shakes me off, so I purposely give him two more pitches just to piss him off.

I get ready for the pitch, and he throws a curve that hangs too long. Bedard is too good a hitter not to grab hold of it. I hear it echo off the bat, and Taz is already hanging his head before the ball sails past the ivy wall and into the bleachers.

And that makes Milwaukee down by one, which means we're in trouble.

Ripley walks over to the mound right away, shaking his head. I jog over, as does our infield.

Easton and Decker glance at me because they know the problems I always have with Taz.

"Interesting call on the first pitch." Ripley doesn't look at Taz or me, and I hope he saw Taz shake off my suggestion. He holds out his hand, and Taz puts the ball into his palm with a little more force than necessary and walks off the field.

We all pat his back, but he pouts as he always does. Such a fucking baby. He's been in the league long enough to be pissed but know he still has to act mature about it. He pitched a great two innings in relief, and now the closer will come in and finish it off.

All the fans clap for Taz as he heads to the dugout, and we remain circling the mound, waiting to see who is coming in from the bullpen.

The lights of the stadium go out, and we all look at each other.

Ripley fights a smile. He definitely knows what's about to happen.

The stadium lights come back on slowly just before the Jumbotron flashes ALL ABOARD! in bold, blinding letters. A train engine bursts from the shadows on the screen, wheels sparking as it barrels down tracks of pure lightning, racing straight toward the fans until it feels as if it might crash through the screen.

"Oh shit," I say under my breath.

Easton's eyes widen, and he turns to me.

I shake my head. I had no fucking clue.

"What the fuck?" Decker shouts over the music.

The music volume comes down a bit.

"Ladies and gentlemen," the stadium announcer says, "it's closing time. Please rise and welcome to the mound the Chicago Colts's newest closer… number fourteen… FOSST-TEERR 'The Reaper' DAVVIISS!"

Foster jogs out of the bullpen and stops at the edge of the infield to let the umpire check his hands and glove for any illegal sticky shit.

We're still in disbelief as he approaches us. This is going to change the entire dynamic of the team, but I can't say I'm not happy to see him.

When he reaches us, the bad boy of baseball fist-bumps all the guys, his full sleeve of tattoos on display. I realize, to no surprise, that he's added to his neck tattoos since I last saw him.

When he gets to Decker, Foster nods. "Happy to see me?"

Decker says nothing, clenching his jaw, and goes back to third base.

"I'll take that as a no." Foster's smile is wicked and dangerous, and he's getting way too much pleasure from this surprise.

"What the hell?" I say.

We don't have time to talk right now, so he smiles and says with a shrug, "Got traded."

"But…"

"I'll tell you after. Let me shut this game down first."

"What—"

"Let's have some fun."

I nod and head back to the plate, but I turn around to

make sure I'm not imagining that Foster Davis is now a Chicago Colt.

I squat to catch his warm-up throws, and I spot Decker standing at third, staring a hole through his twin brother. They're fraternal twins, and besides not looking the same, they couldn't be more different.

This won't be good for the camaraderie of the team, but it's nice to have my best friend back.

CHAPTER
FORTY-THREE

Leighton

We ordered and ate pizza, and now I've made a popcorn and candy buffet table for us to enjoy. Since Hayes had an afternoon game today and he's off tomorrow, we decided to make it a movie night.

Lake wasn't happy at first, but then Hayes said they'd play rock, paper, scissors for who gets to choose the movie. He purposely lost, and Lake picked *Inside Out 2*.

All the kids are in the family room, getting under blankets, already dressed in their pajamas. I'm hoping for some early bedtimes so I can steal some alone time with Hayes.

I love that Hayes has Foster back on his team, and he's Hayes's new roommate, but it's put a dent in our time together. I keep having to push away my fears about Foster being a bad influence on Hayes because I don't honestly believe that. My mom used to say the same thing about Callie, and I always did what I wanted, not what Callie wanted me to.

Dinner was filled with figuring out all the details for Lake's upcoming birthday celebration.

"Decker and Easton want to know if they're invited?" Hayes asks Lake when she comes back into the kitchen.

I look at Lake, since it's her birthday party.

She shrugs. "Sure."

"You just made their day." Hayes tosses some popcorn in his mouth then takes out his phone. "Do you want to give them the happy news?"

"No, you can," she says.

Hayes jumps off the counter and hugs her, although she keeps her arms at her sides. "Smile. You're going to be twelve, and everyone will be here to celebrate you."

She pretends she's annoyed, trying to get him off her, and he only tightens his hold. I join them and put my face in hers and my arms around Hayes's neck and her body.

Hayes slides out and hooks his phone up to the Bluetooth speaker in the kitchen. "Happy" by Pharrell comes on, and Hayes dances over to us. He holds out his hands, and I take one, but Lake shakes her head.

Lincoln and Monroe rush into the room, both dancing, which is mostly jumping around.

Hayes spins me and dances us over to Lake. We hold our hands out to her, and she shakes her head, but Hayes grabs her hand, dancing in front of her as their arms swing back and forth.

I leave them and make a little circle with Monroe and Lincoln.

"Come on," Hayes begs, and Lake finally moves her upper body back and forth.

I watch from the corner of my eye as her hips move. Hayes learned his dance moves somewhere because it doesn't take long before he's got her in full dance mode. The other two kids and I dance over to them, and we make one big circle. Hayes is clapping to the beat, Monroe joining in.

I grab Lake's hand and dance with her. Finally, she's smiling and laughing at Hayes as he falls to his knees and pretends he's singing into a microphone to Monroe.

As the song ends, Lake's laughing and dancing with her brother and sister, and I'm in Hayes's arms. I lean my head on Hayes's chest. Seeing them happy and smiling makes me feel as if we might be turning a corner.

"Movie time!" Lincoln runs into the family room, to the spot he made up himself, and tucks himself under the blanket.

Lake and Monroe follow, but I linger in the kitchen with Hayes.

We look at one another, and he places his finger and thumb on my chin, tilting my head. Then he bends down and kisses me. It's short but sweet, and I already know what to name this feeling developing between us. It might have always been there and just had to bloom, but I love him, and that thought scares me more than it should.

"They're kissing again," Monroe groans.

"Come on," Lincoln calls.

Hayes's hand finds mine, and he leads me to our spot on the couch. I look at Lake after I snuggle into Hayes's chest, and she smiles at me. Smiles like she's happy for me, and like maybe she loves Hayes too.

Lincoln and Monroe are asleep within an hour, and Lake asks to go upstairs so she can chat with her friends. We say okay, and that leaves Hayes and me essentially alone.

"So how are things over at The Stables, The Barn… Paddock? Have they settled on a name yet?"

Hayes shakes his head. He's rarely there, and he tells me Ruby keeps giving him shit for not bringing the kids by. She said she serves chocolate milk. It's just hard to find the time.

"Jagger wanted us to become a little family, but when we have two twin brothers who don't even talk to one another, that makes it difficult."

I sit up straighter and tuck my legs under my body to be face-to-face with him. "I'm sorry, that sucks."

"Yeah, but the plus side is that Ripley's a great manager. He's really been giving me props lately. I've been in the media room every game."

"You are playing pretty amazing."

He smiles, and I feel it in my chest. I'm so happy for him.

"Easton says it's the power of Leighton."

I chuckle. "Me? No."

He holds out his arms, and I turn so I can still face him and rest my back over his body. "I think he's right."

I place my hand on his cheek. "No, Hayes, you've always been an amazing player. And if other people didn't see that, then that's their loss. Last year your mom was going through cancer treatments. You were lost."

"That's just it—you found me."

I shake my head, but he shakes his back. I don't want to be responsible for his success on the field because what happens if he has a bad game? Then am I the reason for his failure too?

"I think you found yourself." I sit up, glancing at the sleeping kids, then straddle him. "Let's take these kids up to bed."

"You okay?" He grabs my hand, stopping me.

"Yeah, of course."

He releases my hand, taking my word. I lift Monroe and he gets Lincoln, then we walk them upstairs and into their rooms, tucking them into bed.

I check on Lake, and she's still FaceTiming with her friends, so I wave hello and close her door.

Hayes is waiting at the top of the stairs outside Sky and Patrick's room. "I was thinking… want me to go in there with you?"

My eyes widen. "No."

He tilts his head. "You shouldn't be in that guest room. Look at all of us in the kitchen earlier—we're all growing. It's okay to sleep in their room so you can have your own bathroom." He twists the doorknob.

"Hayes."

What he hears in my voice, I don't know, but he removes his hand. "No? Okay."

I know he has a point, and I'd rather be brave with him here, so I reach around him, suck in a breath, and open the door. It's exactly how I left it how many months ago, except maybe dustier. All I did was toss the suitcases and duffel bags the police returned to us in here after the funeral.

Hayes follows me in, and I shut the door, so the kids won't find us in here. I know Lincoln doesn't care, but I don't know how the girls will feel about it.

"This is their stuff?" Hayes squats down to the backpack with a phone in the side pocket. "Did you think about looking through their phones?"

"No." I put my arms around myself, feeling as though I'm invading someone's personal space.

"There are probably pictures the kids would want when they're older." He stands, and a relieved breath floats out of me that he didn't pick up the phone. He walks over to me and takes my hands. "I know this is hard, and I've never been in your position, but Leighton, after my mom got sick, all I could do was look at pictures of her. And my first thought was that we didn't take enough. I worried that if cancer took her, the memories would fade, and I wouldn't have enough to remember her by. I know it's hard, but you might want to do it for the kids. You can't just forget them."

Unshed tears burn in my eyes, but he's right. I know he is. I just don't want to see her smiling face knowing what happened after that last picture was taken.

"I'm happy to go through them if you don't want to." His voice is gentle.

I lean my forehead on his chest, and he runs his hands up and down my arms in a comforting motion.

"No, I should do it." I leave his warm body and go over to the backpacks, squatting and staring at the phone in the outside pocket.

It was Sky's. I don't understand why she didn't have it on her when she fell. It makes no sense to me. She was such a picture-taker. Maybe having her phone would've made all the difference.

But I'm never going to get the answer to that question, so I have to let it go.

"I'll have to charge it." I get back up on my feet and white-knuckle the phone.

"I'll be right next to you. Do you want me to go through their bags for anything else?"

"I think one step at a time is all I can handle." I walk to the door and give one last look at the room before I open the door.

Hayes follows me to my room, and I plug her phone into the charger. My libido is gone now, and Hayes must read my mood shift because he holds me, his hands running up and down my arms until we see the screen light up.

I swing my legs over the bed and pick up her phone, feeling more urgent about it now that I see messages coming in. They're mostly from around the time they died, but there's a number that has called and left numerous messages. It's saved under the name Dr. Bonnie Welsh.

Sky never mentioned Dr. Bonnie Welsh. And why would she call so many times?

CHAPTER
FORTY-FOUR

Hayes

Leighton and I are getting ready for the gala that Jagger insisted we attend. Since my condo is filled with Foster's shit until he finds a place, and Leighton's mom is sleeping over at the house to watch the kids for the night, I rented a hotel room for Leighton and me.

But Leighton told me I had to stay in the sitting area while she got ready to make it more like a real date, as though I was coming to pick her up. I really want to ditch the gala and have as much bedroom time as we can squeeze in, but I know that's not happening.

"Ready?" she calls from the other side of the double doors that lead to the bedroom.

I stand from the couch and turn off the sports highlights on the TV. Walking over, I knock on the door.

"Just a minute," she says in a way that sounds far away. Almost as if she's cupping her hands around her mouth. "Who is it?"

I chuckle. "Me."

"Me who?"

"Your date."

"How do I know it's really you?"

"Leighton, it's Hayes, and I really want to see my smokin' hot girlfriend all dressed up, so can you please open the door?"

"Tell me something about yourself before I open it, so I know it's really you."

"My cock is eight inches long, and it's rock-hard wanting to get into that pussy that owns him."

She laughs, and the doorknobs twist. Both doors open, revealing the most stunning, sexy, beautiful woman I've ever seen.

"Damn, Leighton." My hand comes to my face and my thumb brushes along my bottom lip as I soak her in. "You are… I have no words."

She twirls around, but her dress doesn't move since it's molded to her delicious curves. It's the color of the champagne I'm sure I'll be sipping on tonight and goes all the way down to the floor.

"Speechless is good," she says.

I step forward, and my hands go to her hips. "Tell me you're dressed up just for me so I can unzip you, and we can fuck like bunnies for the rest of the night."

She takes my hands and removes them from her hips. "Nope. But maybe I'll meet you in the coat room later."

"I'll be following you around like a lost puppy all night."

She walks to the bed and picks up her clutch, tucking it under her arm. "The sooner we go, the sooner we're back making good use of this hotel room."

"You're so much smarter than me." I hold out my arm for her to walk ahead of me. It is selfish really, because I get to admire her ass and the deep valley in the back of her dress. "I hope I don't get into a fight tonight."

She laughs. For the entire walk to the elevator and down to the lobby, I can't take my eyes off of her. But as soon as the elevator doors open, I secure her hand in mine to make sure that every asshole in a fifty-foot radius knows who she belongs to.

The doorman ushers us to the waiting car I ordered, and I tip him before joining Leighton in the back seat.

I don't want to ruin the vibe we have going, but there are some conversations we can only have without the kids around.

"Did you call that doctor's office that was on Skylar's phone?" I ask, since the minute the car leaves the hotel, we're sitting in downtown Chicago traffic.

"Oh yeah, I meant to tell you. She's a therapist. But she wouldn't give me any information except to say that she was following up on an appointment they had scheduled. She wouldn't even tell me if it was for Sky or Patrick or both of them. But when I googled her, it seems she mostly does couples counseling, so my guess it was both of them."

"They had issues?" I'm surprised, because Leighton's never alluded to that.

She shakes her head. "Sky never said anything to me. I thought she told me everything, but I guess not." Leighton frowns, and I squeeze her hand. "Before the home visit, I was putting my shoes away, and I found an overnight bag shoved way back in the closet with a new bottle of perfume and red lingerie inside. And the kids mentioned that Patrick used to sleep in there sometimes."

"I think it's healthy for couples to go to therapy. I don't think it has to mean there was any real trouble in their marriage." I brush my knuckle down her cheek.

"I just hate that she thought she couldn't talk to me. I honestly thought they had the best marriage. Couple goals and all that."

"Maybe their getaway was about them trying to reconnect."

She nods, but her teeth bite her lower lip. Knowing Leighton, she's working through every bad scenario in her head. It must be hard because she'll never really get the answers she wants.

"Anyway, let's just concentrate on us tonight. We rarely get this." She squeezes my hand.

"You look beautiful." I lean in and kiss her bare shoulder.

She preens under my compliment. "And you look so handsome in your tuxedo. Just so you know." She leans closer and says directly into my ear, "Later tonight, you'll be in the armchair with your tie undone, suit coat open, and I'll be on my knees between your legs."

I reach for the back of her neck and pull her in, pressing my lips to hers. I don't care about lipstick or the fucking driver. She drives me to the brink of insanity.

The driver clears his throat, then there's a knock on the window. Guess we've arrived.

"You have lipstick." She presses her thumb to my lips.

I really want to beg her again to just have this car turn back around. But she deserves a night out that doesn't include the ice cream parlor or our recent obsession with the cookie place.

I climb out of the car and hold out my hand for her.

You'd think she was used to all this, the way she flawlessly lets me guide her out of the car. We walk into the venue hand in hand, and as we're checking in, I spot some of the Chicago Falcons and Grizzlies in attendance.

This is about the last place I want to be, but we pose for pictures as Jagger wants us to, and we socialize, my arm around her the entire time. The only thing fake tonight is both of us acting as if this is where we want to spend our night.

After the meal, when the dancing starts, Leighton's hand slides down to my ass while we're talking to Rowan and

Kyleigh Landry on their way out. All of the Falcons leave pretty soon after dinner, blaming it on babysitters and early mornings.

"We need a baby," I grumble.

"Um… no, we don't. There are already three kids we could use as an excuse to leave, but I think I promised you some coatroom time, no?" Leighton arches a perfectly shaped brow.

My gaze coasts down her body. "Lead the way."

She inches up and kisses me. "Meet me in there in two minutes."

"Be ready in one. I'm barely holding on here." I button my tuxedo jacket closed so my semi isn't obvious to everyone around us.

She giggles and walks away, out of the event space.

I'm about to follow when Jagger clasps his hand on my shoulder. "I'm proud of you. You two look like you're about to tear each other's clothes off."

We were, or at least some heavy petting.

"Yeah, turns out we're the real thing. And I'd like permission to leave this party now so I can spend the rest of my night in bed with Leighton."

Jagger chuckles. "I knew it. I told Quinn you two would eventually find one another in the dark and pull off those blindfolds you've been wearing. Well, happy looks really good on you, man."

"Thanks. I think so too."

So much so that I have a word for it. If someone asked how I know I'm in love with Leighton, I wouldn't be able to explain it, other than that she really sees me.

Jagger pats me on the back. "You're dismissed. I'll talk to you next week."

I shake his hand, and he goes one way. I head the opposite direction toward the exit. The coatroom door is propped up, so I slip inside.

I love that Leighton thought of this. Maybe this will be our thing—sneaking off to fuck in small, enclosed spaces.

It's pretty dark in here, and there aren't a lot of coats since it's summer. Maybe it's not even open this time of year. I feel along the wall, grazing over a hand. It grabs mine and pulls me closer.

Damn, I love when she's this bossy in the bedroom.

My hand slides along her waist, and I bend down to nuzzle her neck the way she loves, but instead of a neck, I hit what feels like a chest. And then I realize that the hand I'm holding is a lot bigger and more calloused than Leighton's.

"What the fuck?" the other person and I say at the same time, pushing away from one another.

A light flickers on, and I turn to my left to see Leighton standing by the door. If she's there, then who was… I turn back around.

"Tweetie?"

"Fucking hell, Carlisle, this is me and the missus's spot."

"Fuck my life," I groan.

"First you spy on Tedi pumping in Ruby's office and now you're trying to grope me in the dark. I'm starting to wonder about you."

"I did not spy on your wife pumping breast milk!"

Tedi pops up next to Leighton in the doorway. "Oh, you were meeting Hayes in here? I love it." Tedi links her arms with Leighton's. "We'll leave you two alone. Sorry for interrupting."

"Tedi," Tweetie growls.

She laughs and pats Leighton's arm, then walks toward us. "So good to catch up with you. But we made this our make-out spot a while ago. You're going to have to find your own." She leans into Tweetie, who wraps his arms around his wife.

"That was a nice way to say get the fuck out," Tweetie says without looking away from his wife.

"See you guys. Don't make another baby," I say, heading toward the exit.

Tweetie flips me off behind Tedi's back. "It might be too late for that. Good night, you two." Tedi presses her lips to Tweetie's as Leighton flicks off the lights.

"You said you'd be in there." I look around to make sure no one else saw what went down as we make our way toward the lobby.

"I just went to the bathroom to take off my panties, but I ran into Tedi and never got that far. We got to talking and well..." She laughs. "Tell me you're not going to want to trade me in for Tweetie now?"

I grab her by the waist and tug her to me, while she laughs the whole time.

"Hell no." I glance at the clutch in her hands. "So, what you're saying is that I can be the one to remove your panties now?"

She nods and bites her lip, which drives me fucking insane.

"Let's go." I tug her across the lobby, and she laughs the entire way.

I hope I can keep my dick at bay until the hotel room, but as soon as we're behind those closed doors, it's game on.

CHAPTER
FORTY-FIVE

Leighton

The hotel door clicks shut, and Hayes presses me gently but firmly against the wall, his fingers already searching for the zipper on my dress. My hands slide up his chest, pushing his tuxedo jacket off his shoulders. His mouth finds mine, urgent and hungry, and for a moment we're all hands and breath—shoes and heels abandoned at the door.

"You have no idea how bad I want you." My voice echoes through the quiet suite. I'm louder than I should be, but for once, it doesn't matter because there's no one here to hear us.

"Yeah, I do." He finds my zipper and draws it down slowly, his eyes never leaving mine.

Then he steps back, though I'm still chasing his mouth. "What… what are you doing?"

"Take it off for me." He leans against the wall, then lifts a finger. "Actually…" His hand finds mine, and he guides me across the room and into the bedroom portion of our suite. He sits in the armchair and loosens his bow tie. "Now, take it off and show me your sexy body."

He slides off his bow tie and tosses it on the floor before undoing the top buttons of his shirt with unhurried precision. His gaze follows my hands to the straps of my dress. I slide one arm free, then the other, the cool air in the suite raising goose bumps along my skin. I start to let the fabric fall, but he lifts his hand.

"Tease me, baby. You know how I love it when you tease me."

God, his voice is all decadence and sin. I'll never get enough of this man. I slow my movements, inching the dress down, addicted to watching his control slip away. His eyelids get heavy, and his breath deepens with every inch of skin I expose. The thick erection tenting his pants makes my mouth water.

Hayes keeps repeating under his breath—"Fuck, damn, I'm a lucky bastard, you're beautiful, you're perfect."

When the dress pools at my feet, he crooks his finger. I move toward him instinctively, but instead of pulling me close, he pats his thigh.

I sit down wearing nothing but my thong, and he positions me so my back rests against his chest, his warmth sinking into my skin. His hands snake up my chest, tracing lazy paths along my flesh that make me shiver.

"Are you cold, baby?" he murmurs against my ear, his voice low and rough, stealing the air from my lungs.

"Not so much now."

His hand drifts lower, fingers playing idly at my waist. Then his hand slides down farther and his fingers drift along the elastic band of my thong, teasing. The pulse between my legs becomes more insistent, more demanding, and I arch, wanting him to move his hand just a little… farther… down.

"You're trembling," he says softly. "I can feel your heart beating through your skin."

"Please, Hayes…"

"I bet you're soaked." His voice is thick with affection and desire.

I nod, and his other hand cups my breast in a way that feels both possessive and tender. His breath stutters against my neck. His erection presses into the small of my back, and he shifts behind me, I swear just to tease me even more. I'm desperate to feel him moving between my legs.

"What do you want, Leighton?"

A million images flash behind my closed eyelids, but when I answer, I distill it down to its core. "I just want to please you," I whisper. "I love pleasing you."

"I know you do. But tonight, I want to watch you come apart on my lap, then I'm going to take you to the bed and make love to you."

I stifle a gasp, his words piercing straight through me.

"Is that okay?" His lips brush my shoulder.

I nod. "Yes."

He slides my thong over, exposing my pussy to the cool air, and runs his finger over my slit before bringing it to his mouth and sucking my juices off.

"God, Hayes…"

He hums low in his throat. "I know," he murmurs, kissing the hollow behind my ear.

My hand finds the back of his neck, my fingers threading through his hair as tension coils tightly in me.

"Please," I whisper, desperate for him to touch me again.

"I've got you." He brings his fingers back to my center, deepening the rhythm, drawing me closer.

Hayes has been a master student because I'm dragged to the precipice only a minute later. When my orgasm comes, it's like a bolt of lightning—a rush of light, a breathless quake that leaves the world spinning.

"Shh," he soothes, pressing soft kisses along my shoulder. "I could watch you fall apart forever."

I stand on unsteady legs as he rises too, his expression is lust mixed with a tenderness I get lost in every time. He undresses, each movement slower than the last, and I crawl up onto the bed, feeling the weight of everything unspoken between us.

He follows, his body a shadow against the soft lamplight. "I want to take my time with you."

We're always stealing minutes between schedules. But not tonight.

He meets me on the bed, and our joining is unhurried and deliberate. We don't need words—it's all there in our locked gazes and shuddered breaths.

Once he's fully seated inside me, his deep brown eyes lock with my baby blues. "I love you, Leighton."

I inhale sharply, every part of me trembling from the truth in his voice.

"You don't have to say it back," he adds. "I have no idea how to explain it, other than that I found myself with you. Who I am and the man I can be… it's all because of you."

My hands frame his face. "I love you too. I never thought this was possible. To have someone like you and to feel this much."

He smiles—a slow, devastating curve of his lips that feels like a forever—and leans in to kiss me.

Then we're making promises and declarations as our hands explore slowly, our movements an easy, romantic rhythm that makes my heart soar. We come together, kissing languidly, our sweaty bodies so entwined that nothing could ever tear us apart.

CHAPTER
FORTY-SIX

Leighton

I dump all the decorations for Lake's birthday on the island. I meant to do most of it last night with Hayes, but after the kids went to bed, I wanted a little more alone time with him. He spent the night but got up and left before the kids were out of their rooms. Eventually, we'll have to talk about sleepovers, but that's a discussion for after I'm awarded custody of the kids.

The doorbell rings, and I drop the balloon I was about to blow up to answer it.

Usually, I'd be running to the door to see Callie. After months of her being away, I'd haul her into my arms, but my footsteps slow the closer I get. Because I told Hayes that today would be the day I confess everything to his sister.

I don't think she'll be too upset. She's made hints about me liking him, so she's not clueless. But I don't want her to ever feel left out or think I'm picking her brother over her.

The doorbell rings. Then rings again. And again.

I open the door, shaking my head. "You're so—"

Her bags drop with a *thunk*, and she drags me into a hug. I'm not sure if there's a Carlisle class on hugging, but everyone should take one.

I wrap my arms around her, and the scent of her perfume and her shampoo brings me comfort. My best friend is home.

"I'm never going away that long again." She pulls back and gives me the once-over. "You look different."

I run my hand down my hair and look down at myself. "How?"

She scans me over me one more time. "I don't know. It's not bad, just different."

I pick up one of her bags. "You're such a dork, get in here."

She takes off her shoes, and I put her bag on the bench before we walk farther into the house.

"Where are the kiddos?" she asks.

"Lincoln and Monroe are with my mom. It's Blueberry Muffin Day, so they're picking up a bunch to see which is better."

She slides up on the counter and takes a balloon from the packaging. "I didn't think Lil had it in her."

I chuckle and get up on the other side, suddenly feeling as if we're twelve again and sharing a bowl of raw cookie dough, gossiping about boys and teen drama. Even back in those days, I was usually tracking Hayes if he was home when I was there. A rush of heat flows through my veins just thinking about how he's mine now.

"What are you thinking about?" Callie interrupts the memory of his lips venturing down my body last night as he kept his dark gaze on my face the entire time.

"Just the stress of the party," I say quickly.

"You have this weird smile." Her head cocks to the side.

I need to tell her sooner than later. If I wait too long, she might be madder. "I have to tell you something."

There you go, girl, rip it wide open.

She drops the balloon from her mouth and rests her hands on her lap. "Is it something with the guardianship?"

"No. They have one more visit with Art and Julianna, then as far as I know, the social worker said she'll be sending her report to the judge in a couple of weeks."

Callie rolls her eyes. "Nice of them to take their sweet time with it."

I shrug. I can't really fault them for wanting to make sure the best decision is made for the kids. Although I'm biased, I know I'm the best one for them.

She pats my knee. "You'll get them. I'm sure of it. How's Mark doing?" She waggles her eyebrows.

"He's not my lawyer anymore, remember?"

Callie frowns. "I had some hot dreams about him." She sighs and looks at the ceiling, pink coloring her cheeks before she snaps out of it. "Okay, so if it's not the kids, what is it?" Her eyes widen. "Did you meet someone?"

You can do this, Leighton. Just spit it out.

"I did."

"Why didn't you start with that? It should've been the first thing you told me when I walked through the door. And I'm a little upset that you didn't bring up this mystery guy during our bestie bitch time." She brings the balloon to her lips, then she sets it back down, seeming contemplative. "Does he check all your boxes?"

"Um… no."

Her head falls back, and I can't read whether it's relief or upset she's feeling. Then she straightens and goes to blow the balloon up again. "Good. I'm pretty sure whatever guy you find off that list isn't going to be very good in bed."

Yeah, definitely not a problem.

When I don't respond right away, she asks, "You've slept with him, right?"

A part of me wants her to blow up the balloon so I can

have some time to form my words. Even practicing with Hayes last night, he just laughed and said he really doesn't give a shit if Callie is okay with us or not, it wouldn't change anything for him. Which was nice to hear, but it does matter to me, and I think he's fooling himself if he thinks it won't bother him if she has a problem with our relationship.

"I have, yeah."

"And?" She quickly puts up her hand. "Never mind. I know how you don't like to kiss and tell."

I always tell her what happens… within reason. But sitting here, it's the first time I realize that I'll never be able to talk to her about my sex life as long as Hayes and I are together. Not that I get super specific, but I won't be telling her over coffee, *your brother's tongue action is top-notch* or *your brother's dick almost broke me in two last night.*

"Okay, what the hell is going on? This is the first time you've seen me in months, and your mind keeps wandering. This guy must be something."

"He is." Hopefully she hears in my voice how important he is to me.

"How the hell did you find time to fall head over heels for a guy while navigating the kids and the custody—" Her eyes widen and her jaw drops. "Leighton…"

I'm not surprised she figured it out. Callie's always been very perceptive. I nod and bite my lip.

"Hayes?" she shouts. The balloon drops from her hands, and she jumps off the counter. "My brother?"

This isn't the reaction I was hoping for. She seems so surprised, and I really didn't see that coming. "Yeah, it's Hayes."

She whips around and puts her hands on her hips. "You're sleeping with my brother?"

I nod and mess with the decorations to distract myself.

No. I need to own this. Let her know how much he means to me.

"I'm sorry." I slide off the counter. "It just happened. I mean, that's not true. I never told you—" Fuck, she doesn't even know about the kiss back in college.

"You bitch."

I'm taken aback by her anger, and I recoil.

"I sent him over here to help you, and you mount him like some horny alley cat."

My chest feels tight, and I have to work to push out the words. "What? No, that's not how it happened."

"I thought you were my best friend."

"I am."

"Best friends don't fuck each other's brothers. I trusted you. Both of you." She pulls her phone out of her back pocket. "I'm going to message him and tell him he can fuck right off."

I cross the room and place my hand on her phone. "No. He has a game, and this is between me and you."

She lifts her gaze to mine, a conniving smile lifting her lips. Then she laughs, placing her phone on the counter.

My shoulders drop. "Seriously?"

She laughs harder and pulls me in for a hug, her laughter ringing in my ear. "Come on, it was funny."

"Do you know how worried I was? I even rehearsed it with Hayes last night."

She smacks a kiss on my cheek. "Of course you did." She hops back up on the counter and picks up another balloon. "Now tell me all about it without any kinky sex stuff." She puts her hand on her heart. "I'm gonna mourn that part of our relationship. I guess it will only be me sharing now."

"Are you sure you're okay with this?" I get up on the counter beside her.

"I just have one question. Do you love him?"

That was the last question I thought she'd ask, but I'm glad she did because I want her to know how much he means to me and how much I care for him. "I do."

Her smile takes over her entire face. "Okay. Now tell me everything."

As we decorate, I tell her all about how I fell in love with her brother and promise her that nothing will come between our friendship.

Now we just need the guardianship finalized in my favor, then Hayes, the kids, and I can have our happily ever after.

CHAPTER
FORTY-SEVEN

Leighton

"Hey, you know what to do." I get Hayes's voicemail after a few rings.

"Hey, it's me again. I'm not even sure if you'll get this, but please call me as soon as you do. I know it was a rough day, but it's only one game. Please… just call me."

"Voicemail again?" Callie asks, and I nod.

We're in the corner of the kitchen, as Lake's friends do a scavenger hunt through the house and backyard. I've fed them. Callie and I took turns painting their nails. I put on ten face masks.

"I'm gonna call." Callie steps away from me, grabbing her phone off the counter and dialing her brother.

I'd be surprised if he picked up for her and not me. I have no idea why he isn't here at the party. My only assumption is that it was a horrible game today. They were leading in the top of the ninth when Foster came in to get only two outs. O'Leary hit a single to third that got by Decker, and one run came in. Although Decker made a great throw to Hayes, he didn't get the tag down, and another runner scored. After that, it looked as though they were so shaken up, they couldn't come back.

In the bottom of the ninth, when the Colts had a chance to get the run back, Easton struck out, Decker struck out, Torres walked, and Hayes worked it to a full count before ultimately striking out. Game over. Colts lose.

But it's not as if he hasn't had a bad game or a loss while we've been together. Sure, he'll seem a little down, but he can easily be cheered up. It's just not like him to let me, and especially one of the kids, down. I can't believe he's not here. Or that he hasn't called.

Callie sets her phone down and shakes her head.

"Who is his emergency contact? Should we call hospitals?" My stomach flips over at the thought, remembering when I received the call about Skylar and Patrick.

Callie frowns. "I'd call my mom, but I don't want to worry her yet. Plus, if anyone called her, she'd call me right away."

I nod. That's true. The Carlisles always keep one another in the loop.

A rush of girls storm through the back door, running toward the staircase.

Lake lingers as her friends try to find the next item upstairs. "So, he's not coming?"

"He's just late. Maybe there was a meeting after the game." I hate making excuses for Hayes. I understand that sometimes things come up, or whatever it is, but a phone call would at least tell me he's not dead.

"Great." She throws up her hands. "Now I'm a liar. I told them all three Colts players were coming, and they acted like I was lying all week."

"Lake..." Even Callie is at a loss for words.

The newly minted twelve-year-old huffs and storms away.

I sigh, picking up my phone and redialing him. "Hey, you know what to do." I slam my phone on the counter.

"Hey, I know. Believe me, if he's not dead in a ditch, his balls are mine." Callie wraps her arms around my shoulders.

Every scenario runs through my mind, but one haunting suspicion that isn't fair to Hayes is the fact that Foster Davis is back. Could they both be wallowing over a bad game in some bar and—no. I can't assume he's cheating or out tying one on. I know Hayes, and he wouldn't do that. He just made love to me last night, whispering how much I mean to him.

Still, the familiar feeling of disappointment mixed with dread swamps my system. My chest feels tight, and it makes me jittery.

But it makes no sense why he would be late.

A fucking phone call. Would it kill him?

CHAPTER
FORTY-EIGHT

Hayes

I t was a shit game.

The fact that we couldn't pull it together in the bottom of the ninth only made what happened at the top sting worse.

Baseball is called a game of failure for a reason. Errors happen—every game, every team, no matter how good you are. The best hitters in the league fail seven times out of ten. That's success in this sport.

The defense controls the pace, which is rare in any other game. The batter steps in alone, outnumbered nine to one. There's no teammate to pass to, no quick assist. It's just you, a bat, and the hope that you can square up a ninety-five-mile-an-hour fastball.

Even then, most of the game depends on the pitcher hitting a spot the size of a postage stamp—and an umpire's judgment on whether or not he did. One call, one inch, one blink—it all decides who walks away a hero and who walks off the field defeated.

All four of us—Foster, Decker, Easton, and me—walk into the media room having not said a word to one another since the game ended. We're processing—most likely our own failures during those six outs.

Foster brushes by me onto the platform and takes the far chair to the right. He's stewing, and if I were Ripley, I'd have made him sit this one out. It always takes Foster a night to regroup, and by the next morning, he walks in ready for a fresh start. It's the way this game has to be played in order to remain sane. It's exactly what I *wasn't* doing last year.

I just want to get this over with so I can make it to Lake's party in time to help Leighton finish decorating and keep Callie off her back since Leighton said she was going to tell my sister we're a couple as soon as she arrived. I'll be pissed off if my sister behaves shitty when I want to be a human shield to Leighton.

Foster and Decker are in identical poses—leaned back in their chairs with their arms crossed and scowls on their faces —so I point at the first reporter.

"Foster, walk us through the top of the ninth. Looked like you had command until the walked Richards. What changed?"

Foster doesn't bother leaning into the microphone. "What do you want me to say? I was ahead zero to two, then I missed the plate and fell behind on the count fast. You can't walk the first guy in the ninth. It's on me."

I look at both sides of me, and it looks as though no one else is going to take questions. Easton is just fiddling with his chains.

"Hayes, you've caught for Foster for a long time," the next reporter says. "Did you notice anything off mechanically in that inning? Did you think about a mound visit?"

I push back my irritation. "Not really. His stuff was still sharp. The fastball had life. I think it's more about pitch selection. I was trying to keep them guessing, but maybe I got a little cute instead of going right at them. That's my bad."

The next reporter I point at always comes right at us, so I'm not surprised when he sets his gaze on Decker. "Decker, that error on the routine ground ball—how tough is it to shake that off in the moment?"

Decker, unlike Foster, sits up and leans into the microphone. "Yeah, that was brutal. Ball took a weird hop, but I still gotta make that play. Ninth inning, two outs, you can't give them any extra chances."

I point at the next reporter, and he sets his sights on Easton. I'm not sure why he's even here. Other than striking out, Easton had a great game.

"Easton, you seemed a little jumpy at the plate in the bottom of the ninth. Had you been more patient, you might have drawn a walk."

"What exactly is the question?" Easton asks. The reporter opens his mouth to speak, but Easton quickly interrupts. "I'm a hitter. That's the player I am. I'm not going to let pitches I think I can hit go by me."

I point at the next reporter and inwardly groan because what else do you want? We sucked today, end of discussion.

"You've had three straight games where late innings got away from you guys. Is it mid-season fatigue? Mental struggle?"

Foster mumbles something that I think might have been fuck you, so I quickly shift closer to the microphone. "We've got the talent. It's about trusting it and not trying to play hero. Baseball humbles you fast when you start forcing things."

With all the usual questions out of the way, it turns into a kind of free-for-all with reporters standing and asking questions.

"Decker, what's the message to the guys after a game like this?"

"Flush it. You learn from it, and you move on. No one in this room is quitting. We've got another game tomorrow. That's the beauty of baseball. We get another chance to come out on top."

The next reporter stands. "Easton, this loss drops your average under three hundred. How do you stay out of your head?"

Easton grunts. "I'm frustrated, obviously. We've all played this game long enough to know the grind. You keep showing up, and eventually it turns."

"Last question," our press guy says from the side of the room.

Thank fuck, I want to get out of here.

A reporter stands, and I'm not sure I've seen her before. She doesn't look familiar. "Hayes, there's been speculation that your recent hot streak at the plate has something to do with off-field happiness. After three losses, could it be your focus has changed?"

"Fuck's sake," Foster mumbles.

I thought that question was going somewhere good, until she did a one-eighty at the tail end.

"I think how I play has nothing to do with my girlfriend—except when I play well, of course." I throw in a wink for good measure.

The room laughs, but the reporter remains standing, not seeming impressed.

"Some people believe a relationship during the season can be a distraction. How do you respond to that?" she asks.

"I don't. The people speculating have never been in my shoes."

The room is somber and still she's standing. What the fuck does this woman want from me?

"Last last question," our press guy says.

I inhale a deep breath.

"Of course." She smiles. "This is to Hayes again."

"Not surprising," I say, trying to mask my irritation.

A few people in the room quietly chuckle.

"You've always come off as pretty private, Hayes. What made you decide to go public with this relationship?"

"I think it's pretty simple. When you love someone, you want the whole world to know."

She finally sits back down.

Our press guy steps forward, hands raised as the reporters call out more questions, and the four of us stand. "Ripley will be right in."

We step out of the media room and run right into our manager, who's holding a little girl who looks to be about six years old, a blonde woman standing next to them.

"How did it go in there?" Ripley passes the little girl to the woman at his side.

"Time of my life," Easton says. "Is this the missus?" He holds his hand out to the woman, who looks a lot closer to our age than our manager's.

Ripley levels him with a deadpan look. "It's my daughter and my granddaughter."

Foster chuckles. I give him a questioning look.

Foster slaps Decker on the shoulder. "Hey, Penelope," Foster says and walks down the hallway.

"Foster. Decker. Always a pleasure to see the Davis brothers." There's a bite to her tone.

I look at Easton to see if he has any idea what's going on, but he looks as confused as me.

The press guy peeks his head out of the press room. "They're ready for you."

"Come on, Hazel, you're going to be my buffer." He picks the little girl out of Penelope's arms.

"Grandpa." She laughs when he tickles her stomach.

"Dad." Penelope's eyes shift from her dad to Decker then back to her dad. "You can't just use her to get the heat off of you." She follows her dad and daughter into the press room.

After the media room door shuts, Easton and I turn toward Decker.

"You know the manager's daughter?" Easton asks.

"It was a long time ago." Decker stalks down the hallway.

Easton and I stare at one another for a beat. Things just got interesting.

"I feel like I don't even know you," Easton says, following Decker. "What kind of friendship do we have if you can't tell me you know the new manager's daughter?"

I laugh, glancing at the clock in the locker room. Shit, I need to get a move on.

We all go in and grab our shit, then leave the stadium to make the short walk over to our building. We'll drop our stuff and head over to Lake's birthday party.

Easton and I are starting to let our attitudes about the shitty game slip away as we head back home, but the mood between Foster and Decker has only gotten worse. The tension in the air is palpable.

"What? Did Penelope distract you so much, you couldn't get your glove down?" Foster snipes at his brother once we've almost reached the building.

"Hey, man, everyone has days." I try to smooth it over.

"Fuck you. You walked him. That run was on you." Decker has his finger pointed at his brother, and Foster looks as if he's liable to break it.

"Plus, it took a bad hop, I saw it," Easton chimes in.

"None of that matters. We didn't get anything done at the plate. It's on all of us," I say, hoping it will cool things off.

Decker stops walking and turns to Foster. "You always blame everyone else. Why did you even come here?"

Foster's grin says he's about to say something he shouldn't. "Too much money to turn it down, brother. I know you can't understand that since we're at two very different pay grades."

"Shit, that's not cool," Easton says.

Ever since Foster got here, there's been a divide—Easton and Decker, and Foster and me.

"It's all right, Easton. It's the truth, and that's where we're different. I don't need money to know my worth." Decker steps closer to Foster.

They're the same height, and they both look as if they could breathe fire right now.

"You're still the player who gets flustered by your emotions. Always so many feelings." Foster shakes his head.

"It's better than being a cold, heartless bastard," Decker says.

Their chests press against one another's.

Easton and I look at each other, then scramble to get between them before it comes to blows.

"Hey, we're in public," Easton says. "Fans are still hanging around."

"We're a team." I wedge myself between them. "Like it or not, you two are on the same side."

My phone vibrates, and knowing I'm already late, I pull it out of my back pocket, seeing Leighton's name on the screen. "Fuck, guys. We gotta go."

I'm about to tuck it back in my pocket when I'm pushed to the ground, and the phone flies out of my hands.

"Jesus. Fuck!" Easton shouts. "Hayes!"

I scramble back to my feet to see Decker and Foster rolling around on the pavement. I pull Foster off his brother and push his chest back as Decker scrambles to his feet.

"You guys need to sort out your shit," Easton tells them. Now he's pissed.

"I'm going to the party on my own. I don't want you assholes there. Go see a fucking therapist and fix whatever is wrong before it poisons the team." I search the ground for my phone, but I don't see it anywhere. "Where the hell is my phone?"

"Hey, man," Easton says, staring at the storm grate.

"Fuck!" I shout at the sky, knowing my phone is now lost to me.

"You broke my fucking nose," Foster says, blood gushing down his shirt.

Awesome.

CHAPTER
FORTY-NINE

Leighton

The birthday party ends, and there's still no word from Hayes. My worry has grown exponentially with every minute that ticks by.

Lake is in her room. My mom took Lincoln and Monroe to Aunt Iris's who said she'll keep them overnight. Of course, my mom couldn't leave before delivering her parting shot of, "I'm not surprised he disappointed you, Leighton. Men always do. When are you going to learn that?"

I hear a key in the door as Callie and I are cleaning up, and I pause throwing all the streamers into a garbage bag. Callie looks up from piling up Lake's birthday gifts and over at me. I drop the garbage bag and rush into the foyer.

Hayes walks in, and his eyes plead for forgiveness before he even opens his mouth. A wave of relief hits me. Foster is behind him, his shirt covered in blood.

"I'm so sorry," Hayes says. "It's over?" He looks at the

half-eaten cake on the counter and the pile of balloons in the family room.

"That's the funny thing, Hayes. Birthday parties have times you're supposed to show up." Callie puts her hands on her hips. "I get that you think you're special and everything, but the party doesn't start when you decide to make it."

"Who's this one?" Foster points lazily at Callie.

"I'm his sister, dipshit. I assume you're the reason for this." She motions with both hands at them.

They both look as though they just got out of a barroom brawl. Hayes's shirt sleeve is ripped, blood splattered on him.

"Why do I always get the blame?" Foster says, but I ignore him.

"Are you okay?" I ask Hayes.

He steps toward me, and I don't stop him. For a minute, I just want to wrap my head around the fact that he's here. He's safe and nothing has happened to him.

"Yeah," he says.

"No broken bones? No accident?"

His shoulders sink. "No, I'm fine. Shit, Leighton, I'm sorry. I lost my phone and Foster broke his nose."

I put my hand up to stop him from talking. "Just give me a minute." I turn and walk out to the back patio.

"Wait. I want to talk about this," Hayes calls behind me.

I shut the door, and the tears that have been on the brink of falling are finally unable to stay at bay. I go to the corner, face the house, cover my face with my hands, and I weep. I sob for all the fears that plagued me during the hours I didn't know where he was.

He's fine. He's good. He's here. He's alive.

"Leighton." He places his hand on my back. "Come here. I'm so sorry."

He wraps his arms around me, and I turn into him, needing to touch him, to let him hold me, prove to me that he's still with me.

Hayes continues to murmur apologies, but I just want to smell him and feel him and try to get rid of this horrible feeling inside me.

After my sobs subside, he explains what happened. "The media ran late. Then Foster and Decker got into a fight on the way back to the condo, and my phone fell into a storm grate. Decker broke Foster's nose, so I've been at the emergency room with him. I was going to leave the hospital staff to deal with him, but then the nurse said they had to check him for a concussion, and he was freaked out because that would mean he couldn't pitch. I wanted to leave, but when I saw how messed up he was before he knew he was in the clear, I just couldn't. I was trying to get here as fast as I could. I should've made more of an effort to call you."

I pull away from him, and he tries to keep me in place, but I need space from him now that I know he's alive.

"Lake is really upset. You let her down." I walk to the edge of the patio. The grass looks way too brown, and Patrick's garden is half dead. I've done a shit job of keeping up with his landscaping.

"I'll apologize."

I'm sure he will, and maybe she'll accept it, or she won't, but eventually she'll let it go. If he messes up again, she'll let it go again, until she's so used to disappointment, she comes to expect it from men. Just like me.

"Hayes, the one thing I told myself when I took on the job of raising these kids is that I would protect them at all costs. I know I have issues stemming from my upbringing. I always expect people, especially men, to disappoint me. To not show up when it matters."

"I have shown up when it matters," he argues.

"Yes, you have. You broke down all my assumptions, and you've been with me through this. There's no denying that. But today really poked at the wound in me. I was so worried that something terrible had happened because it was outside of your character to not show up without a word. Not only did my past resurface, but it brought back that awful phone call I got when Skylar—" I have to swallow past the painful lump in my throat. "I felt like I was waiting for my phone to ring with news about you."

"Leighton." He steps forward, but I put my hand up to stop him. If I allow him any closer, I won't be able to do this. "The situation was out of my control."

"I just need some time." I squeeze my eyes shut.

"No. Please, don't do this. You can't do this."

A tear runs down my cheek at the panic in his voice, and I open my eyes, wiping it away. "I'm not saying never. I'm just saying that there's a lot going on right now, and you need to focus on your career, and I—"

"That's bullshit, and you know it."

I shake my head. "They've been through enough, Hayes. I can't let you—"

"Don't you dare fucking say it, Leighton. I *have* been here. I've fallen in love with you. I've fallen in love with them. I've done every fucking National Day. I've packed lunches. I've read bedtime stories. I've done math homework and talked about preteen drama. But that's not enough, right?"

"I didn't say that."

He steps away from me, and my heart splinters. "You need to deal with your issues."

"What?" I feel as though I've been slapped in the face.

"You want us to be perfect, but there's no such thing. I hate how you were brought up and the tug-of-war your parents put you through. The rumors, the divorce, the affair, the constant disappointment. All of it. I fucking hate that you had to go through all of that, so I was happy to put in the time it took for you to realize that you can count on me. For you to conquer all those shitty beliefs that a man is only going to deliver disappointment to your doorstep. And now one time." He raises his finger. "One time I'm late, and you're ready to call it quits."

I suck back my tears that are begging to be let free again. "You could have called."

He throws his hands in the air. "My phone went down a storm drain, and I don't know anyone's number by heart. I was just getting Foster—"

"Foster," I sneer, and he tilts his head.

"This is useless. You have your opinions, and I'll never live up to the perfection you demand. But I'm telling you, you're not living in reality. You can't give them a perfect life. Do you really think Sky and Patrick had a perfect life? That every day he brought home roses, and she had dinner on the table for him? Fuck no. That's not life, it's a fucking sitcom. We're gonna fight. We're both gonna screw up." He lowers his voice and steps closer. I don't stop him. "What matters is that we keep turning toward each other, not away. That we choose this. Choose *us*."

His words press on the already painful bruise that is my past and panic flares, telling me to abort. Save yourself. Don't let him too close. He'll just hurt you and the kids again.

"I just need some time," I whisper.

He stares at me, and I meet his gaze, using every ounce of the remaining strength I have to show him I'm not backing down.

"Fuck, Leighton, I wish you would've told me I never really stood a chance." He shakes his head, frowning. "I'd already lost before I even tried to win you." He turns away and walks to the door.

Hold it together just a few more seconds, then he'll be gone.

He circles back. "Take all the time you need, Leighton. I hope you find the clarity you feel you need but be prepared for the fact that you might lose one of the best things that's ever happened to you too." He walks back into the house.

I slide onto a patio chair, bring my knees up to my chest

and weep. I'm not sure how long after Callie comes out and slides a chair next to mine, putting her arm around my shoulders.

"Is he gone?" I sob.

"Yeah, he asked to talk to Lake first so he could apologize, but he's gone now." She rests her head on mine, and neither of us says a word.

CHAPTER
FIFTY

Hayes

"This is why I don't do relationships," Foster says from the seat next to me on the plane.

We're headed out of town for two weeks. This stretch is the most brutal part of our schedule. I'd been dreading it since I got together with Leighton, and I thought she had too. She worked out a schedule with her mom since the kids are off for summer, and now that Callie is back, I figured she'd be covered. Guess that's not something I need to worry about anymore though.

"Seriously, man, just call her." Easton, who I thought would understand, thinks it can all be fixed with a simple conversation.

"She doesn't want to hear from me. She wants a break."

Decker isn't saying much. After news about the fight leaked, he and Foster got called into the office for a meeting. Neither has divulged what was said, but both of them have been a little more patient with the other since then. They don't talk to each other—actually, they blatantly ignore when the other one talks—but it's better than what was happening before.

"Doesn't she understand that your phone went in the storm drain?" Foster asks. "Chicks are ridiculous. Just take your sister. She poked me in the fucking chest and blamed me."

Easton points at him. "I saw her first."

Foster rolls his eyes. "This isn't grade school where you can call dibs. She'll make her choice. Figure out who will get the job done in bed."

"Assholes, that's my little sister you're talking about."

It's Callie's business who she sleeps with, but none of these assholes are gonna be on her roster.

Callie's been blowing up my phone. Every day she's texting me some kind of advice. Telling me to give Leighton time. Be patient. But it's all-consuming. How does someone who wasn't even in your life months ago become all you can think about, all you want?

I've picked up my phone to text or call Leighton but stop myself each time.

"She's got a great ass," Easton says, and Foster hums his agreement.

I grind my teeth together.

"Kinda got me hot when she came at me. Like I was a very bad boy, and she was gonna punish me." Foster's shit-eating grin pisses me off even more. "You never told me how hot your sister is, Haymaker."

Easton laughs. "Shit, I had to soothe Decker's ego, and you got to see a hot-tempered Callie."

"Again, assholes, that's my baby sister."

"Oh, now it's *baby* sister." Easton laughs.

The two of them continue to talk shit about my sister.

Callie hates it when her friends crush on me, and I hate it in reverse. Not that I would have a problem if the friend was someone like Decker. My gaze shoots to where he's quietly reading a book. He's the kind of guy I'd like Callie to find. Someone to calm her extroverted personality.

"None of you can give me any more advice?" The fact that I'm asking them shows how desperate I am. Both to fix this with Leighton and to move the conversation away from my sister.

"The longest relationship I've ever been in was a friends-with-benefits in college, and when she got attached, I bailed." Foster shrugs and glances at Decker. "Truth is, I thought we were the same person, Hayes. I'm shocked you're pining so hard."

Decker glances at his brother, blows out his breath as though he wants to say something, but then goes back to reading.

"Oh, our boy was smitten," Easton chimes in. "He was never home."

"I noticed." Foster shrugs. "That's all right. Maybe we'll make your place into a pussy palace now that you're single. What do you think, Hayes?" He elbows me.

I squeeze my eyes shut, hoping God will grant me the patience to deal with these idiots.

"He wouldn't even go eat with us. Bailed on the last two prize dinners we won off the DICs." Easton shakes his head at my apparent blasphemy. "She must have one magic fucking pussy."

I slam my head into the seat rest. She does. And she tastes so sweet. The more sex we had, the more I saw a new side of her come out. She was never shy about taking what she wanted from me. And I can't even think about her blow jobs. How she somehow knew exactly how I like it. God, I'll never get sucked off like that again.

"Regular pussy?" Foster scowls. "Not sure I see the appeal."

"You don't ever want to settle down?" Easton asks him.

"Hell no. Why? So some woman can lead me around by the dick and tell me what I can and cannot do?"

"You're missing out," I say, knowing I'd give anything to be able to walk into that house and have it be how it was with Leighton and the kids. Another chaotic dinner where we're laughing, arguing, or just hearing Monroe talk about her monkey bar record at the park.

Foster gives me the once-over. "Oh right, look at your sorry ass. No thanks. I'm not missing out on shit."

"Eventually she's going to forgive you," Easton says.

I want desperately to believe that, but I also witnessed everything Leighton went through when we were younger. And what I didn't see for myself, Callie and my mom talked about. I thought I was enough to help her overcome all that. Turns out that just like my baseball career, I'm just one step away from being good enough.

Just the one to catch the ball for the first-round drafted pitcher.

Just a throw-in for another guy's trade.

Just the guy to have fun with but not steady enough to have as a serious boyfriend.

I felt on top of the world with Leighton. The way I saw myself looking through her eyes, man, talk about an ego check. But in the end, I didn't have "it" once again.

I look out the window and watch the clouds drift by underneath us, unsure where I go from here.

CHAPTER
FIFTY-ONE

Leighton

The kids are at Art and Julianna's. This is their last visit over there before a final decision is made on who they'll live with. I feel as if I'm in the world's longest competition.

Over the last few days, I've been thinking about Hayes's words, about Sky and Patrick's room… can any of us really move on when we walk by this door that remains shut? It's a constant reminder of what happened, as though we're stuck in time, bound to relive the tragedy. If we want to move forward, we need to move on. At the same time, we need to bring them to life in our memories. Sky deserved to be honored, not forgotten. And right now, this room represents us all trying to forget, trying to pretend as though their deaths never happened.

I rest my hand on the doorknob and close my eyes as I twist it.

Then I push the door open, step in, and instead of shutting it, I leave the door open.

All I can do is stare at the bed and see Sky lying there, her head propped up on her pillow, reading her Kindle until the middle of the night. She'd always tell me how tired she was the next day, but how it was such a good book that it was worth it.

Her walking out of the bathroom in her robe with her hair twisted in one of the microfiber towels she was always buying me so my hair wouldn't be frizzy.

How am I supposed to pack all this up and erase her? Once all these things are gone from here, where does she live? Only in our hearts? How do we show that she was once on this earth? She was a daughter, a mother, a cousin, a friend. She was an amazing human being. She and Patrick both.

I force myself to be brave and walk through the room. It all looks so daunting. But I need to face the pain, push through it, and move on so that all of us can move forward.

When I reach her closet, I take out her UIC sweatshirt and press it to my face, inhaling her scent as if she's hugging me hello or goodbye again.

"I miss you so much," I mumble into the fabric.

"Hello?" Callie's voice calls from downstairs.

I'm tempted to drop the sweatshirt, run out of the room, and shut the door, but I stay put. She swears when her foot hits the third step, and it creaks loudly.

"Leighton?" Her voice is softer as she steps into the room. I emerge from the closet, and she smiles softly at me. "Want some help?"

I didn't think I did. I wanted to do it myself. I told her as much this morning on the phone, which was perfect since she had a podcast recording planned. But she's here, and I've never been so thankful.

"Yeah. Thanks."

"I'll be right back." She holds up her finger and rushes

down the stairs, swearing again when the third stair from the bottom squeaks again. When she returns, she has a box of trash bags and empty moving boxes. "Just put me to work."

We spend the afternoon designating piles for keep, give-away, or trash, and I put together a box of Patrick's things for Art to go through. We share stories and memories about our time with them, and for the first time in a long time, I remember them as the couple they were, not the perfection I envisioned after they died.

How Sky would complain about his boxers not making it into the hamper.

Or Patrick telling us about how Sky is hyper-organized, but she squeezes the toothpaste in the middle. Callie pulls the toothpaste from the drawer and says, "She really did," and we laugh with tears in our eyes.

Sky was always picking on Patrick for not finishing the last few drops of water in a cup.

"They were a great couple though," Callie says, which makes me remember that I haven't told her about the counselor or the bag I found in the closet.

For some reason, I'm not sure I want to share the fact that they might have been having some issues when they died. Let them live on in everyone's eyes as having had a wonderful marriage.

When we're done, we sit on the floor and stare at all the bags and boxes.

"I know you don't want to talk about it, but this is where my brother would be good to have around."

"True. He's good at carrying the heavy stuff." I mean it in more ways than one. Callie opens her mouth to say more, but I shake my head. "Not yet."

"Okay." She nods.

She hasn't pushed me or tried to convince me to call Hayes. I miss him so much. I've almost caved so many times. But after I rehashed everything he said that night, I realized that I won't be a good partner to him until I do what he said —deal with my issues. I just hope I can get through it before I lose him completely. The thought of him being with another woman makes me feel physically ill.

He came into my life exactly when I needed someone like him the most, but I'm still letting those lingering doubts keep us from really moving forward. And when I call him and ask for another chance, I want to do it knowing I won't be waiting for the other shoe to drop.

Callie comes to my side and puts her arm around my waist. "I'm really proud of you. This is some adult-level shit. You really put your big-girl panties on."

I chuckle and lay my head on her shoulder, and she kisses the top of my head.

Then I scan the room, seeing Sky and Patrick's backpacks just by the door. "We still have to deal with those."

"We can donate them as is if you want."

I'm already getting up. "I want to see what's in here. It was with them when they…"

"Okay." She follows.

I pick up both backpacks and place them on the bed. She takes Sky's, and I have Patrick's.

Sky's doesn't have anything out of the ordinary. Clothes, a poncho, and other essentials to go hiking for a day.

Patrick's holds all the navigation essentials. The compass, a physical map of the trails, snacks like trail mix and beef jerky. A water bottle. At the very bottom of the bag, wrapped in a T-shirt, is another phone.

"Did he have a separate work phone?" Callie asks.

We already took out the phone that the police put in the side pockets of each of their bags.

I frown. "I don't think so, but I guess it's possible."

"I feel like they would've told you or asked you when they came for his computer."

She's right. Patrick's work came by shortly after he passed

and took his laptop and all the other work-related security equipment.

"Well, let's charge it up." Callie holds out her hand and grabs the charger that was next to Sky's bed, plugging it in.

"And now let's get everything out before the kids return after dinner." I pick up one of the bags.

Callie was right, having Hayes here would've made it a lot easier to get the bags into the garage, but we manage.

We order dinner to be delivered, and when it arrives and we sit down to eat, I catch her checking the score of the Colts game when she thinks I'm not looking. They've been gone for a week, and they'll be gone for another one.

"How are they doing?" I ask.

"What?" She slides her phone into her back pocket.

I tilt my head. "Come on."

"He's playing like complete shit. Can't focus or concentrate without you." She smiles a little too wide and too fake.

"Callie."

"Okay, he's playing pretty great actually. Hit a home run last night and drove in the winning run, and he's two for three today." She waves. "But he's probably crying himself to sleep at night."

Or finding someone to keep his hotel bed warm.

No. That's just an old pattern of thinking. I know Hayes wouldn't do that. Not so soon.

"I'm happy for him."

"Sure, you are," she deadpans.

"I really am. I want him to have all the success he wants on that field. Honestly."

She pats my hand. "You know what I'm upset about?"

"What?" I fork my lo mein noodles.

"I never got to see you guys together. I bet it was a pretty great sight."

I smile because it really was. The happiest I've ever been.

After Callie leaves and before the kids return, I go back

into Sky and Patrick's room. I'm about to shut the door, but I think I'll have a conversation with the three of them about leaving the door open from now on.

I notice that Patrick's second phone's screen is lit up, and it's vibrating all over the nightstand.

I pick it up and slide my thumb across the screen. "Hello?"

"Is Patrick there?" a deep male voice asks.

"Who is this?"

"Sky?" he asks.

Who is this person, and how do they not know that Patrick and Sky are no longer with us?

CHAPTER
FIFTY-TWO

Hayes

We're finally back from our away games, and we play at home for the next two weeks. Which would be amazing if I had Leighton and the kids as part of my life.

"Just get drunk, and you'll forget it all," Foster says.

"Want me to call Ruby in for some shots?" Easton asks.

The two have been thick as thieves over my problems because they share the same mentality on what they're looking for right now.

"No shots for me," Decker says.

"Figures." Foster gets up to leave but stops short when the door opens. "And we meet again."

Callie puts her hand in front of Foster's face and walks by him. He lets out a low chuckle and leaves the room.

My sister comes straight for me and sits down next to me. "You need to get your head out of your ass."

I glare at her, then pick up my beer and turn my attention

to the television. "I'm doing what she wants. Staying the hell away from her."

Ruby comes into the back room. "Graffiti boy says you guys want shots?"

"No, we're good," Decker answers for everyone.

"Graffiti boy?" Callie asks.

"That's what she calls Foster," Easton fills her in.

"Who puts tattoos all over their body like that?" Ruby shakes her head in disgust. "And on your neck."

Easton laughs, then turns his attention toward my sister. "Hey, Callie, I've got a hookup at Saffire tonight. Wanna come?"

"Ask me after I get my brother to man up."

"Why is he being so crabby? He just sits around here and pouts these days." Ruby gestures to me. I'm sure my sister is about to fill her in.

"It's a girl thing. He's not used to feeling that beating organ in his chest. It's new for him." Callie smiles at me condescendingly.

I narrow my eyes at her. "Cute."

Foster comes back in and sits next to Callie. She slides her chair closer to me. At least she realizes he's the last kinda guy she needs.

"You messed up with the girl?" Ruby asks. "This is why I loved my Falcons. All that drama was over. I can't go through another round of getting you boys to see the error of your ways and figure out how you're going to get the love of your life back."

"Don't worry, you won't ever have that problem with me." Foster raises his hand.

"Me either." Easton raises his hand, then points at Decker. "This one however, you will have to coax through it."

"She broke it off with me," I admit, and my chest squeezes. "All thanks to these fuckheads." I uncross my arms to point at Decker and Foster.

Neither of them says anything.

Foster slides up to the table. "Listen, yeah, sorry, I fucked your plans up, but what have you done to fix it?"

Callie peers over her shoulder at him.

Easton snaps his fingers and points at Foster. "He's got a point. You haven't even fought for her. You're just sitting there, brooding and waiting around for her to do something. Action gets results."

Callie crosses her arms and smiles.

"What?" I say to her.

She holds up her hands. "Nothing, just seeing what you're going to do."

"You guys can fuck off. You don't understand."

Callie shakes her head and sits up again. "All right, let's try this. Hayes, I don't want you to fight for Leighton. Under no circumstances are you to go over there and have an adult conversation with her and work this out. I'll be so mad if you try to win her back. You just used her, didn't you? It pisses me off that you took advantage of my best friend."

What the hell is she even talking about?

"Are you trying reverse psychology on him?" Decker asks.

She shrugs. "It usually works. Maybe I was too direct."

"Oh my god, do you want to be alone for your whole life? You love the girl. Go get her," Ruby says. "What's the worst she can say? No? Again? How did you end up a professional ball player when you're so goddamn timid?"

I look at Callie, and she raises her eyebrows.

Foster picks up his phone from the table. "You know I suck at this relationship stuff, but if you love her, you gotta fight for her, man."

Easton shrugs. "She's the one, and if my family has taught me anything, it's that everyone's got someone out there."

I look at Decker, whom I trust the most when it comes to this kinda stuff. "I don't think I'm the one to ask, except to say that if you let her go, be prepared for her to move on. She won't wait forever for you. So, if you don't want her to find her happily ever after with someone else, get your ass out of that chair and fix it."

Decker is so right. What am I going to do, let some other bastard slot into my spot in her life? My destiny? My fate? Hell fucking no. That spot is mine.

I stand abruptly and the chair falls to the floor behind me. "I'm getting an Uber."

"It's already outside," Foster says.

"And big enough for all of us?" Callie asks.

"Of course." He winks at her.

"You're not all coming." I make my way to the door.

"Oh yes, we are. You two kept me in the dark long enough. I want to see this." Callie follows, and I hear the rest of the chairs scraping along the floor.

I guess this will be a public groveling.

CHAPTER
FIFTY-THREE

Leighton

I'm on a ladder, cutting in with paint in Sky and Patrick's room, when Lake comes in and sits on the bed.

The kids took it well when I told them we needed to remember their parents, but we also need to work on moving forward, that it's what their parents would have wanted for them. I don't think Monroe understood at all, and Lincoln only half. I talked to their therapist though, so I'm hoping she'll be able to help.

"What's up?"

"You know he texts us… well, me," she says.

I glance over my shoulder. "Uncle Art?"

Art better not be trying to swing her preference his way.

"No. Hayes."

My paintbrush pauses on the wall. "Oh."

"Just to say good night or ask us how the day was. He asks me to send him pictures of Monroe doing her National Days stuff. I hope you're not mad."

I put the paintbrush on the tray and climb down the ladder. "I'm not mad. I just wish someone had told me sooner."

She shrugs. "That night of my party, he came up and apologized."

I nod. Callie told me, but I never asked what happened.

"He felt bad and said he was really sorry. Explained the whole thing and..." She shrugs. "It made sense. I told him I was upset and how the girls from school said I was a liar."

I pat her leg. "I think forgiveness is good."

"Then why won't you forgive him?"

God, kids can be so direct sometimes.

"It's adult stuff."

"That's what Mom used to say, and it makes no sense. He hurt me too, and I could forgive him."

I give her a small smile I hope isn't patronizing. "You're twelve, I'm thirty. We've experienced different things, and I—"

"That's what Allison said."

My forehead wrinkles. "You talked to your therapist about it?"

"Yeah, we're supposed to talk about what's bothering us. And we all really miss Hayes."

I suck in a breath. This is why people don't introduce their significant others to their kids.

"She said that Aunt Lily and Uncle Lenny's divorce had a profound effect on you. And until you work through your trauma, this might continue to happen."

I frown. "What?"

She shrugs. "I'm just telling you what she said."

"Is she suggesting I'm going to keep bringing men into this house, getting you guys attached, and then break up with them?"

She shrugs again, and my anger sparks. Who is Allison to judge me or my reasons?

"She said people with your kind of trauma turn their backs on the people and things that cause them pain reminiscent of their past, instead of turning toward the person to fix it. And that until you learn that, you'll be alone." She delivers her words so matter-of-factly that I stare at her.

"She seriously told you that?"

"She just didn't want me to think it was my fault that Hayes isn't around anymore."

I nod a bunch of times and purse my lips, my chest burning. I'm trying to hold it together and not pick up my phone and call *Therapist Allison* and tell her she can shove her advice up her ass. "Did she say anything else?"

"No. But I came in here to ask you a question."

Sure, shred me to pieces with your therapist's psychoanalysis of me, and now you want something.

"What is it?"

"I… we… Lincoln and Monroe were wondering if… um… we could spend a day with Hayes? He hasn't asked, but we were all talking, and we miss him."

I suck back all the tears pricking my eyes. "I'll talk to him and see if we can work something out."

She stands from the bed and blows out a long breath. "Okay. That doesn't upset you? Us wanting to see him?"

I will not put them in the same position I was in growing up. "No." I smack on a big smile. "Not at all. It's understandable."

She smiles. "Great. Jeez, I was so nervous to ask." She starts to walk out of the room but stops. "Leighton?"

I look up from my lap. "Yeah?"

"Maybe you can go see Allison, you know, so you can be happy again."

Knife in the heart. Lodged and twisted.

She leaves as I sit on the bed, everything she said running through my mind.

Have I really been this stupid? To allow this man who

willingly stepped into this chaos with me and wrapped his arms around all of us go? Just because I'm scared of being hurt again? Newsflash, idiot—you're already hurting. More and more with each day that passes.

"Oh god, I really am stupid," I mumble.

I call my mom and ask her to come over to watch the kids, then I order myself an Uber. I don't even bother to see what I look like, just pocket my phone and run down the stairs. I don't even bother to skip the third step.

All three kids are standing in the kitchen, smiling a little creepily.

"Lake, can you watch your brother and sister? Aunt Lily is on her way over."

"I can, yup. Go."

They all smile even wider.

"Thanks." I rush over to them, kiss their cheeks, and tell them I love them.

Then I open the door and rush down the porch steps. My Uber is already here, so I wind through the cars parked along the curb. As I approach, the back door opens, and I rear back.

Hayes steps out and pauses when he sees me.

I suck in a breath.

"Get out." Callie's voice comes from the back seat, and I lean around him, seeing not only Callie but his three teammates in the Uber XL.

"What are you doing here?" I ask, really hoping Hayes is here for the same reason I was running to him.

"I'm here for you. I'm sorry for all the shit I said. I love you. I can't even function without you." He takes my hand and leads me to the curb.

"He really can't," Easton says, getting out of the vehicle.

"It's pathetic," Foster adds.

"I'm the one who's sorry." Tears burn my eyes. "I shouldn't have pushed you out of our lives. I was so scared that something had happened to you, and it dredged up all this shit, but I was wrong for shutting you out. You were right, this life won't be perfect, but it's us, working through everything. Together."

"I should've tried harder to call so you wouldn't have to worry." He puts his hand on my cheek. "And I should've just left Foster at the hospital."

"Thanks," Foster mutters.

"So…" I'm not sure what happens now.

"So, I'm going to kiss you," he says, and I nod like a damn bobblehead.

His other hand comes up to my cheek so both of his palms cradle my face, and he presses his lips to mine. I sink into him, the feeling of home and rightness wrapping around me.

Then our friends and family are cheering, the kids are jumping up and down in the doorway.

"Okay, kiddos, in the house before it gets rated R." Callie forces everyone toward the porch and ushers the kids inside.

The door shuts, and I wrap my arms around Hayes's waist, burying my head in his chest. "I love you."

He kisses the top of my head. "You're the love of my life."

I squeeze him tighter.

We stand there wrapped around each other for a long time.

Before we pull apart, I say, "I think we have to watch out for Lake. She just did some weird psychology thing to get me to see that I was wrong."

He chuckles. "Probably learned it from Callie. We should ban her from spending time with the kids."

He puts his arm around me, and we walk up the stairs, and it feels as if the puzzle pieces fit. Well, except for one.

CHAPTER
FIFTY-FOUR

Hayes

We allow all my teammates and Callie to stay for dinner. Afterward, they take the kids to the ice cream parlor, giving us time alone together. Foster wasn't on board at first, but Lincoln found his new favorite Colts player, much to Easton's displeasure.

Leighton takes my hand and leads me to the stairs. "Come on."

"Baby, it's been so long since I've had you, I want to take my time."

She stops on the second stair and turns around. My hands find her hips, and she bends down to kiss me. "I'm not bringing you up here for sex."

"Good, because after the kids go to bed tonight, I'm gonna spend an obscene amount of time feasting on your pussy before I slide inside you. I missed my playmate."

Her cheeks flush, and she moans. God, I love those sounds.

"Okay, you need to stop with the dirty talk until after I show you this." She tugs my hand, and I let her lead me up the stairs.

She stops at the top, not taking me to her guest room. I realize that Sky and Patrick's bedroom door is open. She pulls me through the doorway.

It looks as though she's in the middle of painting. The space has been cleared out of everything except a ladder—and the picture of Leighton and Sky resting on the otherwise empty dresser.

"What do you think?" she asks.

"I think it looks great. The color's a little feminine for me though." She tilts her head, and I walk over to her. "I love it. I think this will make a great bedroom for you."

"And you?" Her eyebrows rise.

I pretend that my heart isn't leaping out of my chest at her suggestion that I move in here. "You want me to move in?"

"I know it's sudden, but going through all their stuff, it told a story of their life together, and I realized that I want that. I want the different decades of our favorite clothes hung in the closet. Years of makeup in a drawer. I want to accumulate stuff with you."

"So romantic." I chuckle.

"So, I suck at words, but I want to lie next to you every night. I want lazy mornings where we order donuts for the kids so we can stay in bed just a little longer."

I pull her to me and kiss her forehead. "You're taking all my lines. I'm supposed to woo you, and now you're wooing me."

She rests her chin on my chest and stares up at me. "I think we woo each other. That's the whole point, so the spark doesn't go out."

"Baby, the spark is never going away."

"It might. But like you said, that's life, right? We'd find it again."

In this moment, I can't imagine never wanting her.

"So?" She bites her bottom lip.

I stare into her eyes and cradle her cheek with my hand. "I love you, Leighton Sinclair, and I'd love to move in with you."

She blows out a breath and sighs. "I thought you were going to say thanks, but no thanks."

I frown. "Why?"

She shakes her head. "Because I thought I messed this up between us, and you might want to take it slow. That my issues—"

"Never. Let's make a deal. You never kick me out again, and I'll never leave you." I take her hands so she can't pull away and look into her ocean eyes. "I promise to never leave you."

Leighton smiles, and she doesn't try to get free of my grip. "I know. And I'll never kick you out again. I might ask you to sleep on the couch though." She chuckles.

"I'm not sleeping on the couch. I'm putting in a rule that we don't go to bed mad. I'll eat your pussy for hours straight until you forgive me if I have to."

"Jeez, Hayes." She's protesting, but her blush says she loves it when I talk to her like that. "Oh!" She squirms out of my arms, and I want to grab her shirt and tug her back. "There's another reason I called you up here."

"What is it?" My head tilts.

She opens one of the dresser drawers and pulls out a phone, bringing it over to me. I sit on the edge of the bed and pat my leg for her to sit on my lap, which she does.

"I found this phone in Patrick's backpack. It was an extra one. I charged it, and that night there was a call on it. I answered."

My eyebrows lift.

"It was a private investigator that Patrick hired. He claimed that since he hadn't heard from Patrick, he was going to destroy the photos because he had never received payment."

"Did he say why Patrick hired him?"

She shakes her head. "No. He said if I pay him, he'll tell me."

"And did you pay him?"

She shakes her head. "I don't know if I want to know. I mean, there are only so many reasons a man has a second phone, and he hired a PI. Something is up. I could let it all remain a secret…"

"What do you want to do?" If I was her, I would've already paid, but I also understand why she might want to let the secret die with them.

She mulls it over, then blows out a breath. "I think I want to know. Is that bad? Is it an invasion of privacy—"

"You're raising his three kids. It doesn't necessarily mean what you're thinking. It could be something other than infidelity."

She nods. "Okay, I'm gonna call the PI back."

I kiss her cheek and run my hand up and down her back in silent support.

She calls the number, and I hear her end of the conversation. She tells him to send her the bill, and she'll pay it. Then he'll get her the pictures.

It takes the guy a minute to get us the invoice, and since I have my wallet on me and her purse is downstairs, I put it on my credit card. I wanted to volunteer anyway, but I didn't want to overstep.

Minutes after we pay the invoice, she receives an email from the investigator.

"Wait!" she says before we can click on the pictures. "I don't want to do it here. Let's go into the guest room."

"Are you worried about bad energy or something?"

She shrugs. "Just in case. This room is ours now, and I want whatever those pictures show to stay out of it."

I laugh but understand. "Lead the way."

We get into the guest room, and we settle on the edge of the bed, side by side, our thighs and arms brushing.

"Ready?" she asks.

"I feel like I should be asking you that."

"I am."

She nods and clicks on the link, and when the first picture comes up, we say in unison, "What the hell?"

CHAPTER
FIFTY-FIVE

Leighton

My finger shakes as I ring the doorbell.

Their house is decorated for summer with a popsicle doormat, and the potted flowers on each side of the door have pinwheels in them. The banner across the floral wreath on the door says, Welcome Summer.

It all makes me want to throw up.

It took all of Hayes's willpower not to come with me, but I feel as if I'll get more answers if I'm alone.

The lock slides, and I hold my breath, every muscle in my body screaming for me to run and forget this whole thing. Who cares what happened? But I want the truth. And maybe someday the kids will too. Who knows? That's something I'll have to figure out as the years go by, though right now I think that it's probably best that I keep the truth to myself.

The door creeps open, and he rears back when he sees me.

"Leighton?" he asks, because I'm probably the last person he expected to see.

"Can I come in?"

He steps aside. I was worried I wouldn't even get this far.

I walk into the house that smells as though they have a scent pod on the stove. It's nice and not as homey as I prefer, but not as cold as I had imagined either.

"We can sit in the study." He shuts the front door, flicks the lock, and walks to his right toward the kind of room I've only ever seen in magazines.

There are two brown couches across from one another with a long table in between, holding perfect magazines and some sculpture that is definitely for show. I want to laugh at the thing, knowing that in our house, it would probably last a week before Lincoln knocked it over with a ball that ricocheted off the wall.

He settles on the couch across from me, one arm draped across the back of the couch and his ankle resting on his opposite knee. He's the picture of aloofness and relaxation. Or at least he's pretending to be.

I shift to the edge of the couch, reminding myself that I hold the cards here. "I was going through some of Skylar and Patrick's things, and I found this." I place the phone on the table between us.

He glances at it and back at me, shrugging. "I've never seen that phone before."

"I figured. It was Patrick's second phone."

An irritated expression crosses his face as if I'm wasting his time.

"He hired a private investigator," I add.

He flinches, just for a heartbeat, then shifts in his seat, jaw clenching. He relaxes again as he forces himself to embody the aloofness he wants to portray.

"I paid his fee, and he sent me the pictures that Patrick had requested."

"I don't understand why you're here or what this has to

do with me. I wasn't in business with Patrick, and he never told me anything, if that's why you're here."

I unlock the phone and slide it in front of him, opening the picture I saved to the Photos App. "But you were in the business of fucking his wife."

Art glances at the screen, then right back at me.

"Would you like to see another one?" With the flick of my finger, it moves to one of him and Sky outside this house, on the porch. Arthur was wearing shorts and no shirt, kissing her goodbye. "Or this one?" They're at a park, she's pressed against a tree, and again, they're kissing. "Should I go on?"

His chest rises and falls as he draws in big gasps of air. "So what? They're dead now. It doesn't matter."

How did Sky ever feel something for this cold man? Patrick was his complete opposite. So loving and friendly. Never treated anyone badly. I can't figure it out. I'm not sure I ever will.

"It doesn't matter to them, but I'm pretty sure *your* wife doesn't know you were sleeping with your *brother's* wife. And I'm guessing you don't want her to know either. So in order for these pictures to stay private, you're no longer going to contest my guardianship of the children." He opens his mouth, but I continue. "I'm not sure why you contested in the first place if you're in an unhappy marriage, and I don't care. I just want it to end. Sky and Patrick chose me to raise the kids. The kids want me. I am the one who is going to be their caregiver from this day forward."

He says nothing but picks up the phone and goes through the pictures. It's then that I see the weight of what he's carrying. The dark circles under his eyes. The pain that flashes across his features with every new picture he reveals.

When he's done, he sets the phone back on the table. I desperately want to ask him how it started, how and why they found themselves in this position. But they aren't questions I want to ask Art. They're questions for Sky. Questions I'll never have answers to.

"Okay." He nods.

I stand and pick up the phone. "It's up to you if you want to tell your wife. That's not my business. But I do ask that this stays between a select few until those kids get older. The last thing they need is to find out is that their mom and uncle were having an affair."

My anger toward Sky is something I'm going to have to work through, but those kids do not need this in their lives. God, maybe I do need my own sessions with *Therapist Allison.*

"It will."

I give him a nod. "Thank you."

As I leave the study, I hear the couch crinkle when he stands. "I loved her."

I turn at the door, just wanting to leave.

"I think you should know that. We were going to… come out, but Patrick surprised her with that trip, and she said she owed it to him to go and see what came of it. It was complicated." He shoves his hand through his hair. "But I did love her, and she loved me."

Wetness pools in my eyes. How did someone I felt so close to keep all this inside? Part of me thinks it's because Sky knew how I felt about cheating, but still, I would've listened to her and tried to understand.

"Thank you for no longer contesting the guardianship. Obviously, I won't keep you from the kids. You're their family. If you want a relationship with them, you can have it."

"I appreciate that. I love them, but I don't really want to be a parent. That was more Julianna."

"I figured." I walk to the front door, and when I go to open it, Art reaches past me to pull it open for me.

My stomach swoops and a warm feeling invades my chest when I see who's waiting for me.

Hayes sits on the front steps and stands to face us when the door opens.

"Was he worried I'd fight you?" Art asks.

I smile at Hayes. "No, he's just here for me."

I walk down the steps and right into Hayes, who swarms me in a hug as I finally let go of the emotions I put in a stranglehold inside the house and cry into his chest.

"Don't worry, baby, I'm flipping him off behind your back."

And then I'm laughing through tears.

"Come on, let's go home," he says, putting his arm around me and guiding me down the sidewalk.

Now all the puzzle pieces are finally in place.

CHAPTER
FIFTY-SIX

Hayes

Four months later

We got through our first baseball season as a family. I can't lie and say it wasn't stressful at times, but what matters is we came out of it together.

I left Leighton in bed earlier this morning. She's on her first day off in three days, and since I'm in my off season, I'm picking up the slack and giving her a much-needed break.

I walk into Mariano's, grab a cart, and shop for everything I need to surprise them all with breakfast. I open the donut case, picking the glazed for Monroe, Long John chocolate for Lincoln, chocolate cake for Lake, and sugar for Leighton.

It's then I spot a familiar-looking blonde. I hurry to pick out the donuts, put the box in the cart, and try to sneak away before she sees me.

"Hayes? Hayes Carlisle?" she calls.

Now I have more than one person looking at me. If I ignore her, I look like a dick, and there will be bad press about me.

I turn back around. "Hi, Julianna." I glance at her left hand and spot no ring.

Art came to Monroe's school play, and we were wondering why Julianna wasn't with him, but we decided it's their business, not ours, so we didn't ask.

"How's the family?" she asks.

Of course, she knows we're still together. Anyone who looks us up on social media will see pictures of Leighton and the kids at the home games, Leighton and me at numerous functions, or Leighton and me out with our friends.

I nod. "Really good."

She raises her left hand, wiggling her fingers. "I'm sure you're not surprised."

I shake my head, not wanting to get into this drama.

"I knew he was cheating. I just never knew with whom."

"I'm sorry," I say, unsure what else there is to say.

She sighs. "Well, Leighton's probably happy. She got the kids."

I bite my lip, so I don't say they should've been hers all along. Art did drop his petition, and Leighton was granted permanent guardianship. We celebrated by taking the kids to the expensive new steakhouse—along with her parents, Aunt Iris, my parents, Callie, and the three guys. Wish the DICS could have picked up that bill.

"Anyway, I actually have a date tonight—unless you want to fix me up with one of your teammates." She laughs. "Foster Davis looks like a good time."

I have to force my smile. "Yeah, none of them are looking to settle down."

"Not like you. Leighton sure got lucky."

"I like to think she did, but I'm even luckier."

She makes a sound as though she's annoyed but trying to mask it with niceness. "You're sweet. Anyway, I'd better get going. Tell Leighton and the kids I say hello."

"I will." My hands are already on the cart and ready to wheel away.

"Bye, Hayes."

"See ya." I try to walk steadily and not like I want to get away from her, but that was the most uncomfortable conversation I've ever been part of.

I buy all the groceries and Uber back to our place. The minute I open the door, I realize my mistake in leaving to get groceries.

Lincoln is throwing the ball against the wall, Monroe is acting as if she's a marching band, and Leighton has her head in one hand and a coffee cup in the other.

"Shit. I'm sorry." I cringe.

"You got dressed!" Monroe comes over and points at me.

I unzip my coat and show her that I still have my pajamas on.

"You almost got in trouble," Lincoln says. "Do I have to stay in my pajamas all day?"

I kiss Leighton's cheek. "Go back to bed. I've got this."

She shakes her head. "Nah, believe it or not, I miss this when I'm working for three days."

I turn to Lincoln. "It's National Family PJ Day, so we're in our pajamas all day."

I begin unpacking the groceries, tossing the Twix bars in the candy drawer.

"You brought a chill in with you." Leighton abandons her cup of coffee and wraps her arms around my back, sliding her hands under my shirt. "My own furnace."

One thing about the weather getting colder is that Leighton's hands are always cold, and she's decided I'm the only one who can warm them up.

"Donuts!" I say, and Lincoln and Monroe run over, picking out their favorites.

We let them eat in front of the television, and I circle around, keeping my back to them, bringing Leighton into my arms.

"I don't like waking up without you." She still sounds a little sleepy.

"Me either, but they're fed. We could sneak upstairs."

She moans, and my dick twitches in my pajama pants.

Just then, Lake comes down the stairs with a box in her hands, wearing her pajamas. Monroe runs over and skids to a stop at the bottom of the stairs, looking Lake up and down. She gives Lake a thumbs-up and goes back to her donuts.

"What's in the box?" I ask.

Lake looks at Lincoln and Monroe, nodding toward me. "Guys?"

Their eyes grow wide, and they run back over. Lincoln climbs over the couch.

"No climbing over furniture," Leighton calls.

Lake holds the box out to me.

"It's not my birthday?" My forehead wrinkles.

"We know, but, well… you'll see." She nods at it.

Leighton's eyes are welling up with tears, so she must know what's inside.

"Is this a prank?" I ask, shaking the box a little.

"No." Lake laughs.

"Is something going to fly out at me?"

"No. Open it." She pushes it into me.

I take off the lid and unwrap the tissue paper, glancing at them every few seconds. None of them give away anything.

Monroe lies across the counter with her chin in her hands. Lincoln is jumping up and down, and Lake keeps nodding with an expression that says *just open the box.*

I push away the final piece of tissue paper, and tears flood my eyes. I step back and shake my head.

"You deserved it, but since they're idiots, we wanted you to know you're our Gold Glove winner." Leighton's tears are tracking down her cheeks.

"Did you know about this?" I ask.

She nods. "It was their idea. I just helped with the execution."

I pull the baseball glove that they sprayed with gold paint out of the box.

I was passed over again for the Gold Glove, but it didn't sting this year because I realized that I'll take what I have under this roof over what happens on that field any day.

"I don't even know what to say." I pull Lake and Leighton into a hug and wave my hands so Lincoln and Monroe join us. "Thank you, guys."

I kiss the tops of their heads, overcome with emotion.

Lake is only good with affection for a short time, so she wiggles out of our group hug. Then Monroe wants her donut, and Lincoln goes to watch television. Leaving Leighton and me in the kitchen alone.

I stare at the gold glove, and she leans her head on my shoulder. "They came to me right after you found out. I think they feel like they were a little to blame." I start to protest, but she shakes her head. "I told them no, that we come first. Baseball is second. And yeah, you would've loved to get honored with it, but your priorities are different now."

"You said it better than I could have." I slide my arm around her again. "Amazing, isn't it? How good your life can become in such a short amount of time." I look at the room with our three kids in it.

Lincoln is trying to pry the remote out of Lake's hands, and Monroe wants to get involved, so she sticks her hands in the fight. Eventually, the arguing turns into yelling, and someone gets hurt.

Leighton leaves me to sort it out.

I watch them all from the kitchen, my heart overflowing

with joy. Funny how you can spend years chasing what you thought you wanted, and it turns out you weren't even close.

Leighton turns around as she soothes Monroe, rocking her up and down. Our eyes catch, and our smiles match. This life is everything I ever wanted. I just didn't know it.

EPILOGUE

Callie

Five months later

The season starts next week, so we're at Peeper's Alley, celebrating Decker and Foster's birthday, which is weird since they don't really talk to each other. Nonetheless, we forced them to be here and ordered them each their own cake.

As I look around the room, I want to give myself a pat on the back.

Hayes has his arms around Leighton's waist, his head nuzzled into her neck, whispering things I'm sure I don't want to hear. Both of them are clueless as to just how okay I was with them getting together.

Of course I want the credit for all my hard work, but it's better if they think it's fate or destiny or whatever. They're believers that there's one person out there for you, and they found each other. Fools if you ask me, but seeing them together, I can almost believe in kismet.

They really thought I had no idea how they've pined for one another for years, but I appreciate that they respected me enough not to pursue one another. That's why when I saw them together the day of Sky's funeral, I knew it was time. Leighton needed Hayes, and Hayes needed to know there was more to life than baseball. And it worked out beautifully if I do say so myself.

"What are you smiling about?" Lake asks me, going through my makeup in my purse and putting on my lipstick.

"That they have no idea. They're only here because of me, you… well, us."

She smiles and looks at Hayes and Leighton, who are admiring Monroe playing pinball with Decker. Lincoln is competing at darts with Foster and Easton.

Lake is a natural. I barely had to tell her what to say to Leighton that day to get her to finally realize she was pushing away the man she loved because of what happened to her when she was younger.

"Are you going to tell them?" Lake asks.

"Nah, let them think they did it all themselves. But jeez, are they stubborn."

"Tell me about it, I live with them." She rolls her eyes the way only a girl on the verge of teenager-dom can.

We both laugh, catching Leighton's attention. She tilts her head at us. By the end of this party, I need to tell her about the predicament I've found myself in, but that can wait until later.

"Just always remember to use reverse psychology with Hayes. You tell him he can't do something, and he'll see it as a challenge." I shrug. "He's been that way since we were kids."

Lake puckers her lips and stares at them in my compact mirror. "Figured that out already. Told him he wasn't strong enough to take the garbage out the other day, and he proved me wrong by doing my chore for me." She grins at her reflection.

"Smart girl."

"Hey, Callie, why don't you cool it on the makeup?" Hayes hollers across the room.

"Leave us alone. We're talking about boys." I elbow Lake. "Watch this."

His arms unwind from Leighton, and he takes a step in our direction, but she tugs him back. "Boys are dumb, and they smell," he calls.

The whole room laughs.

"Speak for yourself," Easton says.

Ruby comes into the back room. "Chocolate milks." She puts them rather forcefully on the table.

Monroe slides off the stool and runs over to Ruby, stopping right in front of her. "Ruby, do you have bananas?"

I glance at Leighton. "I thought she was done with the National Day thing?"

She and Hayes laugh. "She's on to food days now. Today is banana day."

Ruby ruffles Monroe's brown hair. "No, but I'll send out one of the regulars to get you one."

Leighton steps up, but Hayes goes along with her like a Velcro puppet on her back. "Ruby, that's not necessary. I'll stop on the way home."

"Please, they need the exercise." She leaves the room.

I lean back in my chair. "Curious minds, when you two start procreating, are you incorporating the whole name thing?"

Decker, Easton, and Foster all turn toward them.

"Are you pregnant?" Easton asks, eyes wide.

"No. She's talking about my family and their obsession with family names having a theme." Leighton meets my gaze. "And no, that's ending with me."

"Like what?" Decker asks. "You know in Tedi's family, all the kids' names start with Ts."

"That's like Leighton's family. They're all Ls. Lily, Lenny, and Leighton." I count them off on my fingers.

Hayes turns Leighton around. "I never knew that. You never said anything."

"It's never come up," Leighton says and turns back toward the group. "My mom and her sister are Lily and Iris. Flowers. We're the Ls. And Skylar continued it with these three."

Leighton smiles at the kids as if she's remembering Sky fondly. I know it's been a hard road, but she's doing the hard work to heal, so I'm proud of her.

"How do Lake, Lincoln, and Monroe go together?" Decker asks, as though he's trying to work out a puzzle.

"Streets. Lake Shore, Lincoln, and Monroe," Easton guesses, thinking he's right.

I make a buzzer sound. "Wrong."

He winks at me, and I shake my head and smile. He's always flirting.

"It's actually Lake for Lake Michigan," Leighton says. "Lincoln for Lincoln Park, and Monroe for Monroe Harbor."

"Damn," Foster says, rocking back his head. "You're screwed, Carlisle. How are you going to come up with something?"

"The biggest struggle will be that the name has to match the theme. So, they have to find a fourth Chicago landmark," I add to put some fuel on the fire.

"No, because we're not doing that." Leighton squares her gaze on Hayes, but I can tell it's game over.

"I bet you guys can't figure one out." I throw out one more challenge for my brother to grab onto. It's just too much fun.

Hayes is biting his lip and thinking.

Leighton slaps his stomach. "We're not doing that."

"They have to match. We can't have Lake, Lincoln, Monroe, and Phil." He looks at her imploringly.

"First of all, I'm not naming our baby Phil."

The two of them continue to go at it, and Lake looks at me. I like having her as my little accomplice.

The Davis brothers blow out their candles, and we have cake. I can't help but wonder what they each wished for. I'm sure whatever it was, they were the opposite of one another.

As the night dwindles down, Monroe falls asleep, draped across Hayes as he and Decker are still trying to come up with names for a baby that hasn't even been conceived yet.

All while… my hand falls to my stomach, but I push the thought out of my head.

It's time. I've delayed this long enough.

Easton and Lake are in a competition to see who can get the highest score in pinball. Foster is watching the Falcons game with Lincoln, explaining hockey to him. I'll give it to Foster, Lincoln actually looks interested.

I pull out my phone and send a text to Leighton to meet me out front.

"I'll be back," I say, sliding my phone in my back pocket and leaving the back room. Maybe I could've told Leighton to meet me in the bathroom, but I don't want to chance anyone overhearing our conversation.

Thankfully, the Falcons are away, so the bar is less crowded than when they're playing at home. It's just the two of us when Leighton joins me in front of the building.

"What's this about?" Leighton asks, walking over to me and looking at herself in the reflection of the glass. "I'm looking old. I think the stress of motherhood is showing."

"You're beautiful. Listen."

She pulls her skin up around her eyes and frowns when she lets go.

"Leighton!"

Her head rocks back. "What?" Turning away from the glass, she looks at me with concern.

Okay, now's the moment. You can do this.

"I'm pregnant."

Her mouth drops open, and she stares at me for a beat before she recovers. "What? When? By whom?"

Only Leighton can come up with one question after the other, even when she's surprised.

"I took a test this morning."

"Oh my god. Callie, who is the dad?"

I bite my lip because I really want to tell her. I want to give her the entire story, but he deserves to know first. So, I tell her as much as I can, as complicated as the situation is, without saying exactly who. "It's one of the men in there."

She frowns. "One of the old guys at the bar?"

I stare at her, and she laughs.

"Right." She laughs again. "My excuse is that I'm going on, like, two hours of sleep." She shakes her head. "Just to clarify, you mean the baby's father"—she points at my stomach—"is either Decker, Foster, or Easton?"

I nod.

And it's written all over her face.

This is complicated, and my brother is going to lose his shit.

Before either of us can say anything else, the door to the bar swings open and all the guys come out, kids in tow.

"What are you guys doing out here?" Hayes asks. He steps over and wraps his arm around Leighton's shoulders.

"Just getting some fresh air." I give my brother a smile I hope doesn't look forced.

He nods and turns his attention to Leighton. "The kids wanted to go to Lincoln Park Zoo, and I said I'd have to check with you. These morons have decided to tag along." He thumbs over to where Easton, Decker, and Foster are all crowded around the gate that leads to the entrance of their building.

"Haymaker, come check this out," Easton calls out.

"Sure, we can probably squeeze a couple hours in before it closes," Leighton says, then looks over at me. "You want to join us?"

I glance over at the three guys as Hayes makes his way over. "I think I'm just going to head home. It feels weird being around him when he doesn't know yet." I add the last part in a low voice so only she can hear.

Leighton nods.

Monroe and Lincoln both rush over to us and take us by the hand, dragging us toward the guys.

"What is going on?" Leighton asks, half laughing.

"Come look," is all Lincoln says.

Hayes is holding a cardboard sign, and when we reach him, he turns around to show us.

~~The Barn~~

~~The Stable~~

~~The Paddock~~

The Dugout

"What do you ladies think?" Easton points to the sign in Hayes's hands.

"Does it matter what we think?" I ask.

"Of course it does," Decker says, giving me a soft smile that I return.

"Who gives a shit what they call it. Fine. It's the Dugout. Done," Foster says, watching me.

The man irritates me half the time, but I can't disagree with him, so I shrug. "Agreed."

Hayes meets Leighton's gaze. "What about you?"

She smiles and nods. "I think this place will officially be known as The Dugout from here on."

"Perfect." Hayes leans in to give Leighton a kiss which makes all three kids groan.

It is perfect, just like my brother and my best friend's lives. It makes me wish that mine wasn't such a mess.

The End

ALSO BY PIPER RAYNE

The Dugout

The Hotshot

The Wild Card

The Rulebreaker

The Troublemaker

The Nest

Mr. Heartbreaker

Mr. Broody

Mr. Swoony

Mr. Charming

The Nest Before Christmas

Hockey Hotties

Countdown to a Kiss

My Lucky #13

The Trouble with #9

Faking it with #41

Tropical Hat Trick (Novella)

Sneaking around with #34

Second Shot with #76

Offside with #55

Chicago Grizzlies

On the Defense

Something like Hate

Something like Lust

Something like Love

Kingsmen Football Stars

False Start

You Had Your Chance, Lee Burrows

You Can't Kiss the Nanny, Brady Banks

Over My Brother's Dead Body, Chase Andrews

Modern Love

Charmed by the Bartender

Hooked by the Boxer

Mad about the Banker

Single Dads Club

Real Deal

Dirty Talker

Sexy Beast

Hollywood Hearts

Mister Mom

Animal Attraction

Domestic Bliss

Bedroom Games

Cold as Ice

On Thin Ice

Break the Ice

Chicago Law

Smitten with the Best Man

Tempted by my Ex-Husband

Seduced by my Ex's Divorce Attorney

Blue Collar Brothers

Flirting with Fire

Crushing on the Cop

Engaged to the EMT

White Collar Brothers

Sexy Filthy Boss

Dirty Flirty Enemy

Wild Steamy Hook-up

The Rooftop Crew

My Bestie's Ex

A Royal Mistake

The Rival Roomies

Our Star-Crossed Kiss

The Do-Over

A Co-Workers Crush

Holiday Romances

Single and Ready to Jingle

Claus and Effect

Merry Kissmas

Yule Be Mine

The Baileys

Lessons from a One-Night Stand

Advice from a Jilted Bride

Birth of a Baby Daddy

Operation Bailey Wedding (Novella)

Falling for My Brother's Best Friend

Demise of a Self-Centered Playboy

Confessions of a Naughty Nanny

Operation Bailey Babies (Novella)

Secrets of the World's Worst Matchmaker

Winning my Best Friend's Girl

Rules for Dating Your Ex

Operation Bailey Birthday (Novella)

The Greene Family

My Twist of Fortune

My Beautiful Neighbor

My Almost Ex

My Vegas Groom

A Greene Family Summer Bash (Novella)

My Sister's Flirty Friend

My Unexpected Surprise

My Famous Frenemy

A Greene Family Vacation (Novella)

My Scorned Best Friend

My Fake Fiancé

My Brother's Forbidden Friend

A Greene Family Christmas (Novella)

Lake Starlight

The Problem with Second Chances

The Issue with Bad Boy Roommates

The Trouble with Runaway Brides

The Drawback of Single Dads

The Complication with the Best Man

Plain Daisy Ranch

One Last Summer

The One I Left Behind

The One I Stood Beside

The One I Didn't See Coming

Chasing Forever

Chasing Love

Chasing Home

Love in Apartment 3B

Hit or Miss

Three's A Crowd

Good on Paper

The Abbott Brothers

Rent a Husband

Buy a Boyfriend

Standalones

Don't Mind if "I Do"

COCKAMAMIE
UNICORN RAMBLINGS

YAY! Our first baseball book ever!

To be honest, we were so nervous to write this book for many reasons. First, after everyone fell in love with The Nest series it made us contemplate whether we should have stayed a little longer with our Falcons and the world of hockey. Second, developing an entirely new found family and hoping you fall in love with them is hard. Ugh, the pressure was real.

If you've read a lot of our work, you know we tend to write ourselves into a corner A LOT! So, we were purposely vague at the end of Mr. Charming about Hayes and Leighton's past. We wanted the freedom to do what we wanted when it was time to write their story.

At first, THE HOTSHOT was a straight-up best friend's older brother storyline. But in the end, we couldn't be happier with how it turned out despite all the complications. We fell in love with Hayes, Leighton, and most of all Lake, Lincoln, and Monroe. (Squirrel—any guesses on the theme for their names?) Every story we strive to go a little further, dig a little deeper, and go somewhere we haven't been before. So not only is this our first baseball sports romance, but we've also never done a guardian storyline before either.

Since we're talking about the guardian storyline… that wasn't our first thought when we were plotting THE HOTSHOT, but at this point, we don't remember how we got there. After we decided we were going to incorporate three kids of various ages into our first book of a new series (it seemed daunting since we were just getting to know the guys themselves), ideas were being thrown around like confetti.

Here's just a few things we considered, but later scraped…

- Leighton's guardianship wasn't going to be threatened.
- Patrick was going to be the one who was having the affair.
- Art and Julianna were just going to be Patrick's brother and wife and play no bigger role than that.
- The moms at the school were going to play a bigger role with Hayes.
- Hayes himself wasn't going to be going through a career crisis.
- Hayes was going to go out with Foster, and that made Leighton insecure.
- Hayes and the guys were going to coach the baseball rec league, not Leighton

(Side note: From age nine to fourteen, Rayne's son was coached by an incredible mom-coach, and it opened her family's eyes to how surprisingly harsh some of the coaches, dads, and even the moms in the stands can be to a female coach. They were shockingly nasty at times. She coached that team to a high level of competition, winning multiple championships. We hope someday women like her won't be the exception—they'll be the norm).

There are probably so many more things that changed along the way, but those are the big ones we can remember. One day we'll take better notes, we promise!

In the end, this story was theirs and came out just as it should have. We hope we've made you fans of our new crew, and that you'll be cheering them on from the stands!

As always, we have a lot of people to thank for getting this book into your hands…

Nina and the entire Valentine PR team. The organization, the promotion, the way you keep us on point with deadlines. We appreciate you SO much!

Cassie from Joy Editing for the line edits and who always graciously works with our chaotic schedules.

Ellie from My Brother's Editor for line edits and proofreading. We give you barely any time, but you always come through.

Olivia Winston for giving our manuscript one final look over before we hit publish.

Simone at Buerosued for our illustrated cover. Your work is amazing, and we're so happy to be working with you on this series. You brought Hayes and Leighton to life!

All the bloggers and influencers who choose to read us when you have so many options out there. We're appreciative and honored to be on your list of must-reads and love reading all your reviews, edits, and more.

All the Piper Rayne Unicorns who support us all day, every day. We'd be lost without you answering our polls and telling us what you love and hate. We strive to listen to you and give you what you love about our books with a twist every time.

You, the reader, reading this now in real time, who has an abundance of books to choose from—thank you for picking up one of ours. Word of mouth is always the best form of advertising, and we appreciate you sharing your love for this series with the romance community!

We're sure some of you have your guesses on whose book is next! If you read us, you know we love the mystery of who the baby daddy is. And… after so much debate on what to name the building and so many names making the shortlist, we hope you feel The Dugout is the perfect name for our Colts! We sure do!

See you soon!

xo,
   Piper & Rayne

ABOUT PIPER & RAYNE

Piper Rayne is an Amazon Top 100 and *USA Today* Bestselling Author duo who believes in soft places to land, big laughs, and happily-ever-afters.

Piper runs on tea. Rayne runs on Diet Coke. But they both have one boy and one girl and are married to men who patiently listen to book talk they'll never quite understand.

Piper's the one who turns up the heat and humor—spinning tension, spark, and steam into moments that make you blush into your pillow and grin through the next chapter.

Rayne's the one who tugs on your heartstrings—mixing locker-room laughs, brotherhood banter, and the kind of heart-punch moments that hit when you least expect them.

Together, they create stories that feel like family—sometimes found, sometimes blood—but always the kind that stays with you long after the final word.

At the end of the day, Piper and Rayne write love stories that they hope feel real, funny, with just the right amount of steam… ones that make your heart race and your world a little warmer.